P9-CDT-293

DEATH
IN ROUGH
WATER

BOOKS BY THE AUTHOR

Death in the Off-Season
Death in Rough Water
Death in a Mood Indigo
Death in a Cold Hard Light

WRITTEN UNDER THE NAME
STEPHANIE BARRON

Jane and the Unpleasantness at Scargrave Manor
Jane and the Man of the Cloth
Jane and the Wandering Eye
Jane and the Genius of the Place
Jane and the Stillroom Maid
Jane and the Prisoner of Wool House
Jane and the Ghosts of Netley
Jane and His Lordship's Legacy
Jane and the Barque of Frailty
Jane and the Madness of Lord Byron
Jane and the Canterbury Tale
Jane and the Twelve Days of Christmas
Jane and the Waterloo Map

DEATH
IN ROUGH
WATER

FRANCINE
MATHEWS

**SOHO
CRIME**

Copyright © 1995, 2016 by Francine Mathews

All rights reserved.

Published in 2016 by
Soho Press, Inc.
853 Broadway
New York, NY 10003

Library of Congress Cataloging-in-Publication Data
Mathews, Francine.
Death in rough water / Francine Mathews.

ISBN 978-1-61695-728-5
eISBN 978-1-61695-729-2

1. Folger, Merry (Fictitious character)—Fiction. 2. Women
detectives—Massachusetts—Nantucket Island—Fiction. 3. Nantucket Island
(Mass.)—Fiction. I. Title.
PS3563.A8357 D42 2016 813.54—dc23 2016001860

Printed in the United States of America

10 9 8 7 6 5 4 3 2 1

This book is dedicated to Mark

I don't think we need feel guilty about the killing we do, we do it for life's sake: our own. But I guess for that very reason the killing may put a scared and thoughtful fisherman in mind of his own span.
—JOHN HERSEY, BLUES

Prologue

THE NIGHT WIND was blowing unusually cold for late May, and the stars were blotted out by a bank of cloud. Captain Joe Duarte took the measure of the waters, felt the plunge of his deck, and knew he should head for port. The mounting weather made black sea and sky one, a pitching cocoon through which his trawler labored and rolled. The *Lisboa Girl* had just crossed over what Duarte knew as the Leg—part of the intricate underwater landscape of the Georges Bank he'd been fishing since the age of fifteen. He had turned sixty-eight three months past, and though much had changed in the fifty-three years he'd been on the water, he still called the Bank's bottoms, its gullies and peaks, by the old names made familiar from decades of studying charts in storm and sun: Cultivator Shoals, Billy Doyle's Hole, Little Georges, Outer Hole.

The younger men, using location indicators fed down from the stars, thought in signals instead of words. They moved over the crags of the seabed as a blind man feels Braille, sensing the humps and dips that clutched at their nets. Had they been told to head to the Leg instead of following a GPS, they'd have been lost.

The captain knew the Georges Bank like the profile of a beloved woman, something no locator on a screen could ever replace. It was an ancient shelf of the North American continent, inundated by glacial ice melt twelve thousand years before. The Georges Bank sat more than sixty nautical miles off the present coastline and was larger than the entire state of Massachusetts. To Joe Duarte, it was home. The charted names of the bottoms remained with him like the Portuguese words of his childhood, artifacts of a vanished age. Like his boat. And himself, for that matter. He was among the last of Nantucket's commercial fishermen, and the last of the Duartes to go down to the sea, something they had been doing in Portugal and the New World for over five hundred years.

The *Lisboa Girl*, three decades old and Joe's second trawler, was one of only two remaining draggers to call Nantucket home. She was an Eastern-rigged wooden vessel, meaning that her pilothouse was aft and she launched her nets over the side rather than to the stern. A more dangerous and old-fashioned boat to fish from than the steel-hulled Western-riggers—in heavy seas like this, she'd have to come to a stop and turn broadside to the wind to prevent the net from drifting under the hull and fouling the propeller.

The captain pulled open the pilothouse porthole and stuck his head into the rising wind. It was time to quit fishing and head for home. His rheumatic bones ached, and his eyelids stung with weariness. Maybe it was time to quit for good, like all the rest.

Nobody his age worked a trawler anymore. The younger men skippered boats that cost hundreds of thousands of dollars and carried insurance that drained them of thousands more. Fishing from an island port like Nantucket tacked a surcharge on everything they needed to survive. They weren't fools. They had left long ago for the mainland ports of Hyannis and Provincetown, Gloucester and New Bedford, and the Nantucket fleet slowly died.

Joe Duarte had watched the others go with a grim pride. His boat was paid off. He'd inherited his house on Milk Street. He could afford to stay in the town where he was born—where, at fifteen, he learned his trade from his father and grandfather, and had the youth whipped out of him by the bitter cold of winter fishing. He found the mainland ports too crowded and the towns too suburban. Returning to the harbor of a January night, past Great Point Light arcing its reassurance into the early dusk, he saw the glow from hundreds of Nantucket windows rising out of the midwinter Atlantic with a surging of the heart and a gladness born of deep love. He knew the value of what he had earned with his blood and his years.

Only I've no one to give it to, he thought. *So much for pride. All it buys is loneliness. I've got to call Del. Blood is blood, after all.*

"Holy Christ, would you look at that!"

Jackie Alcantrara, his first mate, was bent over the gray face of the fish-finder, studying the shifting shapes of the schools twenty-five fathoms below. The image rippled like a field of summer wheat. "It's cod, Joe. A friggin' fish convention. Let's go." He moved to the door of the pilothouse impatiently, shouting orders to the two crewmen on the night watch.

Joe Duarte squinted in the glare of the working lights. It was impossible to see much of the Atlantic beyond, but he could feel the pitch of the waves, grown sharper in the last few minutes, and the wind that was tugging at his sparse white hair. They were heading into fifteen-foot seas, over sharp peaks on the sandy bottom, and the net would be torn to shreds. There were no other boats in sight. They were one hundred and fifty miles from land.

Loneliness is a kind of death. I gotta call Del.

"Jackie!" he yelled over the din of the gantry winch, which was paying out the net and the pair of half-ton steel doors that dragged it to the bottom. "Jackie!"

The mate turned to him impatiently, bullet head thrust forward in resentment. He had been a captain himself until last year, and taking orders from Joe was something he fought every day.

"Get the net outta the water, *now!*"

"What the hell are you talking about, old man?"

"I won't have a couple thousand dollars' worth of new net torn apart in a gale, you understand? Get it up!"

Jackie stood stock-still, his jaw working fiercely, his overdeveloped upper body emphasizing all that was squat and Cro-Magnon about him; then he turned and drove a hand flat against the pilothouse wall with a shuddering violence.

"Christ *Almighty*," he said. "When are you gonna go home and die, old man? Tell me that! There's ten tons of cod down there, more than we've seen in months, more than anybody's seen at one time in more trips out than we can count. We're making money here, and you talk about a net!"

The bastard. I'd never have spoken to my captain like that. No respect, these days. No gratitude. I'd better call Felix Harper, too.

On the one hand, everything Jackie said was true. For years, cod on the Bank had steadily dwindled. During the day, they hung around in the mid-depths where only the huge factory ships could reach them; but at night, they dropped back to the bottom, and the *Lisboa Girl* dropped her nets after them through all the hours of darkness. Joe was turning his back on money. But he could sense the weather's gathering menace, and no amount of fish was worth the safety of his boat and men. Jackie was young. He would learn from the weather, from the ones who didn't come home, from the sudden silences on the radio frequencies in the midst of an unexpected gale.

"First Mate Alcantrara," the captain shouted into the wind, "for the last time, *bring in the net,* or I will do it for you." He ducked back into the pilothouse and counted to five. Then he looked through the porthole for Jackie. The mate had gone over to the crewmen and was shouting and gesturing; but still the net was being paid out. *Bullheaded young cuss.* A huge wave broke over the bow as the *Lisboa Girl* dove into a trough, spraying the men standing midships by the gantry.

Joe abandoned the pilothouse and reeled his way across the heaving deck, his hair instantly wet from the blown seas, his face turning red with suppressed rage.

"Tell me what I have to do to get an order obeyed here," he said to Jackie. The mate shrugged and looked away, muttering into the storm. Joe turned to a younger man working the winch. "Get that net back on deck, Lars, double-time, you understand?"

"Sure, Cap'n, if you say so." The blond crewman glanced at the first mate. "But there's an awful lot of fish down there."

"There's a lot of bones, too," Joe said through his teeth, "and not all of them ancient. Bring it up."

Lars, a Norwegian incorrectly known around Nantucket as the Swede, turned back to the controls and eased the lever through neutral into reverse. The winch gave a groan audible even over the force of the wind, and the net started to wind wetly out of the water.

"That's it," Jackie burst out beside him. "I'm through. There's nothing worse than a man who's too afraid to make money. Why don't you stay home and leave the cod to people who know what they're doing?"

Joe Duarte's rage hiccuped inside of him as he shot a look at Jackie's ugly face, but it was quickly replaced by a terrible weariness. He *was* old, too old to be walking a sea-slick deck in the pitching dead of night, too old to slam an obnoxious twenty-eight-year-old on the jaw, too old to weigh whether the catch or his life was more important.

"You think you know what you're doing, huh?" he said. "You think you know how to run a boat?"

"Damn sight better'n you do, old man," Jackie retorted.

"At least I've got a boat to skipper," Joe said, with satisfaction, "instead of a wreck at the bottom of Cape Cod Bay. You didn't learn from that bit of trouble, did you, Jackie boy? You never learn anything. Your skull's too hard and your brain's too small. You can get off my boat, and good riddance."

He had expected the first mate's scowl of rage and the words bubbling at his lips, had expected him to take a swing at him, even, sealing the fate of their sundering after a year of strained partnership. But he hadn't expected the look of horror that washed over the man as he stared at something behind Joe himself, over his head, or the cry of warning that was torn from him too late.

Oh no. God, no. Del.

The full force of the net's steel otter door, rising much too fast from the roiling sea, caught the captain in the back of the skull. It was a massive blow that knocked sense from him with the swiftness of a snuffed candle. He crumpled at his crewmen's feet, at the base of the gantry, the otter door swinging wildly overhead as the Swede struggled to secure it. Jackie reached for Joe Duarte just as the boat heeled over, wallowing in a trough and pitched sideways by the weight of the swinging door. But the stunned man slid out of the mate's reach, into the water, his white head another bit of froth on the surging waves.

"Joe!" Jackie cried, the howling of the wind drowning his voice. "Joe!"

But the old man was gone.

"IT COMES AS no surprise to any of us, dear friends," Father Acevedo was saying, "that Joe Duarte stayed in the water rather than attend his own funeral. He used to say that if the Lord wanted him at Mass instead of on the Georges Bank on Sunday, He'd have sent the fish to church." He paused for the anticipated laughter. "I think we know where the fish are today, dear friends, and we know that Joe Duarte is right where he'd want to be."

The sentiment, however apt, failed to strike a note of cheer in the crowd. It *missed*, somehow, like the funeral conducted without a body, like the blowing gusts of frenzied rain that hammered the first summer flowers into their muddy beds. Father Acevedo meant well. He was Portuguese himself, born and raised on the Cape, and his father had fished with the Provincetown fleet. He'd known Joe Duarte for six years. But when a man was lost at sea, fear cut deep in the hearts of his confederates, a fear hard to laugh off. No one who fished for a living wanted to die for it.

Detective Meredith Folger scanned the faces lining the pews and aisles of St. Mary's. A few shocked smiles met the priest's sally, but most of the mourners simply looked uncomfortable. She caught the eye of Jackie

Alcantrara—Joe Duarte's first mate, the one who'd jumped into the Atlantic after him and come back empty-handed. He'd taken a knock on the head, and the hospital had shaved his skull; the man looked more like a bull than ever, she thought. His heavy-featured face had gone white under his tanned skin, and he wasn't laughing. Merry dropped her eyes to her lap and wished the funeral Mass were done.

Joe's relatives had come from all over Massachusetts—the Ed Duartes from Gloucester, the Luis Duartes from Mattapoisett, and up front, behind the first pew, the Manny Duartes out of New Bedford, the ones his daughter, Del, had been living with. They were all fishermen. A good number of townsfolk had also braved the rain to say goodbye to Cap'n Joe, though few among them still made their living from the sea. There were Portuguese names all over the island, but they tended to be printed on the sides of pickup trucks rather than boats. Not a family among them failed to fish every summer, however—for pleasure or sport, or the occasional killing in the Japanese tuna auctions.

Father Acevedo beamed all around and raised his hands, signaling the end of his homily, and the congregation rose for the Prayer of the Faithful. Merry craned for a look at Adelia Duarte as she stood in the first pew, her two-year-old, Sara, singing a quiet nonsense song to her doll, and marveled again at her calm dignity. She had been absent from the island almost three years, since the pregnancy that had alienated her father. To return under circumstances like these must be an unbearable strain. Yet she showed no signs of the gnawing guilt and regret that her neighbors probably hoped to see—none of the remorse of the prodigal daughter, eyes downcast and shoulders trembling, all hope of reconciliation lost. She had yet to endure the post-funeral reception, when the wives of her father's friends would invade the house with their casseroles and sympathy, sincere or false, a suffocating flock of femininity blessed with men safe and alive.

Merry smiled, and just as swiftly smoothed her features back into anonymous solemnity. Everyone in the church was trying not to stare at Adelia and her baby, and failing miserably. She was too much her father's child to care what Nantucketers said or thought about her life; she was probably looking forward to the struggle.

She had, after all, chosen to wear red today.

"A PRETTY ENOUGH little thing," Jenny Baldwin was saying, her eye on Sara Duarte, who was wandering wide-eyed through the forest of adult legs filling Joe Duarte's living room, "though rather small. But then she *is* illegitimate, and I always find that babies born out of wedlock are *not* robust, don't you? And where did she get that red hair?" she continued, not waiting for Merry's response. "Not from the Duartes, certainly."

"Agnes's hair was auburn," Merry said, recalling Adelia's mother.

"Was it?" Jenny said vaguely. "She died before my time, I'm afraid. Too bad. If she'd lived, perhaps Adelia wouldn't have been quite so—unrestrained. But a girl raised as she was . . ." She clicked her tongue in mock sympathy and raised one eyebrow in the general direction of the red dress. She was the sort of woman who'd learned to click her tongue before she'd learned to form sentences. "Of course, Tom and I were always ready to do anything we could for her—"

"If you'll excuse me, Mrs. Baldwin," Merry said, her own black brows lowering, "I'd like to talk to Del, and I haven't much time before I'm due back at the station. You understand."

"You were great friends once, weren't you?" Jenny Baldwin said, her bleached blue eyes awash with interest.

She's wondering if I know who the baby's father is, Merry thought with distaste. "Yes," she said, "but we've grown far closer since she left the island. Absence has a way of revealing your true friends."

She set down her club soda and crossed the room in search of the red dress, which seemed to have vanished into the kitchen. She had been less than frank with Jenny Baldwin, but anger brought out her contrary streak. Del Duarte was a childhood friend. They had grown apart during the past decade, some of which Merry had spent at Cape Cod Community College, the Massachusetts Police Academy, and her first tour in New Bedford. By the time she'd come back to Nantucket six years ago, Del had her own life. Her pregnancy took her off-island three years later. Merry had no idea who'd fathered baby Sara.

A wall of bodies obscured her view. She eased her shoulder past stocky, weathered Tom Baldwin, Jenny's husband, raising her hand to the small of his back and hoping he'd ignore her. Instead, he turned his head and smiled.

"Merry!" he said. "Good to see you."

"And you, Tom. Where've you been hiding?"

"Oh, inside a foundation or two," he said, his tanned skin crinkling at the corners of his eyes. He'd made more money than most during the recent development boom, and from the look of the signs around town announcing his current projects, he'd plowed the profits back into his business. Merry doubted he'd been inside a concrete cellar for years.

"I hope no one commits a crime today," he said, glancing over at her father, the police chief, who stood surrounded by a knot of Joe Duarte's older friends. From the way he held his hands in the air, spaced about eighteen inches apart, Merry knew John Folger was regaling them with the tale of his latest near-conquest of an elusive bluefish. "With Nantucket's finest trapped in this room, they'd get clean away with it."

"We left Ralph Waldo by the phone."

"How's your granddad doing?"

"Very well, thanks. He never seems to get any older." At eighty-two, Ralph Waldo Folger was competent and eager enough to resume his duties as police chief—relinquished to his son some twenty years before—so that Merry and John could attend Joe Duarte's funeral. She knew he'd be safely tucked up in his favorite armchair, one eye on the storm and one ear on the police radio.

"Sad about Joe," Tom said, twirling the ice cubes in his drink, "but at least he lived a long life."

"Right," Merry said shortly. Tom Baldwin would consider sixty-eight young once he reached it.

"I don't suppose Adelia will be staying on the island long," he continued. "The house should sell quickly, this time of year—"

"—and on this block of Milk Street," Merry finished. "I know. Everyone says the same thing. *Perfect* summer cottage for a young investment banker from New York.

But I haven't had a chance to talk to her long enough to find out whether she's planning to sell or not." She caught sight of Del through the space left by a turning head, and with a smile for Tom Baldwin, wove her way toward the kitchen.

It was like Joe Duarte's daughter to be calmly scrambling an egg in the middle of chaos. She stood by the stove, her long dark hair a shining band against the brightness of her dress, the only cheerful thing in an otherwise drab bachelor kitchen. It was a galley space, narrow and dark, with an ell for a small Formica-and-steel table with three outmoded chairs. The stubby refrigerator was rounded and domed in the mode of the 1940s, the counters were badly fauxed marble, and the linoleum on the floor was bleached of its original color—yellow, probably. A frieze of brown age spots overlaid the wallpaper like the back of an octogenarian's hand; Joe had apparently intended to strip it from the walls, since one section was torn off and hung to the floor with the pathetic droop of a three-day-old lily. The young investment banker from New York would have to sink some money into the place. Merry touched Del lightly on the shoulder, and Del turned to her with an expression partly of relief and partly of weariness.

"*Eh, filha,*" she said, "Good of you to come. It's been too long."

Hey, girl. The affectionate Portuguese phrase stripped away the years as suddenly as a breath of wind. Merry reached out to hug Adelia. "You look great," she said. "I can't tell you how sorry I am about Joe."

Del looked beyond her to the crowded living room. "Can you believe this circus?"

"It's like a bad joke—'How many people can you fit into a Nantucket cottage?'"

"Depends how many have eaten today, right?" Del said, laughing. "Joe'd have thrown them all out an hour ago."

"Or left them the house and camped on the boat."

"But that's what it means to be dead," she said, glancing up at the ceiling. "He's a captive audience somewhere, for the first time in sixty-eight years." Her eyes shifted quickly to the egg drying in the pan. "Whoops. She likes them soft, salmonella or no. Sara!"

She reached for a plate and scraped the egg onto it. Tom Baldwin shouldered his broad chest through the kitchen door, Sara Duarte giggling on one arm. "Here she is!" he said, swooping her into a chair fitted haphazardly with a booster-seat cushion. He turned to Adelia, one hand reaching for the plate. The Baldwins had no children, Merry remembered, but it must not be from choice, Tom clearly enjoyed them. He smoothed Sara's deep red curls, the color of mahogany, and settled himself into a chair, fork at the ready. Merry leaned against the wall and smiled at Del. She didn't smile back.

"I'll feed her, if you don't mind, Tom." Adelia took the fork out of his hand and stood over his chair, her lips compressed.

"Sure," he said, rising quickly. "Just thought you could use a hand."

"I'm never too busy to feed Sara," she said, and sat down. Tom looked at Merry, shrugged, and backed out of the kitchen.

"Feeling a little tense?" Merry said, drawing up the remaining chair as Adelia lifted a forkful of egg toward Sara's obliging mouth. "Or did Tom hit a nerve?"

"Tom's just being Tom," she said wearily. "Hale and hearty and bending over backward to show everybody that Sara would love to have a daddy. That poor Del has her hands too full, trying to raise her kid alone. Why didn't she put her up for adoption, like everyone told her to? So couples like the Baldwins, poor guys, could have a baby of their own? But no. Adelia was always so stubborn, so bullheaded. Never knew what was good for her, and never would listen when people tried to tell her. *Que pena.*"

"You don't really believe they think that, Del," Merry said.

"Oh, I *know* they do." Adelia put down the fork in frustration. "And I've got a headache that will not quit."

Sara kicked her feet against the tabletop, wanting another forkful of egg, then gave up and reached for it with her fingers.

"Okay, so maybe I'm a little raw," Del said, sitting back in the chair. "But you don't know, Mer, how hard it is to come back. To look like I don't give a damn. I can't even cry for Pop in peace. I can't lose it in public. Everybody'd nod and say I feel as guilty as sin. So I try to be a rock instead. You know, half these people are here out of nosiness. They want to see how I handle Sara. And how bad I feel."

"So how *do* you feel?"

"Pretty lousy," she said, laughing shortly. "You know me. I always felt guilt over things I've only *thought* of doing, never mind things I've actually done. I can't get it out of my head that I didn't call him on his birthday. I *should* have called him, Merry. It was three months ago. I thought about it that day, *and I decided not to.* Can you believe that? As if he'd be around next year to call instead. I'm such a fucking idiot."

"Del—you can't think like that."

"Then I guess I can't think at all."

Merry was silent for a moment. She'd known Del for twenty-odd years. Despite the distance that had grown between them, she was probably Del's closest friend on Nantucket. And she knew that if their roles were reversed, she'd have felt the same way. Never mind that Joe Duarte hadn't called his daughter in years; he'd had the last laugh. He'd *died*, the ultimate upping of the ante in a war of silence.

"It'll be over soon," she said, reaching for Del's hand. "You'll be home in New Bed before you know it."

Del squeezed her fingers in response, released them, and drew a deep breath. "Well, yeah, that's what I'd like to talk to you about," she said. "I'm thinking of staying."

"Here?" It was the last thing she'd expected. "So you're not selling the house. From the way the real estate talk is going, you've got at least ten buyers in the living room alone. Do you want your old job back?"

"With Tom?" Del shook her head. Three years ago, she had been Tom Baldwin's personal assistant, and was, by all accounts, invaluable. She was smart, efficient, and organized—the last something Tom had struggled and failed to be.

Del reached for a napkin to wipe Sara's face. It was smeared with egg, like the sunrise smile of a clown. Sara pursed her lips and leaned away, her hands balled into fists.

"He hired a sub for me when I left, and he's not gonna fire her just because I'm back in town."

"Even if you could stand it," Merry said.

Del grinned. "Yeah, there's that," she said. "I'd prob-ably go nuts. Too much a part of the past, you know?" She looked at Merry, weighing her words. "I've got a better idea. I'm going to take Pop's boat out and fish."

"You? *Fish?*"

"Swordfish, actually. You know what they're getting for harpooned ones? It's like a yuppie craze. Somebody figured out that a harpooned fish dies quicker and tastes better than one caught by the long-liners' nets. Whole Foods pays through the nose for it, all over the country. So do restaurants."

"And God knows we have enough of those." Nantuck-et's restaurants were expensive, trendy, and geared to a moneyed crowd. "But Del—a harpoon?"

"I've thrown one before," she said, smiling. "You know how Pop was. He wanted a son and he got me. So he tried his best to turn me into a boy. I've been throwing a harpoon with him on the weekends since I was ten. He'd leave the *Lisboa Girl* at dock and take out the *Praia*—his thirty-footer—with me in the bow to spot. We caught a bunch over the years. You learn the knack. And you never forget the thrill."

"Aren't swordfish pretty scarce?"

"Used to be," Adelia said, "but lately the stocks have been recovering. Some of us think that's due to the shift from longline to harpoon fishing—swords aren't being overfished as badly as they were. My cousins in New Bed harpoon on the side. I went out with them a couple of times to get my arm back in shape, and it reminded me how much I missed being on the water. Pop used to say the harpooner's arm was passed down through the blood, you know, ever since the whaling days. Knowing the sea and loving it is something Duartes are born with."

She paused and looked at Merry soberly. "Pop's dead. I can't bring him back. But now he's gone, I miss a lot of things I thought I'd forgotten. Like hard work and cold spray and the fight to the death. I want Sara to grow up a Duarte."

"You think you can make a living?"

"I hope."

"If the swords play out, you can always switch to tuna." The Japanese paid exorbitant prices—up to twenty thousand dollars a fish—for prime bluefin tuna at auction.

Del shook her head. "They're even scarcer than swords."

Merry ran her fingers through her blonde hair—still damp from the rain and the persistent humidity that came with it—and decided to concentrate on essentials. "Who's going to crew for you?"

"I haven't figured that out," her friend admitted. "I'll think about crew tomorrow. There has to be some guy on the island who's strong enough to work for a woman."

"I'm not so sure," Merry said carefully. "Precious few are willing to take orders from one."

"Nothing's changed down at the station, eh, *filha?*"

Merry was one of the few women on the Nantucket police force.

Adelia's sudden smile was like a snapshot of childhood. "Come fish," she said. "We could be the only girl crew on Nantucket. Think about it. We'd be a tourist attraction."

"We Folgers like to say that police work is handed down through the blood. Something we're born with."

"I was afraid of that. Got any ideas about crew?"

"I might. Give me a few hours." She paused, and eyed the baby. "You'll need child care."

"I know." Adelia lifted Sara out of her chair and straightened the hem of her dress.

"She's beautiful, Del," Merry said, squatting down to Sara's eye level. She had the meltingly soft skin and the faint flush of rose in her cheeks that come with the two-year-old's territory. Her eyes were Merry's exact shade of green. She smiled slowly at Merry and reached a hand out to squeeze her nose.

"Yeah. She's a sweetheart. Gives nobody trouble," Adelia said soberly. "Hard to believe she comes from me."

Merry rose and brushed off her skirt. "What are you doing tonight? After this crowd clears out, I mean."

"Having dinner at your house, if I'm lucky."

"Good. I know just the person to take care of Sara." She gave her friend a swift kiss, touched a hand to the child's head, and was gone.

IT WAS ONLY when the last of the guests had left, and she had begun to collect the scattered glasses lying about the living room, that Adelia realized Jackie Alcantrara was still in the house. Was it a slight cough, an overly loud exhalation of air, that had drawn her to her father's "snug," as he called it? Or the creeping sense of being not quite alone?

The little den at the back of the house had never seemed big enough for more than one person. She'd rarely ventured farther than the threshold, even when she'd been desperate for her father's notice. The space was still dwarfed by the cracked Naugahyde recliner at full stretch and the huge old desk in one corner, piled to its gills with papers, bills, and photographs of prize catches; and there was a strong odor of pipe tobacco embedded in the fibers of the room that brought her father back in a sharp rush. Thumbtacked to the fake dark paneling was a picture of herself, taken at Great Point Rip when she was fifteen, holding high her first surf-caught blue.

Habit stopped her in the doorway, a dishtowel flung over one shoulder and a brace of wineglasses in her hands. Jackie was bent over the desk, rifling through the papers, too intent on his search to notice her approach. At the sight of him—close-cropped bullet head, large animal hands cracked and roughened by weather, awkward, bulky body—she felt sharply afraid. She had made no mention to Merry Folger of the doubts that had troubled her since Joe's death. In daylight, among friends, they seemed slightly hysterical, and that was not her style. But doubt tugged at her nonetheless. Standing before her now, Jackie was the embodiment of her worst suspicion.

"Tell me what you're looking for, and maybe I can help," she said.

He straightened as if he'd been shot, his face suddenly crimson, and shoved his hands in his pockets without a word.

"What's up, Jackie?"

He shrugged. "You might as well hear it from me as anyone else," he said, avoiding her eyes. "Your dad promised me his boat, when he was gone, since he had no sons and he figured you wouldn't be back after . . . And you're a woman, anyway. It's not like you'd need it."

"His *boat*?" Adelia said, aghast. "The *Lisboa Girl*?"
Jackie nodded.

"But it's paid for. Free and clear. There's no mortgage,"

she added, as if this would make it plainer. Boats free
of debt were an increasing rarity among New England
fishermen, and though Joe Duarte's was old, it was worth
at least a hundred thousand dollars. "He musta been nuts.
Maybe he'd give you a break on the price, but—"

"The word was *give*," Jackie said firmly, his color rising again. "And not just the *Lisboa Girl*, but the *Praia* as
well."

"You're dreaming! There's no way he'd give you
both." It was the *Praia* she intended to use for swordfish
harpooning.

"Dreaming? *I'm* dreaming?" Jackie said. "And what
have you been doing for the past three years, Del, besides
spreading your legs for any man in a pair of pants? While
you were bumming around New Bedford with a bun in
the oven, I was working myself to the bone to keep your
dad on the water." He came toward her, his blunt skull
and bear paws made suddenly menacing by the smallness
of the room and the viciousness of his words. Despite herself she leaned backward into the hall, a sick mingling of
rage and fear building in her throat.

"I earned that boat, every foot of her, and the *Praia* too.
If it weren't for me, Joe Duarte would've been finished
months ago, and much you cared about it. So don't tell
me what I know and don't know, or what you're due from
a man you couldn't trouble yourself to look after." He was
swaying slightly on his feet, as though he still felt a deck
heaving beneath him. Adelia knew he'd drunk quite a bit
that afternoon.

"You've got your nerve, coming back here with that
brat after what you've done, acting like you've never
left and nobody the wiser." His voice had grown harsh,

the words slurring with anger. "You'll get what's coming to you, Del—that's the truth, and everybody knows it. There's not a man on the water won't think it's justice when Joe Duarte's will is read."

"His will," Adelia said dully. "Is that what you were looking for?"

"I witnessed it. So I know what it says. I just figured I'd find it before you did, in case you decided to trash it."

"Like I'd do that, Jackie. If Pop wanted you to have the boats, he wanted you to have the boats. But you won't find anything in the desk—Pop gave up trying to, years ago. Now get out of my house."

Adelia felt suddenly weary, as though she were ancient beyond belief, and had survived the last century without a single night's sleep. *Pop gave away his boats. My boats.* It was God's little joke, spiking her plans and cursing her with characters like Jackie. Of course, her father had thought she'd never need her birthright. She'd left him, as Jackie said. The anger in the man before her must have been nothing compared to Joe Duarte's.

"I'll call Felix Harper in the morning." She turned away from the room. "He's Pop's lawyer. He'll be able to answer all your questions." *And mine,* she thought.

"I'll call him myself." Jackie brushed past her heavily on his way to the door. She smelled the sour odor of stale whiskey.

"You do that," she said, watching him swing down the shining-wet brick path and through the picket-fence gate onto Milk Street, his figure hunched against the violent gusts that still battered the island. Her mother's peonies were sodden starbursts against the grass, the hydrangea heads were bowed to their knees in a welter of rain. She looked up at the heavy sky, the lowering dusk, and let the storm's wet fingers brush back her hair. The weather had settled in. Even Joe's seabed must be uneasy tonight, with such turbulence sweeping the air above. The thought of him lost and alone in the Atlantic sent a sharp stab of pain through her stomach.

She closed her eyes and considered dinner at the Folgers' with relief and something else—a renewed conviction. Hysterical or no, her fears would have to be shared. She could not stand another night of brooding about her father's murder.

ADELIA DUARTE CLOSED her door on the stormy dusk just as Merry Folger was drawing up to the geranium-colored portal of Peter Mason's two-hundred-year-old saltbox. The house, with its hundred acres of cranberry bog and sheep pasture, was tucked into the island's moors and surrounded by Nantucket Conservation Foundation lands, but despite its isolation in the late-afternoon gloom, it looked snug and welcoming. Yellow light shone from the windows, the scent of woodsmoke spiraled from the chimney—and Merry's spirits, dampened by funereal thoughts and contagious melancholy, immediately rose. She turned off her car's ignition and thrust open the door.

She was still wearing the quiet navy suit she'd thought proper for the Mass, and her pumps sank into the crushed quahog shells that covered the drive. She jumped quickly to the brick steps and rang the bell, feeling the sudden rush of anticipation that always preceded the sight of Peter. Ney was barking from somewhere within the house. That meant Peter was probably home.

"Detective!"

Not Peter, but Rebecca the housekeeper, her close-cropped iron-gray hair as grim as ever, her blue eyes snapping with interest, and her smile wide with pleasure.

Rebecca, who would love to see Peter settled with a nice young woman and had been trying to get Merry to the house on various pretexts all year. First, the laundry-room window she thought was forced, and demanded that Merry inspect herself—a window that clearly had not been raised or otherwise violated in years. Next, the matter of the missing suitcase, filled, Rebecca swore, with her most personal documents, that had disappeared from the barn storage room. The suitcase was discovered not much later, safely shelved in the stone depths of the storm cellar. After that, Rebecca started talking about her failing memory, and Merry made a point of stopping at the farm without being summoned—knowing how long the gray island winters could be for a woman of Rebecca's years, living with only Peter and his foreman, Rafe da Silva, for company.

"Now isn't that the prettiest thing!" Rebecca said, admiring her suit as she stood aside to allow Merry across the threshold. "You didn't find *that* on-island."

"J.Crew," Merry said automatically. "I've just been to Joe Duarte's funeral."

"That was today?" the housekeeper said. "And I never remembered. I'll have to send that poor girl a card all the same. You'll be wanting to see Peter, of course," she said briskly. "He's on through to the study."

But the sound of voices had drawn Peter Mason from his fire, and when Merry turned toward the hallway leading to the warmth of his favorite room, she found him leaning against the doorjamb, index finger in his book, studying her quietly.

"Merry," he said. "What a pleasure." The way he said the final word made her catch her breath and flush to her black eyebrows, but he'd already turned back into the room and couldn't possibly have noticed. She followed him and took the seat he offered, feeling the comfort of the place steal over her in warm waves. The fire was of driftwood, its multicolored flames cheerily psychedelic, and the sofa was bright against the storm beyond the windows. Rebecca had disappeared, and Merry felt herself relax into the place and the moment with something like relief. She hadn't realized how tense the funeral and the crowd at Adelia's had made her.

"I've been having scotch," he said. "Something about the rain and the damp—when it's raw, I need to drink something earthy. Like bourbon. Or this. What'll it be?"

"A glass of red, if you've got it." A few months ago she'd have refused even a beer, conscious of how it might look for a cop to drink on the job; but she wasn't on the job today, and Peter Mason was no longer a suspect in his brother's murder. "I just got out of Joe Duarte's funeral."

"Of all days," Peter said, glancing out the window. "My own father was buried on a raw day in January. You never forget it."

"Particularly when you've no body to bury," Merry said. "Just word of a death you tell yourself to believe." She accepted the glass of Pinot Peter handed her and let the first sip pool on her tongue. Like the last warm days of September captured in a bottle. She sighed and leaned back into the sofa's softness.

"How's your friend taking it?"

"Del? Like a rock. Mostly because everyone who knew her dad is hoping she'll fall apart. The outcast, returned too late—you know."

He slid into his club chair. "Sometimes this island is way too small."

"She knew what it would be like."

"Were they ever close?"

"Once. After Del's mother died, she and Joe were all each other had. That's one reason Joe took it so hard when she got pregnant and left. Although he'd stopped speaking to her by that time."

Peter's brow was furrowed. "Because of the baby?"

"Because she wouldn't tell him whose it was. She probably knew he'd go after the guy with a shotgun and try to make him marry her, and I doubt Del wanted to marry Sara's father. If she had, she'd be married by now. She wanted to have the baby in peace and ignore all the questions. That wasn't Joe's style."

"He probably died regretting it," Peter said.

"Like Jose da Silva will." Portuguese patriarchs tended to be implacable. The father of Peter's foreman, Rafe da Silva, had rejected Rafe when he was falsely accused of murder. Despite the passage of six years and Rafe's imminent marriage, the two still had not spoken. "That's partly why I'm here."

One of Peter's eyebrows rose. "I'd hoped it was to drink with me—since I hadn't heard Rebecca lost a silver tea service or a pair of pearl earrings. But never mind. Tell me about Rafe while I refill your glass."

Merry studied his back as he stood at the bookshelf-cum-bar, decanting the wine with practiced ease, and wondered what he did poorly. She had never witnessed an awkward moment in Peter Mason's life—except, perhaps, those first few after the discovery of his brother's body in his flooded bog. He had been enraged and embittered then, at Rusty Mason more than anyone else, and anger made him careless with words. She hoped she wasn't going to make him angry now.

"How much do you depend upon Rafe?"

He stoppered the Pinot bottle. "As a friend or a foreman?"

"As a foreman, I suppose."

"I rely on him increasingly. I doubt I'll replace him entirely if and when he leaves me."

"You seem certain he will," she said, feeling relieved.

"Change is a norm, Merry." His gray eyes went flat and cold for an instant, and he sat down again opposite her. "I never expect to hold the people I care about for very long."

She took the refilled glass he offered without comment. Peter's fear of loss disturbed her. It was too much like her own.

"So I have a thorough knowledge of every stage of production at Mason Farms," he continued. "It's vital, and it's frankly impossible to run this place unless you have your finger on its pulse. I make sure I do—if only so I don't look stupid every time Rafe takes a vacation."

"How busy are you right now?"

"Not terribly. The vines have flowered, and the fruit should set fairly soon. After that it's just a matter of irrigation and time. The harvest isn't until fall. The sheep are past lambing, and the shearing, again, can wait for September." He set down his glass. "Now. Tell me what you want from Rafe."

"Adelia needs somebody to crew for her."

"To crew *for* her?"

Merry nodded. "I know. It's unusual. The most women

are ever allowed to do on a fishing boat is cook, right?
I'm sure Rafe thinks so. But he's the best person I could
think of. He's dying to get back on the water—at least, I
imagine he is. Every ex-fisherman I know dreams of it for
the rest of his days. Del's going to harpoon swordfish—"

"She's going to *what* swordfish?"

"Harpoon them." Her voice sounded small even to
herself. "You don't know her, Peter, so this must seem
crazy. But trust me. It's not."

"And a woman wielding a barbed hook on a stick
needs somebody to steer the boat, I'm thinking?"

"That's about it."

"I can't see Rafe as a glorified taxi driver."

"I just wanted your permission, as his employer, to
ask," Merry said. "It would just be part time. A few days
when you can spare him. Adelia knows Rafe from way
back. She'd be thrilled to have his help."

"By all means, ask," Peter said. "Just don't be hurt if he
laughs in your face."

Merry found Rafe drawn up to his desk in the
barn loft, dark head bent over a pile of paperwork. He was
listening to music, one reason he hadn't heard her shoes
on the barn's wooden stairs.

"Girl Scout! How ya doin'?"

Her childhood nickname. "Not bad. You?"

He spun around in the chair. "Saw you at the funeral."

"But didn't bother to say hello."

"I got outta there fast. Didn't want to run into my dad.
He and Joe went to school together."

"Joe's entire first-grade class must have been in the living room. I said hello to Jose. He looked good."

"Yeah, pride agrees with the Old Bastard," Rafe said, slapping a sheaf of papers into a neat, squared pile. "Amazing we can live on an island of six thousand people and avoid each other. But da Silvas were always masters when it came to blood feuds. My great-great-grandfather kept one running in Portugal for three generations."

Merry pulled up a chair. "Do you miss it, Rafe?"

"Fighting with my father? Not at all. I'm smarter than that, Merry."

"I meant fishing for a living. Going out with the boats in the dark."

"All the time," Rafe said. "Even though I know my dad sold his boat to a guy trawling out of Hyannis. I keep thinking it should've been mine."

"It should have," Merry said.

"What's in the blood doesn't die easy. Particularly pride."

"I know." Merry looked at her shoes. A scalloped stain on the leather showed where the rain had done its work. "Del is thinking of staying here," she said.

"Yeah? She gonna work for Tom Baldwin again?"

"She's talking about swordfishing."

Rafe gave a short bark of laughter.

"Harpooning, actually," Merry continued, "off the *Praia*."

"Nobody's sending boats out after sword in these waters, Merry. Most of 'em are picked up off Long Island. Del won't make a decent living. Then she'll be scrambling for a part-time job in high season, when they've been promised to kids from Ireland and the Dominican Republic for months. She'll be desperate."

Merry knew what he meant. Local summer jobs

increasingly went to foreigners who applied through overseas agencies. Some had work permits, some did not. The Nantucket police couldn't do the work of the Immigration and Naturalization Service. So her father told his officers to look the other way, and restaurant owners paid fifteen bucks an hour for dishwashers. Like everything imported, summer help was pricey.

"Who's she gonna get to crew for her, anyway?" Rafe continued. "It'd be different if she had a brother. But no guy is gonna work for a Jonah."

A Jonah. Seaman's term for landlubber—or worse, a bad-luck curse. It was drawn from the miserable story of Jonah and the whale. All women were by definition Jonahs to commercial fishermen. They were some of the last champions of sexism.

"I thought maybe you might," Merry said quickly.

"*Me?*" Rafe stared at her in horror. "You crazy, Girl Scout? I wouldn't set foot on that boat if it were drydocked and for sale. I don't miss fishing that bad."

"Come on, Rafe. At least give it a thought."

"No."

"Flat-out?"

"You heard me. I'd be the laughingstock of every self-respecting guy in the harbor. And then there's Tess. Took me long enough to get her to the altar as it is. I don't want her catching me with another woman a month before the wedding."

"Peter thinks it's a great idea," Merry said.

"I just bet." Rafe laughed outright. "Get *him* on the boat then, he's so sensitive with women."

"Rafe—" She heard the pleading note in her voice, and started over. "Maybe with time Del will find somebody permanent to crew for her. But for now you could do a favor for an old friend. And you'll give her credibility. A little bit of acceptance. Until she gets her head above water and decides whether she's any good at this."

Rafe folded his tanned arms across his chest and stared at her quizzically. "You're trying to make me feel bad so I'll do something I don't want to. You'll be pulling out all the stops and talking about Billy next."

Billy. The IED that killed Merry's brother in Iraq had been meant for Rafe. But it was the foreman who brought it up all the time, not Merry.

"Nobody wants to give Del a break. You know what that's like. They'd rather she failed. But you, Rafe—independent, respected, mature enough to work with a woman—you can give her one."

"You're way too emotional to be a cop, you know that?" he said.

"Yep."

He rolled a pen under his fingers. "Just for a few days?"

"You know you'd love to be out on the water again."

"Might be fun to see the look on the Old Bastard's face." He turned back to his papers. "I'm not saying yes. I'm just not saying no."

Chapter 3

RALPH WALDO FOLGER lifted the lid from his beloved spaghetti sauce, breathed deeply of garlic, beef, and tomatoes, and sighed. The recipe was his wife's, mastered during the final years when arthritis had swollen Sylvie's hands and crippled her legs, barring her from the things she had loved—needlework, garden, and kitchen, in that order. The slow illness, Ralph had told Merry, was God's way of teaching him how to live without her grandmother; had she been taken from him abruptly, he'd have been lost. Instead, they continued to collaborate, in a sense, every time he unfolded one of the yellowed slips of paper on which she had recorded her secrets in her spidery Swedish hand. And so it was that on a night of terrible spring storm the Thursday before Memorial Day weekend, he could grace the house on Tattle Court with the mouth-watering smell of Bolognese.

In contrast to the unrelenting rain and the early dark, the kitchen was warm and filled with a soft golden light. It was a square space nearly one hundred and fifty years old, with somewhat newer wooden cabinets and white-enameled fixtures overlaid with a faint yellowing from age. The walls were painted a strong sea blue that looked shady in summer and cozy in winter, while the floor was of oak that creaked and sloped with the settling of the house. In the center of the room was a large oval table, scarred from decades of use, where the Folgers read their morning papers, piled their discarded mail, left purses and hats and crumpled brown bags of forgotten lunch. As a child, Merry had done her homework here, and Sylvie had put up jar after jar of brightly colored preserves. The room was the soul of the house.

A sudden shriek nearly jolted Ralph Waldo out of his shoes—Sara Duarte, exercising her lungs. Her small hands waved a fork and spoon in midair, and her legs, clad in bright green jersey, were energetically kicking the rungs of the aged Folger high chair. "Skettie!" she crowed. "Sara want *skettie!*"

Ralph Waldo smiled, his strong teeth a bright slash through his already tanned skin. Sara stopped kicking and waving, mesmerized by the sight of him. He knew how utterly strange he must seem to her—six feet tall, white-haired, his brows bristling over a trimmed beard—a Santa in sports clothes, like a card sent from a retirement community in Florida. But Sara Duarte was too little to know about Santa yet. Her wonder was wordless.

"Meredith Abiah!" he bellowed in the general direction of the stairs. "There's a child needs feeding!"

A pause in distant conversation and a hasty clatter of footsteps. The girls were coming down.

He had never gotten past thinking of them as the girls. As children they had tucked themselves into Merry's dormer room to gossip and share secrets. That they were both over thirty now and long past the age of slumber parties meant little to Ralph Waldo. Time had ceased to serve as a responsible marker of age. He felt as fit as he had at sixty—well, perhaps as fit as he had at seventy—and so the girls' passage through their twenties had happened imperceptibly. Even this little one seated at his table, impatient for spaghetti, did not age Adelia in Ralph Waldo's eyes. Sara was simply another girl, with years and years before her, and Ralph could think of nothing more delightful to have in the house.

Merry had tackled him in the living room before Del and her baby arrived that evening.

"I've got a favor to ask, Ralph."

"Does this have to do with Adelia, perchance?"

"How do you envision your summer?"

"My summer?" His favorite season. The time of tomato plants and bluefish on the grill and early-morning walks to Bartlett's produce truck at Federal and Main, followed by a satisfying lunch and nap in his Adirondack chair. "Same as always, I expect. Puttering at this, meddling with that."

"How'd you like some company?"

"What are you proposing, Meredith?"

"It's just that Adelia is thinking of staying."

"And what would she want with an old man's company?"

"Child care. She's got to work, and if she works, she's got to have someone reliable to take care of Sara. You're the most reliable person I can think of."

"A two-year-old?" He quailed momentarily, remembering Merry at that age. Legs that ran as fast as a sandpiper's, and always in the most dangerous direction. A constant stream of semi-intelligible language, punctuated by questions that rarely had adequate answers. The occasional storm of temper that ended in tears and a sudden fall into sleep. The smallness of a soft hand encased in his (to a child) enormous one, and all the sweetness of discovering the world anew, shining and wondrous as it hadn't been in years. Would he be reduced to ferrying her around on his bicycle, as he had seen so many tourist grandpas do, small fists beating on the broad back, the demands relentless for "a *story*, Grandpa, a *story*"?

"It would only be temporary," Merry said, "until Del got her feet under her and could find a good alternative."

Ralph looked at his granddaughter. "Temporary," he repeated, knowing how false that word usually turned out to be.

"I swear."

Of course he said yes.

"I'M STARVING." MERRY automatically stepped around Tabitha the cat and a cluster of recyclable containers piled willy-nilly on the floor. Tidiness was not the Folgers' strong point. "I feel like I haven't eaten in ten years."

"Me, too," Adelia said. "Ralph, if I could have had anything tonight, it would have been Sylvie's spaghetti."

Ralph beamed. "I thought you might. Comfort food. Your dad loved Sylvie's sauce himself, so we'll pretend for a few moments we're all together under one roof, as we were in the old days."

Merry felt her throat constrict as she reached for the grated cheese. Her mother had died about eight years before, Adelia's when she was six. With John Folger running the police force and Joe Duarte out on the water for days at a time, home life was a sporadic thing. Ralph Waldo, however, had tried to fill the gap. He was never too occupied to help them grow up. Although they were both over thirty now, he was still the greatest comfort, with or without his Bolognese. But for the life of her, Merry had no idea how to tell him that.

Adelia squeezed his gnarled hand. "Can I have the cheese, Ralph?"

This would have to do for the moment.

"You two get caught up?" her grandfather asked.

They looked at each other. Sara clattered her spoon against the table with determined purpose, and Adelia reached over to cut the spaghetti into baby-sized bits.

"Del thinks there's something wrong with her father's death," Merry said quietly.

"Beyond the obvious fact that sixty-eight is too young, you mean?"

She nodded.

"Adelia, my dear," Ralph Waldo began, and then stopped. No point in telling a Portuguese Nantucketer that the sea was a fickle mistress; and none in reminding her that men as good as Joe Duarte were lost up and down the coast every year. If her mourning took a turn toward denial, so be it. "What exactly do you mean by *wrong?*"

"I can't get it out of my head," she said. "Ever since the word came that he was gone, I knew something wasn't right. They said Pop was hit by one of the otter doors and knocked overboard. That with the size of the swell and the weight of his clothes, he sank like a stone. That Jackie, who jumped in after him when he saw him fall, was almost drowned himself trying to find him. But none of it makes sense. Joe Duarte was too good a fisher-man to—"

"Have an accident?"

"—to mess with his crew's job. And he was a damn sight too smart to have a net down in rising weather. He'd have smelled it coming, seen it in the set of the waves, and been on his way home before it hit."

"People make mistakes, Del."

"Not this stupid, Ralph. Believe you me," she said, drumming a red-lacquered fingernail on the tabletop. "My Pop was killed."

Ralph Waldo grunted and glanced at Merry.

"Maybe Joe Duarte was hit over the head and thrown in the water," Del persisted, "but not by the net doors and not by the swell. He was murdered."

"How many folks crewed for your dad, Adelia?" Ralph asked.

"Four. The *Lisboa Girl* is a sixty-five-footer."

"Had they been with him long?"

"Nope. Since most guys nowadays want to fish from the mainland, Pop was having trouble keeping a crew together for longer than a season. I don't know any of them, except Jackie, and he's only been first mate for a year."

"That's right," Merry said. "He'd moved off-island."

"Until he sank the boat he was skippering over on the Cape's backside," Del said. "At least, that's what I heard from my cousins. I was in New Bed at the time."

"He sank a boat, and your dad took him on as first mate?"

"Like I said, with only two boats trawling out of Nantucket, it's tough to find *anybody* to crew. Particularly anyone with experience. Besides, Pop and Jackie's dad, Sylvester, were cronies from way back. Ever since Sylvester died of a heart attack, Pop's tried to look out for Jackie."

"My dear," Ralph said gently, "for what you're saying

to be true, the entire crew would have to be lying. And to keep their stories straight, under such pressure, is quite beyond the power of most of the chuckleheads running trawlers for a living. And as I recollect from the newspaper account, the crew was interviewed by the Coast Guard, and the stories agreed."

Adelia looked away. "It sounds crazy, right?"

"I'm not saying that makes it any less likely, understand." He waved his spaghetti fork for emphasis. "Quite the contrary. But even if we accept, for the moment, that your father was helped into the water, where's the *why* of it? Why would an entire crew want to murder their captain?"

"Maybe they were paid to do it," Adelia suggested.

"Because . . . ?"

"Pop left Jackie the *Lisboa Girl* and the *Praia* free and clear in his will."

Frowning, Ralph set down his fork.

"*Both boats*. Or so Jackie says. I'm calling the lawyer to make sure."

"And you didn't see this coming?" Ralph asked carefully. "You two had been . . . estranged . . . for a while."

"If I thought about it, I'd expect him to leave 'em to my cousins Manny or Luis. They're blood, and they coulda used the break. They're running other people's boats because they can't afford the mortgages and the insurance."

"You see what this means, Ralph," Merry said. "Jackie's come into a fortune, and a way to restore his reputation as a skipper."

"If Jackie wanted a boat," Del interjected, "Pop signed his death warrant."

Ralph held up his hand. "Did he know that he stood to inherit?"

"He told me he'd witnessed the will."

Ralph Waldo heard the pain in her voice. Jackie had been Joe's confidant at a crucial moment—when he hadn't given his daughter a thought.

"Think of it," Del pressed. "Guys are lost overboard every year. Especially in storms. All he had to do was take his chance."

Neither Ralph nor Merry answered, and silence fell around the table, punctuated by the lilting waver of Sara Duarte singing as she fingered her pasta. Her spoon was abandoned to one side of her plastic mat, and her hands were covered with dark red sauce. Impatiently, Adelia seized a paper napkin and wiped her child's hands clean, moving on to the smeared cheeks, despite Sara's protests.

"I had a gut feeling things were screwy as soon as they told me Pop was dead," she said. "But when I heard what Jackie had to say—and the way he said it, tough as nails and like he'd just been caught peeing in the bushes— I just knew Pop was murdered." She threw down the napkin and looked at them both, her eyes sharp and stubborn. "So you guys think I'm crazy. I'm not gonna let it slide. Pop deserves better. And I'm the only one who cares about him, now."

LATER, WHEN THE dishes were washed and Ralph Waldo was putting the last scouring on the stainless-steel sink, Merry saw Adelia and her baby out the door. Then she joined him in the kitchen with a towel.

"Leave them to drain," he said.

Obediently, she draped the towel over a hook. "What do you think?"

"I think, Meredith Abiah, that your friend is succumbing to the culture of her forebears."

"Which one is that?"

"In my day, the Portuguese fishing community was always rife with rumor and innuendo. If they weren't talking about good and bad luck—who was carrying it and who was spreading it—they were drumming up the latest conspiracy theory about price-fixing in the Boston fish markets. The Portuguese take nothing at face value that they can embroider and embellish. Joe Duarte was getting on in years, he made a mistake, or a series of mistakes, and he paid a heavy price. But it doesn't surprise me that his daughter prefers a conspiracy theory."

Merry hoisted herself onto the Formica counter, legs dangling. "That business about Jackie inheriting the boats has nothing to do with Portuguese culture. Del's right. Joe should have left them to Manny or Luis. It might be worth looking into Jackie's stories."

"You mean about the boat he sank last year, as well as the boats he stands to inherit?"

Her eyes gleamed. "Exactly. Here's a guy who's involved in two boat accidents within months. Even Del can be forgiven for thinking he's bad luck. Or that there's more here than meets the eye. I'm getting pretty interested in his seamanship myself."

"You can't think Joe was murdered, Meredith Abiah."

"No," she admitted. "Much as I'd like to support Del, I can't say that I do. But she may keep accusing Jackie until I can prove he had nothing to do it."

"Even proof may not stop the rumors," Ralph Waldo said. "The Duartes are pretty good at carrying a grudge."

"It can't hurt to help an old friend, Ralph."

The sound of rain suddenly swept into the kitchen; Merry's father stood in the open doorway, wrenching off his sodden shoes.

"In my experience," John Folger said, "those words are usually a shortcut to disaster. Which old friend are we helping now?"

"Del Duarte," Merry said. "She wants us to find Joe's murderer."

Chapter 4

MERRY TURNED INTO the Coast Guard compound at Brant Point, its square buildings looming as purely white as a Greek fishing village in the glare off the harbor. The previous day's storm had given way to a brilliant May morning of sun and high cumulus, with a fresh breeze that sent the sailboats' riggings clanging metallically against their masts. It was the sort of spring day that came all too rarely on an island affectionately called the Gray Lady for its persistent fogs.

Everywhere about the compound lay desks and cot frames torn out of their rooms, grayed mattresses piled high, chairs overturned on their sides; spring cleaning for the Coast Guard, Merry guessed. She turned away from the postcard perfection of the boat basin and ran up the steps of the main building, lifting her sunglasses to the top of her head as she pulled open the heavy door.

The interior of the station was dim and cool, blinding her for a moment as she stood in the doorway, blinking and searching for a point of focus.

"Detective Folger."

Terry Samson's high-pitched, cracking voice was one no man deserved, certainly not the compact fighting weight that was Terry. He was standing by the refrigerator in the midst of the station's eating area, holding a pitcher of lemonade, looking for all the world like Tom Cruise in *Top Gun*. The sunglasses worn inside were a bit much.

"What can I do for you?" The words fell somewhere between a screech and a whine.

Merry winced involuntarily and turned it quickly into a smile. "Terry. I figured you'd be out on patrol."

"Not this shift. I'm on tomorrow—always seem to draw more Saturday nights than anyone else, and I'm beginning to think the system's rigged. Do me a favor and investigate."

"I'm actually here on a case, if you've got the time to help me," Merry said.

"Anything I can do, Merry, you know that. This concern the boat-borne heroin ring Woods Hole keeps yammering about?"

Heroin ring. First word *she'd* heard. That might be something to offer her father, since he'd told her in no uncertain terms to leave the Duarte mess alone. In John Folger's opinion, the state police should handle Joe's death if it was suspect—and the DA in Barnstable wouldn't like the Nantucket force jumping turf. Merry had enough on her plate anyway, he said. Even now, she was supposed to be calling on an elderly woman in Dionis who claimed to have had her geraniums stolen from their pots.

Some plate.

"You keep a record of boating accidents, right?" she asked Terry.

"Sure. It's all in the MISLE."

"Missile?"

He took a swig of lemonade straight from the jug, let out a deep sigh, and closed the refrigerator door. "Marine

Information for Safety and Law Enforcement database. It tracks over 650,000 vessels in American waters."

"That's a lot." She was momentarily daunted; she knew nothing about the boat Jackie Alcantrara had sunk in Cape Cod Bay. "Do you need to know the registration data for the ship, or could we search for incidents that occurred nearby? Say, in the last year?"

"Sure. Nantucket's part of Sector Southeastern New England, which covers everything from Manomet Point, Massachusetts, to Watch Hill Point, Rhode Island. What do you consider nearby?"

"The Cape. Off Wellfleet, I think."

"Commercial or pleasure boat?"

"Fishing trawler, actually."

"That helps. Commercial captains have to be licensed, so if you've got the captain's name . . ."

"Jackie Alcantrara."

Terry looked at her quizzically. "He was a first mate, last I heard. And Joe Duarte's boat didn't sink."

"Right. This wasn't the *Lisboa Girl*, but a boat he captained last year."

"Got a date?"

She shook her head.

"You looking for insurance fraud?"

"Not particularly. I just want the details of what happened."

"Okay." Terry led her out of the kitchen area and into the duty station where his laptop sat on a desk. He took off his sunglasses and logged into the MISLE while Merry pulled up a second chair.

Not surprisingly, the bulk of the commercial fishing accidents occurred during the rough weather of late winter and early spring, when the Atlantic was fiercely cold, the swell was dramatic, and the water was the color of a submarine's steel hull. These were the months when the New England fishing community eked out a living, waiting for the return of the summer schools, competing with the Canadians, Spaniards, Japanese and Russians for whatever bottom fish remained in international waters. Tough as the work was, nobody could afford to stay home.

Terry punched in Jackie's name and turned up two accident reports within seconds. One was the *Lisboa Girl*. The Coast Guard choppers had been dispatched to the Georges Bank in an effort to retrieve Joe Duarte's body, and they'd continued to look for it for two days after the storm that killed him. Jackie's name was on record as an incident witness.

The second report dated from last April. Merry scrolled through the file.

Jackie had sunk a trawler named *Seaman's Folly* just off Wellfleet Harbor during a sudden squall on April 16. While attempting to race for port, he'd struck an unmarked wreck in seven fathoms of water and the boat had foundered rapidly. The five-man crew was saved, owing to a timely SOS. The boat's owner—a corporation called SeaCon—lost its investment and Jackie lost his job.

Merry looked up from the monitor, deflated. What had she expected? A red flag hidden in efficient Coast Guard prose? The hint that a criminal act had gone undetected?

A *pattern*. That's what she'd hoped to see: something that linked the accidents. But the only commonality was bad weather—and that was business as usual in commercial fishing.

Mortgaged boats carried insurance by law, and as with any accident, the proof of the policy and its underwriter were recorded in the Coast Guard report. The SeaCon Corporation's underwriter was a company called Water Rights. *Insurance fraud*, Terry had suggested. Maybe she should check on the outcome of SeaCon's claim.

"Want a copy of the report?" he asked.

"Email it to me. And Terry—please forget Jackie's name."

He flashed her his Top Gun smile. "I'd like to. Guy's an asshole."

"As a friend or a fisherman?"

"Both. Violent when he drinks. If you're going after him, Merry, watch your back."

"Needs more balsamic vinegar." Tess Starbuck passed Peter Mason the spoon with an air of conviction.

He sipped the liquid tentatively and screwed up his face. "Needs *sugar*, surely?"

Tess sighed and handed him a piece of lettuce. "You're not in the habit of drinking salad dressing straight from the bottle, are you? Try it with something grassy-flavored, and imagine warm duck breast slivered on top. An autumnal taste is what we're going for here."

Rafe leaned in the doorway, arms crossed, and decided not to involve himself in the debate. Too many cooks, and so forth, and besides, his allegiance was murky: his bride-to-be or his boss of six years. The two of them had been experimenting with the cranberry-based dressing for much of the afternoon. It was one of a series of concoctions intended for bottling under a new Mason Farms label. Tess had persuaded Peter to play the role of partner, promising to showcase his produce, cranberries, and spring lamb in ways certain to wow locavore food critics. They were to test the line at the Greengage this summer, and eventually launch it upon an unsuspecting world.

Thank God for Memorial Day weekend and the start of the tourist trade, Rafe thought, and felt a sudden sense of blasphemy. He'd always decried the yearly invasion of off-islanders, claiming they took and spoiled and gave nothing back; but Tess's business had changed his mind. Her livelihood was directly dependent upon the summer people, and the good opinion of a few powerful critics in the mainland enclaves of Boston, Manhattan, and Washington, D.C.

He hated the worry lines around Tess's eyes and the heightened streaks of gray in her rich hair. She had suffered the vagaries of sudden death and accident too often in the past few years. First there was her husband, Dan, lost overboard in a nor'easter, and then her son, Will, had been struck down in a vicious attack. He had survived, but his motor skills were impaired and his after-school hours were spent in physical therapy rather than the hoped-for Nantucket Whalers football practice. By late April, he had finally seemed his old self, despite the migraine headaches that still swept over him without warning, leaving him lost and silent in his darkened attic room for days at a time.

Throughout the off-season, Tess had struggled to make ends meet and nurse her son back to health; the Mason Farms line had been born of frustrated creativity and financial need. Whether Peter had decided to back her out of kindness or a hereditary business sense Rafe couldn't say, but he was grateful regardless.

"This'd be great with the lamb-and-apple sausage, too," Peter said, chewing the lettuce ruminatively. "But that'd be more of a spring salad."

"Right. Slice it thin, layer it with the chevre, and put it on baby field greens." Tess turned from him briskly and sought out the vinegar. "I can see using the dressing with melon and papaya and some green chilies in a fruit salsa, too. But I'll work on that tomorrow, okay?"

"The restaurant opens tomorrow," Peter said.

"Salsa takes maybe twenty minutes. If it works, I'll serve it for lunch. I'll get it to you and add it to the file." Tess was keeping an informal compilation of recipes, thinking long-term of *The Greengage Way*, her pet cookbook project.

"We should enter these in the cranberry festival cookoff," Peter said.

"By October, I'll have the kinks worked out. *Something* should win a first-prize ribbon."

Rafe handed Tess a towel. "I'll run you home."

"I thought Will got his license," Peter said.

"He did." She dried her hands briskly. "Why do you think I've got no car?"

ON THE WAY back to town in Peter's Range Rover, Tess was quiet and abstracted. *Thinking about the food,* Rafe decided. She had come to her business late in life, but it was her passion, born of innate talent and the thrill of making money from what she loved.

"You look tired, hon," he said. "Whaddya say we hit the Brotherhood for a burger and a beer?" Brotherhood of Thieves had changed over the years—from a subterranean burger dive to a full blown restaurant that served two hundred—and Rafe wouldn't go near it once the summer people hit the island. For someone like Tess who charted every day with a complex palate, however, it was blessedly simple.

She slid over and leaned her head against his shoulder. "Can I have an Allagash White Ale?"

"You can have two."

"Nobody's in town yet, really. It'll be our last chance to have the Brotherhood to ourselves."

Once on Broad Street, he managed to find a parking space—something else that would vanish with Memorial Day weekend—and got a table for two in a dim corner of the Brotherhood's ground floor. It was only five, but neither he nor Tess had eaten lunch, and the prospect of food was stimulating. There was a fire burning on the hearth, perfect for the end-of-May chilliness that came off the water of an evening, and Rafe leaned back in his chair with a sigh.

"Get a beer in my hand now, and I'll feel like I've died and gone to heaven."

"You work hard today?"

"Nope." He grinned. "But I was probably thinking too much."

"About what Merry said?" Tess's eyes dropped to her hands. She was worrying at her engagement ring, sliding it nervously back and forth. Sometimes Rafe wished he'd given her a car or something practical instead, but he shuddered to think what she'd have done with a steering wheel in times of mental turmoil.

"You think it's a bad idea for me to crew for Del," he said flatly.

"Not because I'm jealous, Rafe. You don't think that, do you?"

"Of course not," he lied.

"I'm too much of an adult not to trust the man I love, even if he's spending eight hours in the sun on a small boat in the middle of the Atlantic with a woman ten years my junior who's known for her loose morals."

"Adelia Duarte's never been known for loose morals," he said, "and you know it, Tess. She made a mistake, is all—" He bit his tongue. The last thing Tess needed to hear was his defense of a woman she'd decided to mistrust.

"Hi, folks!" A cheery college kid of a waiter, on the island early and clearly ready to enjoy the summer. "Have you seen our specials on the blackboard?"

"Yep," Rafe said, to stem the endless recitation of ingredients he knew would follow. "And I think we've decided."

"Great! What can I get for you this evening?"

He looked at Tess, who was gazing stonily into the fire. "The lady'll have a Cisco burger," he said, "and I'll have a Steakhouse. Medium. A Whale's Tail and an Allagash." He slapped the menus shut and handed them to the waiter with a smile. The kid nodded at both of them and headed for the kitchen.

Tess stood up immediately and stalked after the waiter, all her fury in her thin form. She grabbed him by the elbow. *Changing her dinner*, Rafe thought. She'd probably really wanted the barbecue cheeseburger he'd ordered for her—it was her standing meal at the Brotherhood—but God forbid that the defender of Adelia Duarte should be right about anything.

Tess slumped back down in her seat, avoiding him with her eyes.

"So if you're not jealous, why are you so pissed?"

"Because I can't believe you'd be stupid enough to alienate Peter Mason," she said. "Running around after swordfish—which, believe me, I know as a restaurateur are scarce as hens' teeth—when you can make a steady income and have the stability you do after six years at Mason Farms—" She put her face in her hands in frustration, and Rafe saw with alarm that she had begun to cry.

"Tess," he said, reaching a hand to her shoulder gently, "Peter doesn't mind. This is a slow point in the farming season. I've got some days free. There's no harm in it, girl. And I'd be helping out an old friend."

"I'm just so afraid," Tess said. Her voice was muffled by her fingers.

"Of what?"

"Of you. Of the whole fishing thing. I know you, Rafe—you've never gotten over your love of that life. It's in your blood. The slow season will turn into the high season, and you'll be out there just one more day, and pretty soon you won't be there when Peter needs you for the cranberry harvest, and you'll just gradually slip away. Back to boats and the craziness of the fishing grounds and the relentless work and the lousy money."

"Tess—"

"Well, I've lived that life, Rafe." Her head came up out of her hands, and he saw the reddened wetness where she'd rubbed at her eyes. "I lost Dan to it. We never had a dime we hadn't spent three times over, and we were never out of debt a single day of our married lives. He handed me that debt at the side of his grave, and I'm still not close to paying it off. I've only added to it. Can't you see that financial security is the one thing I need in my life?"

"I thought what you needed was me," he said, feeling suddenly cold.

"Not if you're on a fishing boat. I left that life behind me. I can't face the instability now, or the possibility of—loss. You could die out there like Dan did. Like Joe Duarte did, for God's sake. Don't you guys ever learn?"

"Dan and Joe were exceptions," Rafe said falteringly.

"And you never believe that anything will happen to you, do you?" She laughed, a short, humorless sound. "I'm just starting to make a foothold in a world I love, and I *will not* allow myself or my son to be dragged back down. I want Will to grow up knowing there's something more to life besides gutting fish and mending nets."

"Is that an ultimatum?"

She looked back at him wordlessly.

"Is it, Tess?"

"I don't know."

"Well, you think about it. Because July twenty-third isn't far away. And when I marry, Ms. Starbuck, I intend it to be for richer, for poorer, in good times and in bad, in farming or on the water. And I intend it to be for keeps." He pushed back his chair, pulled out his wallet, and tossed fifty dollars on the table. "Wouldn't want you to worry about the bill," he said, and turned away.

There was a sharp ping on his back followed by a metallic clink at his feet. She'd thrown her engagement ring as he walked out the door.

Chapter 5

PETER MASON HAD watched Rafe and Tess drive away from his open front door, then shut it carefully. He intended to pursue the salad dressing—this time as accompaniment to the marinating chicken breasts Rebecca had left on the counter for his supper. He would grill and slice them into the lettuce he'd pulled from the garden that morning, open a bottle of chardonnay, and tuck into a healthy meal that felt like Memorial Day weekend. All it lacked was company.

He stopped in the act of opening the refrigerator, his eyes focused on the kitchen clock. For some reason the numbered dial had been overlaid with Merry Folger's face. What was he waiting for? He'd been haunted by the blonde detective throughout the winter, the strongest proof he could find that he'd recovered from a decade-long obsession with his college sweetheart. Seeing Alison after his brother's murder had finally put to rest the long ache; he no longer mourned his broken engagement. Instead, he'd exchanged Christmas cards with her. And lately, when the form of a woman invaded his dreams at night, exquisite and pulsating and elusive as fog, she had borne the sharp cheekbones, the eyes green as new leaves, of Meredith Folger.

But what of Merry herself? On every occasion that Peter had seen her during the past eight months, she had seemed much as usual—friendly, warm, and carefully professional. He shut the refrigerator door without retrieving the lettuce and slid into a kitchen chair.

It was important, after all, to approach emotion with logic. Never mind that the two had nothing to do with each other. It was part of his education to consider a problem objectively—and to fear the consequences of impulse.

What if he asked Merry out, for example, and she rejected him? Would it be wiser not to ask at all?

Nah.

He'd wasted too long being safe. It was time to call her.

He picked up his cell phone before he could change his mind.

SHE ARRIVED LOOKING as cool and elegant as if she'd just stepped from a luxury hotel instead of the kitchen on Tattle Court, where in fact she'd been feeding Sara Duarte her supper. She had changed from her jeans into a jade-green washed silk sheath—nothing expensive, but clean-lined and simple enough on her tall, thin frame that it looked like a million bucks. The color exactly matched her eyes. Peter drew a sharp breath when he saw her step out of her new unmarked police Explorer, struck by the fact that she had gone to some effort over his invitation, and too wary to consider what that might mean.

She smiled when she saw his face in the window; and all he could think was, *Where does she get off being so calm?*

The dinner had turned into something more elaborate than grilled chicken salad during the hour preceding her arrival, and he hoped he didn't look too eager, with his smoked bluefish pâté and his corn muffins and the new red potatoes sliced over baby Bibb lettuce—but Merry was a good little eater and dove into the food with a sigh of delight, allowing him to refill her glass with the chilled chardonnay, moisture pearling the side of the crystal until she pressed it against her forehead and closed her eyes, in a gesture at once so sensual and childlike that it tightened his throat.

He had promised himself he would not push her this evening; he didn't want to scare her off. So he focused on grilling his chicken while she told him about Adelia Duarte and her father and the possibility of a murder case, however unlikely. What he wanted was to reach out and take hold of her long, thin fingers, the hands that were tanned and weathered from a lifetime in sun; wanted to kiss her palm and then the forehead she had tried to cool with her glass. He shut his eyes.

"So we're going tomorrow. Do you want to come?"

He blinked and looked back at her, and for an instant, perhaps, she saw the intensity he'd been masking. He recognized it in her face, the way her features went blank in surprise and then recovered. She took a sip of wine.

"Go where?"

"Swordfishing. With Rafe and Adelia and me. It'll be a wonderful day on the water—like nothing you've ever done. Say you'll come, Peter."

He held her eyes a minute, assessing. She didn't blink. "Maybe I will," he said.

THEY LEFT THE Town Pier off South Beach at six in the morning, when the sun laid a white light on the water and the coffee in Rafe's thermos tasted very good. Peter and Merry were braced by the long steel pulpit jutting from the bow, Rafe was at the helm, and Adelia studied the charts. The *Cormorant* was a forty-four-foot sportfishing boat she'd chartered cheap from one of Joe Duarte's cronies, past all fishing now and only too glad to earn something from the custom Brownell he kept loitering at its mooring. They made their way through the harbor to the narrow channel between the jetties and Nantucket Sound beyond. Out past Point Rip, a huge submerged sandbar that signaled its presence with white-rilled waves and a darker shadow on the nautical charts. Then into the broad depth of the Great Round Shoal Channel, and finally, when the coffee was long gone and they'd progressed to Rebecca's muffins, toward the deceptive and shifting bars of the Great Round Shoal itself, northeast of the island, where entire schools lurked in the shimmering depths and many a boat had run aground in decades past.

An hour went by. The great swords were elsewhere.

"Let's head for the wreck of the *Andrea Doria*," Rafe said.

"That's forty miles south." Del looked annoyed.

"If they're in Nantucket waters, they're basking over that ship." Rafe chewed his beard, holding in his temper.

Del scanned the horizon an instant, then shrugged. "*Ta bom*," she said. "Let's go."

Rafe throttled the engines higher and turned the boat toward the waters beyond Siasconset.

Two hours or so passed in surging motion. Adelia took the wheel, one eye on the charts, and Rafe came forward to where Peter sat, quiet in the rush of the wind and sun, his face speckled with the white spots of dried salt from the spray shushing over the Brownell's bow. He was wearing faded Nantucket Reds and Sperrys, his traditional sailing togs, with a heavy sweatshirt to ward off the chill. The wind had raised gooseflesh along his thigh.

"Happy?" he asked Rafe.

Rafe shrugged. "I'd be happier if Tess weren't in such a snit."

"Take her some swordfish steaks this evening and tell her I caught the thing," Peter said. "Maybe she'll get over it."

"Fat chance. If we even *see* a sword today."

"That rare?"

"That rare. Most Atlantic fish are off Nova Scotia, where there's a harpoon fleet. The long-liners fight the harpooners for quotas—catches are regulated, you understand—but if you've got a sport fishing license from NOAA you can go out like Del and catch one per trip. I doubt that'll happen today—swords have been overfished for decades, by driftnets and Spanish long-liners in particular. Those boats'll put out a thousand hooks at a time and take everything they can get. It shows in the catch: the fish coming in to market are half the size of the ones we caught when I was a kid."

"So how big are we talking?"

Rafe pursed his lips. "Couple hundred pounds, maybe. A good sword can weigh half a ton and be fifteen feet long—not that we see many of 'em anymore. But you go up against one of these babies traveling fifty miles an hour, with your feet in that pulpit and a harpoon in your hand, you'd better not blink. Sometimes they even attack the boat. It's the only thing comes close to Moby Dick these days."

Peter looked toward Adelia, who was studying gauges on the bridge. She had the short, sturdy body of a Portuguese fisherman, the muscled arms and the strong legs. She looked bred into this life, as indeed she was. Her long dark hair was pulled through a baseball cap—a *swordfishing* cap, as Rafe had reminded him—and her face was intent and efficient.

"She doesn't look like she blinks much," Peter said.

"Sure don't. But we'll have to see."

"We're at thirty fathoms, Rafe," Adelia called out.

"What's the water temperature?"

"Hovering right around seventy."

"That's it. Start lookin'." He turned to Peter. "Few years ago when I was still working my cousin's boat out of New Bed, the swords used to bask along this thirty-fathom line. Two miles north, two miles south, you won't find 'em, but if they're here, they're *here*, you see what I mean."

He sent Merry into the tower at the ship's midsection to scan the blue-green sea, and took over the wheel. Adelia made her way to the bow and climbed into the pulpit, rolling her shoulders in anticipation. She lashed the steel harpoon horizontally across the bowsprit and fed the strong vinyl line aft, where it lay coiled in a barrel, one end tied to a bright yellow float. Peter glanced up at Merry and saw her puzzled look. He decided to join her.

"What exactly are you supposed to be looking for?"

"You're asking me?"

"Rafe!" he shouted below. "What're we looking for up here?"

"Dorsal fin breaking the surface, you ass. Or a bunch of gulls hovering over something in the water. That might mean the sword is fishing himself. Lot of menhaden and blues in these waters, and swords love 'em. Or with all this sunlight, you should be able to see the body cruising below the surface. Shaped like a torpedo, or a shark—you remember *Jaws*. The sun'll pick out the colors. Smaller ones're blue, big ones look dark gray."

"I see one!" Merry cried excitedly, pointing and jumping in the tower. "Over there, Peter! See it?"

He craned to look and registered something long and blue, almost ten feet it seemed, a few boat lengths away. The dorsal fin was breaking the surface.

Adelia was poised and craning from the pulpit as Rafe brought the boat in alongside the enormous fish, floating just under the surface of the waves like a submerged log. Merry had gone completely still, and Peter realized with a start that she had taken his hand and was holding it tightly.

"Forget it, Rafe!" Adelia yelled. "Shark."

Merry dropped Peter's hand, deflated and relieved at once, he thought, and let out a deep breath.

"Let's keep looking," he said. "You scan that side, I'll scan this."

An hour went by, with Rafe cruising first southeast, then northwest, along the thirty-fathom line. It was noon, the sun high and warm, the breeze cooling now instead of chill. Peter and Merry switched sides, then gave up and descended from the tower to eat some lunch and rest their eyes. They had seen nothing but unbroken ocean—not a tuna, not another shark, and certainly not a swordfish.

It was only once they had torn into Rebecca's cheese-and-tomato sandwiches that Adelia, glancing idly to starboard, caught the first roiling of the fin through the water. "Three o'clock!" she yelled, leaping to the pulpit and drawing the harpoon across her body, dart facing to starboard. "Three boat lengths."

The fish began to run, and Rafe brought the boat around quickly and steadily, down-sun from the fish, a giant, gray-slick mass slicing rapidly toward the bow. Merry and Peter were poised on either side of the fifteen-foot pulpit, tensed and wordless.

"Sword it is," Adelia said, leaning far over the protective bar, harpoon poised. Her scarlet nails flashed in the sunlight. "A nice little one. A marker."

"What's a marker?"

"Hunnerd 'n' fifty pounds or so."

Peter's gaze shifted from the woman to the fish, watching as she led the broadbill with her dart, left hand gripping the shaft, right palm on the harpoon's heel. The fish came closer. Del's shoulders moved. *Strike*.

She seemed poised like a gymnast on the shaft running straight down into the water, the fish frozen by the pin thrust near its dorsal fin. Her shoulders heaved up and thrust downward a second time, almost falling over the pulpit's side, driving the dart deeper into the fish's flesh. Then she yanked the steel shaft of the harpoon upward, pulling it free from the dart and the vinyl line attached to it, just as the big fish surged off into the water.

"There he goes," she said, almost hoarsely, and slid down against the pulpit's rails. Peter, mesmerized by the entire sight, only now came alive and climbed up into the pulpit to offer her a hand. Almost stumbling from relieved tension, Adelia ducked back into the boat and gave a war whoop of victory.

The sixty-fathom line was running out rapidly from its barrel, and in a few more seconds, the yellow floater zipped over the side of the boat and skittered across the waves. The fish was diving, diving, desperate for sanctuary; but the constant tugging against line and dart would eventually wear down its strength.

For fifteen minutes the diving and the plunging continued. Then the yellow ball no longer jiggled on the surface. Somewhere in the depths the great fish had fallen still. Rafe slowly brought the boat alongside the yellow floater, and the rest of them moved to the stern, securing the ball on deck and beginning the arduous task of hauling the line back on board. They had nearly two hundred pounds of fish to pull to the surface, hand over hand, and there was life in the great beast yet. Three times the line they collected was run out by the fish's dying throes, and four times they hauled it in.

"It's a tug-of-war," Merry said.

"Exactly." Rafe was the anchorman behind the rest of them, muscles bulging against the force of the fish, the taut line chafing his leathery palm. "This is where it comes down to us or him. He knows it, we know it. Come on, boy," he said. "I ain't gonna stand here forever."

The dorsal fin and tail broke the surface; the fish circled a few times off to starboard, and then finally rolled on its side. The purplish, fluorescent scales glowed vividly in the sun. Merry gasped as she saw the great dark eye, alive and seemingly fixed directly on her, and found to her dismay that she was crying. Despite her island childhood, she had known such creatures only by rumor, and to witness one fight for its existence was profoundly moving. She glanced at Adelia. All she saw on the other woman's face was weariness, excitement, exultation. She was truly her father's daughter, then.

"Let's bring him alongside," Rafe said, leaving the tail of the rope in Peter's hands. He towed the fish against the side of the boat and lassoed the tail. Then it was a matter of block and tackle, winching the body into the air until it hung alongside, head alone remaining in the water. The purple scales had begun to fade to a silvery gray.

"Seven, eight feet. Two hundred pounds, easy," Adelia said. She reached into her pocket for a knife, leaned over the side, and slit the fish's throat. The water darkened suddenly with blood. Merry turned her face into Peter's shoulder, felt his arm come up around her, and closed her eyes.

They headed for home, the fish soaked with buckets of seawater and shrouded in wet canvas to keep it fresh.

"I probably made a thousand bucks today," Adelia said. "With the price of harpooned swordfish right now, at least a thousand bucks."

Peter whistled.

"Of course, I spent a couple hundred on fuel. And I'm splitting what's left over with Rafe. But still. I could get by with one fish a week. If I'm lucky, maybe I'll find two."

Rafe snorted from his post at the wheel. "This could be the first and last fish you see all season, Del. Don't get cocky."

Merry said nothing, staring out at the late-afternoon light as they rounded Great Point.

"Tired?" Peter asked.

"Just ridiculously sheltered. I'm actually struggling with the idea that my friend plans to kill things for a living."

"That's because you get up every morning trying to save them. Don't you?"

"Not fish," she countered. "People. I'm just being stupid."

"Soft-hearted, maybe." His body was shielding her from the gusting wind. "I, on the other hand, frequently kill baby sheep I raise myself. And cook them for my friends."

Adelia reached past Rafe for a soda in his cooler. "So that's the famous Peter Mason," she muttered.

"I don't know about famous." Rafe was navigating the channel into Nantucket Harbor. "Rich, yeah. But that just happened. An accident of birth."

"And he likes it that way."

Rafe shot her a glance. "What do you want to know, Del?"

"Merry emailed a few times during that murder case last year," she said. "He gave her some trouble, didn't he?"

"It wasn't an easy time. He lost his brother and he got shot himself. Merry thought he might have run Rusty over and left him to drown in the bog. That doesn't make for a good relationship."

"*Que pena.*"

"Whaddya mean, too bad?"

"He's fallen for her."

Rafe hawked and spit into the sea by way of answer.

"How long you lived with this guy?" Del demanded. "You tellin' me you can't see it?"

"That makes two of us," Rafe said. "Merry doesn't have a clue."

Chapter 6

"Name?"

"Joshua Field."

"Spell it."

The kid in the Birkenstocks, Greenpeace T-shirt, and two-hundred-dollar faux-nineteenth-century horn-rimmed spectacles complied, albeit with disdain. Perhaps she still smelled of fish, Merry thought; she couldn't tell. Her olfactory threshold had long since been passed. For reasons she was about to learn, Joshua Field had thrown fish guts and blood over her head as she debarked from Del's boat. A quick dousing under the Town Pier's hot-water shower hadn't done much to cleanse her. Her gorge rose at the memory of the slimy mess, and she glowered at Field. He stared back defiantly.

Never mind. He'd still be sitting in a holding cell when she was warm in her bath.

"Age?"

"Twenty."

"Occupation?"

"Student. At BU."

"Address?"

"Three-twenty Commonwealth Avenue, Apartment Three-A, Boston."

She leaned back in her desk chair and glanced out her office door at the station's upstairs conference area. Only one other guy was in on this late Saturday afternoon of Memorial Day weekend; the rest were either off-duty or out pounding the streets as the first wave of summer residents landed on Nantucket. She'd hoped to have dinner with Peter after Rafe had docked the Brownell, but in the midst of unloading the swordfish and figuring out how to get it to the scales and the wholesalers, Joshua Field attacked. After a moment's stunned silence, Peter punched him flat on his back, an act that galvanized Merry into action; she arrested Field for assaulting a police officer and told Peter to go home.

"So tell me, Field, why's a kid like you pouring fish guts over a police officer's head?"

"I didn't know you were a cop."

"I figured that. Let me rephrase the question. Why fish guts at all?"

"Spawning stocks of Atlantic swordfish are at an all-time low," he said. "NOAA's in the pockets of the commercial fishing industry. So it's the industry that has to pay. Otherwise, swordfish will go extinct."

"So this was a protest. I still don't see where the fish guts come in."

He sighed and thrust his glasses higher on the bridge of his nose. His right eye, Merry noticed, was starting to purple. "National action, pressure on political organs, and the mobilization of the press are important, of course," he said, "but the fish are being slaughtered here in New England. We have to take the fight to the killers themselves. If blood and guts hit them in the face, maybe they'll start to listen."

"Are you a marine biology major or something?"

"Political science."

"That explains your problem." Merry leaned toward him. "Fishermen rip guts out of fish every day. They're not going to be moved by a cup of slime and blood. I admit it had an effect on *me*—but as I've explained, I don't fish for a living. Try that on one of the commercial guys in New Bed and you'll find your head in a toilet."

"Are we done?"

"As soon as I get your prints," she said.

PETER CALLED WHILE she was wrapping herself in a terry robe an hour later, hair fragrant and skin softened.

"What was with that little creep?" he asked.

"Protesting the near-extinction of swordfish."

"Jesus."

"Are you telling me that you never protested in college, Peter?"

"Well—" He had the grace to sound embarrassed. "I *did* throw chicken blood on Nassau Hall once. To protest the university's investment portfolio."

"Its *investment* portfolio? How like a Mason."

"They still owned stock in oil companies," he said patiently. "It was a global warming thing. You kept the kid overnight?"

"Yes. And now he's a martyr."

"At least he couldn't follow you home."

"You can't be serious. He was completely harmless, Peter."

"I'm not so sure." He hesitated, as if weighing his next words. "I wouldn't want anything to happen to you. Be careful, okay?"

Simple phrases. But they kept her distracted and silent over her dinner that night, and twice she had to ask Ralph to repeat what he had said.

SHE WAS ON duty the next day, Sunday. She released Joshua Field, took an address and phone number where he could be reached, and watched him hoist his backpack onto one shoulder and head off toward town. Then she set about tidying the file of a case she'd closed a few weeks back—a fairly simple burglary investigation. She'd been assigned nothing major since, and it was time her brain was put to use. The station was pretty quiet, and Merry felt restless. She glanced at her father's darkened office, considered the hour—one o'clock—and picked up the phone.

Jackie Alcantrara had gone down to the Town Pier to work on the *Lisboa Girl,* his wife told Merry. The lawyer wouldn't let him operate it until it was officially his— meaning after the will had been probated and he'd paid some form of inheritance tax to the state, and God alone knew where *that* money would come from, with Jackie unable to fish—but he wasn't a man to sit at home when there was work that could be done, and one of the things that needed doing was mending net. Merry thanked her, picked up her enormous shoulder bag, and headed for the Town Pier.

The sixty-five-foot *Lisboa Girl* was about thirty years old, Merry guessed—pushing the limit of her intended life span, but kept, through careful dry-docking every few springs, in the sort of shape that allowed her to survive the following January's weather. She was moored not at a slip but at the far end of the dock, one of the few spots that accommodated her size; near her sat the dark blue *Ruthie B.*, Nantucket's only other dragger. The *Lisboa Girl's* hull was of cypress, painted white with racing stripes in the colors of the Portuguese flag; but the steel frame of the gantry bolted amidships was frightful with rust, as were the otter doors that lay at its feet, detached from the net. It was clear to all eyes that this was a boat with a commercial purpose, a workhorse sharply distinct from the thousand-odd other boats moored off South Beach. Industrial or no, Merry found her a cheerier sort of craft than the newer million-dollar steel-hulled draggers that commonly fished out of New Bedford and other mainland ports. And most important, she was an *unmortgaged* boat, free of the necessity of insurance that could cost an owner tens of thousands of dollars a year.

The perfect boat for Jackie, in other words.

To her right, the beach curved sharply out into the water and ended in Monomoy, where splendid old houses and private docks ran down to the harbor; to her left, the two-hundred-foot yacht *Athena,* a dark green corporate cruiser, rocked gently at her mooring on the backside of Old South Wharf. Merry could see the crowds of day-trippers from the Hy-Line ferry tours milling like brightly colored ants among the fishing-shack boutiques that lined the wharf; but a breathless quiet still held where she stood on the Town Pier. It was almost empty this Sunday afternoon, with just the occasional *thunk, thunk* of a flip-flop on the wooden planking or the guttural interruption of a boat engine to break the peace.

She scanned the *Lisboa Girl's* deck for Jackie, and saw only a heap of net unrolled from its drum. He had been mending, but wasn't now. Lunch, maybe? She called his name.

A close-cropped head popped into view through the pilothouse door. He gave her a long look, not unfriendly, but not welcoming either. For an instant she thought he'd pretend she was a stranger, and duck back inside. But Jackie wasn't entirely stupid. He'd grown up with Merry, though they'd never had much reason to chat.

"You here to see me?" he finally said.

"Yeah. How are you, Jackie?"

"What's it about?"

"I'd like to come aboard."

He shrugged. "If you want. It's kind of a mess."

The dragger was crafted low to the water, wide-girthed and rounded as a dory. Merry stretched a foot to the side, grabbed a rail, and hoisted herself on deck. Jackie was slow in moving to help her.

"I understand congratulations are in order," she said. "Hear you're captain now."

A wariness in his eyes. "Who told you that?"

"Felix Harper. Joe's lawyer. And your wife mentioned it when I talked to her just now. Cap'n Joe certainly was a generous man."

"There's a lot'll say I earned it," Jackie said. "The old man was slipping these past few months. His crew was all that stood between him and retirement, and he knew it. I figure I got what I was due."

Merry walked in front of the pilothouse and across the deck, to the side where the steel gantry rose. She imagined the net hauled out of the air, taut and straining overhead; thought of the added weight of swinging steel doors tipping the ship seaward in heavy weather;

and felt how suddenly Joe Duarte must have slid off the canted deck. The knowledge of it came over her like vertigo, a mingling of dizziness and fear. She reached down to steady herself against the boat's side.

"This isn't a social call, is it?" Jackie said. His muscular bulk loomed over her.

"Yes and no," she said. "I realized at Joe's funeral how little I know about fishing, even though I grew up here. I decided I'd like to know more." She touched the rough surface of the detached otter doors. "What do these things do, anyway?"

"The doors?" He crouched down next to her. "You have to understand trawling to understand the doors. The net's funnel-shaped, like a bag, with the narrow end closed by a string." He reached for a length of net and pulled it toward them by way of illustration. "The open end is raised upward by floaters, while the closed end trails along the seabed. That's why we spend so much time mending net," he said, smiling for the first time, "because there's so much junk along the bottom. Rocks pulled up by scallopers, pieces of trash left by other boats, even the sand hills will put a hole in a net. The bigger boats have rollers on theirs that sort of keep the net off the bottom, but the *Lisboa Girl* isn't big enough to handle those."

"And the doors?" Merry said.

"The doors—they weigh the net down. One on either side of the net, eight hundred pounds apiece. That's hardwood sheathed in steel, that is, and you don't get much heavier than that. They slice into the water like a pair of hatchets when the net's paid out. The floaters, now," he said, pointing to the net's upper rim, "keep the top of the net mouth rising while the doors hold the bottom down, and what you end up with is an opening that doesn't close."

"Don't the fish swim out once they realize they're in a net?"

"Doesn't work that way. Fish strike upward when they're panicked, and what they hit is mesh. And the net's being dragged along by the boat at about two knots, so they're scooped into the closed end."

"How long do you leave the net in the water before you haul it in?"

"Maybe an hour," he said, "depending. Sometimes half an hour, sometimes two. You scope out the fish on the fish-finder, and you figure how long it'll take to get a good haul." He hoisted himself to his feet and headed for the pilothouse. Merry followed.

It was a snug space for wheel and charts, with a bank of electronic equipment ranged along an instrument console.

"It's like a plane cockpit," Merry said.

"The *Lisboa Girl*'s not young, but Joe kept her up-to-date." Jackie gestured toward a screen. "That's our GPS for satellite navigation—can't fish without it these days. And this is the automatic pilot, that's the sonar, for depth-finding, and that there's the fish-finder." He flipped a switch and she saw a screen full of murkiness. "Nothing much to see here at dock, of course, but you get the idea."

"I didn't know fishing was so high-tech."

"When you're out alone on the Georges Bank in ten-foot seas, taking ice on the bow and the rigging, and you've got a hundred miles to port, you want everything you can get between you and disaster. You trust your men, you trust your boat, and you trust your equipment; but you never, never trust the sea." He leaned back against the chart table and gave her a level stare. "Now why don't you tell me why you're here."

Merry said nothing for an instant, assessing his calm for signs of the volatile temper people had warned her about. "I'm here because Del Duarte can't get over Joe's death, and I have to help her put it behind her."

"By learning about fishing?"

"By asking you again what happened that day."

"I told the Coast Guard everything."

"But Del doesn't believe it, Jackie. She can't accept the idea that Joe Duarte was fallible, that he could have made a mistake that cost him his life. She's asked us—the Nantucket police—to open a murder investigation."

His fingers clenched spasmodically on the wooden table and then released. He thrust himself away from the charts and pulled open the pilothouse door.

Merry followed him outside and found him standing by the gantry with its now-impotent steel slabs. *The scene of the crime*, she thought.

Jackie swung around abruptly and faced her, the muscle in his jaws working, his gray eyes flat and cold. "You telling me that bitch is accusing me of murder?"

"No," Merry said. "I'm telling you that no one at the station thinks there's any truth in it, but to satisfy Del and calm her down—to help her come to terms with her father's death—we've got to go through the motions."

"To hell with the motions," he shot back. "I've got a living to make, and if she sets out to tie up my boat, she'll regret it. You tell her that from me." He emphasized his point with a blunt forefinger, thrust accusingly in Merry's face. "Del's a spoiled little girl. She needs to grow up and face reality. Just because she left her old man for years is no reason to start blaming me when he goes and dies. Shit." He turned away and spit over the bow, all his venom in the arc of phlegm.

Merry took a deep breath, seeing the rigidity in his shoulders, the stiffness of his neck. "Well, Jackie," she said, "in somewhat gentler terms, that's what I'm trying to do. And it'll help all of us get past this faster if you answer my questions."

There was a short silence, during which he continued to stare out toward the mouth of the harbor, and she held on to her calm by folding her arms across her chest, her hands clutching her elbows.

"Seems a guy can't even make a living anymore," he said. "Between the lawyers and the police and the friggin' stupid women. *I just want to fish.* You know? I want to go out and do what I know how to do. This sitting around is killing me."

Merry refrained from telling him that the sooner he talked to her, the sooner he might be able to claim his boat; it wasn't exactly true. Her father wasn't opening a murder investigation. Nothing would stop the probate of Joe Duarte's will. But as long as Jackie thought Del might—

"Okay," he said, thrusting himself away from the gantry. "Shoot."

She got out a notebook, pen, and her half-glasses. "The weather was pretty bad that night, wasn't it?"

"The storm that hit the island the day of Joe's funeral was nothing compared to what swept through the Bank the day he died."

"But Joe decided to stay and fish."

Jackie's eyes shifted away. "We'd been out for two days and were almost ready to turn for home. The weather came up sudden, and I don't think anybody expected it. Besides, he'd seen a lot of rough sea over the years. You worry about January. You don't worry so much about May."

"You had a net down."

"Most of the other boats had pulled out and were heading for port. We were in about twenty-four fathoms of water, around the Leg—"

"What's a fathom?"

"Six feet."

"And the Leg?"

"—is just a spot on the Bank. That don't mean nothing to you, I know, but it's the only grave marker Joe'll ever have."

"Go on."

"We'd run into some nice-sized cod. They're gettin' rarer and rarer anywhere, even on the Bank, which was famous for 'em, so we wanted to fish while we were still making money, and damn the swell. But Joe got nervous about the weather—he'd lost all his balls this winter, God knows how we got any fish at all—and ordered the net pulled in. The Swede—he's a kid 'bout twenty-three, and Joe had him working the winch—he's so excited about all the fish down there, and pissed about Joe, that he doesn't ease up on the throttle, and the doors come rocketing out of the water twice as fast as they should. Here, look at these."

He reached down and picked up the net, pointing to the yellow chafing strips tied to it at varying intervals. "These are made of fiberglass to toughen the net while it's dragging along the bottom." His blunt, calloused finger moved higher, to some strips of rag. "But these *here* are like flags—haul three in together, and you know the doors are coming up out of the water. The Swede was only hauling in about fifty feet of net. He shoulda seen these rags, and eased off the throttle. But he's feeling angry about the fish that got away, and he gets careless." He threw the net aside in disgust.

"So the doors slammed into this thing here," Merry said, tapping the gantry, "much faster than they should. Where was Joe?"

Jackie dropped his eyes and rubbed at his nose with chapped, red fingers. *Stalling*, Merry thought.

"He was at the helm, at first," Jackie said, "like he shoulda been. But when he sees what's happened, he runs out fast and starts giving orders. Doors that weigh this much, unsecured and swinging wild, can capsize a boat, and the cap'n wasn't about to let that happen. He got in the way, what with the crew trying to secure the doors— you've got maybe thirty seconds to do it, and Joe figured we weren't doin' it right—and all of sudden he's reaching an arm in to do it himself. The boat heels over, the left door comes walloping in, and Joe's out cold from an eight-hundred-pound slap to the head."

He fell silent, and looked away over the mass of fishing boats to either side of the *Lisboa Girl*, to the mouth of the harbor and the sea beyond. "It looks real nice out there today," he said. "A real Chamber of Commerce view. But unless you've seen it, Merry, you'll never understand what high seas in a storm and chaos on deck can be like. How sixty feet of old wooden boat can feel like a milk carton, shuddering with every wave that comes against the bow, lurching into the troughs, while the sea rises like a wall in front of you, swamping your men and tearing at the net you're trying just to get on board. And trying to get on board quickly, so's the weight of the catch don't send the entire boat capsizing with the next wallow." He turned back to her and dropped his eyes again. "Joe didn't panic, exactly. He just picked the wrong moment to try'n run things."

Jackie was definitely uncomfortable about something, but whether it was his memories—or his version of them—Merry couldn't say. "You went into the sea after him?"

He nodded. "Not that it did any good. He wasn't wearing a life jacket—nobody does, the padding's too dangerous around the winches. You get caught in a line and you'll lose an arm. What with the knock on the head and the size of the seas, he never had a chance. He had his boots and his slicker on, and they'd have weighted his body and sent him to the bottom. Almost sent me down, in fact, 'cause I forgot to haul off my boots when I went in after Joe. But at least I wasn't unconscious."

"How'd you get that?" she asked, pointing to his head wound.

He felt it gingerly. "They had to use a grappling hook to haul me back on board, and they hit me in the head with it before they managed to catch my clothing. No big deal. The hair'll grow back." He gave her the vestige of a smile. "I was lucky it wasn't January. The water in May is around fifty degrees, but at least it isn't freezing. Man only lasts a few minutes in January water."

Merry felt her stomach clench and looked up at Jackie Alcantrara. "Did you get a good price for the trip?"

He shrugged. "Nothing like what Joe's life was worth."

For the first time, amid all the bluster about the boat being his due, about Joe Duarte being past his prime, about Jackie himself being all that had stood between the Captain and disaster, Merry saw something like pain for the dead man in the living one's eyes. She read it as a form of truth, and decided that despite Jackie's deliberate omissions and half-truths, he probably had not killed Adelia's father.

"You know how many good men get caught by those doors over the years?" he said. "I could read you a list. Men retired now with one arm, men knocked unconscious and overboard like Cap'n Joe. He wasn't God, Detective. What happened to him has happened a thousand times. You tell Del that, from me. And you tell her I won't be taking no murder rap for what the sea's done on its own."

Chapter 7

"HOW'S BUSINESS?"

Tess turned from tossing the last of the chicken lobsters, claws waving frantically, into a boiling vat of water and squinted at the kitchen's back screen door. The light was behind the face thrust around the jamb, blotting out the features, but she recognized Rafe's voice and the outline of his shaggy head. He'd affected a breezy nonchalance, as though Friday's blowup and Saturday's fishing hadn't occurred, but there was an edge of tension to the words nonetheless.

"Not bad," she said, turning back to the lobsters. "In fact, I don't have time to talk right now."

"Did you get the steaks?"

"Yep."

"How were they?"

"Don't know. Gave them to the cat."

"Tess! Those things're worth a fortune!"

He had a right to be aghast. Almost thirty pounds of swordfish had arrived on her doorstep the previous evening, enough to serve the entire restaurant at a tidy profit; and though she had no cat, as Rafe well knew, she hadn't kept the steaks either. She sent them out to the VFW's

Memorial Day dinner in Sconset, with her compliments and no explanation.

"Do you really think I'd accept anything from that woman?" she said now. "After she's done her best to destroy my happiness?"

"Oh come on, Tess, be reasonable," Rafe said in exasperation. "The steaks were from me. My share of the catch. I had as much to do with landing it as Del did."

"You're quite the partners, I hear."

"Now what's that supposed to mean?"

"You took her to dinner yesterday."

"We got a burger with Peter, and we went dutch, if you want to know. Now stop acting like a three-year-old and ask me into the kitchen."

She turned toward him abruptly, kitchen knife in hand, and despite himself, he leaned back from the doorway apprehensively.

"Do me a favor, Rafael da Silva," she said, advancing on the screen door. "Get out of my backyard and don't come around here again. We have nothing to talk about. Not until you know what you want, who you want, and why. Is that clear?"

"Tess!"

She shut the back door firmly in his face, despite the heat of the unairconditioned kitchen, and sat down suddenly in an available chair. *Damn Adelia Duarte*, she thought. *Damn her thirty-year-old body and her Portuguese blood and her adorable two-year-old and her love of the sea. Damn her for being everything I'm not, and for spending entire days with him. I hate her.*

The inner door swung open, and her chief waiter, Sammy, looked at her with pleading eyes. "Tess, table five is frantic for their orders. I placed them half an hour ago. Whaddya say we give them their food before they leave, huh?"

I hate her. I wish she had never come back.

The door swung closed. From the stove the timer suddenly blared, announcing the end of the lobsters' martyrdom.

I wish she were dead.

She reached for the pot with shaking hands.

MERRY GLANCED AT her watch and turned her car toward home. A thorough canvass of the docks revealed that most of Joe Duarte's crew had left the island for work on boats elsewhere—one in Gloucester, another in New Bedford. She'd managed to find the last and best man to talk to—the twenty-three-year-old winch opera-tor known as the Swede—scraping the barnacles from a pleasure yacht still dry-docked in the Washington Street boatyard. He pushed sunglasses to the top of his white-blond head, crossed his arms over his deeply tanned and completely bare chest, and told her his name was Lars Olafson. He was really from Norway, and he'd been knocking around the New England seaports looking for work since the age of seventeen.

If she believed Lars, he hadn't missed the marker rags on the net; the winch itself was to blame. The throttle hadn't been working properly, and even when Cap'n Joe rushed up and all hell broke loose with the doors, no one could get the thing to slow down. They'd finally thrown the proverbial wrench in the works—jammed the winch itself—but by that time the skipper was over the side and Jackie had gone in after him.

"So how'd it happen?" Merry had asked.

The Swede shrugged. "The engineer didn't ship that trip—had a bad cold, and his wife wouldn't let him outta the house. Maybe things didn't get checked out right."

Or perhaps they did, Merry thought, if the object was murder. Had Jackie fixed the winch so that it would malfunction, anticipating Cap'n Joe's reaction and the probable consequences? Here was a way to kill someone without the entire crew being aware of it—no need for consistent stories, no silence bought with money, no risk of acting with confederates one could not entirely trust. But how risky the method itself would have been! The chances of the wrong crew member being struck by the doors—of other lives being lost beside Joe's, or *instead* of Joe's—were very great. Was Jackie that much of a gambler?

Merry had no idea. But she declined the Swede's offer of a drink, tore her eyes from his flashing white grin, and turned toward home with less conviction of Jackie Alcantrara's innocence than she'd had a few hours before.

"WE'RE GOING OUT again tomorrow," Adelia said, spooning some of Ralph Waldo's kale-and-bean soup into Sara's mouth. "Rafe says he's got the time, and that we might as well see if we can do this more than once. He wants to get the word out to the local wholesalers that they don't have to count on importing all their swordfish."

Merry was half-listening to the wail of sirens from town. "Could you sell to restaurants directly? What about the Greengage?"

Ralph Waldo flashed her a look of warning. Adelia's spoon dipped as she went for Sara's mouth, and soup dribbled onto the mat.

"Shoot!" she said. "Can I have a sponge, Ralph?"

He tossed her one.

"What's wrong with the Greengage?" Merry asked.

"Tess Starbuck thinks I'm a threat," Adelia said carefully. "She doesn't want Rafe fishing anymore, and I'm the reason he is. She gave him back his ring and warned him off the property."

"You're kidding." Merry sat down quickly, a knot in her stomach. There was a time when she'd been jealous of Tess, and wished that Rafe had never met her; but those days were long past. Now she felt responsible. If she hadn't persuaded Rafe to help Del, Tess might still be planning a July wedding.

"This is terrible," she said. "I've got to talk to her."

"Stay out of it, Meredith Abiah," Ralph Waldo said. "No good ever comes from meddling. Tess is a big girl. Acting childish right now, maybe, but she doesn't need anybody to tell her that."

"Is she jealous of you, or just mad that Rafe's fishing?"

"I'm not sure," Adelia said. "Maybe both. But I think if anybody talks to her, it should be me. I put a note in her mailbox today, asked her to lunch. All I need is another person out to get me."

Merry looked at Ralph Waldo. He lifted an eyebrow. "Are you talking about Jackie?"

Del shrugged. "I dunno. That's what makes it so weird." She stood up and reached for her purse, fishing around in its depths. Her red-tipped fingers extracted a folded sheet. "I got hate mail. Came under the door this morning."

Someone had glued letters cut from magazines onto a piece of lined notebook paper.

"The oldest trick in the book." Merry showed it to Ralph Waldo. The persistent whine of the sirens amplified, drifting up through the streets from the waterfront. *That's fire, not police*, Merry thought, and then studied the paper before her.

ADELIA DUARTE NEW BEDFORD WAS TOO HOT TO HOLD YOU, BUT NANTUCKET ISN'T YOUR HOME ANYMORE. GET OUT OF TOWN AND TAKE YOUR BRAT WITH YOU.

It was signed *The Avenging Angel*—again in clipped magazine letters, but culled this time from flowing italic script. An author with an egotistical streak, a desire for self-dramatization.

"So should I be worried?"

"Yes," Merry said. "This isn't exactly normal." She looked up at her friend, her eyes sober. "You think this is from Tess?"

"Could be," Adelia said slowly. "It's the same old stuff about Sara and my morals. The sort of crap a woman would care about."

"It just doesn't sound like Tess Starbuck," Ralph Waldo said. "Too self-righteous."

"Jealousy can turn the nicest person into a raving lunatic," Merry said. "Particularly if she thinks she's got a lot more to lose than just Rafe. Tess's whole life, really, is at stake here—a father for Will, financial security, her happiness. It's not beyond the realm of possibility. That's what makes it so disturbing." She perused the letter again. "I'm not sure I *want* you to go talk to her, Del. She might not be very reasonable."

"*If* she sent the note," Ralph Waldo reminded her.

"Got any other likely candidates?"

"Jack Alcantara comes to mind. Del, my dear, perhaps you should sleep here tonight," Ralph Waldo said.

"I'll be okay, Ralph. I'm staying on Nantucket, and so is Sara, and no vicious creep is going to scare us away."

"Did Joe ever install a security system?" Ralph Waldo asked.

"Yeah. They're called dead bolts," Del said.

Merry was still examining the threatening note. "I wonder if the Avenging Angel wore gloves."

"Probably not," Ralph said. "Most folks don't think paper holds fingerprints."

At that, Merry's cell phone rang. She took the call, noting it was from her father. As she listened, her expression changed.

"I'll be there right away."

"What is it?" Ralph asked as she rose abruptly from the kitchen table.

"The Town Pier's on fire. Everything within shouting distance—boats, sheds, you name it—is going up like a torch."

Chapter 8

MERRY FOLGER STOOD aghast on the shore of South Beach, overwhelmed by the orange flames engulfing the Town Pier. The roar and heat of the fire rolled toward her like the onset of a hurricane, battering her face, assaulting her eardrums, drowning the curses and shouts of the men grappling with hoses on the blackened sand. The crackling light cast a distorted reflection of boats rippling across the harbor, colored it red, and then tore it to pieces with ravenous jaws. As she watched, a blinding flash detonated out past the pier—a ball of flame spiraling upward from a boat's gas tank—and then a concussive *boom!* that startled her out of her skin. Her heart racing, she took a deep breath. And bent double with coughing.

Ash and the acrid odor of burning plastic sifted through the air. Merry narrowed her eyes to slits, pulled the tail of her T-shirt out of her jeans, and held it to her mouth. Ninety-five percent of the craft moored off South Beach—some nine hundred boats even this early in the season—had fiberglass hulls. Fiberglass was toxic when burned. She could pass out just from breathing.

The Town Pier was really two structures—the original wooden one built in the Seventies, and a newer steel addition with a man-made breakwater at the far end. The wooden pier, soaked in tar and oil from generations of vessels, was burning as though designed for the purpose. One glance told Merry it could not be saved. Shadowy figures up and down the half-moon of beach were leaping the protective police barricades, wading out into the water, and swimming to their boats in the hope of saving them. Her throat constricted at the sight. Patches of oil flamed on the water, unmoored boats drifted in all directions, and any swimmer in the night harbor could be injured or killed. She should jump into crowd control. But where was her dad?

It was almost impossible to pick out one person from the many battling the fire. South Beach was only about twenty feet deep at its widest point, and the scorched sand was a bewildering morass of bodies, hoses, trucks, spotlights, and debris. Access to the pier was blocked by the airport crash truck, one of the few island vehicles designed to approach intense heat without its windshield cracking. Inside the cab, the operator was outlined against the flames and the sweeping arc of foam the truck was spraying desperately at the burning boats.

The fire chief, Walt Munn, had reacted quickly, Merry thought. Only four men at a time out of the department's staff of eighteen worked each ten-hour shift at the firehouse, but tonight there were at least thirty battling the flames in front of her. Fire department vessels equipped with water cannons divided their spray between the docks and the buildings immediately bordering the beach—the houses on Washington Street, the marina sheds, the harbormaster's office and public showers. Between the guys on the shore and the ones on the boats, Munn must have called in volunteers as well as full-time crews, and still it was not enough. In the hellish glow off the water, Merry saw despair and exhaustion on the men's sooty faces.

But the chaos of South Beach was nothing compared to what was happening beyond the waterline. The Coast Guard was trying, and failing, to maintain order. As far as the eye could see in the fire-lit night, boats were heading for the jetties and Nantucket Sound, almost ramming one another in the mad scramble to put danger behind them.

It was, from any point of view, a disaster.

"Meredith!"

It took an instant to recognize her father beneath a layer of sweat and soot. His regulation blue Nantucket police uniform was a mess. A gas mask dangled from his chin; he'd removed it to call her.

"Dad!" She dropped her shirt and sucked a lungful of air; big mistake. Coughing, she closed her streaming eyes and breathed into the handkerchief John Folger shoved in her hand. He was one of the few men she knew who still carried one. She made a mental note to start carrying one herself, and tied it thankfully over her nose and mouth. "What can I do?" she shouted over the din of the flames.

Her father rubbed a hand across his face, leaving wet black marks on his nose and cheeks. "It's like a steam bath inside this mask," he said. Merry held her breath and passed him the handkerchief. He mopped his forehead and mouth and handed it back to her, damp and smoke-laden. She tied it over her face anyway.

"Keep these idiots back from the wharf area," John Folger said, gesturing toward the crowds of sightseers who had walked down from town for a better view of disaster.

"All we need is some summer kid blown up while he's taking a selfie." He handed her a bullhorn and made as if to move on.

"How'd it start?"

He stopped and fixed her in his vivid blue gaze. "That's what I want you and Hank Burrows to find out," he said. "A fortune in boats went up in smoke tonight, and somebody's going to be sued. We have to establish cause, and establish it well."

Hank Burrows was the deputy fire chief. He was also the island's trained arson expert. A disaster at one of the piers in high season was the town's worst nightmare. The fire department staged annual drills with the police and Coast Guard, in the grim hope that if they prepped for disaster, it would never come.

"You don't think it was an accident," Merry said.

John Folger laughed brusquely, at the arsonist, not her. "A cigarette may take out Yellowstone, but for this, you'd need a drum of lighter fluid and a plenty long fuse. The fire was reported half an hour ago, just after it got dark. I got here in five minutes, maybe less. And it was already beyond saving."

Merry swallowed. That someone could have set this was difficult to believe. Nantucketers had a terrified respect for fire—the legacy of the Great Fire of 1846, which had raged for an entire night and consumed fifteen square blocks of the town's heart. For more than a year, the islanders had gone homeless. No native could forget that, despite a century and a half's passage.

She pushed aside the handkerchief and lifted the bullhorn to her lips. "Clear the area," she bellowed, her voice transformed and falling away from her, one more inhuman sound in the general cacophony. "Stand away from the police line. You are in extreme danger . . ."

A boat exploded five hundred yards away from her, sending plastic and metal and sheets of fire sky high with a deafening boom. The crowd gasped. A few people cheered. In the slight illusion of silence that followed the concussion, Merry and the thrill seekers watched the scattered pieces of what had been a Boston Whaler rain down like a fountain in the roiling, angry harbor. She had instinctively ducked and clapped her hands over her ears when the boom fell upon her; and now, recovered, felt incredibly stupid. She raised the bullhorn back to her lips.

It was three in the morning before the fire was under control, but the sightseers had left hours earlier. In the dead watches of the night only the islanders remained—the exhausted firemen, the owners of houses threatened on Washington Street, the police struggling for order and the Coast Guard. Daylight would show that over a thousand feet of pier and three hundred boats had been destroyed—a cold and objective statistic. But the ruins were still warm and smoking at dawn, and there was nothing objective about the anger Merry saw on the faces around her, the frustrated rage of those forced to clean up after someone else's devastating mess.

It was after Merry left, on the 5:00 A.M. turn of the tide, that the body drifted to shore.

Chapter 9

MERRY WOKE AT seven, only a few hours after she had stumbled into bed, and forced her smoked-seared eyelids open. The shower had done little to erase the rank smell that permeated her hair and skin; now her bed would reek of it, though her closet had escaped. She had shed her clothes in the backyard.

The sound of Ralph whistling from the kitchen drifted up the stairs, and she fell back into her smoky pillow with a sigh. If God were just, her grandfather would skip the bacon and eggs today in favor of oatmeal. She didn't think her stomach could take the combined odors of melted fiberglass, tar, and pork belly grease.

When she appeared in the kitchen a half hour later, her blonde waves falling damply helter-skelter to her chin, Ralph Waldo paused by her chair and thrust his nose in the general direction of her scalp.

"I'm going to have to shave it off," she said. Her voice was hoarsened by smoke inhalation, despite the gas mask she'd eventually managed to find. When she coughed she tasted smoke.

"Takes me back a century or two to the first days of whaling," he said. "The smell of a tryworks melting down blubber must have been about like this. Wear it proudly."

"And wear it somewhere else, right?"

"It'll pass off. Another few days, you'll be right as rain."

"Or would be, if Dad hadn't made the fire my summer project."

"I think it's becoming the entire town's," Ralph said soberly. "Your dad's set up a crisis center at the station."

"For boat owners reporting lost vessels?"

Ralph Waldo set warm cranberry muffins and a bowl of blueberries in cream before her, the two freshest scents in the world. "The station phones have been ringing all night. Your father never made it home."

Merry took a bite of muffin and closed her eyes appreciatively. "We'll be dredging for rudders and somebody's boat-rail barbecue all summer long."

"There's something else," Ralph Waldo said. "They've found a body."

Merry's spoonful of blueberries stopped in mid-ascent. She stared at him, her face expressionless. "Just one?"

"So far."

"There ought to be dozens, the way people panicked last night," Merry said bitterly. "We train and train for a disaster like this, and when it happens, we realize we should have trained more. There has to be some way to keep people out of the water." She raked her hands across her face, trying to force the bone-deep weariness to recede. "Was it a man or a woman, Ralph?"

"They think it was a man."

"That bad, huh?"

"Must've been caught in a burning boat."

"Jesus." She pushed away the bowl of blueberries, nauseated by her own smokiness and the images it conjured up. Blackened, unrecognizable skeletons, the skin shrink-wrapped by heat over the bones, the teeth gaping. Bodies caught in seaweed and stinking masses of fish gone belly up from so many hours of heat on the water.

"I can't face it, Ralph."

"Try to eat something, Meredith Abiah," he said gently. He was the only person who used her middle name—from Ben Franklin's mother, a Nantucket Folger—usually when he felt tender or indignant. She was thankful it was the former this morning. Though she never allowed her father to see her weaknesses if she could help it, Ralph saw everything.

"I was just getting interested in Joe Duarte's death," Merry said, lifting her head and meeting his bright blue eyes. "That threatening letter Del got only makes her doubts more justified. But all that seems irrelevant now, doesn't it?"

"That reminds me," Ralph said. "In the craziness over the fire, she left her cell phone here. You'll want to drop it off, I expect." He pulled up a chair and teased an edge from one of her muffins. "I thought we'd agreed Joe Duarte's death was an accident."

"We had. But then I talked to the Swede—one of Joe's crew—after I talked to Jackie Alcantrara. Their stories didn't match up."

"Funny. I don't remember that from the newspaper accounts."

"The Swede wasn't interviewed. He was off-island at the time—I checked. And since he was technically responsible for the accident, I suppose it's always been his word against the others'."

"He worked the winch?"

She nodded. "Jackie says he was careless and brought

the metal doors in too wild and too fast. That's why Joe jumped in to lend a hand; then he got hit and went over."

"It's happened often enough before."

"That's what Jackie said. Only the Swede doesn't agree. He says the winch *couldn't* be stopped—that it had to be jammed. Something had gone wrong with it."

"Something that didn't show up in the rest of the trip?" Ralph said skeptically. "It wasn't the first haul they'd pulled. They'd been out two days, or so the newspaper said."

"That's true. But things can break down, can't they? Or be tampered with?"

"Maybe." Ralph reached one long arm to the stove and pulled his percolator toward her cup. "Maybe this Swede is feeling too responsible, and thinks he'll shift the blame. Remember, Meredith, nobody else on the crew mentioned jamming the winch. Everybody said it was human error."

SHE SPENT THE morning down on South Beach with the Nantucket Fire Department. Hank Burrows had requested the help of an arson expert from Boston, who was arriving that afternoon. Until then the scarred wreckage of pilings and hulls was cordoned off from all but the tide. What threatened to drift out to sea was dragged ashore in pieces by volunteers working with the exhausted Coast Guard crews. Uncertain what might be relevant, they saved everything they could. All police personnel were on call, including the summer interns. John Folger had pulled them off foot patrol and set them to the task of labeling debris as the fire department's divers retrieved it from the water.

The banality of the morning after, Merry thought, *when even disaster can be handled with logistics and a smartphone.*

She was given the job of debriefing witnesses among the boat owners and residents of Washington Street. It wasn't hard to do; most of them were on the beach that morning, scavenging among the detritus for signs of a familiar vessel, gone past recalling. There were insurance forms to fill out, and dreams to be mourned; but most of all, there was anger to vent, and the wide-open beach was the place to do it.

On her third canvass she found Marty Bremen. He was a weather-beaten guy of fifty, a New Yorker by birth, who spent each summer in a house on Union Street his family had owned for two generations. He installed his wife and kids every Memorial Day weekend, put the boat in the water, and flew back to the city for the work week.

"This year," he said, "I should have waited a day to take the *Gemini* off its trailer. But yesterday was perfect fishing weather—"

"You were out on the water?"

He nodded. "Shoulda stayed out all night, in retrospect."

He'd left the pier in the late afternoon with his eldest son, a kid of fifteen who was just getting the passion for blues, and they'd come back late with their lights on.

"What time was that?"

"Geez, I dunno. Eight-thirty, nine, maybe? Just light enough to still see, and dark enough not to see much."

"Did you notice anything wrong at the pier?"

"Not on our approach, no. But the explosion came when I was mooring up. Like an idiot, I tried to help, instead of heading right back out to sea."

"You're sure it was an explosion?"

"Couldn't have been anything else, Detective. A loud boom, like a gas tank exploding, and a helluva sheet of flame."

"Where'd it come from?"

He turned and gestured vaguely toward the ruin of the pier. "From the other side of the dock, couple of boats down from mine. I didn't get a clear view of what happened, but Charlie Roundseville"—at this, Marty looked past Merry's shoulder in search of Charlie—"was having a party on his yacht, *Calypso*, only a few slips away. The explosion must have shaken more than the martinis."

Charlie Roundseville was a tall, rangy-looking guy in his mid-thirties. He had a tailgate picnic set up on the back of his Range Rover and was offering wine to various passersby. Last night's party, it seemed, had simply moved to the beach. Merry was wearing her police uniform, something that, as a detective, she rarely donned; but official authority went with it, she figured, and authority was needed. Charlie Roundseville was hardly awed, however. He greeted her with an outstretched glass.

"Officer! May I offer you a drink?"

"Too early, I'm afraid. You're Charlie Roundseville?"

"The same. But you have the advantage of me, Miss—"

"—Detective Meredith Folger. I'm in charge of the police side of this investigation."

"So there's an investigation?" He glanced triumphantly at one of his guests. "I win the bet, Jamie. Arson."

"What makes you so sure?" Merry asked.

"My own eyes, Detective. Sure you won't have a glass?" He uncorked a bottle of California Pinot and sloshed it into what looked like a plastic champagne flute. "Salvaged the picnic basket from the boat when all hell broke loose," he confided. "These were in it."

"Mr. Roundseville," Merry said, "could we start from the beginning?"

"Certainly. It's the end, after all, that's so damn depressing. What do you want to know?"

Charlie Roundseville owned a house on Orange Street. He had made what Merry gathered was an obscene amount of money running a hedge fund, and now devoted himself to spending it on himself and his friends.

"You had a party on your boat last night?"

"Drinks and hors d'oeuvres. I'd intended a brilliant launch of the summer season, but losing my eighty-foot yacht was not part of the plan."

"You were on board when the fire started?"

"We'd intended to go on to dinner in town, but it was a great night, Detective, and nobody wanted to move. We bagged the reservation at Ventuno."

"When did you realize something was wrong?"

"Nine o'clock or so."

"Could you be more precise?"

"Jamie!" Charlie called. "What time was it when the first bomb or whatever blew? He always has his alarm set," he confided to Merry in a wine-scented mutter, "so he can check messages. The damn phone beeps every five minutes."

"Every fifteen," Jamie said indignantly.

"See? Ass. What time did the fire start?"

"Right after eight-forty-five."

"Some use, anyway," Charlie said, turning back to Merry.

"So you think it was a bomb."

"Sure of it."

"Could you describe it for me, please?"

"Well—" He hesitated. "My slip is—was—number nine. The boat in seven—that's just next to mine on the left as you're facing the dock"—he waved toward the blackened skeleton of the pier—"was a pretty little antique sloop named the *Sea Devil,* belonged to a woman, Nancy Harding. It's hard to picture now, of course. The explosion came from number five, just to the left of her. A huge boom! And then the sounds of falling debris and crackling flame right after. We were sitting on deck, some of us, while the rest were in the cabin. The boat rocked and pitched like we'd been hit by a typhoon. I remember looking over my shoulder and seeing a wall of flame jump from number five into Nancy's sloop. The furled sails went up first, and then it was the mast, and the planking between the two slips was blazing. I jumped onto the dock and threw my wine at it. Stupid thing. Alcohol can't have helped."

"Probably not," Merry said gently, "but it's the sort of impulse we all have."

"Exactly. Well, then some people got out of their boats and started throwing buckets of water on the flames, but they seemed to simply get higher. Marty Bremen pulled out his cell and called 911. A few people fired up their engines and tried to motor out to sea. The ones who left right away got lucky. The rest of us just tried to form a bucket brigade to douse the fire, but—" Charlie stopped and took a sip of wine. "I don't know this for certain, you understand, but I've been thinking about it ever since. *We couldn't put the fire out.* There was oil all over the place. Water was useless. And that's what made me think of a bomb. Something like cigarette ash on gasoline wouldn't have had the explosive power. Somebody rigged the dinghy and made sure the dock would burn, too."

"Who owned the dinghy?"

"I'd never seen it before," Charlie said. "Slip five is reserved by the mooring company for short-term rental. It'd been empty the day before."

"Did you see who tied it up yesterday—or do you remember what time?"

He shook his head. "We didn't come down until cocktail hour yesterday. It was moored then."

"Could you describe it for me?"

He snorted in derision. "A vessel to sink rather than sail. A little wooden dinghy, maybe twelve feet, couple of decades old, with oars and a lot of old crap stowed in the bottom. Needed scraping and painting desperately. The sort of dinghy you see all the time, and never look at twice."

And I'll bet the skipper's description matches, Merry thought: a nondescript guy in a faded polo and shorts, probably former military with explosives training. Or maybe just a guy who'd worked construction and knew how to blow things up. The sort of guy no one would notice, the sort of guy nobody did.

Chapter 10

WILL STARBUCK WAS out of breath from pedaling the four and a half miles between his door and Mason Farms. He would not have noticed the distance last year, but that he was able to ride the bike at all this Memorial Day weekend was cause for thankfulness. The previous fall, a murderous trap had knocked Will from his saddle, leaving him with a fractured skull and damaged coordination. This was his first trip to Peter's under his own power in over six months.

He laid the bike in the tall grass by the drive and pounded up the back steps to the kitchen. Rebecca was ironing, and that particular smell of damp linen and moist metallic heat had crowded spring out of the room.

"Where are you going in such a hurry?" she exclaimed.

"Peter here?"

"He's in the study."

Will shot down the hallway before she could ask another question and paused long enough before Peter's closed door to permit an impatient knock. Before the invitation to enter was half spoken he'd turned the knob.

"Will!" Peter was in his favorite armchair, a last mug of coffee to one side and his tanned face just lifting from a nursery catalogue. "Where's the fire?"

"So you know about it then," he said, disappointed. "I thought I'd be the first to tell you."

"There's such a thing as the news," Peter reminded him, "although rarely does it offer such spectacular footage of Nantucket." He flipped the catalogue closed, stood up, and stretched his hands over his head. "Matter of fact, I ran by South Beach this morning. Got up early, saw the pictures on TV, and thought of the boat Adelia Duarte rented. We used it only two days ago. I can't believe it's gone."

Will felt himself flush. Peter had an uncanny way of voicing the things he most wanted to discuss but lacked the courage to say. He met the older man's eyes and looked down, feeling exposed and young.

"What is it?"

"I just wondered," he said, "if maybe Rafe wouldn't be fishing anymore. I sort of miss seeing him around here."

"It hasn't been that long," Peter said, momentarily amused. "Only a weekend." Then he read the unhappiness in Will's face and adopted a more sober expression. "I imagine you miss him around the Greengage," he said. "I remember from my own parents. Three days of silence and tension can be a lifetime."

"It's just that it's making my mom crazy," Will burst out. "She's moping around the house, ignoring everybody, and she's not cooking right. People's orders have been late all weekend. She's mixing them up. The restaurant is really important to her, you know? Only now—it's like it doesn't matter. It's a lousy way to start the season." He kicked at a coffee table leg and slumped down on Peter's sofa. "I keep thinking Rafe'll come by, and she'll snap out of it. Or that I should get him over to the house. But what if I screw things up?"

"You're afraid you'll make it worse."

Will nodded. "Then it'll be my fault. If I leave them alone, it's their problem. But how can I leave them alone? It's my wedding, too!"

"You're right, of course. I hadn't thought of it that way."

"Pete," he said imploringly, and then hesitated, his face flushing. "Do you think *you* could . . ."

"Talk to them? But what if I screw things up?" Peter smiled. "Playing matchmaker isn't my strong suit, Will. I'm better at nursing grudges. Besides, what could I do? Tess doesn't want Rafe fishing. She particularly doesn't want him fishing with Adelia Duarte. I'm afraid that kind of attempt to control Rafe only makes him resist her harder. If it comes up now—this clash of wills and lifestyles—it's bound to come up later. Better they learn how to live with it before the wedding."

"If there is a wedding," Will said.

"Has your mother canceled any of the arrangements?"

He shook his head. "Nope. But maybe she just hasn't thought of it yet. She isn't very organized these days. She's talking to herself like a total space. I'll ask her a question, and she won't even answer. It's worse than when Dad died." He paused. "Rafe's made her really happy, I guess. I don't want that to change. Things were pretty bad a year ago."

"I know."

"Where is Rafe, anyway?"

"He's gone into town," Peter said. "To see a guy named Jackie Alcantrara."

"Who's he?"

"The man who owns a boat Rafe's thinking of renting."

"Give me one reason to help Del out," Jackie was saying. "What's she ever done but shaft me?"

"So the *Praia* wasn't lost in the fire?"

Jackie shrugged and said nothing. He'd told Rafe he'd been working on the *Lisboa Girl* when the fire started, and from his excellent position at the far end of the pier, had had no difficulty in fleeing the harbor early. But Rafe didn't know whether the *Praia* had been moored off South Beach or not.

"You don't have to help Del out," he said, starting over. "You can view it as money in your own pocket."

"Or the lawyer's."

"You own the boat," Rafe said patiently, "or will. Any rent the lawyer collects will be deposited in the estate. It'll go to you eventually. It's a way to make money when you're just sitting at dock."

"That Felix Harper guy won't even let me take the *Lisboa Girl* out. What makes you think he'll rent the *Praia* to Del?"

"I called him."

"You did? Without asking me?"

"You own the boat, Jackie, not the lawyer."

"Shit." Jackie pulled a toothpick out of his mouth and stared venomously at the point. "Everybody's trying to run my business. *Felix.* You know what that means? In Latin? *Happy.* I guess he's pretty happy right now, all the money he stands to make before I get what's my due."

"He told me he's planning to call you. Thinks there's no reason why you can't work the *Lisboa Girl* a similar way—pay rent to the estate and take her out to fish."

Anticipating Jackie's pique, Rafe had suggested the idea to Felix Harper. "Until Joe's will is probated, that's the only solution. So he's not giving Del any special favors. He's treating her the same as you."

"Me, pay rent to work the *Girl*? Pay it to myself? What a bunch of crap. It's killing me, da Silva. You know the blues they're hauling in right now? The schools started early this year. I'm burning money every day I sit at home."

"Then view the rent as money in the bank, and get back on the water. Or go to the Cape and hire out on somebody's crew. The legal stuff'll only take a few months."

"Nobody'd hire me," Jackie said, shoving the toothpick back in his mouth and rolling it from side to side with his tongue. "*You* know what that's like. People think you carry bad luck, they don't want you on their boat."

"Do you?"

"Do I what?"

"Carry bad luck?"

He shrugged, but Rafe saw the truth in his studied indifference. No fisherman, any more than a baseball player, could discount luck. There were the obvious codes everyone knew—a knife stuck in a mast was a bad omen; a hatch cover placed upside down was equally foolhardy; but whistling on deck was sure to raise the wind. Jackie was probably making rituals even now from the way he wore his socks, the route he took moving about the boat, whether he positioned his fisherman's cap with the bill forward or back. One day his luck would break.

"Where's the *Praia* now?" Rafe pressed.

Jackie said nothing for a minute, then shifted his flat

gray stare to Rafe. There was no emotion in his eyes, neither anger nor bitterness nor amused contempt. They reminded Rafe of a fish.

"Whaddya want with that slut, anyway?" Jackie said. "Heard you're getting married. You settin' Del up on the side in case you get bored?"

Rafe twitched with the impulse to slam him, but he controlled it. What Jackie wanted, after all, was a fight. He was dying to punch somebody over something and feel like a winner for once.

"You like just lookin' at those boats? Or you gonna make some money off 'em?"

"Ah, hell," Jackie said, and spat. "The *Praia's* on a trailer at the Washington Street boatyard—or was, before last night. Talk to the goddamn lawyer. Maybe Del'll harpoon herself in the head one of these days and solve all our problems."

THE BOSTON ARSON expert, Jim Hayes by name, was lifting pieces of debris from the collection on the sand, examining each for possible blast patterns. He was a little man, five feet six at most, but they were all—the other police officers, firemen, herself—studying him as though he were a modern prophet.

He'd arrived by helicopter just after one, and listened to the fire chief's report of last night's blaze and Merry's account of the morning's interviews. That the fire was caused by some sort of explosion seemed apparent, and Hayes said nothing that might counter the assumption. The issue was whether the blast was natural—an electrical short on a boat with a full gas tank—or a deliberate act of sabotage.

Hayes looked up and searched the attentive faces, his own lighting when he spied Merry.

"Detective! When the explosion occurred—any of your witnesses mention the color of the smoke?"

Merry looked blank. "It was dark. Almost nine o'clock at night."

"Yeah—but there are lights here on the dock. Lights on the boats. Nobody mentioned smoke?"

"I can interview them again. Is it important?"

"I wouldn't be asking otherwise. Explosives 101: white smoke means commercial gunpowder, black means military-grade plastique."

"I'll find out if anyone noticed."

"Another thing. I need police divers trained in evidence collection."

"Of course."

"The tides have been through here once since the fire," he said, "but the collapsed part of the pier is acting as a dam against too much drift. Heavy debris won't have shifted much. We'll have to crane the pier wreckage out of the water eventually to get at any evidence that may be trapped beneath it. But that can wait until tomorrow. For now, it's vital we get what evidence we can from the harbor floor."

"The water isn't very deep there anyway," Merry said. "It ranges from two to eleven feet at mean low tide."

"Where are we now?"

"The tide was almost out when the fire started," she said, "so it was low again this morning around nine A.M. It's heading in right now, and should be high in another two hours."

"Good." He turned to walk toward the waterlogged remains of the marine superintendent's office.

"Mr. Hayes?"

"Yes?"

"What are our divers looking for that the fire department hasn't already found?"

"The dinghy that blew up, of course. And pieces of the bomb."

"You really think they'll find *that* after the fire that swept through here?"

"Detective, do you remember the Boston marathon bombing?"

"Naturally."

"Within twenty-four hours of that incident we'd found pieces of the pressure cookers used to contain the explosives, the backpacks that hid them, and the ball bearings that served as shrapnel. *Ball bearings*. In the middle of downtown Boston. Compared to that, this should be a piece of cake. If a device caused this explosion, I expect your divers to find every last piece. They'll answer to me if they don't."

"We've only got one trained team, a pair of police officers who are SCUBA certified," she said evenly. "If that's inadequate, import some of your people from Boston."

"I will." He marched off, leaving Merry feeling out of her depth.

After she'd heard all that Charlie Roundseville had to say that morning, she'd headed directly for the harbormaster's office in search of the marine superintendent, Mitch Davis. She found only Scottie Flanagan, a scalloper by winter and Mitch's assistant during the summer months. He was spiking his coffee mug with Bailey's and staring gloomily out at the devastated beach. The office, built by Visitor Services with funds Nantucket skimmed from the hotel taxes paid by tourists, had been doused with water and saved from last night's flames, but the shingles were darkened with smoke and everything inside was completely begrimed with ash. The heat and the force of the water hoses had shattered the windowpanes; the floor was swimming with broken glass and sodden paper. Merry noticed Scottie's brown bag of coffee had spilled, sending dark grinds all over the filing cabinet. She tried not to wonder whether the coffee he was drinking had come from the floor.

"Would you look at this, Meredith? The town'll be sued by every son of a bitch who lost a boat. And where's Mitch? That's what I'd like to know."

"He hasn't shown up?"

"Not today. He was here most of the night, but weren't we all. Coulda seen Elvis, you looked hard enough."

"It was probably arson, Scottie. That's a criminal offense. If we find the guy, the town'll be awarded damages, and the boat owners can sue for civil redress. So cheer up. But first, tell me who'd be likely to want to see this place burn."

"The Town Pier?" He looked blank.

"I admit, it seems far-fetched. But think for a minute. Who holds a grudge against you or Mitch?"

"That's crazy, Merry. Scottie Flanagan's everybody's friend."

When he's in the bar, and he's buying, she thought. "I know, Scottie. I know. But if, as we think, the fire was deliberately set, then someone went to a lot of trouble to make life lousy for you and Mitch. Have you thrown anybody out of the marina? Crossed anybody in business? Slept with somebody's wife?"

She'd added the last as a joke, to conjure a smile from the man; he had been talking a good line about the boatmen's wives for decades now, but she knew he was completely devoted to his Carol.

Scottie's weathered features were puckered with thought.

"There's something," Merry said. "Come on, tell me."

He looked up at her from under his eyebrows, like a hesitant dog. "Nothing but the same old bizness, Mere. Can't believe somebody'd set a fire over it."

"You never know. What is it?"

"Just the board of selectmen, is all."

"The *selectmen?*"

Nantucket's local form of government was a board of selectmen, who met every Wednesday to consider island business. They controlled the purse strings as well. Any proposal to initiate, fund, or terminate anything had to be approved by the board.

"They've never been happy with our upgrades for boaters," Scottie said. "It's one thing to offer cable TV hookups over in the boat basin, and concierges for restaurant reservations—the boat basin's a commercial business. But this is Town property, and the selectmen don't want island taxpayers footing the bill for summer people's comfort."

"Aren't there some locals who win slip rentals in the lottery?" Merry asked.

"Sure. But they're not the ones who need hot showers or ice machines down here. Local taxes didn't really pay for those, either—Visitor Services did, and their funds come from tourist taxes. But it's a sore spot for some people. Mitch went around the selectmen when he got Visitor Services to put money into the Town Pier. And we *still* have Nantucketers who complain about their taxes going to off-islanders."

It was unlikely that a deranged local politician or disgruntled Nantucket boat owner had torched the pier in a misguided assault on the tourist showers, but Merry made a mental note to call Mitch Davis. She turned to the subject of slip five.

Scottie was able to pull up the dock plan on his laptop, which had been safe at home during the fire. The dock plan showed the numbered slips and the names of the seasonal renters. There were one hundred available slips at the Town Pier, most of which were allocated by lottery to seasonal renters. A few slips were reserved for commercial fishermen, whose leases ran for five years—the *Lisboa Girl* had one of these. Others were assigned to the police cutter and Harbor Master boats. A few were for transients, rented out on a first-come, first-served basis. Slip five was one of these.

"That was the slip next to Nancy Harding's sloop— poor Nancy, that's quite a loss, that is," Scottie said. "Insurance money won't come close to replacing such a pretty little vessel. There aren't many of them in good condition to be found anymore, even if she wanted to buy another."

"Slip five was rented this weekend I gather," Merry said.

"I guess so."

"You don't know?"

"Mooring company handles the rentals. Boaters call up the Lewises—they're the operators—on the boat radio and tell them they're comin' in, and the Lewises collect the fees by launch every evening. No one in particular is here to greet every boat."

Merry's heart sank. "You're kidding."

"Is it important?"

"Very."

"You saying it was that boat caused all this trouble?"

"The party on the *Calypso* saw it explode."

"I'll be damned."

"Try to think, Scottie. Were you here when the boat came in? Did the owner ask for the mooring company's number?" She searched for a marker meaningful to the old man. "Did he buy ice, maybe?"

"Don't remember the boat coming in," he said doubtfully. "Just that there was one there after it'd been empty awhile."

"That'd be when? Friday?"

"Thursday night. If he'd come as late as Friday, the slip would already have been rented."

"And you don't remember the operator?"

"You'll have to call Cindy Lewis for that. I remember the boat, though. Hardly worth docking, come to think of it; little dinghy with an outboard putt-putt and a pair of oars. He wasn't going much past Coatue with that."

"Did he come and go much?"

"Not that I noticed."

"Try to think, Scottie. Maybe you saw him Sunday."

"I don't watch every boat that moves in the harbor, Meredith," he said testily. "I've my radio to listen to, and my paper to read." He closed his eyes and was silent a moment. "I'd have to say the boat was there all day

Sunday. I was up and down the docks a bit, and I never saw it gone."

"And Saturday?"

"That's it," Scottie said, his eyes flying open. *"Saturday."*

"What about it?"

"You saw him yourself, Meredith. Here at the dock, when you got back from fishing with Del. He's the kid who poured fish guts over your head."

STANDING NOW ON the beach, watching Jim Hayes disappear toward the fire truck, Merry thought again of what Scottie Flanagan had told her. The arrival of the arson expert had prevented her from following up the lead on Joshua Field. But she had radioed a request that he be brought back in for questioning. It was time she checked whether Field had been found. She had to radio for Hayes's divers anyway. She headed to her Explorer and raised the dispatcher.

"Sunny, I need the Potts brothers and their diving gear down at South Beach," she said. Tom and Phil Potts were islanders and members of the division of criminal investigation, detectives like herself. But unlike Merry, they were avid divers. "Any word on the Field kid?"

"I sent a uniformed officer over to the Baldwin place," the dispatcher said, her voice fogged and broken by static, "but nobody's home. Probably at the beach."

"The Baldwin place?"

"That's the local address he left. Tom and Jenny Baldwin. We'll have somebody try again later, okay?"

Chapter 11

PETER MASON SHOWED up at South Beach right around the time the Potts brothers did. He took one look at the way Merry's cheekbones stood out sharply under her green eyes and recognized her exhaustion. Whenever Merry pushed herself too far, her bones seemed to surface and betray the frailty of her long, thin frame. He resisted the impulse to put his arm around her and settled for inviting her to lunch.

The Potts brothers were safely in the hands of Jim Hayes, she had asked every last question she could ask, and the prospect of sitting down for an hour far from the smell of burned plastic and dead fish was too much to deny.

"Can I have a drink?" she said.

"You can have several."

"One will be enough to put me to sleep."

"I've been hoping you'd pass out in my car."

Merry looked at him closely. Peter adopted many moods with her, but he had never flirted before. It was a day for strange revelations and unexpected turns of events.

"SO YOU THINK this Field kid was crazy enough to set fire to the wharf?" he asked.

They were sitting in Arno's, a lively restaurant on Main, where they'd had to wait only fifteen minutes for one of the two tables by the window. This was the *good* table, the one for four people on the opposite side of the room from the reception desk and the line of hopeful tourists. Arno's was noisy with the clatter of cutlery against china and unceasing conversation, amplified by the wood floors and two-storey brick walls. Merry relaxed into the din and the color, the normalcy of tourist life, though it was clear from snatches of conversation floating around them that nearly everyone was discussing the previous night's disaster.

"What I don't understand is why he'd do it the night after he was released," she said. "Sort of stupid, don't you think?"

"He'd have been smarter to have a Greenpeace buddy set off the bomb while he was safely in a police cell."

"We can't be sure he's a member of Greenpeace. He was just wearing the T-shirt. And there's a big difference from tossing fish guts over a woman's head and blowing up the wharf. I could see that kid knocking a hole in somebody's boat and sinking it, but a *bomb?* It's too sophisticated."

"Hardly," Peter said. "A bomb is just a battery attached to an open circuit and some explosive. Something—a timer, a trigger—closes the circuit, and it detonates. There are instructions on how to build one all over the internet."

"Except Field seems like he'd be more comfortable harassing tourists on Main Street. Protest is glamorous to him, not violent. Understand?"

"I think so. But Scottie Flanagan saw him moor that boat," Peter pointed out.

"True," Merry said. "Dammit."

"Eat your sandwich."

Peter's fingers felt for hers, a cool, dry caress that was gone almost before she registered it. "Otherwise, the beer will go straight to your head. It's tempting to get you drunk and have my way with you—but you *are* still on duty, and as hot as you may look in uniform, I prefer to ravage you in green silk. So eat."

Merry choked on her beer. That Peter might want to ravage her in anything was impossible. For an instant she felt dizzy and closed her eyes.

When she put a word to her feeling for Peter, she called him a friend. Anything else positively terrified her. He seemed beyond her in so many ways—his wealth, his education, his experience of the world. He came from a tribe that got what it wanted, regardless of cost. He'd learned to control that impulse over the years, maybe, but Merry thought she had surprised a predatory look in his eyes more than once during Friday's dinner. Today of all days she wasn't ready for it.

Peter appeared not to have noticed her confusion. He was calmly eating a Caesar salad. What had he ordered her to do?

Eat.

She picked up her panini and tore into it.

"MERRY! HOW NICE to see you," Jenny Baldwin said. "Won't you come in?" It was Tuesday morning, and Merry was standing on the Baldwin doorstep in Monomoy. At her side, or rather looming over her five feet ten, was Howie Seitz, the previous summer's police intern from Northeastern's Criminal Justice program. He had graduated the Friday before Memorial Day and come directly to the island, the only new hire her father had been able to make. That John Folger had chosen Howie of all people surprised Merry; but she had to admit she'd grown to like the big lug. Seitz had been one of the volunteers on South Beach the night of the fire; to be in on the chase a few days later gave him a definite sense of importance.

"I'm afraid this isn't a social call, Mrs. Baldwin," she said. "Do you have a young man by the name of Joshua Field resident in your house?"

"My, aren't we formal, Meredith," Jenny said, amused. "What's Josh done now?"

"Is he here?"

"Don't tell me you're still mad about those fish guts."

"I'm too busy to hold a grudge, Mrs. Baldwin. Where is Joshua?"

Jenny held wide the screen door and motioned them into the house. The harbor's blue water gleamed from a window at the end of the long center hall, airy and cool. Merry felt rather than saw the faded chintz sofas, hydrangea blooms in large green bowls, rag rugs scattered across worn board floors.

"Josh!" Jenny called up the staircase. "Detective Folger is here to see you!"

There was an instant's silence from above, as though a small animal were crouched in its burrow, awaiting a dog's renewed digging. Then, to Merry's surprise, there came the sound of Joshua Field's easy descent of the steps. She'd half expected him to try an upstairs window, one that gave out on an eave of the roof, perhaps, or the back porch's overhang. But no. Martyr ever, he was coming to meet his doom.

At his appearance she wasted no time. "Mr. Field, I'd like you to accompany us to the station for some questioning in connection with the fire that consumed the Town Pier Sunday night."

There was a silence, during which Joshua Field broke into a grin and Jenny Baldwin's hand came up to her throat.

"You're not arresting him!" she said, her voice shrill and strangled. "Tom won't stand for—"

"No, Mrs. Baldwin, I am not arresting him. I would merely like to record a statement as to his whereabouts and knowledge of Sunday night's events. Mr. Field?"

The strongest impression Merry retained of the afternoon was not of Joshua Field's supercilious smile, nor of his aloof passivity as Howie helped him into the backseat of the police cruiser, but of Jenny Baldwin standing motionless by the door as they pulled away, her expression blank, one hand poised uselessly on the knob.

JOSHUA FIELD, IT turned out, was Tom Baldwin's nephew. He had decided to spend the summer between his junior and senior years working construction at one of Tom's sites on the island, using the happy circumstance of free room and board as a means to wage his anti-swordfishing campaign. He was about to leave for work when Merry nabbed him; and his chief concern, once he was conveyed to the station, was whether he could call his foreman and tell him he'd be late.

"Make that absent for the rest of the day," Merry said.

"You can't seriously be going to hold me for this," Joshua said calmly. "It's police harassment. You have a fire at the wharf, and you decide to pick on the kid who dumped fish guts on your head. It's not going to work, Detective. Certainly not after my uncle gets back from Boston tonight and hears about it. He'll have your job."

"Mr. Field," Merry said patiently, "the police chief is the only person who controls my job, and he happens to be my father. He remembers your uncle as a skinny little guy he used to haul out of the dunes for groping girls on Saturday nights. Your uncle won't piss off my father. Arson, on the other hand—with one person dead and several million dollars' worth of damage to the Town Pier—makes him very mad."

"I *hate* it when the chief's mad," Howie Seitz offered distantly.

They were, by this time, seated across a plain wooden table in the station's upstairs conference area, which doubled as the sole interview room. Merry punched a recorder's button and Howie opened his iPad. "Mr. Field, I'm going to record your statement for police records. I would like to note that those present for the Nantucket police are Detective Meredith Folger and Patrolman Howard Seitz. Mr. Field, could you please state your full name and date of birth . . ."

What the hour and a half of repeated questions, attacks from varying angles, and ingenuous suppositions on Merry's part boiled down to was a firm denial of any involvement in anything like a bombing on the part of Joshua Field. Yes, he'd moored the old dinghy at the pier on Thursday night; he and his uncle had hauled it out of the tall grass at the edge of the Monomoy property and taken it across the harbor to the slips, because the Baldwin dock had been destroyed during last winter's storms and Tom had not yet repaired it. Tom's other boat was already at the pier, and it seemed a simple thing to place the dinghy there. Tom was leaving for Boston and in a hurry, so he'd handed Josh some cash and told him to reserve the next few days until he got back. They'd lost both the dinghy and Tom's forty-foot fishing boat in the fire; he'd be the last person to have triggered a bomb when his uncle's pride and joy was moored nearby.

"Are you aware," Merry asked him, "that witnesses saw your dinghy explode at approximately eight-forty-five P.M. Sunday night, seriously damaging the neighboring vessel and triggering the fire that engulfed the wharf within seconds?"

For the first time, Field looked disconcerted, but he recovered quickly with a characteristic shrug. "I can't explain it," he said. "I wasn't near the boat all day. After you released me, Detective, I went home, had a shower, and fell asleep, since I didn't catch a wink in that cell all Saturday night. Aunt Jen can swear that I was in my room until dinnertime, when I got up and ate with her. Afterward we saw the movie at the Dreamland, which let out at ten-fifteen. You can check all of that."

He was right, of course. She couldn't arrest Joshua Field. She had no proof that he'd built or placed a bomb in his uncle's dinghy. It was just possible someone else had noticed it was the most derelict craft at the Town Pier, perfect for sabotage, but how had the bomber known the dinghy wouldn't be used that day? Was the bomb placed at random a few minutes before exploding? It was far more plausible that Field had done it. But until she could prove it—

"Thank you, Mr. Field," she said. "That will be all for

today. Please stay on-island and be available for police questioning."

"Don't worry, Detective. I'm not likely to run from *you*. Or your father."

"THAT LITTLE TWERP tell you anything?" John Folger asked as she walked into his office a few moments later.

"Not much. Says the boat's his, but the bomb isn't. We've got nothing so far to link him to it. I'm going to tell Jim Hayes in case he wants to check Field's clothing for explosive residue."

"Do it. The crime lab in Boston just called. They've identified the body. It's the Harbor Master, Mitch Davis."

"Mitch?" Merry was bewildered. "Scottie Flanagan said he hadn't come in yesterday, but I didn't know he was actually *missing*."

"His wife has been calling the emergency center every hour on the hour. She got us his dental records a little while ago. That's all the crime lab needed."

"Ralph said the body had been burned in a boat," Merry said.

"After he was dead."

She stared at her father. "What?"

"Mitch was murdered, Meredith. Boston found a thirty-eight slug in the back of his skull."

Chapter 12

ADELIA DUARTE PULLED the dark green sweatshirt over her head and reached back to flip her long hair free. She could hear the faint tolling of the Unitarian Church's curfew bell drifting over town from Orange Street, and out of long habit, she counted the fifty-two strokes. Nine o'clock on a Wednesday night. Early for bed, but she and Sara were both worn out, and Rafe would be knocking on her door at seven. She was tired tonight with something deeper than physical exhaustion. She had ignored her grief for her father for too long, and the strain was beginning to show.

A faint breeze stirred the threadbare curtains at her window and sent the ancient shade slapping against the glass. She turned and sniffed the air, wondering if a storm was kicking up; but the scent of the wind was clean. Good weather brought breezes to Nantucket at this time of year; it was when the rainclouds descended that the world seemed to hold its breath.

Del was fresh from the bath after a day spent cleaning house. She had begun with her father's "snug" and its bulging rolltop desk and worked her way to the attic shelves. Joe Duarte's lifetime accumulation of junk had been sorted, packed in boxes, and set out back near the

trash cans for disposal. Less easily discarded were the
collections of mounted fish, the decades-old photographs of trolling buddies long gone, and the carefully
stored memories of her dead mother. These last had
given her pause.

She found the simple white cardboard box high on
a shelf in the guest-room closet, its ancient and exu-
berant script proclaiming it to be from Filene's. *For Del*
was written on the lid. Her mother's wedding dress. Had
he forgotten it was there? Or kept it in the hope she'd
retrieve her respectability someday and walk down the
aisle on his arm? Del opened the box.

Resting on top of the yellowed silk was a photograph
of Joe and Agnes, freshly married and posed on the
steps of St. Mary's. She raised it to the window, wanting to see more clearly in the fading afternoon light.
All that her parents could not have known was written
on their hopeful faces. No sense of the back-breaking
work, the stormy nights her mother had spent in fear, the
inevitable disappointments, her early death.

Del closed the box and set it back on the shelf,
smoothing the aged cardboard gently with her fingertips.
She was not ready to explore further. Or to examine the
emotions that had plagued her for three years. Even now
the memory of that morning—she queasy with morning-
sickness, unable to stand the smell of tobacco that clung
to her father's shirt and hair, and Joe's face blank with disbelief—made her feel like vomiting. She'd been unable
to come back or pick up the phone, waiting for some sort
of bridge she could not build herself.

Now that Joe was gone, Del could push aside the memory of his stubborn pride and rejection. Even his legacy to

Jackie Alcantrara. Her sense of loss and guilt was stronger than anger.

Without me, your dad would've been finished months ago. Jackie's words rang in her mind. Had her absence hastened Pop's drift toward old age? Had pain worn away at his mental strength, his drive for living—dulled the edges of his fisherman's sixth sense? *Was this why he had died?*

She did not know what his final days were like. And the not knowing was a large stone she stumbled over whenever he came to mind. She had cleaned the house partly in the hope that she would find something—a letter, perhaps, addressed to her in his crabbed hand. But there was nothing. Pop was gone. He was past explanation or redress, past anger or forgiveness, past being hugged or told that he was loved.

If she could find his murderer and avenge his death, maybe she'd feel less like she'd killed him.

Del looked around the room, at the walls grayed with neglect, at the windows crying out for cleansing, at the familiar candlewick bedspread her mother had bought in Hyannis thirty years ago. There was at least this house, the one thing Joe had left her. Del chose to see it as a sign: *He wanted me to come home.*

A faint sound, like a cat mewing, and Del stiffened. One ear was always cocked for her daughter, even when she slept. She turned from the guest room—she preferred it to her father's bedroom, still haunted by his smell, his lingering presence, perhaps even his ghost—and crossed the hall to her own childhood bed.

Sara's face floated like a small flower against the pillow, one fist tightly curled around the neck of a stuffed toy. Not that it *had* a neck, exactly; it was a whale Ralph

Waldo had bought her at the Whaling Museum's gift shop. Ralph would spoil her unmercifully this summer, and Del was inclined to let him. Sara had gone too long without a grandfather.

Del smoothed the child's cheek, and her eyelashes fluttered. No sign of fear or discomfort; the mewing must have been part of a dream. On occasion she wondered what a two-year-old dreamed of; one more thing she would never know, and Sara could never tell her.

The doorbell rang.

Del turned swiftly and ran down the stairs. She had left her cell phone at the Folgers' house Sunday night and wanted it back, but hadn't wanted to bother Merry until the Town Pier investigation was a bit more under control. Maybe this was Merry now, cell phone in hand. But as Del opened the door, her brows knit in confusion. She stepped back.

"Hello," she said, surprised. "I didn't expect you at this time of night."

RAFE DA SILVA was no stranger to the dawn hour, and normally he took his time as the first light of five-thirty stole up from the shoreline to the east, enjoying the way it picked out the drops of dew glinting among the green cranberry vines. He'd drink his coffee, watch the sheep, and think about very little.

Today, however, he was hurrying through his duties with Peter's flock of merinos, intent upon the prospect of swordfishing with Adelia Duarte. Felix Harper had seen his way clear to renting her the *Praia* under a simple contract with Joe Duarte's estate—much as he had determined she could stay in her father's house free of rent or further obligation, as long as she paid the utilities. *Big of him*, Del had said, with a disgusted snort; it was galling to have to ask a perfect stranger if she could sleep in her own bed, or take out the boat she'd handled since she was a teenager. But that's how things were, and Felix, Rafe reflected, wasn't all bad; he might think about writing a will with him himself one of these days. Or would, if he knew where he and Tess stood. She still wasn't talking to him, and if the marriage was off, he didn't much care what they did with his things once he was gone.

At the thought of Tess he felt a familiar ache. He did not know how to reach her, other than to quit fishing, and everything in him rebelled at the idea. But he doubted whether a swordfish was worth trading for happiness, even as he loaded his gear into the back of the Range Rover.

He'd make an appointment with Felix Monday.

Rafe whistled for Ney, the big half-breed working dog both he and Peter adored, and the shaggy mutt's ears swiveled in his direction. He made the sign for bringing in the sheep, and Ney went into action, turning and wheeling among some sixty ewes with breathtakingly silent ferocity. Of all Mason Farms' inmates, Ney enjoyed his work the most.

And what about me? Rafe wondered. *Do I enjoy mine?* A question his father would never have had to ask; fishing, for all its backbreaking labor, its poor pay, its cold and wet and exhaustion, was a way of life, not work.

And that's the difference, he thought. *I work here, and it's fine. I can't think of a much better way to make money, or a fairer guy to work for than Pete. But out on the water, I'm*

*living the life I was born into, the only one that feels as natural
as breathing.* How to make Tess understand?

"DID YOU SEE this, Ralph? They're saying the Nantucket police are dragging their feet on the worst case of
arson in the island's history. As if we've been sitting out
on the beach all week working on our tans!"

Merry Folger snapped the *Inquirer and Mirror* in irritation and bent over the article for a second time.

"Be glad they haven't got that fellow Field for an
exclusive interview," Ralph Waldo said mildly.

"Oh, they have—that story is the sidebar to this one.
He fed them a whole line about police persecution of
political activists. Do me a favor, would you?"

"Hide the paper?"

"At least until I'm gone. Dad sees this, and I'll get
another lecture over breakfast about the importance of
public relations, particularly during tourist season, and I
don't think I can listen to that today."

"Feeling beat?" He set a bowl of blueberries on the
scarred oak table and pulled out a chair.

"It's been a long week, whatever the paper says."

With the discovery of Mitch Davis's murdered body,
John Folger had turned the arson investigation over to
the state police at the order of the Barnstable DA. To
make Merry feel better, he appointed her liaison with
the state police, and she had to scramble between South
Beach and the police station and the state post out on
Liberty Street. No link was found between Joshua Field
and the fire. But the arson expert, Jim Hayes, thought he
had figured out the bomb.

The device was enclosed in a bait box, which Tim

Potts had found on Thursday in blasted pieces, and the detonator, Hayes informed her, was triggered by a curious apparatus he'd never encountered before. After twenty-four hours of study and attempts at reconstruction, he hit upon its mechanism by pure chance as he dangled it from the side of a substitute dinghy at the water's edge.

The trigger was encased in waterproof plastic and suspended straight down in the water from the mooring line, probably at high tide. The mooring line had detonator cord twined along its length that ended abruptly in the hinge of the bait box. As the water receded throughout the day, the boat lowered toward the bottom, until the trigger touched sand at mean low tide and blew the detonator. The cord in turn ignited what Hayes believed was several pounds of plastic explosive—it was the only form of nitroglycerin stable enough to use in a rocking boat—and fed on gasoline sprayed onto the dock by the exploding outboard motor.

"Very clever," Hayes said. "The boats in these first few slips are in five, six feet of water at the low, and a good bit of their lines are dragging on the bottom. With a dinghy as small as that one, it's way below the level of the dock even at high tide. Not the sort of boat anybody's going to study for very long, if they even notice. And no need for a timer, no need for remote control; just a guy with a tide table and an alibi somewhere else."

The timing of the tides suggested the bomb had been set up in mid-afternoon, a few hours on either side of the 2:54 P.M. high.

Merry could envision it all: an average guy—Field or an accomplice—strolls down the dock, bait box in hand, in the middle of a busy Sunday when most of the boat owners are out on the water. He putters around the dinghy, stows the bait box, checks the mooring line—and takes the opportunity to attach a wire with a trigger mechanism and a deadly leash of detonator cord. Then he goes home to Monomoy, and when the plastic bag and its trigger hit sand that evening, he's enthralled with two hundred others by the flickering images on the Dreamland's wide screen.

"It hasn't been a picnic for your dad, either," Ralph said, breaking into her thoughts. "Remember that the next time he's yelling at you. Now, what are you doin' on your day off?"

"Swimming at Surfside," she said, stretching luxuriously, "with a magazine and an umbrella and nothing else. I don't want to speak to anybody, I don't want to run into friends, I don't want to have to read anything longer than two-syllable words. How 'bout you?"

"Young Sara is coming to call," Ralph said, "on account of Del's fishing. Matter of fact, they're probably at the door."

But it was Rafe da Silva standing on the front step, Sara in his arms, and Merry knew as soon as she saw him that something was terribly wrong.

"What is it?" she said, her voice as flat as the look in his eyes.

"It's Del," he said. And that was all.

RAFE HAD CLOSED the door of the house on Milk Street, though he'd found it just barely ajar upon his arrival at seven-thirty that morning. Merry made a mental note about his fingerprints on the knob, knowing he'd have smeared any left by someone else. She wrapped a bandanna around it now—she carried one in the makeshift evidence kit that sat in the back of her Explorer—slipped plastic covers over her shoes, and walked into the Duarte living room.

She drew a sharp breath and half-swallowed a wail of anguish.

Adelia Duarte lay sprawled in the middle of her father's living room, one arm bent under her and her eyes staring at the ceiling. A rich swath of dark hair spilled across the carpet, the last flag she'd left flying in the moment of surrender. The ends were smeared red with dried blood. She was wearing sweatpants and a sweatshirt of dark green that Merry recognized; after-dinner, before-bed clothes she pulled on to watch TV. She'd never gone to bed last night.

But the most horrible thing, the brutal fact that forced Merry's breath from her body, was the harpoon canted rakishly in the middle of Del's chest. The lacquer-tipped fingers of her right hand were still clenched around the steel shaft, as though she had attempted to wrest it from between her ribs; but her time was too short and the dart had been thrust well home. There was a look of wonder on Del's face. In her final moment she'd understood that the line was set and reeling her in.

Merry felt Rafe's fingers grip her arm. She shook him off and knelt at Del's side. She couldn't touch her, couldn't pull the harpoon from her body, couldn't close her eyes. She could only say her name, *Del, Del, Del*, while the memory of an old pain swelled in her mind. She had been here before, keening over her mother, over her brother Billy. Keening over blood. She wanted Ralph and her father. She crumpled in a heap and allowed herself to sob.

"Mer," Rafe said, low and urgent. "Mer, I'll call the station, okay?"

When she didn't answer, he sidestepped toward the kitchen phone, cursing himself for his stupidity. He'd thought of the Folgers first when he'd opened the unlocked door and seen Sara sitting cross-legged in fouled diapers, one thumb in her mouth and the other twirling a piece of hair, by the side of her mother's body; but he should have called the station. John Folger would kill him when he saw the state Merry was in.

Chapter 13

"DARNED IF I know," Dr. John Fairborn said to Chief Folger. "She was a strong, healthy woman. Rigor usually begins fairly quickly in that case, and lasts longer. I'd say it's fairly well established."

"Thanks, John," Chief Folger said in exasperation. "That tells me nothing."

"I can't give you an exact time of death. Only the detective novelists do that," the doctor said. He stood up from his kneeling position by Adelia Duarte's corpse and tiptoed backward in his plastic booties, mindful of the evidence. "The normal range for onset of rigor is two to six hours after death. It's pretty well established two to six hours later, and can last for twenty-four to forty-eight hours after *that*. So *you* tell me when she died."

The chief knit his brows with the effort of mental calculation, working backwards from seven in the morning. "Sara was hungry this morning, but she wasn't starving. Her diaper needed changing, but I wouldn't say she'd spent more than a few hours in it dirty. So we'll rule out the idea that Del was killed before dinner yesterday and skip the twenty-four to forty-eight hours' bit."

"Even assuming she was killed no earlier than dinnertime last night, the state of her rigor still fits a range of anywhere from seven P.M. to three A.M.," the doctor said. "Not to mention the cadaveric spasm."

"The what?"

"Cadaveric spasm. See the way the hand is clenched around the harpoon shaft? It went through her ribs and into her heart, Chief, and she died almost instantly, clutching at the weapon. Her muscles contracted and froze. That looks like rigor, even if it happened only two minutes ago. She might have been killed by the guy who discovered the body. Though I doubt it. She's cooled too much for that."

"Okay, okay," John Folger said, with sudden distaste. Fairborn's casual familiarity with a corpse never failed to disturb him. He glanced at Del's face, the hand still clenched on the harpoon, and turned away. She was too close to be discussed so irreverently. Why did he care *when* this had been done to her, anyway?

"You've got to realize, Chief," Fairborn said, "I just don't assess rigor that often. I attend *births*, not deaths. Other than that Mason guy last year, we haven't had a murder in a decade. Not that I'm complaining. Give me an induced labor anytime."

Nantucket had no coroner. Unattended deaths—bodies discovered by a neighbor, for example—were routinely examined by Fairborn and a few other island doctors on call to the police, and then shipped to Sandwich for autopsy. In serious cases—where murder was suspected—the corpse flew to the state crime lab in Boston. Adelia Duarte would be following Mitch Davis's corpse there.

"She's got several slashes on the right forearm," Fairborn continued, "and a puncture wound in the left shoulder. The slashes are probably defensive—she was holding the arm up before her face—and the puncture is where he missed the first time."

"You figure it was a guy?"

"Not necessarily. I was just being sexist," the doctor said. "The wound is *very* clean. Even without looking at the dart, I'd say it's got to be pretty sharp." He hesitated, assessing Del's chest. "It went right through the ribs here, and angled upward toward the heart. Not a blow that had to penetrate the sternum. A woman could have done it. *This* woman sure could have. She was adept at using this thing, wasn't she?"

"So I understand."

"It doesn't seem like a woman's weapon, all the same. More like something the victim picked up to defend herself with, and then had it turned against her. That's my bet."

"So there was a fight. She wasn't just surprised."

"By a six-foot-long harpoon aimed at her chest? I don't think so."

"She was supposed to go harpooning with Rafe this morning. That's why he found her."

"Then she probably had the weapon waiting by the door, and tried a little preventive action when whoever it was threatened her. Big mistake."

"Preventive action" sounded every inch like Del Duarte. John felt a wave of sadness wash over him. A less confident woman might have called the police when trouble started. A less confident woman might still be alive.

"What about her hands?" he said, hunkering down to examine the scarlet-nailed fingers clenched around the harpoon.

"You want me to open them?" Fairborn looked for Clarence Strangerfield, the crime scene chief, and found him on the other side of the living room, labeling a plastic jar containing a brownish liquid that was probably Del's blood. "Clarence!"

"Ayeh?"

"You're done photographing and sketching?"

"She's all yars."

Fairborn bent down and reached for Del's fingers with a grunt. "I'll have to break them," he said.

Chief Folger nodded once, and then studied the far wall intently. Anything but look at Del, or toward the door where Merry still sat with Rafe on the front steps. There was the cracking sound of small bones. He winced.

"Clarence," Dr. John called over his shoulder, "we need a plastic forensic bag. And your labels."

WHEN THE FIRE department's black body bag had zipped closed over Del and the emergency crew had pulled away, John Folger stood a moment in the doorway and stared down at his daughter's blonde head. It was bent to her drawn-up knees, the curtain of hair hiding her face. He saw that her shoulders were still; no sobbing or grief to read from above. Her hands were linked over her ankles, the slender, tanned fingers pressed white from the effort of holding on.

"Meredith," he said, cupping his palm over her hair, "we need to go home now." She didn't move. He looked at Rafe da Silva. The younger man said nothing, his eyes worried. John Folger lowered himself to the steps between his daughter and the foreman and threw an arm over her shoulders. "Sweetheart." He shook her slightly.

Her head came up from her knees, eyes unfocused. "It's my fault," she said.

"*Your* fault? There's *no way* this is your fault." John Folger shifted around to hold her close. "You couldn't have known this was going to happen to Del."

"Oh no?" She reared away from him. "Because I'm too stupid, right? You'd have to be an idiot not to have seen this coming. She thought Joe was murdered. She told us that. God knows who else she told when we didn't believe her. *Somebody* must have known she wasn't happy with the accident story. She'd even gotten a threatening letter—and *I*, I told her to bolt her door at night. She must have thought I was nuts. Her instincts were right. I mean, what would it take for me to believe her? *Getting killed?*"

"She bolted her door?"

Merry nodded.

"And it was unlocked when you arrived?" This to Rafe da Silva.

"Yep. Standing open, actually."

"She must have let the guy in, then," John Folger said.

Merry thrust away her father's restraining arm and stood on the brick path in front of him. "I'm going to find whoever did this to Del and I'm going to make sure he fries. He's not going to get away with this."

"With what, Meredith? With making you feel responsible?"

"With Del. Lying in there like that—like a—like an *animal*—"

"Meredith. Calm down."

She hesitated, then studied her Sperrys, angry and embarrassed at once. "You know what I mean," she said.

"Yes, I do. But you're in no shape to investigate anything." His stomach knotted, but he pushed on. "I'm giving you two weeks' vacation, Merry. You can help Del far more by settling her affairs and taking care of the baby. That's what she'd have wanted, I think."

"Since I failed her so badly?" his daughter said bitterly. Her face went white and then red. She opened her mouth to say something—an appeal, John Folger sensed—and then read the futility of such words in his face. She turned away, one fist slicing through the air in a gesture of rage and hopelessness, and walked off toward the Civil War monument on Main.

Rafe got to his feet with a grunt. The two men stood looking after her—the tall, thin frame, moving swiftly and surely across the uneven brick sidewalk.

"Poor little Girl Scout," Rafe said.

PETER MASON LOOKED for her where Ralph Waldo had told him she would be: in the shallows off Jetties Beach, swimming laps vigorously up and down the shore. He had walked through the few sunbathers of early June to stand at the base of the lifeguard's chair, eyes narrowed against the glare off the water, searching for the form knifing through the waves. The Sound here was calmer than anywhere else on the island, buffered by the curve of land, the series of bars reaching toward the Cape, and the outflung arm of the stone jetty that kept the harbor channel from completely silting closed. Windsurfers wheeled and rocketed in its protected waters, and toddlers played.

It wasn't difficult to find her; she was the sole swimmer in the water. She'd gone out past the bar, wanting a place her feet couldn't touch. Calling to her would be useless, and disturbing to the sunbathers. Peter pulled his T-shirt over his head and kicked off his shoes, stepping onto the smooth pebbles that marked the beginning of the surf.

Even the Sound was chilly in the first week of June— less than sixty degrees, he guessed. The shock of cold crept up his legs to the edge of his shorts; a surging wave slapped at his groin. He gave up and dove into the Sound, moving powerfully in a crawl, out past the line of breaking surf and the bar. Where the sandy bottom abruptly slid away, Peter stopped, treading water and shaking his hair out of his eyes, his breath coming in quick gasps.

He surged upward to look for Merry. She was moving toward him, having turned in her lap while he edged out from shore, and her golden arms were slicing purposefully through the water. Heading for the jetty as she was now, she moved with the current, and in a very few seconds she would be upon him.

Peter waited, wondering why he'd come and what he would say. He hadn't thought clearly when Rafe had told him about Del. He'd gotten in the car out of blind instinct, certain he could help if only he could find her. *Hubris,* he thought. Why should she talk to him at a time like this?

She must have glimpsed his body motionless in front of her. She swerved to avoid him. He reached out a hand as she passed and she came to a spluttering stop, outrage on her face until she understood who he was.

"Peter." She was breathless from exertion, her eyes wide and green under the black brows. Wet, her hair had darkened to the color of blond wood, swept back from her forehead and revealing the hard, unvarnished structure of her face. Cheekbone and brow hollow and lips were blue from cold, the cords in her neck straining with the effort to keep her head above water.

What do I say?

He reached for her instead, pulling her toward him, her body like carved stone in the wet Lycra, and incredibly her legs slid around his waist. She clung to him, all of her chilled by seawater and death, her cheek against his shoulder, and as Peter breathed deeply to ease the knot at his center, he felt her begin to shake. Salt tears and salt sea. Merry, alive within the circle of his body. He felt pierced by joy, and closed his eyes against it. *In the midst of death we are in life*, he thought, inverting the Biblical phrase with purpose. It seemed the only honest thing to do.

He carried her halfway to shore, until the furrowed mouth of the bar bit at their feet and she dropped away from him. She was done crying, but kept her face averted for all that, the sun and wind sweeping wisps of wet hair like a veil across her eyes. He should have felt awkward, should have retreated from the feeling that had gripped him in the water, but he knew that *that* had been real, and this was not.

"I've only got one towel," she said abruptly.

"I'll use my T-shirt."

"Then what will you wear?"

"A wet T-shirt?"

Her lips started to tremble with what might have been laughter, but a horrified expression superseded the smile and she turned away, pulling her towel from a bag lying on the sand.

"Del wouldn't want you to stop smiling, Merry," Peter said gently, "even though she died and you didn't. You know that."

"She didn't *die*, Peter," Merry shot out. "She was *murdered*. Stuck through with a harpoon like a butterfly on a pin." She turned back to him, her rage on her face. "And here I am swimming with you, *laughing* at you—"

"—as though it had never happened. Yes. That doesn't make you a criminal."

"No," she said. "No, my stupidity did that."

"Merry—"

"I should have saved her, Peter. I should have known."

She fell silent, toweling off purposefully, pulling a shirt over her head, slipping on her shorts. She looped the handles of the beach bag over her right shoulder, ran her fingers through her hair, and set off for the parking lot without looking at him. He followed, sobered, his wet shorts clinging to his legs uncomfortably. He'd go shirtless.

He caught her up at her gray Explorer, and held on to the car window frame as she opened the door. She looked at him finally from her place behind the wheel, her face a picture of misery. He slid the back of his hand up her cheekbone, and she flinched, leaning away from him.

"Your father won't give you the case."

"Why should he give the case to somebody who's already blown it? I had my chance. In my own kitchen, when Del told me Joe's death wasn't right."

"I thought you looked into it."

She laughed in contempt. "I verified my own conclusions. That she was in denial out of grief. Then I went to work on something more important, because my daddy told me to." She lifted the keys to the ignition, then dropped them back on the seat. "She'd be alive if I'd taken her seriously, Peter. I can't get around that."

"Why? Because you'd have stayed with her night and day? There's nothing easier than killing a person, Merry. All the bodyguards in the world couldn't have saved Del if someone wanted her dead."

"Don't tell me what I want to hear, Peter," she said. "From you, I expect the truth."

She pulled the door away from him, and he let her go.

Chapter 14

"TESS," RAFE SAID.

She was sitting slumped over the kitchen table, chin resting on one hand, and she stiffened perceptibly at his voice. He waited for her to look around. She didn't. But she didn't tell him to leave, either. Rafe approached her slowly and stopped a few feet behind her chair.

"Del Duarte was killed last night," he said, and waited. "Or maybe early this morning. They don't know."

Tess did not respond.

Rafe reached a hand toward her shoulder and then lost courage, his arm dropping to his side. The rigidity of her neck, her immobility, caused the hair to rise on the back of his head.

A pile of fresh beets lay leafy and red on the table, their spiky roots tarnished with soil. The eleven-thirty lunch crowd was only an hour away, and Rafe knew the salad Tess intended to fix—the beets boiled and napped in a raspberry vinaigrette, on mesclun, with a bit of goat cheese—but she hadn't made much progress.

"I found her. We were supposed to go fishing today."

Tess's chin dropped and she studied her hands, palms upward, as though her fortune could be read there. She might never have heard him. Then she pushed back her chair and started to walk out of the room. Something in Rafe snapped.

"Don't you even give a goddamn?"

A hesitation, and then she looked at him. "How was it done?"

"She was stabbed through the heart with her harpoon."

A light came over Tess's face, like the lifting of a cloud. Rafe felt slightly sick. The corners of her mouth twitched, and he thought she was about to say something; but to his horror, she threw back her head and began to laugh.

"Tess," he said, shocked.

The laughter grew more hysterical. "Do I give a goddamn, Rafe? You bet I do. I could scream her death from the housetops."

"You don't mean that."

"Oh, yes, I do."

Rafe backed toward the door.

"I wanted her to die," Tess said. "And now I'm free."

"Jesus," Will breathed. He was standing at the door, his face white, his stark eyes fixed on his mother.

Rafe steered him toward the hall and pulled the door shut behind them. "She been this bad all week?"

"Not exactly. The past two days have been really weird. She's looked like hell. I don't think she's been sleeping. Then she drinks coffee all day to stay awake, and her nerves are completely shot. She fired Sammy yesterday for saying an order was late, then called him this morning and begged him to come back. We might as well close the restaurant down."

"I didn't know," Rafe said.

"Of course you didn't," Will snapped. "How could you know anything? You're just *gone*. Like we don't even

matter. *You're* the reason Mom's such a mess. I could—"
He stopped, frustrated and spluttering, his fists clenched.

"You could punch me in the mouth," Rafe said dryly.
"I don't blame you. I'll call Dr. John. Have him stop by
and talk to Tess. Maybe she needs something to quiet her
down, let her sleep. In the meanwhile, stick the 'Closed'
sign on the door. We'll figure this thing out."

Will nodded, his dark blue eyes too large. The kid
never got out from under trouble, it seemed. Rafe pulled
Will's head to his chest in a quick embrace, ruffled his
hair, and opened the door.

But the thought of Tess rode with him all the way
home.

MERRY SAT ON the side of her bed near the open
window, her hands lying uselessly in her lap. A breeze
sent the smell of wild roses wafting through the room,
the pervasive scent of Nantucket in summer; the June
sun was pitilessly bright. From the kitchen below came
the hot, bursting odor of blueberry muffins and the
sound of Ralph Waldo dragging a chair across the floor.
He was singing to Sara, and her childish, tuneless voice
attempted to keep pace.

> "*O do you know the muffin man,*
> *the muffin man, the muffin man,*
> *O do you know the muffin man,*
> *Who lives in Drury Lane?*"

A squeal of laughter and the sound of clapping hands.
The day was starting, full of simple things and the ease
of summer; Merry felt it, heard it, breathed it in. Del was

dead. The sharp pain of having survived overcame her. She closed her eyes, and saw Peter Mason's face.

The smooth wet skin, the hard slope of his shoulder where her cheek had lain; the sense of peace in his arms. For a few seconds, while the water buoyed them and they drew breath in unison, she had felt a relief and a completeness as solid as remembered childhood. She was inches from abandonment, from crawling into his bed and never coming back.

But relief had turned to self-loathing. She had failed Del, and her first impulse was to use Peter and hide. She was despicable.

She had driven aimlessly around the island after leaving him, heading first out to Madaket and then back along the Milestone Road to Siasconset, feeling caged by the monotony of the moors. She had struggled just to *think*—of who might have wanted Del dead. The murder had to be spontaneous, not planned. No one but Del could have known the harpoon would be waiting, sharpened for the morning hunt, by the front door. Whoever killed Del was moved to sudden violence. The door ajar, the lights burning, the baby unharmed—the visit wasn't meant to end in murder.

Jackie Alcantrara was given to sudden rage, Merry knew. Jackie was the most obvious suspect. He disliked Del, and she had all but accused him (to the Folgers, and how many other people?) of having arranged Joe Duarte's death. Merry had told Jackie outright that Del was requesting a murder investigation. Suppose he had stopped by the house on Milk Street last night, hoping to talk things over—tried to strike a deal with Del, the *Praia* for her silence, perhaps—thinking that he could buy her off. It would be like Jackie's limited intelligence. If *he* could be satisfied with a boat, no questions asked, why couldn't she?

But Del flew into a rage, brandished the harpoon, and when Jackie tried to disarm her, was killed in the skirmish. With Del lying in a pool of blood on the floor, Jackie panicked and ran out the door. The neighbors might even remember him.

"Meredith!"

"Up here, Ralph."

"You're wanted on the telephone."

She thought of asking him to take a message, but it might be Matt Bailey, the most obvious of her fellow detectives to be assigned Del's case; and much as she despised Bailey and chafed at the notion of his handling a murder investigation, it would not do to ignore him. She rolled off the bed and headed for the phone in her father's room.

"Merry."

"Peter," she said. She looked about her wildly, the receiver to her ear, as though in search of protective cover. "Did you find a dry shirt?"

He laughed, and the carefree sound felt like a blow to the solar plexus. "I do own more than one."

A pause.

"You still there?" he said.

"I don't feel much like talking."

"I called to see if you felt like coming over for dinner tonight. You needn't speak, just eat."

"I can't."

"You can't eat?"

"Well—actually, I'm starving," she said, surprised.

"Life reasserting itself, Merry. It's not something to fight."

"But you are, Peter," she said, and bit the words back too late.

"I thought I might be," he said, his voice grown very quiet. "That's not what I intended when I came looking for you this morning."

"I know. You wanted to help. But you can't help me right now, Peter, you can only make things worse."

"Because I make you happy."

"Because you make me guilty."

"Same thing. Merry—"

"Don't argue this one, okay? It's how I feel."

The terrible stillness of a phone line burdened with too much to say. He cleared his throat.

"Look," he said. "You need to do something *positive*. Sitting around helpless for two weeks will only make you crazy."

"And you think dinner at your house is something positive?"

"No," he said patiently, "but I think finding Del's murderer might be."

She hesitated, confused. "What are you saying, Peter? That I ignore my dad, run roughshod over the department, and light out on a personal vendetta?"

"Sounds like a good idea to me."

Chapter 15

MERRY SLIPPED OUT the back door in the 6:00 A.M. silence of Friday morning, her Sperrys in one hand and her car keys in the other. She felt like a teenager or an errant spouse, but Sara Duarte was still asleep upstairs, and she didn't want noise to set off a baby alarm that would rouse the household. She needed to get to the station before her father was even showered.

She had tossed and turned all night, debating Peter's words. "Your knowledge of Del could be vital to finding her killer, and you'll feel in the long run like you've helped," he said. "Once you've got the information, you can hand it to the guy running the investigation, and nobody'll be the wiser."

The idea was compelling. But she would need to be back on duty to make it work. The station meant access to evidence—Clarence's forensics—and a plausible reason for tooling around the island asking questions. She would tell John Folger the arson case was a necessary distraction from Del's death, and that she'd defer the vacation he'd offered until she was better equipped to enjoy it.

But first she wanted to see that evidence.

MATT BAILEY COULDN'T type, never carried a laptop, and took all his notes longhand. Yesterday's paperwork still sat on his desk in the darkened office he shared with another detective. Merry outranked him, and had a private room—one more reason he resented her. His first and foremost grievance was her refusal to go out with him.

Merry set her enormous purse on the floor next to Bailey's desk, fished around in its depths for her half-glasses, and switched on the lamp. A spotlight fell on Del's wide-eyed face. They'd printed the pictures quickly.

She shifted the papers and found the crime scene chief's summary.

It was written in Clarence's dry manner. Del's injuries were noted sparingly, pending the state crime lab's autopsy findings. Merry recognized the significance of the defensive cuts on the right forearm, Del had not been taken completely by surprise. She paged quickly to the end of the report, where Clarence described the blood retrieved from Del's floor—and noted two different samples, A positive and O.

Merry flipped back to the top and began reading in a more organized fashion. Clarence's sketch of Del's living room, with the position of the body carefully triangulated and a notation of the blood pattern on the floor, she gave only cursory attention. She knew the living room well, and Del's image was seared in her memory. It was the rest of the house that interested her.

Clare had dusted the doorknob for fingerprints and come up with nothing. When he sprayed the weathered wooden shaft of the harpoon with ninhydrin, however, he hit pay dirt. The killer thought to wipe the doorknob but didn't know unpainted wood retained prints—not surprising, really. Most people thought a surface had to shine in order to show the ghost of a finger. The problem with the harpoon, however, was the sheer volume of prints it revealed.

Merry sat back, chagrined. The first element to be lost from a print was water; some fingerprint processes depended upon reaction with it, and could only pick up fairly recent deposits. Ninhydrin, however, reacted to the amino acids fingers left behind when they touched a porous surface. The spray was capable of picking up traces of touch that were days old. Her own prints were probably on the harpoon somewhere—she'd undoubtedly gripped the shaft during the swordfishing expedition, as had Peter. And Rafe. And Del herself. There was no telling how many people had handled it recently, and very little hope of proving conclusively that a particular print was deposited in the act of murder. She read on.

Joe Duarte's study had been ransacked, the contents of a filing cabinet strewn across the floor. The cabinet's metal surfaces were carefully wiped clean of prints.

This brought Merry up short. In her mind's eye, she'd thought of the killer—all right, she'd thought of Jackie—harpooning Del in the midst of a fight, and running out the door. She hadn't allowed for a jaunt farther into the house, dying woman ignored and caution thrown to the wind, in order to steal some files. *Files?* What crime of passion turned on *files?*

Clarence had endeavored to find out. In Del's room, which the murderer had apparently not entered, the crime scene chief discovered several items of interest neatly stacked on her bureau. First among them were two

threatening letters, composed of newsprint, and repro-
duced in Clare's notes.

I WARNED YOU ADELIA DUARTE GET OUT OF TOWN.
I'M LOSING PATIENCE, the first simply said.

LEAVE UNDER YOUR OWN POWER WHILE YOU STILL CAN,
the second began. THE LIFE YOU SAVE MAY BE YOUR OWN.

Both were signed *The Avenging Angel*.

"A cliché wrapped within a cliché inside a cliché,"
Merry muttered. The poisoned penman might have
cribbed his—or her—notes from a *Threatening Letters for
Beginners* manual. These two must have arrived in the
days following the Town Pier fire. Merry hadn't spoken
to Del since she'd shown her the first letter that night.

Clare had sprayed the paper with ninhydrin—again,
few people thought of fingerprints when they forged a
check or sent an anonymous note—and had come up
with some beauties. He intended to search for a match
among the station's existing prints, but these should also
be mailed to the state crime lab for comparison with its
database. That could take some time, of course, and it
would be useless if their killer wasn't already in the com-
puter. More than likely he wasn't.

The final item on Del's dresser was an inventory of
the file cabinet. *Trust a former office administrator*, Merry
thought. She must have gone through Joe's papers at
some point after the funeral. Everything he'd stored was
carefully noted, as were the items Del discarded and the
files she added for herself. Clarence had cross-referenced
the inventory and the cabinet's remaining folders, and
discovered that only one was missing. Del had labeled it
"Personal Documents." Whether Joe's or her own, Clarence couldn't say. The inventory told them nothing more.

In the galley kitchen, everything had appeared ordinary to the crime scene chief, except for a bottle of Glenfiddich scotch standing open on the counter. Near it stood two clean glasses. Clare had poured the scotch into a sterile container for analysis, dusted the bottle and glasses, and transported them to the station in plastic. The bottle revealed beautiful thumb and forefinger prints that bore no relation to Del's or those he'd found on the threatening letters.

Probably Joe's, Merry thought sourly.

The glasses had no prints at all.

Now, that's bizarre, she thought. *Del offers the murderer a drink, which he pours, and after a bit of scotch, the killer stabs his hostess, tosses her filing cabinet, and carefully washes the glasses, drying them with a towel to remove all prints. But he—or she—thoughtfully leaves the bottle for Clare to dust. Huh?*

The remainder of the report concerned the particulate matter vacuumed from the scene and the body. Clarence was struck by the lack of surface dirt on the premises— Del had apparently cleaned thoroughly only a little while before. Nonetheless, the crime scene chief found a few large links of copper chain embedded in the rug near the body, probably torn from a piece of the perpetrator's jewelry; some fine blond hairs; and sandy grit—probably from a shoe. Del was wearing green cotton fleece. Her hands, unclenched by Dr. Fairborn, had torn at clothing made of beige raw silk and linen.

Merry sat back in disbelief. Jackie Alcantrara's hair was mousy brown, and she doubted he had ever worn silk of any color in his life. Linen might be a possibility—but on a Wednesday night, when he'd probably been mending

net or working winches on the *Lisboa Girl* all day? Indigo
from a pair of jeans was more like it, or the cotton fibers
of a Hanes T-shirt.

She pulled her half-glasses from her nose and
flipped them shut. First thing to do was discover Jackie's whereabouts Wednesday night. She glanced at her
watch. Seven A.M. Time to beat it before Matt Bailey
accused her of turf-jumping. She snapped off the light
and threw her bag over her shoulder.

Jackie Alcantrara lived in a twenty-year-old frame
house off the Surfside Road, not far from the high school.
Merry stopped for Scotch oatcake and coffee at the
Downyflake off the Rotary and pulled up in Jackie's drive
a few minutes before eight o'clock.

His truck was gone—like any fisherman, he'd have
been up at dawn and on the road not long after. She
eyed the house and noted what appeared to be a fresh
paint job. The lawn, too, was neat and newly landscaped.
Either the Alcantraras had a generous landlord or they'd
bought the place and put some money into it. But where
had *that* come from?

Merry rang the bell.

"Constance Alcantrara?"

She was a short bleached blonde with sharp brown
eyes, a tendency toward plumpness, and a fixed simper. In her cotton knit stirrup pants and matching
large tunic she looked, Merry judged, a good five years
older than Jackie's twenty-eight. She stared at Merry
blankly.

"Yes?" Hot pink fingernails with small gold charms at
their tips grazed through the blonde fringe.

"Detective Meredith Folger. Nantucket police."

Wariness replaced the blankness for an instant, and then the simper returned. "What can I do for you, Detective?"

"I'd like to talk to you about Adelia Duarte."

She stood back and held the door wide, the smile more fixed. "Please come in."

The living room shared space with the dining area, and both were done in baby blue and pink. Hearts and flowers in the same shades were stenciled on the walls at ceiling line, and sprays of lace and dried blooms were tucked into pictures, nailed above doorways, and springing from every corner. The sofa was of ruffled gingham, and magazines were stacked in a rack coyly made in the shape of a pig. An open box of chocolates and a mug of coffee proclaimed it breakfast hour in the Alcantrara household.

Constance bent to clear the sofa with a hostess's flutter. "There!" she said brightly. "Now we're ready for guests. Would you like some coffee, Detective? Or herbal tea?"

Merry declined and sat down in a padded rocker. She winced.

"Oh, let me take that for you."

Merry reached back and felt for the hard knob that had driven into her back. The head of a rag doll, tough plastic surmounting calico and nylon lace. She handed it to Constance and pulled out her laptop.

"I feel just terrible about Del," Constance began. "But then, everyone does. The poor thing had such a *tough* life. But then I have to say we make our luck."

"When did you hear about her death?" Merry said.

"Well," Constance said, leaning forward conspiratorially, "I ran into Margot Grant yesterday afternoon—you know, she works as dispatcher at the firehouse, and she'd just run across the parking lot to Stop N Shop to buy some tomatoes—and she told me there'd been a rescue squad sent to the Duartes' that morning. She filled me in on all the details." Her round lips were pursed and her eyes avid. "I understand she was *impaled* by a harpoon. Would you like a chocolate?"

"No, thank you," Merry said. Never in a million years would she have imagined bullet-headed Jackie, with his simmering rage and blunt words, tied to this refugee from a bad soap opera. "And did you tell your husband, Mrs. Alcantrara? Or did he hear the news elsewhere?"

"Call me Connie." She reached for a piece of Russell Stover's and sat back into the cushions, primed for a long gossip. "Jackie's been out fishing for the past few days, but I managed to raise him on the radio and give him the news. He said he'd start back today when his lockers are full."

"You have a radio here in the house?"

"In the kitchen. That way he can let me know when he's due, and I can have something nice and hot waiting when he pulls up in the truck."

"Whereabouts was he when you raised him?"

"The Bank."

A full day's trip out of port. "And he left to fish when?"

"Wednesday morning."

Twenty-four hours before Del's body was discovered. He'd have made the Georges Bank by the time she was killed, if indeed he didn't fish somewhere nearer shore that first day, and return to the harbor under cover of darkness for the express purpose of harpooning her. Then he could have reached the Bank during the night and had his alibi fixed. Merry would get Terry Samson at the Coast Guard office to check a log of radio calls. The fishermen always gave their coordinates when they buzzed the Brant Point station.

But that sort of calculation and scrupulous timing didn't fit with the found weapon, or what seemed to be the spontaneous nature of the crime. *Damn.*

"He managed to find a crew, it seems," Merry said.

"Not really a *crew.*" Connie pulled a face. "Just that Swede. He has nothing better to do, I guess. After what he did to Joe Duarte, I'd rather Jackie fished alone."

"What the *Swede* did?"

"Letting the doors in careless like that. It's criminal."

"Happily, it worked out to Jackie's benefit," Merry said carefully.

"Well, it's an ill wind as doesn't blow *somebody* good. Jackie deserves everything he gets, believe me, Detective. And once that lawyer said he could fish—as if he should have to ask anyone's permission—there was no holding him. Wait another week, I said, and hunt up some real crew, but Jackie was heading out, and I wasn't going to argue."

"The news about Del must have been a shock."

Connie shrugged. "I don't think so. He always said she'd come to a bad end."

Her indifference made Merry burn for an instant, and she had to look away from Connie Alcantrara's self-satisfied face. "Why did he think that, Mrs. Alcantrara?"

"Connie," she said automatically. Merry's questions seemed hardly to bother her. Merry wondered for an instant if she'd expected the police visit or simply enjoyed the attention. "Well, you can hardly blame him after the way Del behaved."

"Over the boat, you mean?"

Connie laughed and took another chocolate. "Those Duartes. Always acting like they ruled the world, and both of 'em dead. No, I meant the way she ran after Jackie a few years ago. Practically threw herself at him, trying to get him into bed. As if she'd be the sort of woman he'd find *attractive*. But she never had any morals, did she? I mean, *that baby* came along somehow, didn't it?"

The idea of Del throwing herself at Jackie was too ludicrous to be believed. But why would Jackie tell his wife such a story? "Did you know Jackie at the time?"

"Oh, I met Jackie three years ago, at the Rose and Crown," she said smugly. "*All* the girls were crazy about him. He couldn't *shake* them off. But I knew just how to handle *him*. I acted like I'd seen his type a thousand times before, and I was looking for something *better*. He bit right away. We were married two years ago."

"And was Jackie working for Joe Duarte at the time?"

"No," Connie said, and clammed up, a slight sharpness in her eyes.

Of course not. He was skippering the boat he would sink a year later.

"This is a lovely house," Merry said.

"Isn't it?" She leaped at the conversational change. "We were so lucky to get it. The owner came down a bit in the price. Not that there was anything wrong with it, you understand," she said hastily, "just that—well, he liked us, and knew we were just starting out."

A sympathetic gesture. Something no Nantucket property-holder would be fool enough to make, with real estate prices as they were. "How long have you been here?"

"Just a year."

So right after Jackie sank his boat and lost his job, he'd bought a house.

"Do you work, Mrs. Alcantrara?"

"Connie," she said. "No. I used to do nails at the On-Glaze"—this was a salon on West Creek Road—"but Jackie doesn't like his wife to work. A man should be able to support his family, Jackie says."

Then he's one of the few fishermen who can afford to be a chauvinist, Merry thought. Like almost everyone else, draggers depended on two incomes to make it. As first mate, Jackie might have cleared forty thousand dollars the previous year—if it was a good year. So how was he keeping his wife in chocolates and dye jobs?

"Thank you, Mrs. Alcantrara," she said, closing her laptop. "You've been very helpful. What do you do in the evenings when Jackie's at sea? It must be very lonely."

"Oh, heavens," she giggled. "I can never find enough time for all I do. I was tied up every night this week."

"Really?"

"Uh-huh. Monday was book group. We're doing Elin Hildebrand because she's local. Tuesday I went to the Dreamland with Margot. Now what did I do Wednesday? Oh, yes. I watched TV. Reruns of *Sex & the City*. I have to do that when Jackie isn't home. He says it's a chick show."

On the evening of Del's death Connie Alcantrara was alone. She could easily have decided to visit Del instead of watching a show she'd seen countless times before. But it would be risky; someone might have seen her car on Milk Street. And Merry couldn't quite see Connie wielding a harpoon. *Too icky.*

"And last night I worked the bingo table at the high

school. A benefit for the Worship Center." The Nantucket Worship Center was an interdenominational group that held services out of the school.

"May I ask *you* a question, Detective?"

"Feel free," Merry said.

"Now that Adelia's dead, what will become of that lovely house on Milk Street?"

"I suppose it will be sold."

"And her estate goes to—?"

"Her daughter, I would think. I don't know if she left a will, but even if she didn't, Sara's her next of kin."

"Well, that might be enough to bring the father forward," Connie said, interest lighting her eyes. "That house is worth a bundle. Which means the baby is, too."

"I hadn't thought of it that way," Merry said stiffly.

"Then I suppose you'll be arresting that Dave Grizutto," the other woman said comfortably.

"Excuse me?"

"The baby's father. *Dave Grizutto*. He bartends at Brotherhood of Thieves. Don't tell me you didn't know? Jackie says it was all over the island once she left."

Not for the first time, Merry wished she'd been more involved in Del's life the past few years. She knew Dave slightly—and remembered vaguely that he and Adelia had dated—but thought they'd broken up long before Sara was conceived.

"He wanted the money, of course," Connie persisted. "Or he wanted Del. And she spurned him. So he killed her. It's obvious, isn't it?"

"Nothing about murder is obvious, Mrs. Alcantrara."

"Connie," she said. "Do let us know if we can help with that baby. Dave Grizzuto is *not* the person to handle so much money. She'd be far better off in a *stable* family, don't you think? And we're practically family anyway. Joe *did* leave Jackie his boats. Which tells you something— he didn't trust that daughter of his. I can't get over him leaving her the house."

Chapter 16

"DETECTIVE FOLGER," BILL Carmichael said, slapping an empty manila file against his thigh, "I thought you'd gone on vacation." *Fine time for it, too,* his tone suggested. The state policeman in charge of the arson investigation looked harassed. His eyes were deeply embedded in their sockets and threaded with reddened capillaries.

"I decided work was more important right now than time off," Merry said.

"I see. Or rather, I don't, but never mind." He brushed past her to his office and slumped behind his desk. Involuntarily, his eyes fluttered closed, and he grimaced, rubbing a hand against his forehead. Carmichael's sandy hair was receding, and the dome of his skull had burned and peeled. Merry took the chair opposite his desk and waited for his eyes to open.

His cell phone buzzed. He ignored it.

"You alone here?" Merry said, glancing around.

"Well, there *are* only three of us, and a secretary," he said irritably. "Sam's on patrol, Chuck has the day off, and Dottie stepped out for a cigarette. I assume you dropped in to hear what we've got, right?"

"If there's anything new," she said.

He laughed shortly. "The phone never stops." Carmichael reached across the desk and stabbed his cell. "I'm not supposed to do that, but what the hell. It's either silence or insanity. I've got boat owners calling when they can't get anywhere with your emergency center; I've got reporters calling; I've got my bosses calling, and the fire chief, and your dad, and Lisa Davis. *She's* calling me at home—not that I blame her. And I can't tell her a thing, except that the bullet that put Mitch away was a thirty-eight to the back of the skull. Small hole where it entered, helluva mess inside. The guy is toast and he's got no nose, Merry, but can I tell her why? Nope."

"The weapon didn't turn up in the water or on the beach."

"And it won't. It's probably in somebody's boat locker. And the boat's probably all the way to Long Island Sound by now."

"What do you mean?"

"I mean it was a random killing, that's what I mean. It can't be anything else. Think about it. Mitch is out there on the beach in the middle of a bunch of panicky boaters who're trying to cross the fire barricade to save their stinkin' boats. He tries to stop some guy, words flare up, the guy's half nuts because he's losing a fortune in fiberglass, and so he hauls off and shoots the jerk who's trying to save his life. Then he gets in his boat and beats it."

"And yet the body was burned, not left on the beach."

Carmichael shrugged. "What wasn't burned that night? Mitch couldn't exactly get out of the way." He shoved a toothpick between his teeth and commenced rolling it from one side of his mouth to the other, his eyes hard and bright. "There's no way we're going to track this one down."

"We could broadcast an appeal for witnesses," Merry said. "If he was killed the way you think, somebody might have seen it."

"I've done that," Carmichael said patiently. "Posted bulletins on the radio and the news. Now I've got the joy of sifting through all the garbage that'll come in for the one nugget of real information."

"I'll help."

He looked at her from under his eyebrows, glowering. Nothing was going to cheer Bill Carmichael today.

"Have you talked to Mitch's wife?"

"I told you, she keeps calling me."

"I mean about who might've wanted him dead."

"Oh, for crying out loud," he said, slapping the desktop in frustration and thrusting his chair back against the wall. "Nobody wanted Mitch dead. *That's the problem*. According to Lisa, he was the local pick for Miss Congeniality. Everybody loved him. The town will never recover from his loss. And you know, she's probably not just painting a rosy picture. Sometimes nice people die for no reason at all, Detective. And we can't assign the blame."

"I know," Merry said. "So you've decided Scottie Flanagan's theory is not worth looking into."

"What, that he was killed in revenge for his toilets?"

"Hot-water showers. And ice machine."

"Maybe you guys have time to follow up leads like that," Carmichael said, "but the *state* police do not, my dear."

"Okay, okay," she said. "It was just a thought. Anything further on Joshua Field?"

"Abbie Hoffman in Birkenstocks?" Carmichael said. "Nope. There's nothing to tie him to the bomb—to its construction, that is. Just to ownership of the boat it was in. Even there, it's his uncle's boat. He'll probably be sued for civil damages, and he'll get a lawyer who'll show that anybody could've rigged that device without the Baldwins' knowledge. It'll go nowhere."

"Were his fingers tested for plastic explosive trace residue?"

"My, my, my, didn't *we* study hard at the academy," Carmichael said sarcastically. "Your arson guru had it done. I think he hoped he'd find a dead Iranian at the bottom of the harbor, with a note proclaiming 'Death to the Great Satan' tacked to his head. He was sure the explosive was Semtex imported from Slovakia. When in fact he's now determined it was American-made plastique you can steal from any construction site. And the timer was from Radio Shack, not Switzerland."

"Joshua Field works construction."

"And we do so much blasting on Nantucket. That sand sure gets tough for the backhoes to handle. Come on, Mere."

"So what about Field's hands?"

"Clean, of course. That's not surprising. Three days elapsed between the bomb and the test."

Merry waited a second while Bill Carmichael toyed with his toothpick, his eyes drifting elsewhere. She recognized the expression. He was half attending to her and half focused on the thoughts that couldn't stop whirling in his brain. She was the same way herself—asking questions about Field, and wondering whether Dave Grizutto had been in touch with Del since her return to the island.

"Bill," she said, rising from her chair, "somebody built a bomb and destroyed the pier. *Somebody did that.* Until we can figure out why, we can't begin to focus on who."

"Maybe there was no *why*, Detective. Maybe there was just a torching for kicks. The classic profile of an arsonist is a guy who gets a sexual high from watching things explode and burn. You've got to admit the pier was a hell of an orgasm."

The station door opened and shut. "Bill!" a woman's voice called. "I brought you coffee!"

Carmichael groaned. "Just what I need," he said. "More Colombian speed. You taking off?"

Merry nodded. "I'll be in touch."

"Heard your friend bought it the other night."

The casual way of describing Del's death struck Merry like a slap on the cheek.

"Sorry to hear it."

"Thanks, Bill," she said, and left, avoiding his eyes.

Once back in her gray Explorer, she sat for a moment with her hands in her lap, staring blankly at the steering wheel. Nothing could be simpler than finding out whether Del had seen Dave Grizutto before her death. She had left her cell phone on the Folgers' dining-room table Sunday night. In the aftermath of the fire, Merry had never found time to return it to her. And she knew Del well enough to expect every one of her appointments to be carefully noted somewhere in the phone's calendar. A chill rose up Merry's back. *My God*, she thought. *She might even have put down a date with death, days in advance.*

RAFE DA SILVA stood up to ease his aching back and rested his chin on the handle of his spade. "So you think I ought to talk to Merry?"

He sounded doubtful and anxious, even to himself. Peter squinted up at him from his place in the dirt, half-way down the row of tomato plants he was staking. "Well, talking to Tess hasn't gotten you anywhere."

"Except deeper in the hole."

He had stopped by the house on Quince Street that morning and found Will sitting morosely in the empty kitchen and a *Closed* sign on the restaurant door. The second weekend of the summer season, and the Green-gage was turning away business. Tess was upstairs in bed, half conscious under the effect of Dr. John's Valium. When Rafe bent over her pillow, he was shocked at the ravages the past twenty-four hours had written on her face. She stared fixedly at the ceiling, her fingers limp, her chest barely rising and falling with the effort of breath. Every inch of her cried out *depression.* He held her fingers and received no pressure in response; nor did she bother to turn her gaze in his direction. He brought Will back to the farm for a few hours and put him in Peter's study with a book, under the careful eye of Rebecca.

"I wonder if this hasn't been coming for a long time," Peter said.

"Tess's blowup?"

"The whole thing. She had nerves of steel those first few months after Dan drowned. You remember. Sold the scal-loper, refinanced the debt, put in a commercial kitchen. All between March and June, with Will walking around like a zombie. Then Will gets sent to the mainland for psy-chiatric work, and she runs the restaurant alone."

Peter ripped at a piece of sheeting with his teeth and tore it into a thin strip. The rag went under a tomato plant's armpit and looped in a figure eight around the six-foot stake.

"Just as she's through her first successful season, and Will's back on the island starting school again, he gets pitched from his bike and ends up in Mass Gen. So Tess has to be stoic for the next six months until he's out of the woods. And make ends meet somehow in the off-season, when the restaurant's closed. *Anybody'd* have a nervous breakdown once they got a breather."

"Maybe," Rafe said. "It's just not like Tess."

"Of course it isn't," Peter said. "If it were, you wouldn't think she was crazy. And you certainly wouldn't think she was a murderer."

There it was, the word he'd been skirting. *Murder*. The fear that had gripped him since he'd heard Tess's weird laughter yesterday morning, seen her rejoicing at Del's death. *Murder*. He couldn't seem to get away from it.

"Go talk to Merry," Peter said, standing up and dusting off his bare knees. Small grains of grit had embedded there and left a pattern like ostrich skin. "She'll probably tell you Tess didn't do it. You need to hear that, Rafe."

"I'm not sure it'll help," he said, swallowing. He lifted his chin from the spade and turned back to the beans he was cultivating. "She scared me bad, Pete. I'd never seen Tess so—*evil*. I can't get it out of my head. Maybe I've never known her at all."

"You know her," Peter said. "You just don't know all of her. There's ugliness in every one of us. Deep feeling—jealousy, fear—brings it out." He stopped. Rafe had seen more of the ugliness of life than Peter could possibly imagine. "Few of us can admit that we're happy when someone we hate is dead. It's a nasty little secret."

"Very nasty."

"But Tess was honest about it. That suggests she had nothing to do with killing Del. And with Del gone, you'll find the Tess you knew again, Rafe."

"But can I trust that it's the real Tess?" the foreman said, stabbing at the dirt with his spade.

Peter said nothing. He understood that trust could be broken as easily as a dropped glass.

RALPH WALDO FOLGER peered down at Sara Duarte as she lay sleeping in her collapsible crib. To his relief, her breathing was steady and shallow. The previous night she had cried out in her sleep, a terrible sound that brought all three Folgers running from their beds, afraid of what they might see. Sara did not even awaken with her shriek; whatever fear grazed her unconscious with dark wings flapped on into oblivion.

Ralph wondered about the memory of a two-year-old. Had Sara seen or heard something the night of Del's death? Probably not. She would certainly have cried out and run to her mother's side. And in that case, she would be dead.

They had brought the child's things to Tattle Court before the Duarte house was sealed, and Sara seemed to have adapted to her new surroundings happily enough. Del had died without appointing a guardian for her daughter; even now, Felix Harper was discussing the formal adoption process with Del's New Bedford cousins.

A sound in the doorway behind him; Merry. "She's

sleeping," Ralph said in a gruff whisper, and backed out of the room in stockinged feet.

"No more nightmares?"

"Not yet."

Merry looked past him toward the crib, her black brows drawn down. "What'll happen to her, Ralph?"

"Felix is handling it."

"I'm not sure he should be."

"Now, Meredith—"

"*We're* the people who loved Del," she said. "We should be taking care of her child. It's what she'd have wanted."

"Her family loved her, too. Don't discount that. Those cousins took her in three years ago, and stood by her."

"I guess," she said, unconvinced. "But Sara's so small, Ralph. She can't say what she wants, so we decide her life for her. She may hate us someday."

"You've just pronounced the ancient law of parenting," he said dryly. "Take it as cautionary advice. How's the arson investigation?"

"Fine. Bill's got everything in hand. Not much news on the prosecution front." She glanced at him, the green eyes softening. "You don't have to remind me, Ralph Waldo. I'm not on Del's case. I'll behave."

"Never occurred to me you wouldn't," he fibbed.

Chapter 17

FELIX HARPER'S OFFICE was in a Federal-style shingled house on South Beach, with roses growing up both sides of the door and a miniature brass lightship basket for a knocker. Other than the discreet wooden sign at the foot of the slate walk that read FELIX HARPER, ATTORNEY, it might have been any other island home—of a wealthy off-islander resident for a month, Merry thought. The place had the carefully tended perennial borders lining its picket fence, the fresh paint trim, and the clipped expanse of lawn that characterized the retreats maintained *in absentia* for the fashionable seasonals of New York and Connecticut. Felix was doing well.

Merry lifted the handle of the lightship-basket knocker and let it fall with a thud.

Del's cell phone calendar showed several appointments with the lawyer, one reason Merry wanted to talk to him. Other entries were equally interesting. Del had lunched with Tom Baldwin a few days after his nephew had thrown fish guts over Merry's head—looking for her old job, perhaps? She had also seen Dave Grizutto—or so Merry assumed. The notation said only "Dave, 7:30"; but it sent a chill through her nonetheless. Del talked to him the very night of her murder.

It was Mrs. Harper who opened the door, a small, sparrowlike woman with white hair the texture of cotton candy and bright blue eyes. Faded pink lipstick was smeared in the crevices of her lips, and her skin had softened into well-worn suede the color of parchment. She wore a Fair Isle sweater and vivid pink linen shorts, and she held a trowel in her hand.

"The peonies," she announced. "Just readying them for the show. And how can I help you, dear?"

"Detective Meredith Folger," Merry said. "Nantucket police. I was hoping to see Mr. Harper."

"Fil!" she called over her shoulder. "Are you engaged? There's a lady to see you."

A low murmur from within, and the sky-blue door opened wider. "Through to the left, dear, and Fil will show you out. Mind you make him ask if you'd like some lemonade. It's sitting on the counter."

Merry worked her way past the dining room's Chippendale side chairs with their needlepointed seats to the study off the hallway beyond. A dim circle of light cast on a desk piled with papers illuminated a pair of hands, the left one holding a pen, and the right braced against a yellow legal pad. At her appearance, Felix Harper ducked into view and stood up, pulling his reading glasses from the bridge of his nose. Tall, gaunt, and distracted, with dark hair just beginning to feather into gray, he was a good thirty years younger than the woman who'd answered the door.

"Yes?" he said. "How can I help you?"

"I'm Meredith Folger, Mr. Harper. With the Nantucket police."

"Ah, yes. Is this a follow-up, then, to that fellow who came by yesterday?"

"Detective Bailey?"

"That was the name."

"Only sort of," Merry said. "I'll be honest. I'm not assigned to Adelia Duarte's case. I was just an old friend of hers, and I wanted to talk to you."

A faint wrinkle on the pale skin, and he raised a hand to his brow. "Please sit down," he said. "I'm not sure I can help you, but perhaps—" He paused. "Mother did make some lemonade. Would you like some?"

"She'll be so pleased you remembered," Merry said, smiling. "I'll have a glass."

He tucked his height under the doorframe and disappeared down the hall. Merry looked around the study. Black-and-white photographs of a much younger Felix, racing a Swan in turbulent seas, were tacked to the walls. Floor-to-ceiling shelves held a motley collection of books, some leather-bound, some paperbacks, all of them carefully dusted. *Mother*, Merry thought. Mother probably had arranged for the framing of the two diplomas—one from Harvard College, one from Harvard Law—positioned over Felix's desk in full view of any client's chair.

An ice-cold glass of lemonade descended from the heavens.

"Thank you," she said, and smiled up at Harper. He looked uncomfortable, and hastened to put the desk between them.

"In what way might I be helpful?"

Merry took a long draft of her drink, sighed, and set it down carefully beside her chair. "My family is taking care of Sara Duarte at the moment."

Recognition and comprehension dawned on his spare face.

"I understand you've been discussing Sara's future with Del's relatives," Merry continued, "and I wondered whether you've reached any conclusions. Also whether the house will be sold, and how the funds from the sale will be disposed of, and so forth. My father, Police Chief John Folger, has asked me to help settle Adelia's estate."

The lawyer fiddled with a signet ring on his finger "Miss Duarte died intestate, as no doubt you know," he said. "In Massachusetts, that's not really a problem—her property will go to her daughter, once the estate is pro-bated and the death duties are paid. I don't think the child will have much to live on unless the house is sold, and its proceeds retained in trust by her guardians."

"That's the question," Merry said. "Who are likely to be Sara's guardians?"

"I've been debating that with Adelia's cousins, Yolanda and Manny Duarte. They're roughly the same age as the deceased, they're quite fond of young Sara, and they have two children of their own. They would be logical adop-tive parents."

"But? Don't they want the responsibility?"

"They may not be allowed the chance," Felix said. "There is the issue of Joe Duarte's will to be considered."

"*Joe's* will?"

"Indeed. It may have some force and effect in the mat-ter—although not in the way he envisioned." The lawyer leaned forward and cupped his hands. "Mr. Duarte's will provided for his granddaughter's care in the event that his daughter predeceased him."

"Wait a minute," Merry said. "Joe Duarte dealt with the issue of Sara in his *will?* He'd never even seen her."

"So I understand. Nevertheless, his will states that

if Adelia Duarte predeceases him, his granddaughter's financial affairs are to be placed under the guardianship of Jackie Alcantrara, one of the legatees of his estate. Apparently Mr. Alcantrara was someone Mr. Duarte trusted."

"No way," Merry said, flabbergasted. "That's insane. Did Del know about this?"

"She was informed at the reading of the will. At the time, the provision seemed meaningless."

"Because she was alive. She hadn't predeceased him."

"Exactly. However, her death makes the will's provision an interesting one. Had Miss Duarte found time to draft a will of her own, assigning the child a guardian, it would, of course, have superseded this. Unfortunately she did not, and Sara Duarte is"—he hesitated before the colloquialism—"up for grabs."

"Along with her inheritance," Merry mused.

"The provision is not, strictly speaking, enforceable. Miss Duarte did not predecease her father. But there remains the possibility that Mr. Alcantrara will attempt to have it enforced, as the sole legal provision for Sara Duarte's future. I have informed Yolanda and Manny Duarte of that fact. If they proceed with their plans for the child, they may face a court battle."

"What a mess," Merry said. Connie Alcantrara's avid face and purposeful questions rose in her mind. She understood better now the woman's willingness to talk; her morning chatter was anything but idle. Had Jackie, who witnessed Joe's will, told her about the guardianship provision? Was this added incentive to murder—or a suggestion that the Alcantraras were innocent? For if monetary gain had been their primary object, wouldn't

Adelia have predeceased Joe—and not the other way around?

"That would be too obvious. They'd be afraid someone would put two and two together. Better to get the boats and hope for the kid."

"I'm sorry?" Felix Harper said.

She looked up and realized she'd spoken aloud.

"Nothing," she said. "Just thinking too much. Mr. Harper—Del stopped by to see you twice in the week she was on the island. Did she come to talk about the will?"

"Yes," he said hesitantly. "About the house, and renting the smaller of the two boats. And some other—matters."

"Could you give me some idea what those matters were? It could be helpful in determining her state of mind before she died—what concerned her, and so forth. That might shed some light on her activities, and possibly on the identity of her murderer."

"I understand," he said.

"Was she thinking of writing a will herself?"

"I don't know."

Merry waited.

"She was certainly concerned about her daughter, however," he finally said, relenting. "She wanted to discuss the nature of trust funds—how they were administered, how funds were safeguarded, the appointment of trustees, and so forth. Almost prophetic, when one considers it."

"Right," Merry said thoughtfully. "But she never got to set anything up."

"No," he assented. "Which means that the hundred thousand dollars is just sitting there, waiting to be drained for death duties. It's a crying shame. A trust would have protected all of it."

"Hundred thousand *what?*"

"Dollars," Felix Harper said. "The amount she wanted to place in trust."

"Did Joe leave that much to Sara?"

"No, Detective," the lawyer said. "I don't know where Miss Duarte came by the money. She wouldn't say."

"Del had a hundred thousand dollars?"

"She still does, I suppose. In an account in the Pacific National Bank."

"SO THE WAY I see it," Matt Bailey said, kicking his chair back and putting his feet up on Merry's desk, "this Alcantrara guy and his wife had everything to gain and nothing to lose. It's an open-and-shut case."

"Based on what evidence?"

He shrugged. "According to your dad, Del thought her father was bumped off, right? And then *she's* bumped off. Who benefits? *Jackie Alcantrara.* Both times."

"Right," Merry said. "But besides that, what *evidence* have you got, Bailey?"

"That's confidential until the arrest is made," he said, pulling his heels to the floor.

Merry rolled her eyes. "Get out of my office, will you?"

He stood up, his expression injured. "I didn't think you'd let a little thing like envy ruin your judgment," he said.

"Believe me, I haven't."

When he had slouched off to his own cubicle, Merry put her head in her hands. The chump would arrest Jackie Alcantrara on the basis of a hunch. She wondered what John Folger would think when he read Bailey's report. She was fairly certain Bailey knew nothing about Del's hundred thousand dollars, but he had latched onto two facts: Jackie'd gotten the boats, and Jackie might get the house if he won custody of Sara. John Folger, however, would be looking for more than just motive—he'd expect to find opportunity and means in Matt Bailey's report. And Merry doubted they were there.

She called Clarence Strangerfield. The crime scene chief was off-duty today, but he might answer his cell.

He did.

A few minutes later, she was driving toward his Sconset home.

"COME ON, CLARE," she said. "Quit holding out on me."

"I would nevah hold out on you, Marradith. But yar not on this case."

All she could see of Clarence Strangerfield was his hindquarters—considerable when viewed from the best of angles, but truly formidable in his current position in the rose bed. He had an insecticide pump firmly in hand and was sending clouds of something noxious billowing about the leafy canes.

"Neither is Matt Bailey," Merry said. "He signed off about twenty-four hours after he signed on."

"Now, Marradith. Bailey may lack yar interest in finding Miss Duarte's murderah—"

"The jerk's going to arrest Jackie Alcantrara."

Clarence sat up so quickly he stabbed his forehead on a thorn and swore under his breath.

"I know he can't have talked to the guy—Jackie's been at sea for the past several days, and isn't due in until tonight. Never mind that he was supposed to be on the

Georges Bank when Del was killed. I figure Bailey thinks he was lying, and that the coordinates he gave to his wife were pulled out of the air. I haven't had time to check whether he radioed them to the Coast Guard as well. I can understand skepticism about the alibi—I was thinking up ways Jackie could've gotten in and out of port long enough to kill Del myself. What I want to know is whether Bailey's even bothered with the evidence."

"O' carse not," Clarence said. "Have you been doin' a bit of investigatin' on the side, Marradith?"

"I've just talked to a few people," she said evasively. "Dad told me to settle Del's affairs. I've been settling."

"And you wouldn't have peeked at my reparht, now would you?"

"Maybe peeked."

Clarence set down his spray gun deliberately and pulled off his gloves. "You'll get yarself fired one o' these days, Detective. And you'll *still* be pokin' yar nose in othah people's business."

"Clare, she was an old friend."

"I know."

"And I let her down."

"Ow, come off it."

"I did. She tried to tell me there was something wrong with her father's death, and I dismissed it. If I'd taken her seriously, she might not be in a refrigerated locker in Boston."

"Don't think about that paht, Marradith." He turned one knee to the earth and raised the other for support, grunting as he thrust himself to his feet. "Yar not responsible."

"If I'm not, no one is."

He looked at her, eyes narrowed. "Whaddya want to know?"

"If, as seems obvious, Del was killed because she'd discovered something incriminating about Joe's death, then Bailey's right to look for suspects among Joe's crew—Jackie chief among them, since he benefited under the will. I would be doing the same. But I'd hate to see Bailey blow the case by arresting Jackie too early. If he can't make the charges stick, Jackie'll be free a few hours later and covering his tracks with a vengeance."

"Ayeh," Clarence said grimly.

"Jackie took only one crew member with him on this fishing trip. The Swede—the guy who operated the winch that accidentally killed Joe. But their stories differ. Jackie says the Swede brought the doors in too fast because he was careless. The Swede says he had no choice; the winch was jammed. Interesting that they're out on the Atlantic together when Del dies, isn't it? That way, the Swede can say Jackie was on the Georges Bank the whole time, and vice versa."

"You think they were conspirin'?"

"I'd like to know where the other two crew members were while Jackie and the Swede set up their alibis. Scuttlebutt has it they've taken jobs on the mainland—but that doesn't mean they weren't on Nantucket Wednesday night. Bailey isn't even bothering to think beyond his feet—which he'd prefer to leave propped up on the desk in front of him."

"Now, Marradith."

"Has Bailey checked Jackie's closets for linen or silk clothes?"

"Nothin's come to me for analysis, far's I know."

"Nothing from his wife's closets, either? *Her* alibi is nonexistent."

Clarence shook his head.

"What about fingerprints?"

"He may plan to get 'em aftah he arrests the fellah."

"Oh, that's brilliant."

"If you've seen the repaht, you'll know about the two different blood types," Clarence said carefully. "Guess they'll be drawin' blood, too."

"Clare, you've got to talk to the chief before Bailey does anything."

"He's *yar* fathah, Marradith."

Chapter 18

JOHN FOLGER WAS pulling at his salt-and-pepper mustache as he read over Matt Bailey's report. The detective prided himself on his intuitive leaps, as he called them. John's preferred words were less flattering. While Bailey saw himself as an intellectual path-blazer who cut investigation time in half, his chief considered him lazy. His failure to do the scut work of investigation too often resulted in a false arrest or an unresolved case.

John had given Bailey Del Duarte's murder in the hope that it might galvanize him. But as he read the cursory paragraphs, the chief admitted that handing Bailey responsibility was rather like giving pen and paper to a dog—you hope he'll learn to write, but more often than not, he'll chew the pen and urinate happily on the paper. Once Del Duarte's death was behind them, John decided, Bailey was going to be counseled. He'd been counseled before, of course, by the training officer; he'd done his forty hours of mandatory, in-line training the state expected every year; and nothing had changed. It was time he was counseled into another career.

The chief slapped the file closed in irritation and reached for his intercom buzzer, intending to call Bailey into the office; but he stopped in mid-reach. His daughter was leaning against the doorframe silently, watching him, and he didn't like the look in her green eyes. She was both wary and intent, which meant she was going to say something she was sure would make him angry.

"What is it, Detective Folger?"

"Do you have a minute, Chief?"

He nodded toward the captain's chair opposite his desk. She closed the door behind her and sat down, tucking her hands between her knees and drawing breath.

"I decided to forgo vacation," she said.

"So I see."

"Time off would just leave me thinking, without any distraction, and that wouldn't be good for me right now."

"Probably not," he said gently. "How's Sara doing?"

"She was asleep when I stopped by the house. No nightmares."

"Good." He waited.

"I talked to Bill Carmichael," she began again. "Nothing much has developed in the arson investigation. They've tracked the plastic explosive by its residue, and can say that it's American-made, probably construction-grade. They should have the manufacturer and batch pinned down soon."

"Uh-huh."

"Nothing can be traced to Field."

"Have you talked to Tom Baldwin?"

"Not yet. I'm planning to."

"Good. I'd like your sense of how he reacts to questioning. Maybe he knows more than he'd like us to believe."

"Maybe. Carmichael thinks Mitch Davis was shot by an enraged boat owner. Completely random."

"Could be." Not our jurisdiction, his tone implied.

"Dad—"

"Yeah?"

"Bailey told me he's planning to arrest Jackie Alcantrara."

"Really," he said, raising one eyebrow. "Feeling good about it, was he? Spreading the joyful news?"

"He called it an open-and-shut case," Merry said, meeting her father's bright blue eyes.

"And it's not."

"You know it's not."

John Folger sighed and tipped his chair back against the wall, legs dangling like a child's. "No, it's not, Mer. I'll be honest. I don't know what to do." His chin lifted and he studied her a moment. "I thought you'd be pleased to hear Jackie was being fitted for handcuffs."

"Not if it means the case is blown," she said.

"Ah."

"He's got an alibi, Dad. He hasn't been in port for three days. And he has a crewmember who'll say the same thing. That doesn't mean he's innocent—just that Bailey hasn't done his homework. No attempt to match fibers found at the scene to fibers in Jackie's closet. Or his wife's, although his wife has no alibi at all and is panting to adopt Sara and her future income."

Her father's face looked suddenly guarded. "You've talked to Jackie's wife?"

Too late, Merry caught herself.

"Isn't that Bailey's job?"

"Felix Harper told me the Alcantraras might contest Sara's adoption," she said, stretching the truth. "I thought I'd better check Connie out. You *did* tell me to take care of Del's affairs."

John Folger didn't answer.

She rushed on. "Bailey hasn't bothered to find out what the other two members of Joe Duarte's crew were doing on the night in question. They might have been at a pizza party with seventy witnesses. Or they might have been shoving a harpoon into Del's stomach."

"You sure you're working on arson, Meredith?"

Her eyes dropped to her lap. "I know it sounds like I'm ratting to Daddy about a fellow detective. I know how it looks. But Dad, he's screwing this up! And I can't stand it."

"I know," her father said. "And I know you came in here expecting me to be angry because you're walking around the margins of Del's case. Normally, I would be."

Merry didn't say anything.

"But I'm actually relieved you're asking these questions. I've been asking them, too."

"So does Bailey arrest Jackie?"

"I don't think so." The chief tapped his fingers on the desk in a rough approximation of chopsticks, his face abstracted. "What if we do this? I tell Bailey he hasn't got enough to support an arrest. I send him out to Alcantrara's to collect samples. I have him hit the Cape to interview the remaining crew members."

"You have him get everybody's fingerprints," Merry said.

"I have him get fingerprints."

"And search the trash," Merry said.

"The trash?"

"Del received threatening letters. Three of them, in fact, before she died. They were made up of clipped newsprint, magazines—the usual thing from a first-time poison penman. Maybe the shreds are out back of Alcantrara's."

"You think Jackie would bother with that?"

"No, but it sounds just like his wife."

"Will that satisfy you?" her father said.

"It's a start." She hesitated, then plunged on. "You could always have me take over the case."

There was a silence. John Folger looked at his hands. "I can't do that, Meredith."

"Dad—I'm not going to fall apart just because it's Del."

"I know you believe that," he said.

"It's not just belief. I'm fine."

"You don't look fine."

She rolled her eyes. "So maybe I haven't been sleeping well. Neither have you, if it comes to that."

He grunted assent. "Bailey needs to win or lose this one, Meredith. It's his last chance."

"Does he know that?"

"He should. But he probably doesn't. Judging by this report"—he flipped one edge of the manila folder contemptuously—"he thinks he's done a dandy job just by stating the obvious. He'll bullshit his way right off the force."

Merry stood up, walked toward the door with her hands in her pockets, and turned. Her face was expressionless. "So finding Del's murderer is less important than finding a reason to fire Bailey?"

"You know that's not true."

"That's what I hear you saying."

"Meredith—" he said, and drew a breath. She was right, he'd had too little sleep, and his temper—volatile at the best of times—was hair-trigger right now. "I'm not going to tell you to keep away from this case, okay? If it makes you feel better to skulk around on the side, making sure you turn over every stone Bailey misses, go ahead. But trust me to do the same. I'm not going to let him arrest Jackie because he inherits under Joe's will. Give me some credit, Detective. We'll find Del's murderer."

Merry looked at him, her green eyes hard. "I won't meddle directly. But if I find evidence or information—"

"Just get it to me, okay?"

"Okay."

"When's Jackie due?" he asked, thinking about the fingerprints.

"His wife figured this evening. He and the Swede left port the day before Del died, and with only two men working the tiller and the nets, they'll take a while to get a full hold."

"The Swede? Isn't that the guy who was careless with a winch?"

"So Jackie says. The Swede tells a different story. The winch was jammed, he says, and couldn't be slowed."

"Maybe they'll fight it out on the high seas."

"Dad—"

"Yeah?"

"Send Howie to find the other two guys who crewed for Joe Duarte. He's a better interviewer after one summer than Bailey is after ten years."

"That's because you trained him, Meredith," John Folger said.

RAFE DA SILVA already had a seat at the counter in Black Eyed Susan's. His blunt fingers were clasped around a bottle of Michelob. At the sight of him, Merry immediately thought of Peter.

"Hey, Girl Scout," Rafe said, standing up to greet her. "You were great to come by."

"Anything's better than sitting at home."

"I hear ya. How's Sara?"

"Actually, better than I'd have expected."

"Good. I was worried when I saw her sitting there next to Del. Seeing that kind of thing can't be good for a kid."

"No," Merry said. "I'll have a glass of wine. Some Pinot Noir."

"Been hanging around Pete too much," he said, grinning.

"Oh, and Tess hasn't converted you?"

Rafe's smile faded.

"Judging by your face, things are still bad."

"Bad to worse."

"I'd have thought Del's death—I mean, you're not going to fish anymore, right? That hasn't helped?"

"Well—that's why I wanted to see you tonight, Mer," Rafe said.

The waitress set a glass before Merry's nose. She thanked her and took a sip. "Tell me about Tess."

"She went a little crazy the other day. Thing is, I don't know whether it happened *after* Del died, when I saw her—or before."

Merry's green eyes slid up from the rim of her mug and studied Rafe. "Crazy how?" she said.

He shrugged. "She's sedated, right now. Dr. John's orders. I can't get any response from her when I visit. Neither can Will. You can imagine what that does for the kid."

"How's she running the restaurant?"

"It's closed."

"Whew." Merry ran a fingertip down the side of Rafe's mug, tracing a pattern in the condensation. "And before she was sedated?"

"After I left Del's the other day I went by the Greengage to tell her the news. She went into some kind of fit, Mer, laughing and crying, like she'd won the lottery or something."

He paused, the air between them filled with the clatter of other people's cutlery and conversation.

"So she's glad Del's dead," Merry said slowly. "I don't like that, but I can't say it's crazy. I've hated people out of jealousy before. It can make your reactions a little—extreme."

"Right," Rafe said. "I figured that's all it was. I mean, it's not like she must've killed Del—right?"

"Right. Are you seriously worried about that?"

"Yes. The way she was acting freaked me out. I wondered if . . . you could find out, once and for all."

"Whether Tess killed Del?"

He nodded, unable to put it into words.

"That's a hell of a job to hand me, Rafe. Find out whether one friend killed another."

"But it *is* your job, Merry," he said suddenly. "When you're a cop on an island this small, it's always going to be people you know doing things you don't want to know about."

"And you'd rather I did this than Matt Bailey."

"*That* stupid son of a bitch? He couldn't find his own mother in broad daylight," Rafe said. "I can't believe your dad put him in charge of Del's case."

"Well, there's a story about that. You don't have time for it, believe me."

"I don't know why this had to happen," Rafe said wistfully.

"Del's death?"

"That too."

WHEN SHE'D LEFT Rafe, Merry walked the few blocks to Brotherhood of Thieves and slung a leg over a stool in the downstairs bar.

"What'll it be?" the barmaid said.

"Can I have a glass of water?"

The woman slammed a dripping glass on the bar, where it settled into a pool of wet.

"Thanks," Merry said. "Is Dave Grizutto on tonight?"

"He comes in at seven."

Merry looked at her watch. "Ten minutes. Do you know if he's here?"

The barmaid sighed and shoved her way through the half-door toward the kitchen. Merry watched her lean through the service entrance, her throat working. The kitchen door swung closed and the barmaid returned.

"He's coming," she said. "Want some chips?"

"Sure."

She recognized him immediately, walking with easy grace through the low-ceilinged room, head slightly bent to accommodate the space. Dave was tall, tanned, blond, and good-looking, with a casual dimple in his resting expression that widened to dazzling charm when he smiled. It was a manner that served him well tending bar. He could defuse a drunken argument, calm a harried waitress, mollify the recipient of a late order. College-age girls hung on his stools and left sizable tips in their disappointed wake. He belonged on a beefcake calendar, bare-chested and lazy-eyed for the camera, but Merry sensed he would be profoundly uncomfortable there. Dave's looks were an accident his personality had not quite caught up with.

"Merry Folger," he said, extending a hand. At close range, she saw the strain around his eyes, the hollows beneath them. Two lines ran from the corners of his mouth to his nose. He'd been keeping late nights, or broken ones.

"Hi, Dave. I hoped I'd find you here."

"Am I ever anywhere else?" A trace of bitterness in the words. He had to be about her own age, Merry thought, and he'd been tending bar at the Brotherhood for years.

"Do you have a few moments to talk before you go on? Somewhere less—public?"

"Sure. Let's head for the back. If I take a table, the manager'll kill me. Not that there's one to take."

She followed Dave through the service door to a small room off the kitchen. "The chef's office," he said. "He orders everything from here. The rest of us use it for phone calls." He sat down in a straight-backed wooden chair and motioned Merry toward its mate. The room barely contained them both, but it had a door that closed, and when Dave shut it, the silence fell welcomingly on her ears.

"You're here to talk about Del," he said quietly.

"Yes."

"As a cop or a friend?"

"I have to be both."

"I can understand that." He looked at her once, looked away. "It might almost be a relief, I suppose. To have something official to do. A distraction."

"I'm sorry, Dave."

"Coming from you, that word almost has meaning." His voice broke, and he rubbed at the bridge of his nose with a thumb and forefinger.

"Dave," Merry said, aware that time was short, "did you get to see Del while she was back on the island?"

A deep, shaky breath, and nothing.

"I only ask because she said something about dropping by here the night she died," Merry said. A white lie, but so what. "I wondered if she'd seemed nervy. Or frightened. Anything out of the ordinary that might give us a clue to what happened."

His hand came away from his face, and she was struck by the grief in his eyes. "How's Sara, Merry?" he said. "What's going to happen to her?"

"She's staying with us. Del's lawyer is working out the adoption."

"So *you're* taking her?"

Merry shook her head. "I'd love to, but Del's cousins are first in line. And there's some chance that a clause in Joe Duarte's will may foul things up. He named Jackie Alcantrara Sara's guardian in the event of Del's death. It's not clear whether that's enforceable, but there's a chance Jackie will try for it."

"No way!" Dave burst out. "Why would that guy want Sara?"

"For her money. That's pretty crass, but it's what I'm guessing."

Why do you care, Dave? Merry studied the bartender's angry face and compared it to the baby's waiting at home. There was not the slightest resemblance between them. Where Sara's features were slight and delicate, Dave's were large and blunt, much as Del's had been. Where Sara's eyes were green, Dave's were bright blue. She was petite for her age, he was enormous. And her auburn hair bore no comparison to his blond.

Blond hair had been found on the floor, however, near Del's body.

"As if Del had money to leave," Dave muttered.

So the hundred thousand dollars hadn't come from him. "There's the Milk Street house," Merry said. "It's worth quite a lot."

"That asshole Alcantrara." Dave stood up and reached for the door, as though he intended to hunt Jackie down that very minute. "He gets Sara over my dead body."

"Dave—"

"She's mine, Merry," he said, turning and stabbing at his chest with a stiff finger. "Sara is *mine*. And the last person who should have her is Jackie Alcantrara. If the bastard goes to court, he'll run into me."

There was a moment's silence.

"Sit down."

The bartender sighed, then slumped back into his chair.

"Did Del say you were Sara's father?" Merry asked.

He shook his head. "She denied everything."

"Then why are you so convinced?"

"Who else could it have been?" he burst out. "I was always with her, Merry. I loved her. I wanted her, for God's sake. I wanted to marry her. Even after she told me she was pregnant, and that she was leaving. I tried everything I could think of to make her stay. I even followed her to New Bedford, did you know that? For three months. I worked at a bar down near the seaport, just so I could see her, try to talk some sense into her."

"But you finally came home."

"What else could I do? There's only so long a guy can feel like an ass."

"And she never admitted you were the father?"

"No. Even I began to wonder, after a while. I mean, why wouldn't she tell me the truth?"

"Maybe because the truth would hurt."

"There was no one else," he said in a small voice.

"Dave," Merry began, and stopped, searching for the words. "Del and I grew apart over the past few years. She never told me who the father was. But I did think she'd ended her relationship with you several months before Sara was conceived."

His eyes slid to hers, slid away. He shrugged, nodded assent. "She decided to stop seeing me. That's true."

"Do you know why?"

He laughed shortly. "Because Del was always threatened by commitment. I asked her to marry me, Merry, and she told me not to call her again. You explain that."

Maybe she couldn't marry someone she didn't love, Merry thought. *And maybe she'd met someone she did.* "When would this have been?"

"Three years ago."

"And Sara is two."

"Right. Which means we broke up in June and Del got pregnant somewhere around September. It wasn't by me, is that what you're saying?"

"I don't have to."

He stood up, turning in the small space like a caged animal. "It may still have been me," he said. "I wasn't done with Del. I've never been done with Del. We got together, on and off, I saw her now and then. Do you know what it's like to ache for someone like that, Merry? To ache *physically*, until you think you'll scream or smash a glass in a customer's face from the pain of not having her? I couldn't live with that. She had no right to expect me to."

A cold finger moved up Merry's back as comprehension dawned. "Did you rape her, Dave?"

"It wasn't rape," he said swiftly, turning on Merry. He was very tall against the office's single swinging bulb, and she shrank away from him involuntarily. "It wasn't rape. I'd never do that to Del."

There was a note of defensiveness in his voice Merry could not accept. She wondered, for a moment, if he was prone to violence; if the calm exterior and the easy charm hid a volatile temper. Perhaps this was what Del had seen, and why she wanted to break away. There was no way of knowing, now. But Matt Bailey could look in Dave's closet for fibers that matched those on Del's floor. He could take a sample of his blood, a piece of his hair, an imprint of his thumb and forefinger.

"Sara doesn't look much like you," she said.

"She doesn't look much like Del, either."

"So you've seen her?"

Too late, he caught himself. His eyes flicked to Merry's, then flicked down to the ground. "I've seen her," he whispered. "I had to see her."

"Did Del bring her to the bar?"

He shook his head. "I wasn't working the day that— that day. I stopped by Del's house."

"The night she was murdered? What time, Dave?"

He did not meet her gaze. "Around seven," he said.

"And how was she?"

"Same old Del. She turned into this person I could never reach once she knew she was pregnant, Merry," he said, sitting down opposite her once more. "She'd stand in front of me with her arms crossed and her face distant, and she'd make small talk. Like we'd never been more than passing strangers. She built up an amazing wall. And all I wanted to know was why she thought that was so necessary. But I could never get her to talk about anything real—to be herself with me. She was polite and untouchable and a complete stranger. Sometimes I wanted to shake her until her teeth rattled in her head—" He stopped, and looked down at his hands. "That is not an admission of guilt."

"Did you argue, Dave?"

He shook his head. "We never got that far. I was trying to give her space, keep my distance, reestablish contact. I played with Sara. I figured with Del back on the island, maybe with time, whatever had gone wrong three years ago could be put right. Maybe she'd see me with Sara and recognize that the kid needed a father. I was trying so hard, Merry, and it was like talking to myself."

"There was nothing wrong when you left?"

"Not a thing."

"What time was this?"

"About eight. An hour was long enough. Besides, Del had been housecleaning all day and she looked pretty beat. She wanted a bath and an early bed."

"Did she say anything that suggested she was worried, Dave?"

"To me? She said nothing even remotely personal to me. You forget, I'm the stranger." He smiled crookedly.

"All I heard about was swordfishing. And how good your grandfather was with kids. And how tired she was, and shouldn't I be going? She gave me the politeness and the door."

"And a drink," Merry said. "Let's not forget the scotch."

"Scotch? What scotch?"

"The Glenfiddich. It was sitting on the kitchen counter when we found her."

"Well, it wasn't when I left." He snorted. "Del didn't drink scotch. She rarely drank hard liquor, and when she did, it was Stoli and cranberry juice with a dash of club and a lime."

That used to be true, Merry knew, but maybe Del's tastes had changed in New Bedford. She studied Dave's cleft chin and warm blue eyes. He was a deceptive guy—nothing about his appearance, his temper, or his life was quite what it seemed. He revealed only a bit of the truth, to himself as well as to her. But now he spoke with absolute authority.

"You're sure about that?" she probed.

"I'm a bartender, Merry. I've got half the resident population's drinking habits memorized, not to mention the preferences of some steady tourists. Del didn't drink scotch."

"I guess the bottle was Joe's," Merry said thoughtfully, "or left over from the funeral reception." Although that still didn't explain two glasses. Or why the scotch was on the counter.

"Joe drank Jack Daniel's," Dave said, "and he was too cheap to keep much of anything else in the house. When I went to dinner there, I always brought the wine. It was the only safe thing to do."

"That your favorite poison?" she asked.

"I don't play favorites," he returned. "Do you?"

Merry merely smiled and closed her laptop. "I've kept you too long," she said. "Your manager will be screaming."

He shrugged. "I don't really care anymore," he said. "I kept this job in the hope that Del would come back to Nantucket one day. She did. Only things didn't turn out the way I'd planned. Maybe it's time I moved on."

"Just don't do it for a few weeks, okay?" Merry said, attempting to keep her voice light.

"Because you suspect me of murder?"

"I don't suspect you of anything. I'm not on Del's case."

"I doubt that," Dave said, and opened the office door.

SLEEP ELUDED MERRY, as it had for several nights past. Her brain was filled with a constant command, urgent and unanswerable. *I have to find Sara's father. I have to find Sara's father.* The best way to avoid all the court battles, the tug-of-war over a child, was to know the truth.

Jackie would want to see the will enforced, and the Duartes would do everything they could to stop him. Dave Grizutto would insist on his paternity to convince himself that Del had really loved him. Merry doubted that Sara was Dave's child. It was not like Del to deliberately lie; but to avoid causing him pain, she could easily justify keeping the truth from Dave. Instead, her silence had allowed him to ignore reality, up to the very night of her death.

—Unless Del finally told him about Sara's father, hoping that hard facts might slap him into sense. She might even have shown him the birth certificate. Had jealousy and rage taken over? Had Dave snatched up the harpoon and plunged it into Del's chest, fleeing with the file marked "Personal Documents"?

As the town clock tolled midnight, the refrain hardened into conviction. *I have to find Sara's father.*

Chapter 19

TOM BALDWIN STARTED life as an unskilled construction worker, with a day that went from six-thirty to four, and though the afternoon hours at his office now stretched until dinnertime, he still left the house while most of the world was asleep. This Tuesday morning in June was no different. The streets of the town were empty of life as his heavy tires wallowed along the cobble paving stones, halting patiently at every stop sign before moving through the empty intersections.

He imagined the traffic that would choke the one-way streets for the rest of the summer as vehicles snaked from Steamboat Wharf along South Water, up Main, and out Orange Street to all the island points beyond. Block by block, every car would stop—for the pedestrians, who believed Nantucket was an island for walking, and the bikers, who thought cars should be banned. Life in high season would be far more efficient if the selectmen would allow traffic lights, but commercial lights of all kinds were expressly forbidden by the historic preservation ordinances. Tom grimaced. If he had his way, Nantucket's future would pay less homage to its past.

The island was governed in traditional New England fashion, by a board of selectmen who presided over a few elected officials and the annual town meeting. Tom had crossed swords with the selectmen in the past—over zoning ordinances, sewage and water rights, tax provisions. He proposed enlightened schemes for the management of the island's property that would have brought in significant tax dollars, and he was thwarted as often as he was pleased. He was an outsider—by birth and occupation—and that marginal status cost him. But soon he would enter the holy of holies.

One of the most significant posts in island government was that of finance director. The finance director was appointed by the selectmen and served, in essence, as the chief financial officer for Nantucket, town and county. The finance director supervised everything to do with money—long-range planning, budgeting, all the contracts and procurement for government projects—and so finance director was the job Tom Baldwin wanted. The incumbent had died suddenly, to Tom's intense satisfaction, and the head of the board of selectmen was a personal friend. Over drinks at the Cliffside Beach Club two days ago, Jerry Swain had all but told Tom that the post was his for the taking.

The developer crossed Broad Street, heading for his office on Easton, and took a moment to glance toward the yacht club on his right. The boats hardly bobbed in the slack tide; a gull posed on a piling, arcing its wings and opening its beak in a soundless cry. A redheaded waitress moved among the breakfast tables on the terrace of the White Elephant, the hotel perched on Brant Point, and he felt a sudden pang. The beauty of young, redheaded women, moving with sinuous grace among the tables; like his mother, before too much hard work and childbirth turned her creamy Irish skin to leather. His eyes flicked back to the road and he cleared his throat, shaking off the past.

There was a car parked next to his reserved space—a Ford Explorer. Not a staffer's car; he knew them precisely. A client? Too early in the morning. A tourist, perhaps. He'd have to have it towed.

"Good morning, Tom."

"Meredith Folger! You're up and at 'em."

"I've a lot to do." She stood with a hand extended, professional and neat as ever in her straight khaki skirt and silk camp blouse. She managed to endow the simplest clothes with a bone-deep elegance, he thought, like Greta Garbo. It was no accident he'd thought of the reclusive actress in looking at Merry; something about the cheekbones and the hollows of the eyes was the same. She was about five foot ten, much taller than his wife, Jenny. But he had never viewed her quite so poetically. Perhaps it was the unexpectedness of her presence, or the breath of memory that had stirred his thoughts earlier.

"What brings you to my neck of the woods?"

"I'd like to talk about the Town Pier, if you don't mind, Tom."

"Of course," he said. "It *would* be about Josh, wouldn't it?"

He showed her into his office and shut the door. "My assistant isn't here yet, but I can make some coffee," he said.

"Don't bother. I've had some." She settled into one of his leather club chairs and pulled a laptop out of her large purse. Half-glasses perched on the end of her nose.

"What can I say, Merry?" he began. "Josh left an old

dory at the Town Pier, but he didn't wire it up. You're barking up the wrong tree if you think he's an arsonist."

"I don't," she said. "At least, he doesn't strike me that way. Maybe he's got a psychological fascination for the blue glow of flame, but if so, I can't detect it. He doesn't seem desperate for attention, or in search of a tool over others, or in need of venting deep-seated hostility through destructive behavior. But then, I'm neither a psychiatrist nor a parent."

"Neither am I."

"No. You're just a relative who's given him board and a job for the summer. How come?"

"Alice—my sister—was recently divorced by her husband of nearly thirty years. Josh hasn't taken well to the change in his home life."

"I thought he was pretty much at school."

"He is. Funny, but a lot of marriages fall apart when the last child leaves for college. That's what happened to Alice. Jack looked around, saw the kids were gone and his only responsibility to them was financial, and he decided to seize on a second youth. Ward off death for a while. He changed jobs, changed towns, changed partners. It's not uncommon."

"No. And Josh?"

"His grades started slipping. He switched majors, from business to political science. Started protesting anything and everything. Alice thought he needed some focus—a different place, new interests, hard work for decent pay. I figured it was the least I could do."

"And how's it been?"

"Fine."

"Just fine?"

"I'm a little old to become a parent overnight. I'm not very good at it, Merry. I don't know how to talk to kids—at least, not like a dad. You know. Fatherly. Inspiring. Warm. Reassuring. So I settle for being a geriatric older brother, and I'm not too good at that either. I imagine Josh sees through both."

"Has he made any local friends?"

"I don't really know. Jenny might."

"I just wondered. If he'd taken up with someone who knew he had the boat, and saw an opportunity to frame him, it might give us a lead."

"You really think this was done by a kid?"

She shrugged. "I'm not in charge of this investigation, Tom. The state police have it. I'm just helping out."

"Which means you're not at liberty to tell me anything."

She smiled by way of an answer. "Do you ever use plastic explosive on your construction sites?"

He looked his surprise. "On Nantucket?"

"I understood you had building sites elsewhere."

"On the Cape, yes. There's one or two developments off Route 28."

"And outside Boston."

"Braintree."

"And—in the Berkshires?"

He shifted behind his desk and raised one foot to the opposite knee, cradling the ankle. "I've a site in the planning stages just outside of Lenox."

"There's a lot of rock in the Berkshires."

"There is."

"If it's not inconvenient, Tom, we'd like to have the name of the site manager there."

"What's going on, Merry?"

"I just do what I'm told, Tom."

"That's a damn lousy attitude to take with a friend."

"Sometimes police work is unfriendly."

He looked at her a moment, assessing. He'd always dismissed her status as a cop, considering it a sinecure provided by her father, equivalent to a college kid's life-guarding at Daddy's country club. He realized now that Meredith Folger was in her early thirties; she'd out-grown the college-kid phase when he wasn't looking, and assumed the family mantle of authority. If she was asking for the manager's name, he knew her father wanted it, too; and if he stonewalled, he'd only bring the chief of police to his door. He reached over to his keyboard and pulled up his contacts, although he could have recited the man's name and phone number from memory.

"Here it is," he said, copying it onto a slip of paper and straining across the desk. As he did so, a pile of paperwork slid to the floor at Merry's feet. She bent to collect it.

"Looks like a lot of work," she said.

"All speculative at the moment." He thrust the pile back on his desk. "It's been delightful, Detective, but my day starts early for a reason. Forgive me, but I'll have to cut this short."

"No problem, Tom," she said, smoothing her hands down the length of her skirt. "Just one more question. Did Del want her old job back?"

He stopped short and stared at her. "Del?" he said,

"Del. Duarte. She had lunch with you a few days before her death. I just wondered why."

"We were old friends," he said.

"I know. That's something we have in common. You're

handling her murder very well, by the way. I thought you might bring it up. If you're respecting my grief, I appreciate it, Tom."

Was she mocking him? The green eyes were as cool and careful as ever; he couldn't tell. He felt the skin on his forehead moisten slightly, and a wave of anger washed over him.

"I handle *everything* well, Detective Folger," he spat out. "I lose an expensive boat to fire, and I shrug it off and talk about insurance. My nephew's facing a criminal indictment, and I tell my sister with a straight face that he's adjusting to life quite well. A young woman I regarded almost as a daughter dies a brutal death, and I'm back at work the next day. Handling things is how I get through *life*, Detective. How do you do it? By turning the knife in the wounds of everybody you meet?"

"It was just a thank-you, Tom," she said quietly, and picked up her purse. "I take it Del didn't come looking for a job?"

He shook his head. "She didn't need anything from me, Meredith. She'd decided to make her own way."

After she left, he picked up the phone and dialed Jerry Swain at home. Swain was independently wealthy and spent the summer sailing; he never left the breakfast table before nine o'clock. It was time to tell him that Tom Baldwin was his man. He'd waited a day, to make it convincing; but he wasn't kidding anybody. The finance director post was everything he'd ever wanted. Strange, to be worth ten million dollars, and still feel that way.

MERRY DROVE THE familiar roads without seeing them, thinking about Tom Baldwin. Her job had been to study his reaction to questioning, and he'd given her plenty of material. The notion of Josh and arson did not ruffle his calm; the request for the name of his Lenox site manager irritated him; but the mention of Del positively blew a fuse. What had happened at that lunch to make Tom Baldwin so defensive? Had Del in fact *asked* for a job, and had he refused her—and felt guilty in retrospect?

And what in the hell is Windy Harbor? Merry thought. The name had leaped out at her from Tom Baldwin's blueprints, scattered at her feet. A development of some kind, but she wasn't able to study it long enough. The name didn't ring a bell. The day before, she'd obtained a listing of Baldwin Builders' fifteen current projects from Tom's helpful secretary. She'd swear Windy Harbor was not among them. *Speculative*, he'd called it; and he'd been anxious to tuck it out of sight. Not before she noticed an unfamiliar name—Oceanside Resorts—and a Delaware incorporation, written in small block letters on the lower left-hand corner of the top sheet. Had Tom come by a competitor's plans? Or was he forming a partnership with another developer? Big business was very hush-hush.

And with everything else on her plate, Merry thought irritably as she parked the Explorer on Chestnut, why did she care?

Chapter 20

MATT BAILEY WAS leaning against the evidence locker when Merry walked in. He had a mug of coffee in his hand and a bleary expression around the eyes, both habitual at eight in the morning. He rarely looked fully awake before noon, nor did he make much effort to work until after lunch. He claimed that he accomplished more in a few hours of focused attention than the rest of them did with halfhearted efforts throughout the day, and no one was interested or outraged enough to challenge him. It was simply one more way Bailey tried to spin his performance.

"Mer! Hey, everybody!" he yelled in the general direction of the dispatch room. "I want it known that I was actually in the office today before Detective Meredith Folger. Sleeping on the job, Mer? Not enough to do?"

"I had a breakfast meeting," Merry muttered, wishing for the strength to ignore him. She tried instead to sweep by, head high. He grabbed her arm.

"Got the case just about wrapped up," he said, in a confidential tone.

"Oh yeah?" Poor Clarence must have been working overtime. Jackie Alcantrara had limped into port Saturday morning with a thunderous look on his face, the

Swede in smiling good health, half a hold's worth of bottom fish, and a busted oil pressure gauge. His engine had died, off and on, for the better part of twenty-four hours, and he was ready to walk away from the *Lisboa Girl* without a backward glance. Bailey had chosen that moment to request his fingerprints, and Jackie had actually swung at him. Without the Swede to restrain him, he might have started a fistfight in the middle of the boat basin. Bailey was presently nursing a grudge.

He had followed Jackie home in order to hear both crewmen protest their innocence and affirm each other's whereabouts on the night in question. Then he surveyed Jackie's closets and found candidates for beige linen and silk fibers among his wife's clothes. The trash was next, where he'd come up with plenty of magazines to store in his police-issue SUV, without explaining to Connie Alcantrara why her outdated *Peoples* and *Cosmopolitans* interested him. Then he'd rousted Clarence from his Saturday peace and told him to get to work.

The crime scene chief had replied mildly that most things could wait until Monday, *except* his weekend, and had shut the door in Bailey's face. He'd been closeted in his tiny lab most of yesterday, however, and despite her antipathy for Bailey, Merry admitted she was interested to know what Clarence had found.

"You want to talk about it?" she said.

"Sure. Never too busy to offer a few pointers to a colleague."

"Drop by my office when you've got a chance."

"So the way I figure it, Jackie goes to sea in search of an alibi and has Connie do the number on Del," Bailey was saying. "She's wearing her beige silk blouse and her beige linen pants, and some of her blond hair gets left behind on the floor. We haven't found a piece of copper jewelry yet, but if it broke in the struggle, she may have gotten rid of it." He sat back in his chair and raised his heels to Merry's desk, the picture of complacency.

"Her hair is dyed."

"What?"

"I misspoke. Forgive me. Her hair is bleached, and *then* dyed."

"So?"

"Oh, for crying out loud, Bailey, don't you remember any of your training? Bleached hair has dark roots. The blond hairs at the scene didn't. Which means they were from a *naturally* blond person. Like the Swede. I suggest you take a sample from *his* head." Merry pulled her half-glasses from her nose and stared at him balefully. "Or wait until Howie gets back from the Cape and ask him if one of Jackie's old shipmates happens to be blond. Connie didn't do it. The mere notion of her shoving a harpoon in Del's chest is laughable. Del would have had her disarmed and decked in thirty seconds."

"I wouldn't be so certain, Detective," Bailey said stubbornly, staring over her head. Lines of pique settled around his nose and mouth, and with a resolute gesture, he stood and turned for the door. "You can't know what Del or Connie would have done, and it's unprofessional to suggest your *feelings* should carry any weight. I'd hoped the daughter of the police chief would look at the evidence instead of following her gut instinct. But women are usually emotional first, and rational when it's too late."

"Has Clarence had a chance to look at the prints, Bailey?"

He stiffened. "I've asked him to send them to the state crime lab for expert matching."

Meaning that Clarence was no expert in Bailey's mind. Jackie's prints must not have looked like those on the threatening letters or the scotch bottle. Interesting. Jackie had all but ruled himself out of suspicion. At the very least, he'd bought himself some time. Even in the case of murder, Bailey wouldn't get the results back from Boston in under a week.

Sometimes an alibi is just an alibi, she thought. *But if not Jackie, then who? It has to be one of Howie's guys. He's been gone all weekend. Maybe he'll show up today.*

Bailey let himself out.

FUNNY THING ABOUT plastic explosives. They were useful in the detonation world because the plastic medium stabilized a highly volatile substance—nitroglycerin— into something that could be cut, torn, molded like putty, and dropped on its head without destroying its handler. No need to worry about transporting *this* stuff like a newborn baby. Those sweat-tingling moments immortalized in a thousand movies, when the nitroglycerin tube falls through the air under the close-up lens, only to be caught at the last second by an agonized hand—those moments had gone the way of John Wayne's rattlesnake smile.

Merry had pored over the technical manual Jim Hayes left for her education. The arson expert had taken a liking to her—perhaps because she was so openly humble on the topic of his expertise, so frank in admitting she knew nothing about explosives beyond Hollywood's special effects.

Though it burned with destructive force once trig-gered, plastic explosive left behind a residue that the clever could read as readily as a signature. The bait box recovered from the shallows of South Beach, for example, which had held this particular bit of explosive, told Jim Hayes not only the name of its manufacturer, but the number of its batch. Plastech Explosives Incorporated—the manufacturer in question—was only too happy to avoid liability for arson and sent its shipping records to Bill Carmichael at the Massachusetts State Police. Merry now had a complete list of those professionals—road engineers, construction companies, Navy SEAL units, and the like—who had received explosive from the batch. Baldwin Builders was not among them. Nor was the name Joshua Field. She had even searched the list for Boston University, thinking perhaps a chem-istry lab had obtained the explosive and Field had pocketed it before leaving for the summer. But here, too, she struck a dead end.

It was just possible, she reasoned, that Baldwin's Lenox site manager ordered plastique under his own name. And so she was poring over the list—which was organized not by alphabet but by shipping date—for a Barry Hei-necker. Or Hemecker—it was tough to tell from Tom's handwriting. There were three hundred entities listed over ten pages. She went through them several times, ticking off the names with a pencil point. No Heinecker. No Hemecker. Nothing to connect Lenox to Nantucket. And that left her—or Bill Carmichael—with a case-by-case investigation of each recipient of explosive, hoping against hope that somebody'd had some plastique stolen, or failed to receive the expected shipment, or could point to an employee with a lifelong grudge against Nantucket Island. Prospects, at the very least, looked tedious.

She picked up the phone and dialed Lenox. Nothing but an answering machine in a closed office. Merry tugged on her hair and studied the list of names for a moment; it swam beneath her eyes. Interesting as Jim Hayes had managed to make bomb investigation, her heart wasn't in this one. After a moment, she thrust the list under a pile of reports and opened her laptop. Time to start looking for Sara's father.

"DID YOU EVER get to the fruit salsa? With the cranberry dressing?"

There was no answer from the inert form in the queen-sized bed. Peter Mason shifted uncomfortably in his chair and glanced out the window, preferring the bustle of tourist life to Tess Starbuck's silence. Then he cursed himself for a coward and got up.

Her face, when he sat down on the edge of the mattress, was turned away from him. He knew she was awake by the line of eyelash visible against the pillow; the lids were at half-mast. But for all her connection to the conscious world, she might as well be in dreamland. He reached a finger to brush back her hair. Its auburn brightness was dimmed and slack. She flinched and moved away from him.

"What do you want us to do, Tess?" he said softly.

No answer.

"Leave you alone, right?"

Her breathing quickened for an instant, then fell back into shallowness. Peter felt a wave of impatience grip him, and thrust it away with effort. He wanted to pull Tess out of bed, show her Will sitting despondent in the empty kitchen below, show her the blank tables in the restaurant, the produce rotting in the refrigerators. Instead he sighed, and looked away. And the doorbell rang.

Will's light feet, running to answer it with the haste of every sixteen-year-old. A murmur of voices, indistinguishable. And then Merry Folger, standing in the bedroom doorway in a slim khaki skirt that made her seem taller and thinner than she was, a blouse the color of melon, her hair like corn silk.

Merry nodded in his direction, her face carefully composed, and looked at the woman in the bed.

"Tess," she said. "I know you're not feeling well, but I need to talk to you. It's important."

Tess's eyes fluttered, but she made no sound. Merry pulled up a chair, set her purse on the floor, and leaned toward Tess's face. "I've got to talk about Del." She looked at Peter. "Has she been given medicine recently or something?" she whispered.

He shrugged his ignorance. "I've been here for fifteen minutes, and she hasn't spoken yet."

Merry nodded and looked back at Tess. "I hear you had an interesting reaction to Del's death," she said carefully. "Under the circumstances, I can pretty well understand it. I can even see how you'd be happy she was dead."

Merry might have been talking to a mannequin, for all the response she drew.

"I'm partly responsible for that, I suppose. That's one reason I'm here. I suggested Rafe help Del out, as a friend. But you saw it differently, didn't you? You think Del lured the man you love back into a world you don't trust, and he seemed to like it there. And he was in no hurry to reassure you about what that meant. Your distance and your silence didn't do a thing to keep him off the water, and in fact, they seemed to drive him further away and closer to Del. That must have been pretty threatening, Tess."

Merry paused—assessing how far she should go, Peter thought.

"I mean, Del was a good ten years younger, and Portuguese to boot. It must have played on your worst fears. And instead of abandoning the whole business in order to save his relationship, Rafe decided to be macho and force you to accept his point of view. So you decided to work on Del, isn't that right?"

Tess shifted under the covers and looked full at Merry. Her eyes were devoid of expression, but her gaze was steady.

"She got the first threatening letter two days after you first fought with Rafe. What did you do—walk out of the Brotherhood and fume all the way home? Think of all the things you'd say to Del Duarte if you just got the chance? Only a cat fight would be demeaning, wouldn't it, and hardly the sort of behavior for a middle-aged woman. Better to look cool and unconcerned. Beat Rafe at his own game. But Rafe didn't call to apologize that night, and when he stopped by Saturday you warned him off the premises with a kitchen knife."

Tess's head turned away.

"You probably tossed and turned until midnight, thinking about the ring you'd thrown at his back, feeling remorse, feeling scared, feeling anger. I bet you got up at two in the morning and started leafing through magazines. Crazy ideas always seem logical to the sleep-deprived, don't they?"

The still form on the pillow moved; it might have been a nod.

"'Get out of town and take your brat with you,'" Merry said. "I started thinking about the tone of those notes after Rafe told me how worried he was. I'd assumed they were sent by whoever killed Del. But they sounded like the words of an angry woman—a woman who resented Del's sexuality and youth and freedom, a woman who wanted her to disappear. Even the last one—'The life you save may be your own'—had the predictability of a cliché.

"They were like the threats a cheerleader would leave in a rival's locker. What were you going to do when the notes failed, Tess? Egg and toilet-paper the front of her house?"

Wincing at Merry's harshness, Peter looked at the woman in the bed. He'd instinctively been gentle with Tess, fearing her fragile spirits, avoiding the outbreak of emotion he sensed was building.

"She had no right," Tess whispered. It was a dry and guttural sound. In the dimness of the shuttered room, Peter could not be sure that she was weeping, but he thought it likely from the break in her voice. He looked at Merry in alarm, but the detective was unmoved.

"No right to take Rafe away from you."

"No right."

"And that made you hate her."

"I wanted to hurt her."

"Call her a slut, talk about her past, make her feel shame and anger and a desire to leave."

Tess nodded.

"She didn't take Rafe away from you," Merry said. "Rafe loves you. He always will."

Something between a grunt and a snort emanated from the bed—a laugh, Peter realized. "Not after what I've done."

"Rafe won't love you?"

"Can't."

"He liked to fish with Del. But that's over now, isn't it? Because Del's dead."

Tess was weeping in earnest, now.

"Did you go to see her the night she died, Tess?"

"Never saw her. Never—"

"You never faced her in person, did you? Just through the patchwork notes, like a coward, unsigned and left at her door. Do you feel like a coward, Tess?"

A shuddering sob. Tess turned her face to the pillow.

"Did you kill Del?" Merry's voice was very quiet, the words might almost have been unsaid.

A pause, filled with shaky breath. "I wanted her dead," Tess said suddenly, clearly, raising her head from the pillow. "I wanted her dead. I'm glad she's dead. I'm not sorry."

"I don't think that's true," Merry said. "I think you're so sorry she's dead that you can't get out of bed in the morning. Or the afternoon. I think you need Dr. John to help you live with how sorry you are, until you've had enough Valium to believe you're not sorry at all. But wanting her dead isn't the same thing as killing her, Tess. Even though you think it is."

She reached for Tess's hand and pressed it, hard. "Stop feeling guilty about what you can't help. Guilt won't bring Del back. Guilt will only poison your life and accomplish your worst fear—it'll drive Rafe away permanently. Admit that you got what you wanted, talk over your feelings with Rafe, and go on. That's the only way to live with what's worst in yourself."

"Won't want to," Tess whispered, slumping back into inertia again.

"Rafe? Rafe won't want to talk? You're the most important thing in his life, Tess. He told me so himself."

Merry stood up and looked at Peter. He nodded once, and bent to kiss Tess on the cheek. She closed her eyes, the tears visible even to him, now, and turned away.

"One last question," Merry said. "Why the fancy signature, 'The Avenging Angel,' in italic script?"

"I wanted her to know," Tess said. "The sort of person she was dealing with."

"I see," Merry said.

Vanity, all is vanity, Peter thought. They left Tess where she lay.

Chapter 21

"DO YOU THINK that was the right thing to do?" Peter said, as he followed Merry down the stairs.

"I don't know," she said frankly. "I haven't the faintest. I figured I'd just see how she reacted to my version of events. Maybe she'll wake up and fix dinner for Will tonight. Or maybe she'll cut her wrists in the bathtub, and *I'll* be the one devastated by guilt in the morning."

"But you don't think so."

She looked over her shoulder. "No. It might be worth sending Rafe over tomorrow morning, though. Just to see how she's faring."

"I'd no idea Del was getting threatening letters."

"There were three altogether. None of them sounded like it was written by a man, and since the chief suspects in Del's murder are male, that left me looking elsewhere. One other woman was a possibility, but I couldn't quite see the motive. Then, when Rafe talked to me, I just knew."

"I thought cops avoided gut instinct."

"Do me a favor, okay? Don't tell anybody down at the station that I guessed about this. Particularly a guy named Bailey."

"Who's he?"

"The jerk trying to solve Del's murder."

"Ah." Peter followed her to the door of the Explorer and watched as she got in, her narrow skirt making it a tricky business with the Ford's high running board. This was the everyday beauty of life, he thought; the appreciation for a strong thigh outlined in strained khaki.

"Had lunch?" he asked suddenly.

She shook her head, staring at the wheel.

"Thinking about it?"

"Peter—"

"I know. You don't want to see me right now. Too busy, too distracted by death. Too scared to eat with me."

"Scared?" Her chin went up.

"That's what I said."

"I'm not scared. I'm just not hungry."

"Right. Since when have you ever turned down a square meal? You've got fear written all over you."

She slammed the car door and rolled down the window. "It'll have to be quick," she said.

"Follow me."

HE LED HER up the Cliff Road past his shuttered ancestral home—inhabited now only in July when his sister, Georgiana, arrived with the children—to the gentle overhang of trees and the hand-painted whale that marked the quahog-shell driveway of Something Natural. The shingled house with the wide porches and the constantly banging screened doors had been an island institution for decades, serving fresh-baked bread and sandwiches to bathers returning on their bikes from Madaket or walking up the twisting roads from Jetties Beach.

Peter had miscalculated, thinking that one o'clock in

the afternoon was past the daily rush. There was a crowd lounging in polo shirts and bathing suits on the porch by the pickup door, waiting for completed orders. Sunburned girls, their hair matted with seawater, perched on the railings near too-tall boys, leather thongs braided around their wrists and baseball caps worn bill-to-the-back. He was recalled sharply to his own college summers, the immortality of every moment, the sense of expansive future, the pleasure of a good sandwich when hunger was sharpened by sea air. At least the last remained to him.

"It's not going to be quick," he said, when Merry appeared from the parking lot.

"Of course's it's not," she replied. "And don't tell me you didn't know that."

"Want to go somewhere else?"

"I want a cheese, avocado, and chutney sandwich on seven-grain," she said. "Make that half." A whole sandwich on Something Natural's bread was impossible to finish.

Peter ordered half a lobster salad for himself and two bottles of Nantucket Naturals lemonade, then walked back to the picnic table where Merry was sitting. She was surveying the sky doubtfully.

"Gonna rain," she said.

"Nah." He set down some napkins and put the lemonade on top as an anchor. "It can't. There are no tables inside."

"Peter—why this? Why now?"

"Because I have to eat every four hours. I get lightheaded if I don't."

"That's not what I mean."

He looked at her, saw the panic in her eyes, and knew it for what it was. "Why *you?* is what you're asking."

She waited.

"I should have ordered chips or something to tide us over. They said it could be twenty minutes."

"Now who's scared?"

Peter stopped and took a deep breath. She was right.

"I've never been less scared in my life," he said. "*That's* why this, why now. Because I'm ready." He swung a leg over the bench and leaned toward her across the plank table, wanting to feel her cheekbones under his fingers. "You know the names of all my ghosts, Meredith. But they have no power over me anymore; I've given myself up entirely to the living. To you."

That silenced her; she looked away, unable to hold his gaze, and fumbled for the lemonade jar on the table beside her.

"It's taken me a while," he said. "I know that. My timing could have been better. But most things have their season of growth. All winter, while the rain and snow fell and the ice formed over the cranberry vines, and gray day followed gray day, I'd sit by the fire and consider taking a walk. And it would occur to me that I wanted to walk with you. I wanted you in an over-sized sweater and a pair of boots tramping through the moors in the mist. I wanted you sitting by the fire after-ward with your hair burning in the reflected light of the flames; I wanted you rolling my glass of sherry between your hands; I wanted your laughter and words to fill my silence."

Peter's voice grew quieter. "I wanted you warm beneath the down of my bed in the dark. I just didn't know how to begin." He closed his hand over her wrist and felt her pulse, racing like a bird's. "I'm not going to tell you I love you, Merry," he said quietly, "only because I can't bear to watch you run."

Merry took a deep, shuddering breath and stood up, loosening his hold. "I can't do this, Peter," she said. "I can't give it the attention it needs. Never mind that I can't even *begin* to understand what you see in me." She turned her back to him, her arms crossed protectively over her chest. "I don't have the mental energy to explore any of it. No—that's not it. The whole question *saps* me of mental energy. It consumes my thoughts. And I need all my ability to find Del's murderer. Nothing can be allowed to stand in the way of that."

"Fair enough," Peter said. "I'm not so selfish as to demand your attention when it's justifiably elsewhere."

She looked at him quickly, suspicious of such ready retreat.

"As long as you're honest with me."

"Haven't I been?"

"I hope so."

"What do you mean?"

"I wouldn't want you to use Del's death as an excuse, Merry. Nothing would be easier. Telling yourself you're focusing on what's meaningful, when in fact you're avoiding it."

"Nothing is more meaningful than Del's death," Merry said tensely.

"Work can be an admirable way—a face-saving way—to ignore the truth."

"What makes you so goddamn certain I give a shit about you anyway?" She was angry now, the black brows knitted contemptuously, her back up like a cat's.

"I'm an egotistical bastard."

"You are, you know. And you have no idea what I think or feel."

"Oh, yes, I do."

"You *can't*."

"Why not?"

"Because it's all I have left."

He saw it then, like a flash of light—how Merry fought him, fought herself, to keep hold of her stability; how the arms buckled under her breasts were a metaphor for her entire emotional state. She'd girded herself with an iron resolve *not to feel;* because if she once allowed feeling in, it might consume her.

"Merry," he said.

She saw in his face all that she had told him, and sat down on the bench. She put her head in her hands. "I can't, Peter," she said. "I can't face it."

"I won't hurt you."

"You can't *help* but hurt me. That's all people do to one another."

"Not all," he said. He reached a hand to the nape of her neck, feeling the warmth of it, the coolness of her blonde hair grazing his skin. Her mouth was like a partly opened shell, awash with seawater and mystery, giving up nothing; it drove him deeper and deeper, drowning.

Merry broke away. The first drops of rain fell on his cheek, and he let them, stunned.

"Aren't our sandwiches ready yet?" she said.

IT WAS MID-AFTERNOON by the time Howie Seitz arrived back on the island. He'd spent the past three days traveling from Gloucester to Mattapoisett to Province-town, and had managed to catch the one-fifteen ferry out of Hyannis by the skin of his teeth, weaving his way among the line of packed cars waiting patiently to board in the rain that had already doused the Cape for much of the morning. He found a seat on the lower deck by the port rail, the side for disembarking, and settled his large frame with a copy of the *Globe*. Once they were an hour out on the Sound he'd think about lunch; but the crowd at the upper-deck snack bar was always heaviest at departure. Something about taking to sea—even for two hours and fifteen minutes—drove people to eat; the lesson of Robinson Crusoe, perhaps. If by some inexplicable mischance they were all wrecked and cast away, at least the bulk of them would be well fortified with chili.

Howie mulled over the past few days with a flutter of uneasiness. He was uncomfortable with Bailey running this investigation—the detective would never know if he had missed something vital. The guy cut corners, neglected evidence, ran with his first idea and fit the pieces to the size of his personal puzzle. That made Howie feel too responsible, like a tightrope walker without a net. It was Merry Folger he hated to fail. She would listen to his recital, read his notes, and find the gap he should have noticed. He wished the chief had put her on the murder.

He found her sitting in her office, staring at a crack in the opposite wall, since she had no window to serve as a suitable focus for daydreaming. He rapped a knuckle on the open door and hovered.

"Seitz! Just the man I wanted to see. How was Gloucester?"

"A dead end. The guy had already left. But I found him in Mattapoisett," he said. "The fishing business is pretty unstable, I guess."

"Pull up a chair. You talked to Bailey yet?"

He turned red. "Your office is first along the hallway. "

She refrained from comment. "Why don't you run through it from the beginning."

"Okay." He pulled his notebook from his back pocket, even though he knew the contents by heart, and sat down, shoving a hand through his dark curls. "Let's see. Charley MacIlvenny is the guy in Mattapoisett. Formerly Gloucester, for all of a week. Formerly Nantucket, where he joined Joe Duarte's crew last October. Formerly Hyannis, where he captained a boat that unfortunately sank in that same month of October."

"It *sank?*"

Howie nodded, uncertain of the significance. "Hit an unmarked wreck while racing for port in a storm, and sank pretty quickly, apparently."

"Did MacIlvenny own the boat?"

Howie looked back at his notes. "I don't think so. He talked about the owners, how after the boat sank he couldn't get hired as captain anywhere, so he went to work for Joe."

"Go on."

"I asked about the night of Joe Duarte's death, and his story pretty much tallied with Jackie's. Said he was standing across from the Swede waiting for the net to come up, and that it was winched in too fast and Joe got clobbered on the left side of his head."

"He said nothing about *why* the net was winched in too fast?"

"Just that it was a pretty confusing night. The storm was hitting hard, and Jackie and Joe were yelling at each other, and first the order was to drop nets, and then it was to pull them up, and they weren't sure who to obey."

"Jackie and Joe were yelling about the net?"

Howie nodded. "Jackie wanted it dropped, and Joe wanted it raised. From the way Charley tells it, Joe was so mad he wouldn't have seen Moby Dick coming over the side that night. He was right in Jackie's face, telling him he'd better figure out who was captain, who gave orders on his boat, and so forth, and Jackie was giving it right back. Charley figures the Swede was just distracted."

"So that's why Joe Duarte was messing around the net," Merry said thoughtfully. "Del couldn't figure out why he hadn't left something that routine to his crew. Jackie never mentioned a fight. I wonder what else he's keeping to himself?" Her eyes flicked back to Howie's. "What'd Charley have to say about the night Del died?"

Howie looked uncomfortable. "He was busy," he said.

"Getting to Nantucket and back? Or what?"

"Busy. You know."

"No, Seitz, I don't."

"He was with a—girl. Woman. Whatever."

"Ah. All night?"

Howie nodded and looked away.

"You talked to her?"

"I had to track her down first, and that wasn't easy, believe me. Charley remembered she was called Kiki, and he had a rough idea where she lived, but couldn't tell me the address or her full name. Talk about drunk. Those two must've been—" He paused, and reddened again. Merry wondered how much older than himself he thought she was.

"But you found Kiki?"

"Yeah. I had Charley drive me to what he thought

was her apartment complex, and then I waited around until the manager came back, and found out her name is Christine Benson. Kiki's her stage name."

"I see. An *artiste*."

"She's a sort of—dancer."

Exotic, by the look on Seitz's face. "Gotcha. And according to Miss Benson, Charley was not on Nantucket at the time of Del's death."

"So she says."

"Okay." Merry sat back in her chair. "What about the second guy you interviewed?"

"Rick Berkowski. New Bedford born and bred, currently crewing on the *Jenny Lyn* out of Provincetown. Joined Joe Duarte's crew in January after his boat sank—"

"No way," Merry said, though she'd been half waiting for the words. "Where'd this one go down?"

"Hit an unmarked wreck near the Nantucket Shoals. Pretty far from port."

"About forty miles."

"There was a New Bedford trawler near enough to pull off the crew."

"Lucky for Rick. Men die in a matter of seconds in January water."

"They couldn't save the boat, though. Sank in ninety fathoms."

"How convenient for the owners—since I very much doubt Rick was skippering his own boat. When it came time to file for insurance, the wreck was probably hard to locate. Sending divers ninety fathoms down in the middle of the winter is no picnic, either. Wonder how long it took the insurance company to pay out?"

"You think the sinking was deliberate?"

"I think it's just too much of a coincidence that three of Joe Duarte's crew were former captains who'd sunk boats in the past year. It's not that common. Scuttling vessels for their insurance is, however."

"Wow," Howie said. "You think Joe put those pieces together?"

"If he didn't, it's because he chose not to," she said. "A man who's been on the water as long as Joe was knows to mistrust coincidence." She leaned across the desk. "I've got a job for you, Seitz. Find out who owned those two boats—you should be able to get the information from Terry Samson at the Coast Guard. And note down who insured them. Something stinks about the whole story."

Howie stood up, his face alight. Merry was pleased. He'd done good.

"Where was Rick the night of Joe's death?" she said.

"Down below. It was his turn to sleep."

"And last Wednesday?"

"He doesn't remember."

"What?"

"That's what he says. Can't remember what he did last Wednesday. Thinks he might have been watching TV."

"Alone?"

"He's not married."

Merry sat very still. "What color's his hair, Seitz?"

"Dirty blond," he said.

"Thanks. Be sure and tell Bailey that, would you?"

"Of course, Detective. Anything else?"

"Don't tell him about the insurance stuff yet, okay?"

RALPH WALDO WAS in the backyard culling lettuces from his vegetable garden when Merry got home.

It occurred to her that he'd been practically housebound since Sara Duarte had come to stay. Not that he couldn't have taken Sara with him on most errands—he could, and did. But he had abandoned many of his normal pursuits, his quiet routines, his visits to old cronies or to check library books out of the Atheneum.

"Hi, Grumpus," she said to the white head bent over the soil. "I decided to come home early."

"Glad to hear it," he said, rising with a grunt. "I could use the help."

"Sara giving you trouble?"

"Apparently the honeymoon is over," Ralph Waldo said. "She's been fussy all day. Started crying after breakfast, and its been like King Lear ever since—howl, howl, howl, howl, howl. The worst of it is, I can't help her, my dear." He tossed some Bibb lettuce in a basket and turned toward the back door. "All she says, over and over, is *I want my mommie. Mommie.* And to that, Meredith Abiah, there is no answer in the world I can give."

"No," Merry said. "I'm so sorry, Ralph. We've left you here to hold everything together, Dad and I, while we ran around looking official. It isn't fair. Should we get a babysitter tomorrow?"

"Oh, it's all right," he said. "I'm fond of the little thing. One more stranger right now is the last thing she needs. It'll pass, with time. If she could get more sleep she'd be less unhappy. But she had nightmares again last night."

"I slept through them," Merry said, feeling guilty. "Did you get up?"

"Twice. Both times she'd fallen back to sleep."

"I wonder what she sees."

"I don't think she has the vocabulary to tell us yet. I only hope it passes before too much longer."

"Ralph," Merry said, following him to the kitchen, "I called the state Registry of Vital Records this morning."

He set the lettuce down on the counter near the sink and turned on the water. "About Sara?"

"Yes."

Ralph Waldo turned the leaves under the water. Tiny black grit flowed out, a dead bug or two. He shook the heads lightly and searched in a cupboard for the salad spinner. "You sure that's a good idea?"

"I didn't get far enough to do any damage," she said. "I was told that when the parents of a child aren't married, access to the birth certificate is restricted."

"They wouldn't send you a copy."

"No. I'd have to get a court order to see Sara's records. From a Boston court."

"Even though you're a police officer, and this is a murder investigation?"

"Even though."

He dropped the lettuce in the salad spinner. It was an old-fashioned one, with a pull cord that turned the inner basket instead of a handle. "Sara loves to pull this, you know," he said. "She laughs and laughs."

"We can't keep her, Ralph."

"There was never any question of that."

"But she's going to be tugged in several different directions, whether she's aware of it or not. Jackie Alcantrara's going to try for her, according to Felix Harper, and with the provision in Joe's will, he's got a fighting chance. The Duartes won't let her go that easily. And then there's Dave Grizutto."

"Who's he?"

"Bartender at the Brotherhood. He thinks he's Sara's father."

"Is he?"

"I doubt it."

"And you think finding the real father would help," Ralph Waldo said slowly.

"It might save a two-year-old a lot of mess. You know what'll happen. She's living here on borrowed time. She'll be declared a ward of the state, and put in foster care while the hearings and the trial dates are set, and Dave Grizutto's DNA is tested for paternity purposes. Then she'll be taken from her foster parents and awarded to *somebody*—the Alcantraras, quite possibly. Connie Alcantrara doesn't have a motherly bone in her body, but she sure knows how to spend money. It'll be a nightmare."

"Even if you find Sara's father, she could still face a trial," Ralph Waldo said. "He might not want her. Or his custody could be contested. He hasn't exactly been active in Sara's life."

"True. I still think it's worth a chance."

"Do you?" Ralph Waldo's voice tightened with anger. When he turned to face her, she saw how offended he was. "Is it Sara you're thinking of, Meredith Abiah, or are you just itching to know?"

"Hardly *that*." She studied him an instant. "I'm surprised you're so opposed."

"Those records are restricted for a reason," Ralph Waldo said. "Del didn't tell anybody when she was alive, and I'm not sure she'd want it known once she was dead."

"She certainly wouldn't want Sara turned over to Jackie Alcantrara," Merry said.

"Then she should have named a guardian."

"But she didn't." He was being very stubborn; but Merry knew what was right. "I'm going to request the court order, Ralph."

"Fine," he said, his bearded chin jutting out. "Just don't blame me once Pandora's box is open."

But it was Jenny Baldwin who really took the lid off, the following morning—though it was not the box Ralph had in mind.

Chapter 22

IT WAS MERRY who ran into Jenny Baldwin at the Downyflake.

Coffee and fresh baked goods seemed particularly necessary this Wednesday morning—Del's autopsy report had come in late the previous afternoon. Overcome by longing for a raspberry bramble, Merry rose an hour early and drove out to the Rotary.

She took a long draft of coffee, gazing through the window at the fire station across the street. It was a gray morning, with yesterday's threat of rain realized. Along the South Shore beaches, fog had rolled in off the Atlantic; by nightfall it would blanket the town, racing like a hasty ghost under the occasional streetlight. The perfect night to stop by Del's, for a warm dinner and some good conversation; the sort of visit Merry had intended to make, and put off because of the Town Pier fire.

The state crime lab's report said that Del had suffered a punctured lung, a broken rib, and a ruptured chamber of the heart. Her death had taken perhaps a moment from harpoon thrust to completion. Analysis of her stomach contents showed primarily half-digested pizza and some alcohol—but it was determined to be red wine, not scotch, despite the two carefully washed highball glasses on her kitchen counter. Del had probably put her wine-glass away herself. She rarely left dishes out to dry.

Pizza and red wine, Merry thought. *The mundanity of final moments never recognized as final.* Del had cleaned all day, felt exhausted, ordered pizza for Sara and herself, and washed it down with table wine she probably kept corked on top of the refrigerator. Had she known it was her last meal, what would she have eaten? A beloved dish from childhood? Something fattening? Nothing at all?

Merry sighed and bit into the bramble. It was an airy, smooth pastry in the shape of a hockey puck, filled with raspberries and what she thought was walnuts. She needed a second one to be sure.

"Detective Folger! Now if that isn't a coincidence!"

She looked up and saw Jenny Baldwin's bleached blue eyes staring at her intently. The developer's wife was wearing neat and emotionless separates of the kind seen everywhere among a certain class of people in New England—flowered skirt in pink and blue, deep pink polo shirt with the collar buttoned clear to the neck; tennis shoes, which she would call "tennies," or "Keds"; and a deep blue hairband drawn severely back from her forehead. A lightship basket dangled from one arm, its chocolate patina and modest ivory decoration suggesting respectable age and provenance.

"I was planning to stop by the station and talk to you right after I got these doughnuts home for the boys," Jenny said. "Do you have a moment?"

"Sure. Sit down."

Jenny transferred the purse from her right arm to her left, tucked one hand behind her skirt, and slid into the banquette opposite Merry.

"Want some coffee?"

"Had some. What's that you're eating?"

"A bramble." Merry didn't offer her any. She could get her own. "What can I do for you, Jenny?"

"Well, it's probably nothing, and I really should talk to someone less senior than yourself, I'm sure—"

Flattering me already, Merry thought. *Must be really thankless.*

"—but you're the only person I know down there, and I'd so much rather talk to a woman."

"I understand."

"I just feel so *violated*."

Dear God, don't tell me she was raped. Merry sat up and put the bramble back on its plate. "Did something happen, Jenny?"

"My upper left-hand drawer," she said.

"Your drawer."

"It's been pilfered."

"Really?"

"Well, it must have been. I mean, I always keep a little store of money tucked into my jewelry box, just for emergencies, and when I happened to put some earrings back yesterday afternoon, I noticed the money was gone."

"How much are we talking about, here?"

"A fifty-dollar bill."

"And you last saw it when?"

"Oh, I don't know. Maybe a week ago. I haven't actually used the money for ages. I just keep it there."

"You don't think Tom could have taken it? Intending to replace it, I mean," Merry added quickly, not wanting to offend. "Maybe he was short of cash, and didn't have time to stop at an ATM."

"Well, I thought so too. And so I asked him, last night. He actually laughed at me. 'You think I'm that desperate for money?' he said, and that was the end of it."

"And—your nephew?"

"Joshua didn't know it was there. How could he?"

Merry relaxed against the seat. Every petty thief knew to check the upper left-hand drawer of a woman's bureau for valuables. Over the past ten years on the island, more upper left-hand drawers had been robbed of cash and jewelry than she could count. Tourists wrapped their treasures in bathroom towels and hid them behind the headboards in their hotel rooms. The crooks knew that, too. But if the loss of fifty dollars felt like violation, Jenny had led a charmed life.

"Did you notice whether anything else was missing?"

"Well, that's it. This morning I decided to do a thorough search of the drawer. After all, I keep some jewelry in there. And the bracelet is gone."

"What sort of bracelet?"

"My copper one. It's not very valuable, which makes it so strange. They left my pearls, and an emerald pendant, and some *rather* good pieces of onyx. And they took the worthless copper."

Merry's attention was suddenly riveted. "Could you describe it for me?"

"It was very simple, really. Just copper links with a bar in the middle that had my name on it. Tom gave it to me for back trouble. They say that copper worn around the wrist can cure you of pain."

"Did it?"

"Not at all. It just turned my wrist black. So I stopped wearing it. I'd almost forgotten about it until this morning."

"You know, Jenny, I'm glad you stopped to talk," Merry said, gathering up her purse. "But I think we'll have to go to the station anyway. We found part of a copper bracelet the other day, and I'd like to see whether you think it's yours."

Merry sent Jenny Baldwin home with her doughnuts and instructions to appear at the police station as soon as she could. Then she drove over to Fairgrounds Road and relayed the news to Matt Bailey.

"We'd better print her," he said grimly.

"Oh, come on, Matt," Merry said. "You really think Jenny Baldwin would innocently report the theft of a bracelet she knew she'd worn to kill Del Duarte? *That* makes a lot of sense. About as much as her motive for Del's murder. She has none."

"It makes more sense than a burglar stealing it, and then leaving it by Del's body."

To that, Merry had no answer.

Jenny duly arrived, and was shown the tiny plastic evidence bag Clarence produced, with its pitifully few links of chain.

"Well, I don't know," she said doubtfully. "You didn't find the bar with my name?"

Be glad we didn't, Merry thought, *or Bailey would have drawn your blood days ago.*

"Thaht's all we have, I'm afraid," Clarence said. "Makes it hahd to say, doesn't it?"

"It certainly does. Where did you find it?"

Clarence looked at Merry, and Merry at Matt Bailey. The latter's expression was portentous. "On the living-room floor of Adelia Duarte's house," he said. "Do you have any idea how part of your bracelet was present at the scene of a murder, Mrs. Baldwin?"

"A murder? My bracelet? But I didn't *say* it was my bracelet," she squeaked, in what Merry judged was genuine bewilderment. "I can't know that from these few links. I just came down to talk about a burglary."

"I'm afraid I'm going to have to fingerprint you, Mrs. Baldwin," Bailey said.

Merry groaned.

"And I'd like permission to take a few samples of your clothing from your closet."

"You can't do this," the woman gasped. Her fingers clenched and unclenched convulsively on the handle of her lightship basket.

"Jenny," Merry said, "is there any chance you wore the bracelet to Joe Duarte's funeral reception? Perhaps you lost it then."

"Maybe I did," Jenny said, grasping at straws. "I'm sure I did."

"Could you come with me, Mrs. Baldwin?"

"You can't take my prints unless you arrest me," she said. "I want to speak to a lawyer. Merry—"

"You're right," Merry said. "He can't. But there's no reason to be afraid of prints, Jenny. You've got nothing to hide, right? So the prints don't mean anything. It might be better to do as he says."

The woman's eyes were wide and frightened, and ten years seemed to have dropped into the lines of her face. Little as she liked Jenny Baldwin, Merry felt moved by pity. If the woman objected and got a lawyer, Bailey would simply write up a request for a search warrant an hour later, and be at her house by the following day. It would be a simple matter then to find prints everywhere.

Jenny took a deep breath. "Of course I've nothing to

hide," she said, avoiding Merry's eyes. "I'll do as you say. But believe me, Tom will have quite a conversation with your father. This is the first time we've asked you people for anything. A *simple burglary*. I understand now what Josh meant about police persecution."

"It doesn't help to threaten the police, Mrs. Baldwin," Matt Bailey said stonily. "Come with me, please."

Clarence watched her go thoughtfully. "She cahn't have lost the bracelet at Joe Duarte's reception, Marradith, though it was nice o' you to suggest it. Thaht house was clean's a whistle. Del had vacuumed. If she hadn't, we'd have found more fibahs and whatnot from that crowd a' people than we'da known what to make of. Those links were dropped ahftah Del cleaned."

"That doesn't make them Jenny Baldwin's," Merry said stubbornly.

Clarence grunted. "Guess I'll be wanted directly." He braced himself against the arms of his chair and thrust himself upright. "Not that young Bailey is so enahmahed of my opinion. He'll be wantin' to send those prints to Bahston next."

But the state crime lab's expertise was unnecessary, as it turned out. Jenny Baldwin's thumb and forefinger clearly matched the prints on the bottle of Glenfiddich. It was merely a matter of time, Bailey said confidently, before they found the right fibers.

Merry wasn't so sure. She looked at the sensible cotton clothes Jenny was wearing, and had always worn. Beige linen and silk? It didn't seem likely.

Bailey went ahead and arrested Jenny, despite Merry's protests. He didn't have enough of a case, she said; there was too much unexplained. But Bailey felt that Jenny

Baldwin was spooked and scared and acting guilty. She had tried to avoid having her prints taken, threatened the police with retribution, and virtually taunted him to arrest her. And if he sent her home now, with *her* money she'd be out of the country in a matter of hours.

Tom Baldwin arrived, breathing fire and demanding to see John Folger. Felix Harper arrived, blinking as though from too much exposure to sunlight, and sat by Jenny while her statement was taken. Bailey took away her lightship basket and locked her in a cell reserved for women, where she huddled like a skittish dog on one corner of the steel bench, staring at the commode and the opposite wall.

"This is ridiculous," Merry said angrily to her father. She was in his office with the door closed, knowing full well she was violating collegial protocol. Bailey was running the investigation; Bailey thought he'd found a murderer. If he was wrong, let him hang himself. Only she couldn't quite leave Jenny Baldwin in the role of gibbet.

"Ask him *why* Jenny Baldwin killed Del. He doesn't know. Neither does Jenny. Because she didn't, Dad."

John Folger looked at her from under his heavy eyebrows—Folger eyebrows, *her* eyebrows—and sighed. He wanted the whole thing to go away. "How'd her prints get in the house?"

"Her story is that she brought the bottle to the funeral reception as a gift," Merry said. "Everybody brought something. She didn't know the Duartes never drank scotch—that sort of thing happens all the time. Look at all the well-meaning bottles of Campari we've got sitting in the pantry at home. The *real* question is why the Glenfiddich was placed out on the counter, with the murderer's prints nowhere in evidence, when the autopsy says Del didn't drink it that night. Bailey doesn't want to think about that. It's too complicated. He'd rather believe Jenny drank enough for two, washed and wiped the glasses, and helpfully left the bottle there with her prints all over it."

"Where was she the night Del died?"

"Lying down in a darkened room with a compress to her head, according to her statement," Merry said. "No witnesses. She was supposed to go to a private party at the yacht club with Tom, and begged off at the last minute because of a migraine, which she says she often gets. Her nephew was out with friends. So she has no alibi. In your experience, isn't that often the case with the innocent? I'd be more suspicious if she produced three complete strangers all willing to swear she'd sat next to them at the Boston Symphony."

"Why are you so sure she didn't do it, Meredith?"

"Because I can think of no reason for her to kill Del." Merry sat back in her chair, arms folded, a challenge in every line of her body. Her father plowed ahead anyway.

"And it wouldn't be because this lets out Jackie—who, I must say, *has* an alibi and left no prints or fibers at the scene?" he said.

"You know what I think of alibis."

"I also know what you think of Jackie."

"I think we're looking at something a little more complex than Jenny Baldwin virtually handing us evidence that incriminates her."

"Meaning?"

"The murderer deliberately left a bottle on the counter that was filled with something Del never drank. Why do that? Unless the murderer knew it had Jenny's prints on it. He left it for the same reason he dropped a part of her bracelet on the rug by Del's body—not enough to look too obvious, not the part of the chain that had her name, for instance, but just enough to look plausible."

"You think she's being framed," her father said slowly.

"Don't you?"

"I don't know, Meredith. Like you, I stumble over motive. Why would Jenny kill Del? I've no idea. But why would someone want us to *think* she did? That's even harder."

Merry ran her fingers through her blonde waves in exasperation. "I don't know, Dad. But I'm sure Bailey won't give either question the consideration it deserves."

"She's being arraigned tomorrow?"

"The sheriff is escorting her by plane to Barnstable. Tom will post whatever bail is necessary. And we'll have two very angry people back on the island, with power and influence to turn the entire Nantucket establishment against the police. You know what this could do to our funding?"

"Don't even talk about it. It's worse than you know."

"What do you mean?" Merry asked.

"Tom Baldwin just informed me he's just been appointed town finance director," her father said. "And I'm under no illusions as to what his wife's arrest means for the police budget. Particularly after that fiasco with his nephew and the fish guts. The arson accusations. We're beginning to look like we have a vendetta against the Baldwins."

John Folger stood up and rubbed balled fists against his aching lower back. "It is not too much to say that my job may even be on the line. What a mess, Meredith. What a mess."

Merry felt cold. For her father to be imperiled by Bailey's stupidity was insupportable.

"You could release Jenny, Dad," she said. "Apologize to Tom. Tell Bailey to build more of a case before he reads people their rights."

"I could," he said slowly, looking off into space, his attention focused somewhere between L3 and L4 of his vertebrae. "In fact, I think I have no choice. As for you, young lady . . ."

"Yes?"

"That business of the scotch bottle. Find out *why.*"

Chapter 23

A MASS OF vegetables were spilled out again on the table, and Tess was sitting in a chair with her back to the door. Rafe was paralyzed by the sight of her, uncertain how to begin. It was too much like the last time he had seen her—only today the vegetables were zucchini, not beets. He must have made a small movement, or expelled a heavy breath, because she turned; and that quickly relief washed over him like a sudden summer storm.

"Hey, girl," he said, and Tess smiled, extending one hand. His ring was shining from her third finger. "You feelin' better?"

She nodded. "Much."

"You look good."

She stood up when he didn't approach the table, and clasped her fingers together awkwardly, as if aware of the flash of the diamond and uncertain of its effect. "It's good to see you."

"And you. Life hasn't been the same."

"No." Tess looked behind her at the squash, and then faced him. "We should talk about all of this."

"Only if you want to."

"I don't. But I need to say some things, and you need to hear them."

Rafe nodded, too thrilled by the peace in her eyes and the color in her skin to care much what penance she felt compelled to perform. But at the thought of penance he remembered his own conviction, seized that morning in the shower and acted upon not long after breakfast.

"I came here to talk myself," he said. "I've got some explaining to do." He took the three steps across the kitchen to her side and put his arms loosely around her. She sighed like a tired child and sank into his chest. Rafe felt a circle of quiet and peace, of rightness he knew only with Tess. "I should have tried harder to understand how I upset you," he said carefully. "The fishing business, I mean. I was trying to settle a score with my father, seems to me, only I was using you to settle it."

"No, Rafe, it was me—"

He laid a finger across her lips, silencing her.

"I didn't have enough courage to face the Old Bastard himself and tell him how much he'd destroyed me when he threw me off his boat. He tried to cut my legs out from under me, Tess, as you know better'n anyone. I forgot that for a while, out on the water; felt like I'd come into my own, on my terms, and the hell with everything else."

"I understand. I—"

"The hell with everything else, including you. So what if you didn't want to see me ruin my place with Pete, or throw myself into a thankless job with lousy pay and worse prospects? So what if I stirred up a lot of bad memories—of Dan and his death and the way he lived his life?"

Tess opened her mouth, and Rafe let his arms drop to his sides. "I was back on the water, doing what I was supposed to do years ago, before the mess in New Bed. That feeling of getting my own back—despite my father and his pride—was pretty powerful. I think I lost you some-where in all that, Tess."

It was a long speech for Rafe da Silva. He felt drained and sat down, staring at a mango-colored zucchini blossom half wilted on the wooden table. He traced a finger along its green veins and waited for her voice.

"I lost faith too quickly," Tess said, sitting down opposite him. Their knees in faded denim were almost, but not quite, touching. "You're not Dan. You don't have his crazy optimism, his stubborn persistence. He couldn't understand when he was beaten, and start fresh." She looked down at her hands. "He kept taking the scalloper out, year after year, and painting houses in the summer, and the bills kept mounting. He always thought he'd catch a break."

"I'm sorry, girl," Rafe said.

"But you're not like that." Tess took his hand and gripped it tightly. "You know life isn't fair. You know what people can do, and how to protect yourself. I should have trusted that."

"There's something else." Rafe covered her fingers with his, smoothing the rough skin. "You should have trusted me to love you. What did Dan do, to make you so sure I'd be gone with the first pretty face?"

A look of wariness came over her. "That wasn't Dan," she said. "That was just me. There's so little place for women over forty in this world. Especially among men. Men want taut thighs and flat stomachs and smooth skin. They want *youth*, Rafe, and that's escaped me."

"You're the youngest person I know," he said, his mouth dry.

"I have brown age spots on my hands. My hair is turning

gray. I have lines that run from the corners of my mouth
to my nose—they used to disappear after a good sleep,
but I don't get much of that anymore. I have a stomach
paunchy from childbirth and saddlebags on the backs of
my thighs. I *saw* Del Duarte. I remember what that was
like—to feel beautiful, strong, worth looking at. Don't
tell me otherwise," Tess said, as he started to protest. "I
don't need flattery. I know what I am. I'm not thirty-one.
Or was it thirty-two? I'm not Portuguese. I can't give you
a darling two-year-old, or a day in the sun at the helm
of a boat. I can't harpoon swordfish. I can't read naviga-
tional charts. That woman was everything I'm not. And
it scared me to death."

"I should have understood that, too," Rafe said.

"Why? I never talked about it. I couldn't. Why point
out every way someone has you beat? The thoughts and
fears just grew in my mind. Until I did what I figured
would make you hate me."

"The letters."

Tess nodded. "Stupid-ass things. Merry Folger was
right. Like a cheerleader egging another girl's locker."

Rafe shifted in his chair; he had no answer for this.

"I've had plenty of time to think about it. I can't
change what I did. But I can accept how I felt and go on.
Merry showed me that, too."

"I guess the Girl Scout was a help," Rafe said.

"She told me you still loved me, when I thought that
was impossible."

He leaned forward and kissed her. "Understand: I don't
want a thirty-year-old, a twenty-year-old, or anything in
between. I want Tess Starbuck. That's something you've
got to *know* as well as believe."

"I'll try," Tess said.

"Want to have dinner tonight?"

She shook her head. "I'd love to, Rafe, but it'll have to wait. I'm completely booked. The high season is kicking in, and I'm back in business."

He surveyed the table. "Need help?"

"Have you ever stuffed a squash blossom?"

He wrinkled his nose. "What for?"

"Deep frying."

"For crying out loud."

Tess threw back her head and laughed, a sound he hadn't heard in weeks. "Tell you what," she said. "Go home. You'll be saving me a trip out to Peter's. I've got that salsa he's been waiting for. Finally."

HOWIE SEITZ WAS at something of a loss. Merry Folger had told him to find the owners of the crew members' sunken boats and track their insurance claims. Matt Bailey had told him to get back to Provincetown, in search of Rick Berkowski's blond hair and fiber samples. But when he'd stopped by Matt's office to say he'd be setting off for the mainland the following day, the detective had snarled at him and nearly given him the back of his hand.

It seemed Matt was stewing about some setback with the chief. He'd had the entire case sewn up, he told Howie, until Merry Folger had stuck her goddamn nose in his business and worked her way around her father. She should be fired, and would be if Daddy weren't protecting her. And if a real chief were ever appointed to take Folger's place, and his daughter was out on her ear, she'd probably scream gender discrimination. These women

were all the same. Why did she think she was on the force
in the first place? Much less a detective with a rank senior
to his own? *Because* of gender discrimination—against
white men. She'd gotten the preferences and the breaks
because she was Daddy's little girl and the force wanted to
show it could hire and retain women. Well, what went up
must come down. She'd get what was coming to her one
of these days, and so would he.

Howie broke into this rambling diatribe as politely as
possible, and asked the obvious question. Were the crew
members of the *Lisboa Girl* no longer under suspicion?

"They never would have been," Bailey said contemptuously, "if Merry Folger hadn't wanted Jackie Alcantrara's
balls in a sling."

Howie refrained from pointing out that Matt himself
had been eager to arrest Jackie only Saturday morning.

He adjusted his sail to the shift in wind direction.
"What would you like me to do?"

Matt rubbed his chin and looked thoughtful. "Find
some dirt on Merry Folger," he said. "That bitch deserves
to be brought down."

Howie escaped as quickly as he could.

He was surveying the Coast Guard's database, thanks
to Terry Samson, who had adopted a knowing air at the
mention of Merry's name as though they shared confidential information. It was easy enough to find the accident
reports. MacIlvenny's dragger was owned by a company
called SeaCon, Berkowski's by MariTrans Shipping, Inc.
Both companies were listed as having offices in New Bedford. The insurer for each was the same: a company called
Water Rights, based in Boston. Howie checked the information about Jackie Alcantrara he'd copied from Merry's

file earlier that morning. Jackie's boat was also owned by SeaCon and insured by Water Rights.

"This is too weird," Howie breathed. "Thanks, Terry. You've been very helpful."

He rode his patrolman's bike back to the station and tried calling the New Bedford numbers for SeaCon and Oceanfree. The numbers were out of service. He searched the internet for newer contact information and turned up nothing. He was stumped.

"Call the insurance company," Merry said, barely looking up as he hovered in her doorway. "If they settled the claim, they'll know where they sent the check."

Howie went back to the phone and called Water Rights' number in Boston. This time he was successful.

"So in all three cases, SeaCon and MariTrans were reimbursed for the replacement value of the boats," Merry said.

"To the tune of four hundred thousand dollars apiece," Howie said. "A total of one point two million."

"After which, they appear to have gone out of business."

"Yep."

"This stinks."

"I thought so too."

"Did the insurance company offer any contacts at either company?"

Howie peered at his notes. "A guy named Jerry Dundee from SeaCon. Nobody at MariTrans. I've got a number in New Bedford for Dundee, but when I dialed it, it was disconnected."

"Wasn't it just," Merry said, bemused. She tapped a pencil against the desk for an instant, in a gesture so like her father's Howie almost gawked; then the green eyes slid back to him. "It's time to talk to Jackie Alcantrara," she said matter-of-factly. "But I'm going to have to ask you to stay here. He might not be as forthcoming with two people taking notes. Not that he's forthcoming anyway. But I've got a hunch he'll talk to me."

"What do you want me to do while you're gone?"

"Doesn't Bailey have anything for you?"

"Not really."

"Well here," Merry said, sliding out from behind her desk.

"You can learn how to fill in these forms sooner rather than later."

"What are they?"

"A request for a court order. In the case of a murder investigation, when the police are the requesters, the probate court should waive a hearing and issue a summary judgment. That'll save us a trip to Boston. But I need these filed as soon as possible."

"You want to see the baby's birth certificate?" he said, wide-eyed. "Why? You think the baby's *father* killed Del? To keep it quiet, I mean?"

Merry stopped stock-still, her face frozen. "Thank you, Seitz. I'd never thought of it that way."

Chapter 24

BECAUSE DEL DUARTE had adamantly refused for years to name Sara's father, Merry had assumed he was no longer in Del's life. So few of her old Nantucket friends were. Look at Dave Grizzuto, whom Del treated like a stranger. Merry had imagined Dave tearing out of the Milk Street house, clutching a birth certificate that denied his claim to the baby, having struck Del down in a jealous rage. Would another man have killed Del because he *was* responsible for Sara's existence? And what if Del had been blackmailing him?

Merry found it hard to imagine her friend in that role; but there was that hundred thousand dollars no one could explain, sitting in an account at the Pacific National Bank. Maybe the man was tired of paying through the nose for a secret he wanted kept. Maybe he'd shown up at Del's door Wednesday night to talk reason, and when tempers flared, had stabbed her with a convenient harpoon. Merry knew she needed to identify Sara's father more than ever.

She found Jackie Alcantrara the first place she looked—at his new berth in the boat basin, mending net under the eyes of gawking tourists. No wonder, Merry thought; the *Lisboa Girl* looked like a vagrant among the sleek and pricey vessels lined up along the Old South Wharf, the sort of rusty fellow picking among dustbins that tourists self-consciously avoid, sensing the arrival of an unpleasant odor on the next shift of wind. Whether Jackie was aware of his effect was uncertain; he appeared oblivious to everything but his nets.

"How long do you think you'll hold out?" Merry said.

Jackie looked up, located the source of the voice, and studied her dispassionately. "How long will you?"

"That's different."

"No, it's not. The costs are just as high for both of us. You could do better on the mainland, maybe even get your own place. You're what—in your thirties? And still living at Dad's."

He stated it as a simple fact, and she had to admit he was right. She had spent close to six years on the Nantucket force, which made her a veteran. The island was considered a first tour for young officers. Real estate prices and the cost of imported goods made it impossible to buy a house or raise a family on a policeman's salary. Merry was different because of her father and grandfather, the house on Tattle Court. But how long, as Jackie said, could she stick it out? She wasn't getting any younger. She'd turn thirty-three in a few months, and had no home, no boyfriend, no marriage, no kids.

Peter Mason's face flashed into her mind. But he wasn't a solution. He was everything she would never be— wealthy, self-possessed, independent. He had the freedom to do whatever he chose, without financial constraints, while she thought of cost before she thought of anything else. Maybe that explained their present conflict. He had decided to acquire her, much as he might a new car. His voice rang in her memory. *I wanted you in an oversized sweater and boots, I wanted you sitting by my fire, I wanted you in my bed.* He'd made it sound far more beguiling, of course, but the basic theme was the same. Want, want, want. She would be another one of his possessions, living in *his* house, as dependent as ever. Another brick in the wall of her resistance to Peter slid into place.

"Can I come aboard?" she said.

"I was just about to leave."

"Can we talk for a bit?"

Jackie shrugged. "I'd like a beer. Feel like the Rose and Crown?"

Merry waited while he locked the pilothouse and swung himself over the side. She wasn't particularly fond of the Rose and Crown, a cavernous beer hall on South Water named for a famous shoal off Nantucket. But she followed Jackie down Straight Wharf, happy to stay one step off his pace, and up Water Street to Broad. Maybe a little alcohol would loosen his grip on the truth.

Jackie chose a high table near the door with four bar-stools grouped around it and took up a position staring out the window. He ordered a Bud and knocked back half of it when the waitress set it down, immediately ordering another. Then his gaze drifted back to the window. He was, Merry realized, checking out girls.

"When did you decide you wanted Del?" she asked.

He started as if stuck by a cattle prod, but his gaze never wavered. He took a swig of beer. "That's bullshit," he said.

"It was Connie—your wife—who gave me the first clue. She talked about how Del had thrown herself at you and made you feel like a hunted man. It was the sort of story I could see you telling, to explain something of Del's that Connie might have found—a picture forgotten in a drawer, maybe, a token you kept for memory's sake."

Jackie belched.

"Or the sort of story you'd use to heal your wounded pride," Merry said. "Even a suspicious wife would prefer it to the truth—that Del didn't think you were worth a second glance. Have you always impressed women with your sexual prowess, Jackie? Or just Connie? Is that why you married her?"

He slammed down the beer and stood up. "I don't have to listen to this shit."

"I'm requesting Sara's birth certificate from Boston," Merry said, clear above the bar's din. "Joe Duarte thought you were the baby's father. That's why he gave you his boat and named you Sara's guardian. Isn't that right? He hoped one day Del would come back and you'd all be a family." She laughed deliberately, to provoke him. "Where did he ever get such a crazy idea?"

"You think it's crazy?"

"Yes. I do."

"Because Del was too high-class, is that it? Too good for me? That's a laugh."

The waitress returned with Jackie's second beer, and he hesitated, eying it. "She wasn't so high-class she couldn't get herself knocked up. Walking around like a princess, with those tits and that ass waving in the breeze, wearing those shorts and her hair hanging loose, acting like she's too good to touch, and all the while—"

"Sit down," Merry said. "You can abuse Del all you like. You can abuse me, if it makes you feel good. But we're going to talk about this one way or another. It can be here, over a beer, or it can be out at the station. You decide."

He took a long slug of the beer, still standing, uncommitted. She thought for a moment he'd fall back on his customary swagger and head for the street, but her tone had implied too much. Merry was just another woman to him, but she was also a cop with a murder on her hands. Jackie sat down.

"You couldn't forgive her for ignoring you, could you?"

"She was just a bitch."

"All that frustration. All the wanting, and the anger. Knowing she gave someone else what she refused to give you. And then she left Nantucket and you knew you'd never have her. So you picked up Connie—poor Connie, who's so easily impressed. Did you tell Joe you'd fathered the baby when you needed a job on his boat?"

"He'd have thrown me overboard if I'd tried that," Jackie said, snorting. "I worked up to the idea. He knew I'd always been hot for Del. He could tell. I used to hang around their house, do chores for the old man, hoping I'd run into her. He knew. Everybody knew. And *she*—"

"—acted like you didn't exist. It must have been galling."

"I wanted to shake her," Jackie said, his fingers white around the sweating glass. "I wanted to bust her till she couldn't move. I wanted—" He stopped, breathing heavily, his eyes slightly glazed.

"Let's not go into exactly *how* you wanted to hurt Del," Merry said matter-of-factly. "Did you?"

He shook his head. "I never got to touch her. Then, or when she got back."

"But you let Joe think you had."

Jackie shrugged. "Once I had the job, I got close to the old man. He was lonely enough. Once in a while I'd let things drop—like I'd talked to Del, or knew more about her than he realized. Just a few words, here and there. Finally he asked me about it. Forced me to tell him what he wanted to hear. I let him think what he chose. Told him Del figured I didn't make enough money, and that's why she refused to marry me; she wanted more than a fisherman for a husband. So she left me, and I married Connie. That made him mad. Like she'd turned her back on her father's way of life. And he got to thinking. Maybe if I was better off financially, maybe—"

"Del would come back. Connie would conveniently disappear. Joe would no longer be lonely."

"He thought the kid should have a proper father," Jackie said defensively. "And he was right. I *should* have custody of the kid. The way Del was living, can you blame her dad for wanting to find it a good home?"

Merry looked at his bestial face, thought of Sara, and stifled the urge to scream. "So he died thinking all this was true?"

"Guess so."

"And that's why you have a boat."

"He left it to me, fair and square. Anybody'll tell you the same."

More swaggering self-justification. She could see how Jackie's life had gone—a poor fisherman's son in the middle of an increasingly wealthy resort; his father's death, his father's debt; the boat he'd counted on inheriting sold to pay off its mortgage; the dogged reliance on the only trade he had ever known, the chance at easy money skippering for SeaCon. The rationalizations, the years of self-deceit, the fantasies used to shore up a flagging ego. Jackie was all-powerful, Jackie was always right, Jackie

made the rules. Jackie was a winner, not like the rest of
the poor schmucks who made an honest living.

"You're used to taking things that aren't yours, aren't
you, Jackie?"

"What's that supposed to mean?"

"I'm just thinking of SeaCon. Your former employer.
How much did they pay you to scuttle the boat?"

He stared for a moment, flabbergasted. "You're full of
shit."

"Am I?"

"You know it."

"They collected four hundred thousand dollars. What
was your percentage? Forty thousand? Or less? Enough to
put a down payment on Connie's house, but not enough
to buy your own boat. Of course, you'd made other plans.
You were getting a boat from your future father-in-law.
Once he was dead, of course."

"I didn't kill him," Jackie said automatically. "What
happened was an accident—"

"—and anybody'll tell me the same," Merry finished
for him. "Right. How much did they pay you, Jackie?"

He said nothing.

"Come on," she said patiently. "I know about Rick
Berkowski. And about Charley MacIlvenney. We've
talked to them." *Not about this exact topic,* she thought,
but it's true enough. "Everybody got a nest egg once they
scuttled the boats. The mortgages on them must have
been low for SeaCon to make a profit. What were you
guys skippering—boats repossessed by the bank and sold
at auction for a fraction of their value?"

Jackie didn't answer. Merry wasn't certain he was even
listening. She plowed on.

"Say SeaCon and MariTrans picked them up at bargain-basement prices, paid for them with mortgages, and insured them at replacement value. Then they paid their captains to scuttle the boats in a convincing fashion—preferably in deep water during the winter when the weather made it hard to locate the wrecks—collected insurance for the boat's full value, paid off the low mortgages, and pocketed the difference. And promptly went out of business."

Merry paused for breath, waiting. Jackie looked slightly whipped—by her words or by downing too much beer too quickly.

"How much is left after Connie takes her share, Jackie?"

"Not enough," he whispered. "Not a goddamn enough. Charley and Rick tell you all this?"

"They didn't have to," she said. "It's pretty obvious. Someone was going to figure it out sooner or later. You're just killing time, Jackie, until you're indicted for fraud along with SeaCon and MariTrans. You know that, don't you?"

He laughed harshly. "Those guys'll never take the fall," he said. "It'll be jerks like Charley and Rick and me. They'll be long gone by the time you catch up with them."

"Unless you help me," she said. "You could make a better deal for yourself with the DA if you tried, Jackie. It wouldn't take much."

He looked at her, considering. "What'd you give Rick and Charley?"

"I haven't yet. I wanted to talk to you first. I figured you'd know more. And have more to lose."

"What do you want to know?"

"Where's Jerry Dundee, Jackie? Where do I find the big fish?"

He snorted. "You really think he's the big fish? You think Dundee's your man?" He threw back his head and laughed. Something in his face made her realize she'd lost him, and she sat back, disappointed, casting about for another hook.

Jackie leaned close to her, his breath oppressively beery. "You've got a lot more work to do, Merry Folger." He reached out and actually pinched her cheek, in a gruesome attempt at condescension. She reared backward. "Good luck," he said. "If all you've got is Jerry Dundee, I'll sleep easy. You're not gonna be indicting *me* anytime soon. Call me when you've got a case."

"I know about the fight, Jackie," she said.

"What fight?"

"The one you had with Joe Duarte, the night he died. The shouting match that drew him out of the pilothouse in the middle of a storm, to handle a job he should have left to you. Only you weren't following orders, were you? Was it deliberate? Did you hope he'd be distracted, not notice when the winch brought the doors in too fast?"

Jackie shoved his stool away from the table and slapped down a twenty-dollar bill.

"The Swede says the winch was broken." Merry rose and faced him. "That he *couldn't* control it. Did you have a hand in that, Jackie?"

"You're out of your fucking mind," he said.

And with that, to her mingled relief and dismay, he really did leave the bar.

Merry gave him five minutes, then walked the few blocks to the Brotherhood.

It was too early for Dave Grizutto to work his shift, but she was in luck; he was having dinner at the bar.

"Looks good," she said.

"Blue cheese burger. Amazing what a little mold can do for a meal, isn't it?" He set down his food and wiped his mouth with a paper napkin. "You're becoming a regular."

"Thought I'd test your fabled knowledge of the island's drinking habits. Does Jenny Baldwin like scotch?"

"Only if it's Glenfiddich," he said immediately.

So he had Jenny's tastes pegged, too. Had he set her up that night at Del's, leaving her favorite drink on the counter? Her bracelet links on the floor?

"Why?" Dave asked. "Need a hostess gift?"

"Not exactly. You know her well?"

A wariness came into the bartender's eyes. "Why do I think this isn't an innocent question?"

"Because I'm a cop," Merry said, exasperated. "I can't ask somebody the *time* without causing panic. Come on, Dave."

"Sorry," he said. "You're right. Anybody else asked me that, I wouldn't think twice. I know Tom better than Jenny. He's in and out of here all the time, talking business, meeting clients, that kind of stuff. Jenny just comes looking for him once in a while. Sometimes she seems to expect him, takes a table in the corner and drinks her scotch, and he never shows."

"That happen often?"

"Three times that I can remember."

"Funny," Merry said. "She's not the sort of woman who'd seem comfortable here."

"Because the bar is near the tables?" he said, amused.

"You know. The tourist crowd, young people, everybody

here around midnight trying out the various liqueurs you guys keep."

"And she's too garden-club," he said.

"Something like that."

"The hairband and the sensible shoes."

"Exactly."

"I think Mrs. Baldwin has everybody fooled."

Merry sat up and looked at him; but his eyes were turned carefully away. He took a bite of his burger and a swig of Coke. "You want anything?"

She shook her head. "Tell me what you meant, instead of changing the subject."

He laughed. "Never try innuendo on Merry Folger." He set down his glass and pushed his half-eaten burger to the side. "Let's just say that I think Jenny is lonely. All is not well in the Baldwin household."

"Did she come on to you, Dave?"

"As much as that sort of woman ever does. Her signals were subtler than a twenty-two-year-old's, but she was signaling all the same." He looked at her with something like embarrassment. "You'll think I've got a big head."

"Not at all," Merry said, mulling it over. "I figure you know what you're looking at."

"She drank a bit too much scotch once," he said. "Back in May. She was here late into the evening, and it was pretty obvious that she was waiting for Tom and he wasn't going to show. She finally abandoned the table when the waitress pressured her to order, and moved over here."

"And that's when she—signaled?"

"She asked when I got off and what I planned to do that night," he said carefully. "So, yeah."

"And you told her—"

"That I would be here another three hours, had to close up, and was exhausted. I was going home to bed. I thought that was a clear enough refusal."

"Jenny didn't?"

"She said that sounded like a lovely idea."

Despite herself, Merry grinned. She could imagine Jenny's bleached blue eyes bloodshot with drink, her loosened inhibitions, the voicing of a thought she'd never have allowed to the forefront of her brain in normal circumstances. She *would* use the word "lovely," as though a tumble with Dave were comparable to a fine piece of china, or a good view of the Sound. She had no vocabulary for the coarser things in life.

"So, Dave?"

"So what?" He ran his fingers through his blond hair, and then grimaced, studying the strands caught on his fingers. They glinted in the candlelight. Like the hair found on Del's floor, Merry thought.

"Did you take her home?" she persisted.

He snorted. "I excused myself, called Tom Baldwin at the Yacht Club, and had him pick her up. Apparently he'd forgotten they had a date."

"How did Tom treat her?"

"Pretty coldly."

"That's sad."

"It always is, Merry."

"Maybe if they'd had children—"

"Who knows? There'd just be a few more lives damaged by the mess."

Merry thought about the Baldwins as she drove toward Tattle Court. Were Tom and Jenny close to divorce? That might give Tom a motive to frame Jenny for murder, leave her bottle and bracelet on a dead woman's floor. But why go to such lengths? And why kill Del?

Because Tom was Sara's father? And Del intended to tell his wife?

Or was Dave Grizutto only giving her half the story? He admitted he'd visited Del the night she died, and he knew about Jenny Baldwin's taste for Glenfiddich. Perhaps his relationship with the developer's wife had gone farther than Dave said—so far, in fact, that he was ready to be done with it. When he'd killed Del in a fit of passion, and taken Sara's birth certificate, he'd set Jenny up for the murder.

It was still too speculative. Merry had no evidence that Dave killed Del; he had only said he'd been in her house.

No evidence *yet*.

She glanced at the passenger seat of her Explorer, where a napkin and a glass sat carefully wrapped in plastic. She'd said good-bye to Dave and watched him walk back toward the kitchen. Then, taking advantage of the Brotherhood's habitual semidarkness, she'd casually dropped his empty Coke glass into her voluminous purse, in case Dave's prints matched any Clarence had found on the harpoon.

It was a matter of seconds to wipe a Kleenex across the bar, scooping up a few of his blond hairs for comparison with the ones found near Del's body.

Going bald was a bitch, Merry thought. A man could lose so much more than just his looks.

Chapter 25

ON THURSDAY MORNING, Chief John Folger released Jenny Baldwin, purse in hand and muttering darkly about the future of the police budget.

Matt Bailey sulked and said he couldn't move forward on a case that was blown.

Merry, feeling guilty about Bill Carmichael and the overloaded state police, glanced at the list of Plastech Explosives customers, considered starting at the top with a call to a contractor in Madison, Wisconsin, and decided she couldn't face it.

Feeling grumpy and dissatisfied, she looked over the Request for Court Order forms Howie Seitz had completed, dated them and signed her name, and scanned them to the Boston probate court. It was a glorious June day, and her windowless cubicle was more than usually oppressive. What she needed was a drive out into the moors. Rebecca's face at the screen door of the Mason Farms saltbox rose in her mind, but if she drove anywhere, it would be to Tom Baldwin's offices to inquire about his schedule the previous Wednesday night. And, in a roundabout fashion, the state of his marriage.

Tom was unavailable, his assistant told Merry when

she entered the air-conditioned dimness of the South Beach Street office. Merry gave the woman the once-over, curious about Del's replacement. She was a neat, cool, elegant blonde, dressed in androgynous separates; the sort of woman who went with the neutral-toned furniture and the generic prints on the walls. Everything about Baldwin Builders was rose and beige, including Tom's assistant, as though she had been acquired with the lamps. An off-island import, Merry decided; very unlike Del. But then, Tom's lifestyle these days was more upscale than it had been when Del worked for him—and he would use the word "upscale." In Del's day he'd rented a place on Washington Street, not far from the Town Pier, and it hadn't looked like the interior of a Hyatt.

"Do you know where he can be reached?"

"He's at a selectmen's meeting," the assistant said. There was an overtone of the British Isles in her accent, not pronounced enough to be native, but quietly suggestive of breeding and culture. Probably as bottled as her hair color.

Merry's brow wrinkled. "I thought they met on Wednesday nights."

"They do. This is a special meeting. To consider the future of the Town Pier. Something has to be done as soon as possible, and as Tom's now finance director—"

"I see."

"He should be back in an hour or so, if you'd like to call round again."

There it was, "call round," a carefully cultivated Anglicism. Wouldn't Del laugh, Merry thought.

She thanked the woman and left, making her way

toward 16 Broad Street and the Town Building, past Steamboat Wharf, where a car ferry had just arrived. A flood of early weekenders rolled off its gangplanks, cars packed to the gills, pedestrians pushing baby strollers and bikes, a huddled mass waiting impatiently at the taxi stand for one of the few vans circulating the island. The taxi problem was notorious; every summer it grew worse. Merry had seen new arrivals actually come to blows over a place in a cab, and more than one driver had been accosted when he refused a fare.

When she arrived at the Town Building's conference room, it was to find the door barred and the sign CLOSED MEETING propped up on an easel.

"Excuse me," she said, walking back to the lobby receptionist, "is it the selectmen's meeting that's closed?"

It was.

"I had understood it concerned the fate of the Town Pier."

It did.

"But isn't that rather important? I mean, shouldn't they call a special town meeting or something?"

The receptionist looked at Merry coldly over her glasses and inquired whether she represented a news organization. Her temper flaring, Merry pulled out her badge and flashed it at the woman.

"The selectmen are merely considering preliminary proposals for the pier's replacement, Detective . . . *Folger*," the receptionist said icily, lifting her glasses to peer more closely at the badge. "Proposals do not concern the public. Once the pier becomes a budgetary matter, it will of course be under consideration as business for next spring's town meeting."

"I thought the point was to get the reconstruction under way quickly."

"That is correct."

"So conceivably it could be done *before* the next town meeting?"

"I could not undertake to say. That is a matter for the selectmen to consider."

Decidedly hush-hush. Too much that concerned the Town Pier was hush-hush. Merry thanked the receptionist, walked back down the hall, and pushed open the door marked LADIES, all with exaggerated emphasis for the woman's benefit. By the time she emerged, the receptionist was occupied by the telephone. Merry crept up to the conference-room door and crouched with one ear to the crack between the double doors.

She was in luck. Tom Baldwin was speaking.

"The Windy Harbor plan submitted by Oceanside Resorts is admirable in several respects," he said. Strange how a familiar voice altered when detached from a face; instead of Tom's avuncular heartiness, this voice sounded suave, persuasive, commanding. "It provides for multiuse facilities that will bring significant tax dollars to Nantucket and improve the shoreline along South Beach. A condominium complex with private moorage, a boat-servicing complex including a dockside restaurant, a shopping arcade providing goods to residents, a small, sixty-five-room hotel, and retail space for galleries, clothing stores, upscale food emporiums, lightship basket shops—"

Oceanside Resorts. Oceanside Resorts. She'd heard that somewhere. She groped for it in her mind, half listening to the conversation behind the door.

"You still haven't explained how you're going to turn a piece of town property into private holdings." This from Patrick Mayhew, a longtime Nantucket resident near the end of his tenure as a selectman. There was an audible sigh from his fellows.

"It'll be *leased*, Pat," came one impatient voice. Jason Summerfield, a recent transplant from Manhattan. "We'll sign a long-term lease with Oceanside, oversee the construction and cleanup, and sit back while they take care of our problems."

Oceanside. Merry sat back on her heels as though she'd been sucker-punched. Small print at the lower left-hand corner of a blueprint sliding from a pile in Tom Baldwin's office. Blueprints that looked pretty final only days after the fire. Blueprints that must have been drafted months earlier.

"Have you run this by the zoning office, Baldwin?"

"Not yet. This is merely a preliminary sounding of the board—"

"Well, I for one don't like it," Mayhew said testily. "We don't need more building along the harbor. Those fishermen's shacks selling T-shirts and whatnot on Old South are eyesore enough. They serve a purpose, of course; they keep the day-trippers occupied and out of the upper end of town. But do we need more of that, I ask you?"

"This is entirely different, Patrick," Tom Baldwin said. "The plan under consideration is geared toward an affluent clientele."

Upscale, Merry thought.

"We're talking condos with harbor views, starting at eight hundred thousand dollars. Eventually, perhaps, it could be extended to Old South and provide a welcome face-lift to the area."

"And what about all the seasonal boats coming in and out of the moorings? Fifteen hundred boats a summer."

"The moorings will be unchanged," Baldwin said. "Oceanside will simply run them."

"And take the jobs from a few more Nantucketers."

"Why are you so opposed to a plan that admirably solves our problems?"

"Why are you so ready to embrace this Oceanside? What do we know about them, anyway? You've only been finance director for a day and a half, and already you're jumping up with a contract to fill. Sure you're not acting as their agent?"

"Good God, Patrick, what are you suggesting?"

"Patrick," Jason Summerfield broke in, "Tom is merely doing his job, and superlatively at that. He's presented an option for solving a major headache. You mentioned fifteen hundred boats mooring off South Beach. That's an accurate number. Only they're unable to moor off South Beach right now, and if we don't move our tuckuses, they're not going to come in all summer. The place is a wreck. We need action, we need improvement, we need a deal that'll bring in *more* tourist dollars than the old pier ever did. And we need it yesterday, not next spring."

"Detective Folger," said an icy voice behind Merry.

She tried to leap to her feet, shamefaced, and discovered her legs had gone numb from the knee down. To sprawl in supplication about the ankles of the lobby receptionist was the cherry on the sundae of her day.

Merry took refuge in Congdon's Pharmacy, blessedly air-conditioned and provided with a spare, neat 1950s lunch counter where real islanders ordered grilled cheese sandwiches and old-fashioned sodas. She had both, stirring her black-and-white desultorily with a straw, licking the foam from the bottom, and trying to fit Tom Baldwin into arson. She'd taken a moment to call Howie Seitz on her cell, and he'd found Oceanside Resorts halfway down the list of Plastech Explosives' customers. Coincidence was not an option here.

For her money, Patrick Mayhew had Tom Baldwin pegged. He was an agent for Oceanside, and he must have believed a bomb was the best door-opener to the South Beach property. There was the obvious tie, of course; it was Tom's dinghy that had blown. The fact that he'd been miles away in Boston was irrelevant. He could have hired someone to destroy the pier, and allowed his own expensive yacht to go up in flames in order to look more convincingly innocent. His boat had undoubtedly been insured—and maybe he was tired of it, anyway. But how to establish his connection to the bomber? And what did the pier have to do with Jenny Baldwin's prints showing up in Del's house?

That was the immediate problem. If Merry revealed how much she knew about Oceanside, Tom would run before any connection with Del was made.

She sighed and pushed away the remains of her sandwich. Her head hurt. A sure sign she was subconsciously working out the tangle. Deciding the best antidote for weariness was to ignore it, she paid her bill and headed back to Tom Baldwin's offices.

The master builder was at leisure, Merry was told, and would be with her in just a few minutes. After perhaps half an hour with a magazine in her lap, she was ushered into his private sanctum.

"Detective," he said, not bothering to rise from behind

his desk, "I understand the Nantucket police are now eavesdropping on the town government. Are things going completely to hell out there at the Rotary, or is your father just past his prime?"

Hence the half-hour wait. She was intended to feel humbled. "I know you must be upset about your wife's arrest," she said, taking a chair he didn't bother to offer.

"Upset? I'm *irate*. The poor woman has done nothing to deserve such persecution. She came to you thinking she was coming to a friend. And she got a night in a jail cell. It's something she won't soon forget, I assure you."

"Tom, her fingerprints were found in Del Duarte's house."

"On a bottle she brought to Del," he said dismissively.

"There is also the bracelet."

"A few links of chain. Which no one can say is hers."

It was definitely possible Baldwin had framed his wife, Merry thought; nobody could be this dense about evidence unless he wanted to seem stupid. "What I'm trying to say, Tom, is that the bottle and the chain were deliberately left there to incriminate your wife. Del didn't drink scotch. There were no other prints on the glasses. So whoever murdered Del wiped the highball glasses clean and left Jenny's prints to be found on the bottle, along with the remains of her chain."

Tom grinned at her derisively. "Implicate my wife? Why would anyone do that?"

"I don't know. But it happened. And the killer must have known Jenny had no alibi. Who besides you and Josh were aware she was alone in bed that night?"

"I suppose everybody at the Yacht Club knew it," Tom said, thinking. "I told them why I showed up at Paul Harris's party alone."

"Paul Harris?"

"Old friend from Boston. Just got married for the second time. Cutest little thing you ever—" He stopped, realizing who he was talking to, and recovered. "There were about twenty or so people."

"When you arrived, or throughout the course of the evening?"

"When I arrived. The invitation was for seven-thirty. I showed up a good fifteen minutes later."

"And were some of the guests friends of yours and Jenny's?"

"Just about all of them."

"Any of them have a reason to kill Del and frame your wife for it?"

"What the hell kind of question is that?"

"The sort I'm forced to ask every day."

"No."

"Any of them leave early?"

"What's early?"

"Before midnight, I suppose."

"Hell, yes. I was home myself by ten-thirty. I get up every morning at five."

"And Jenny was in fact in bed?"

"Sound asleep," he said dismissively.

"Was your nephew home?"

"Not yet. His crowd don't call it quits until the wee hours."

"Did you have any reason to step out, Tom, during the party?"

"Did I take a whiz, are you asking? I should think so. And no one came along to hold my hand."

"The bathroom wasn't exactly what I had in mind."

"Are you accusing me of murdering Del Duarte and framing my wife?" At this, he finally rose from behind the desk and leaned menacingly toward Merry. Tom was not a tall man—not much taller than herself—but he was bulky, his shoulders broadened by years of hard lifting and pounding. He was aware of his strength, she knew, and was consciously using it.

"Should I be?" Merry asked.

"You people don't know when to stop." His voice rose unpleasantly. "But the rest of us may do it for you. There's more than one way to control a rogue elephant. You can trip it, you can trap it, or you can shoot it in the head."

"If by 'the head' you're referring to my father, Tom, I'd be careful what you say. He has more friends than you do."

"We'll see how many he has left when I'm through with him," Tom said. "Now get out of my office, Meredith. And don't come back."

Chapter 26

IF THURSDAY WAS bad, Friday morning looked positively awful. Bailey had stirred himself enough to collect
fabric samples from the Baldwins' closets, and Clarence
was hard at work attempting to match fibers. Merry had
given Bailey her notes about Tom Baldwin, though she
had little hope he'd grasp their significance. Bailey's
ineptitude sat in her gut like a bad clam—sickening, persistent, and ruining her day.

So when the phone rang in her office and Peter's
warm, dark voice came over the line, Merry was frustrated enough to resent him wildly—merely for having a
life independent of murder and fraud.

"I'm pretty busy, Peter," she said, doing her best to
sound both efficient and irritated.

"I'm sure you are. I won't ask you to dinner."

"Good. Can I do something for you?" There was the
hint of a clock ticking behind every word.

"I ran into Lisa Davis yesterday afternoon while I was
out riding. She used to baby-sit for Georgiana at the Cliff
Road house."

Training on his bike, of course. Running into the help,
chatting over a rose-covered fence, enjoying the summer

day without a care in the world beyond the betterment of his quadriceps.

"Who's Lisa Davis?"

"You don't know? I thought you'd have talked to her by now. Mitch Davis's wife. Remember Mitch? Got a bullet through the head during that arson case you're investigating?" Peter never sounded irritated himself. His voice simply got quieter when he was angry.

"I'm not heading that investigation. The state police are."

"What exactly is making you so busy, then?"

"Cleaning up after everybody else," she snapped. "All the work and none of the recognition, if you must know. What about Lisa Davis?"

"She's not doing too well, Merry. I thought you might drop by and talk to her."

"Because it takes a woman to understand another woman's grief?"

"No," Peter said. His voice was almost inaudible. In another mood, Merry would have heard that as a warning. Today, fed up with the smug Baileys and the bike-riding Masons of the world, she didn't care.

"Because nobody seems to give her any information," Peter continued. "Whoever is handling it over at the state police has told her it was a random killing in the middle of a crisis, and that they doubt they'll ever have a lead."

"Sometimes that's the truth, Peter," Merry said. "I'm certainly not going to second-guess the state police."

"What has gotten into you today, Meredith Folger? I'm trying to have a simple conversation here. About something I think matters. I'm asking for your help, and you're biting my head off."

"I said I'm busy, Peter. I realize that's something you can't understand. Thanks for calling." And she hung up.

Merry studied the name Oceanside Resorts on the list of Plastech Explosives customers. She should give the information to Bill Carmichael over at the state police, though she would be unable to answer his obvious questions—why Oceanside, when she had no clear link between the company and a bomb, other than Tom Baldwin pushing their bid for the pier reconstruction, and Tom Baldwin's boat blowing sky-high. It was too soon for the Massachusetts police to muscle their way into Oceanside's doors; more of a case should be built. And despite herself, Merry admitted, she didn't want the state disturbing Tom Baldwin's complacency. She was certain he was into something fraudulent up to his neck, and his wife's fingerprints had been found in Del's house. If the state police rolled up his network prematurely, she might never find out why. She could explain all that to Bill Carmichael, of course, or at least let him know Lisa Davis's concerns. But he'd already said Mitch's wife was pestering him unmercifully, and knowing Bill, he was probably ignoring his cell phone.

Mitch Davis. He'd been shot in the back of the head. Bill thought he'd walked away from an irate boater just as the guy pulled the gun out and fired at him; but in the smoky dark, would an irate boater manage to hit the exact center of the base of the skull? The entrance wound *had* been rather precise, hadn't it? And what about burn marks?

Merry walked down the hall to Clarence's office and knocked. He looked up from a report he was writing and smiled at her. "I'd love to be able to tell you that

Dave Grizutti fellah's prints are on the hahpoon," he said, "but they're not. Hairs are a match, howevah. He was definitely there."

"Never mind that," she said. "Do you have your notes on Mitch Davis?"

"Mitch Davis? O' carse." Clarence was scrupulously neat. Everything was labeled, everything sorted, everything filed. He pulled open a desk drawer and reached into a mass of folders. "Here 'tis."

Her brows knitted, Merry studied the crime scene chief's notes. Though the murder had been turned over to the state police, Clarence had obtained a copy of the crime lab's autopsy report and appended it to his file. Mitch Davis *had* been shot in the center of the base of the skull by a .38 caliber pistol, at close range. He had the burn marks to prove it.

An execution, Merry thought. Bill Carmichael must have recognized it. So why wasn't he doing anything about it? She flipped the file shut. Peter was right. She should talk to Lisa Davis.

THE DAVISES OWNED a neat new Cape Cod off Bartlett Road. This was the southwestern end of the island, abutting Bartlett Farm's acres of produce, the Ram Pasture conservation area, and eventually, down Hummock Pond Road, Cisco Beach.

A child's three-wheeler lay overturned in the gravel drive, and the pots of geraniums on the front stoop looked parched and neglected, their dead flower heads left to wither and straggle above the riotous petunias. Merry walked up the slate path, wondering if anyone was home. But as she mounted the steps, there came from somewhere inside a high-pitched wail, followed by the distinct sound of a slap. Good thing Peter's sister had found another baby-sitter.

Lisa Davis was a younger woman than Merry had expected, perhaps all of twenty-eight. Mitch had been a good two decades older. His wife carried a little girl who looked to be about two, and a boy of perhaps three clung to one leg. It was the latter who had been crying; the track of tears still trailed from his wounded eyes.

"I'm Meredith Folger, Mrs. Davis," Merry said. "With the Nantucket police. Would you have a few minutes to talk?"

"*Would* I?" she said, her eyes widening. "I've been trying to talk to somebody for days. Ever since Mitch—" Her eyes welled with tears. "Ever since Mitch—" She stood back and held open the door. "Please come in."

Merry followed her to a spare living room, furnished with the sort of furniture newlyweds consider necessary—a careful dining-room table and chairs, from their appearance hardly ever used—mixed with the odds and ends of a bachelor's existence.

"You're Peter Mason's friend," Lisa Davis said, leading Merry through the dining area to the small kitchen. She slid the two-year-old into a high chair and pulled out a stool for the older boy. Two peanut butter sandwiches cut in fours sat on plates beside small glasses of milk. "We were just having lunch. I hope you don't mind."

"Go ahead."

"It was such a relief to run into Peter yesterday. He's so comforting, isn't he? I always feel things are okay when I talk to him. Even when they're really bad. I suppose it's because he's the closest thing to family I have on the island."

Merry looked sympathetic.

"He thought you might know something," Lisa said, recovering her train of thought. "I can't get any information out of that Carmichael guy."

"What is it you wanted to know, Mrs. Davis?"

She slumped down in a chair opposite her son and leaned her head against one hand. "Why no one wants to believe Mitch was killed for a reason," she said. "The same reason the wharf was burned. I mean, come *on.*" Lisa grimaced at Merry in exasperation. "You think the whole thing was random? All that destruction? If they want to find out who torched my husband's pier, they'd better find out why somebody thought they had to shoot him. Chalking it up to some faceless boater doesn't work. At least, it doesn't work for me."

"You think Mitch's murder and the arson were linked," Merry said.

"Of course they were linked."

Merry pulled out the remaining chair, slid her purse to the floor, and sat down. "Tell me about Mitch's work."

"That's what's so sad," Lisa Davis said. "It was going so well. He was so proud of it, you know? All the changes he'd made."

"How long had he been marine superintendent?"

"Almost five years. Ever since he left the Coast Guard, right after we got married."

"You met here?"

"Oh, no," she said, surprised. "I'm from Providence. That's where Mitch was stationed. We met when I worked at the Coast Guard headquarters as a secretary, right out of college."

"And when he got out of the service, he took the marine superintendent's job here."

"He liked the idea of living on an island, and staying close to boats, that whole harbor sort of life. I understood it. I thought Nantucket was beautiful. Of course, I had no idea what it was going to be like in the winter months." She smiled ruefully. "But winters were good in another way—Mitch had so much free time. Other than issuing scalloping permits and making sure the catch quotas were kept, there wasn't a lot to do. He was able to be much more of a parent to Tod and Whitney than most men ever are." At this, her eyes filled with tears again.

"Daddy," said the boy faintly, and dropped his sandwich. He pushed his plate away and put his head down on the table, arms hanging slack at his sides.

"You can be excused, Tod," Lisa said firmly, and turned toward her daughter, attempting to force a corner of bread into an unwilling mouth. "They eat next to nothing since it happened," she said to Merry. "And they're so quiet. It breaks my heart. Not that I'm Little Mary Sunshine myself. It's been hard on all of us."

"Could you go back to the mainland for a while? See some family?"

"I will," she said, "just as soon as I figure out what's going on with the police. They haven't released Mitch's body yet. I can't even plan a funeral." She set down the rejected sandwich and wiped her daughter's mouth. "Would you like some iced tea?"

Merry shook her head. "How did Mitch feel about the job once he got into it?"

"I think he saw it as a challenge," Lisa said. "He had to work against a lot of attitudes. People in town tended to disregard the pier area—other than collecting the trash and whatnot. The selectmen, for instance, never want to part with a dime."

"Scottie Flanagan told me. He said Mitch ruffled some feathers."

"Oh, Scottie," Lisa said, shrugging. "The selectmen just didn't want to pay for stuff they thought most islanders wouldn't use, so Mitch went to Visitor Services. Got tourist money to pay for a tourist facility. I think the selectmen were pleased. There really weren't any hard feelings."

"Then why would someone want Mitch out of the way?"

Lisa hesitated, assessing Merry's face. Whatever she saw must have reassured her. "He was being pressured about something. He wouldn't tell me what it was." She glanced at her daughter, then reached over to pull her out of her high chair. "Go play with Tod, sweetie."

She waited until the child ran out of the kitchen, then turned back to Merry. "He told me it would be dangerous for me to know. Whatever it was clearly upset him. He'd meet with that Jerry Dundee, and afterward he'd be so angry he couldn't speak."

"Jerry Dundee," Merry said dully. "Jerry *Dundee?*" The SeaCon employee Seitz had tried and failed to locate.

"You know him?"

"I wish I did. His name keeps turning up in the oddest places."

"He wasn't an islander," Lisa said. "But he used to show up at the marine super's office and bother Mitch."

"Your husband told you this?"

"Not at first. Dundee called here once and left a

message. Mitch got really mad—that's how I found out all about it. I heard him call the guy back and tell him he was never to bother his wife again, or come near his home, and that if he did, he'd have Mitch to reckon with."

"Wow."

"Mitch was very strange after that phone call. He went into the kids' rooms and held them in the dark. I couldn't get it out of my mind. He was threatened by that guy. And he wouldn't tell me why, or how; he wouldn't let me help."

Lisa looked down at her nails, bitten to the quick, and picked at a cuticle. "And then he was killed—"

"Do you know when he last saw Dundee?" Merry asked.

"The call to the house was a while ago—April, maybe. I didn't always know when Mitch had a run-in with him. I used to be able to tell—he'd come home so mad. But then I think Mitch started covering up. So as not to worry me."

"Dundee had been harassing him for a while?"

"At least a year."

Merry sat back and mulled this over. Jerry Dundee, insurance defrauder and sinker of boats, had been pressuring the marine superintendent for the past twelve months. Pressure that culminated in Mitch's death and the destruction of his pride and joy. A warning to others, similarly ill-disposed to accommodate Mr. Dundee? Or a means to an end?

"Mrs. Davis," Merry said, "you mentioned that Dundee left a message in April, and that Mitch called him back. Is there any chance that you still have that number?"

She shook her head. "He didn't leave it. Just his name and that Mitch should get in touch. Mitch must have known the number."

"Did your husband keep his contacts in his phone?"

"Yes," she said. "Normally he'd have had it on him when he was—" She paused, looked down, recovered. "But the night of the fire he left it in his truck. I'll go get it."

She disappeared into the bedroom, down a hallway off the kitchen, and reappeared almost immediately. "I already punched in his access code. You can pull up the contacts. He had his wallet with him, so if he kept the number there, we're out of luck."

"They haven't returned his things to you?" Merry said.

"His wallet was stolen. I thought you knew."

Merry scrolled through the list of names. But there was no sign of a darker presence, no unexplained threat. Jerry Dundee's was not among them. "Did he have anything else, like an actual address book or a calendar where he might have penciled in appointments?"

"He kept one last year," Lisa Davis said. "The smartphone is brand new. He used to say that if one fell in the water while he was working, he'd lose everything. But even Mitch finally forced himself to go digital."

"Would he have kept that calendar?"

"I don't know. Maybe." She left the room once more and Merry heard the sound of rummaging in distant drawers. Lisa returned with a shabby black spiral-bound weekly calendar and handed it wordlessly to Merry.

She leafed through it, starting with the previous January. Mitch Davis's handwriting was surprisingly clear—as crisp and precise as he'd always kept his uniform. There were cryptic references to shellfish permits, boats' names, and what Merry took to be National Marine Fisheries Service regulations, the minutiae of the scalloping season.

He'd even noted the weather for various days. And on a Tuesday in July, nearly a year earlier, Merry discovered what she was looking for. In his precise hand Mitch had written the single word "Dundee." The number had a Providence area code.

Merry studied the notation an instant, debating her next question. But there was no avoiding it, she would have to be brutal. "Why did your husband leave the Coast Guard?"

There was an instant's tense silence, short enough for someone less observant to ignore. Lisa's eyes slid away for the first time, unable to hold Merry's gaze. "He'd been in twenty years," she said. "That was long enough."

ON HER WAY back to the station, Merry called Howie and gave him the Providence number. Then she called Terry Samson at the Coast Guard station. Maybe Mitch Davis *had* simply retired; but if not, Terry would find out. She was willing to bet that Jerry Dundee had something on the marine superintendent—an episode in Providence he was using to blackmail Davis. Unsuccessfully, it would seem. Mitch had faced him down, and Mitch had died. The flaming pier rose vividly in Merry's mind, the memory of choking smoke and horns blowing chaotically. The prize must be worth a hell of a lot.

Chapter 27

"MITCH DAVIS LEFT Providence under something of a cloud." Terry Samson closed his office door. "This is highly confidential, you understand."

"I do," Merry said. "I appreciate your telling me anything. I know it isn't easy to talk about a colleague's record, even a dead one."

"I spent four years in Providence," he said, "and another three at Woods Hole. I don't need to twist any arms back there or ask for any favors. I remember what happened to Mitch."

"Did you see him much once you were both working here?"

"Not socially. But the Coast Guard has to deal with the marine superintendent all the time—he's the harbormaster. He has jurisdiction within the harbor, we have it beyond the jetties. And sometimes things overlap. If Mitch ever thought force would be necessary in apprehending a nasty boater, he didn't hesitate to call. We respected each other's turf."

"So what happened in Rhode Island?"

Terry hesitated. "I only know what the Coast Guard *said* happened. But I have to believe there was another story."

"Of course. There always is. But the Coast Guard's version is what matters—if that's why Mitch left."

"Oh, it's why he left, all right. Though he'd had a clockwork career up to that point. He was a lifer—graduated from the Coast Guard Academy, did tours in Hawaii, Miami, Woods Hole, Providence. That's where he ran into the wrong end of a propeller, metaphorically speaking."

"Personal differences with a boss?"

"I wish." Terry looked over his shoulder, though they were completely alone. "He was in charge of a mission to apprehend some heroin dealers—Dominicans, they run the stuff up from the islands and hand it off to relatives in the states—who were going to meet at a certain coordinate off Providence Harbor. He made the arrest, seized both boats, locked up the money and the drugs, and headed for port. Only when he got there, the money was gone."

"How much money?"

"Close to a million."

"Whoops."

"Mitch couldn't explain it. He'd had the only key to the evidence locker on the boat. The entire vessel was searched. So was every man jack of the crew. Nothing. The service undertook an intensive investigation of Mitch's private life—found out he was recently married to a much younger woman, had significant credit-card debt, a mortgage on a new house, the whole nine yards. They concluded privately that he'd probably tossed the money overboard to a confederate and that it was in a numbered Caymans account by that time. But they couldn't prove anything. They could only court-martial him for dereliction of duty. He resigned first."

"His place doesn't look like the house of a man with a numbered bank account," Merry said thoughtfully. "What do you think of the story, Terry?"

"I think somebody else had a copy of the key, and wasn't telling," he said. "I'd be interested to know which of the crew resigned once the mess blew over and Mitch faded away."

"I would, too," Merry said, "but I haven't got time for that. I imagine this was a big deal in Providence, five, six years ago."

"It was all over the news for a few days."

"So anybody looking for dirt on Mitch Davis would find a significant paper trail."

"Unfortunately."

"How'd he manage to get the job here?"

"He'd resigned, he wasn't court-martialed. Enough people were suspicious of the official story and close enough to Mitch to give him a good recommendation. If he didn't want to talk about the past, I guess he didn't have to."

"But if he'd deliberately kept the incident from the selectmen, he might be worried he'd lose his job if the past was dug up."

"He might. Was Mitch being blackmailed?"

"Maybe."

"Is this related to the other questions you were asking? About insurance fraud?"

"I'm beginning to wonder," Merry said.

TRACKING JERRY DUNDEE, Merry had momentarily forgotten Del; but as she walked into the police station, her friend's face rose before her with a painful urgency. Clarence was placing a package into the evidence locker, and through the clear plastic, Merry could plainly see beige clothing. Linen and silk beige clothing, she had little doubt.

"Jenny Baldwin's?" she asked.

Clarence looked at her and winked. "A-no," he said. "Guess again."

"I don't have time."

"Pawh spahrt."

"Come on, Clarence."

"Her husband's."

"Tom's? Tom's fibers were near Del's body?"

"Ayeh."

"You realize what this means."

"Don't have time, Marradith," he said, giving her some of her own medicine.

"He *framed* her. Jenny, I mean. He killed Del and left his wife's bracelet sitting by the body. He left her fingerprints in the kitchen."

"I reckon that's what young Bailey thinks, too. He just left to arrest the poor bahstahd. Fax arrived, by the way."

"From Boston?"

"Ayeh. Yah got that ordah you were lookin' fahr. I left it on yahr desk."

Merry dashed to her office. There it was, and in record time, too.

"There is no Jerry Dundee at the number you gave me," Howie said, leaning around her doorjamb.

"Aw, shit," Merry said. "You're kidding me."

"Nope. I called up and asked for him, and they said, 'Mr. Dundee is no longer employed by Oceanside Resorts.'

Period. I asked for a forwarding number, I asked how long he'd been gone, I asked—"

"Wait a minute. Did you say *Oceanside Resorts?*"

Howie nodded. "The name you had me look for on the Plastech list. Was this guy sinking boats with explosive?"

"Seitz, you're marvelous," Merry said. "Call Oceanside back. Tell them you're an interested investor, tell them anything that comes to mind. Ask them to email their quarterly report. Then dig up everything you possibly can about who runs the operation. Go to the Providence police, if you have to. And plug Dundee's name into the NCIC index, okay?"

The National Crime Information Center database could tell Merry most of what she needed to know about a suspect in a matter of minutes.

"What are you going to do?"

"Request an official copy of Sara Duarte's birth certificate," she said, waving the court order. Though it hardly mattered. The only possible connection was staring her in the face.

AT MERRY'S REQUEST, Tom Baldwin's questioning was delayed until the following morning—Saturday. She and Howie spent the remainder of Friday researching the corporate history of Baldwin Builders, contacting incorporation offices in Delaware, business offices in Providence, and the Water Rights Insurance Company in Boston. Merry and Howie ordered pizza at five o'clock and spent the next three hours deciphering the trail of evidence. The final piece of information they got was from the Registry of Vital Records and Statistics in Boston. Although she had known what it would say, Merry stared at it, unseeing, for a while.

At eight o'clock Saturday morning, Baldwin was sitting handcuffed in the station's conference area. Felix Harper was beside him, fastidious as a cat. Merry had been unable to brief Matt Bailey prior to the session. He hadn't picked up his calls the previous night and he arrived late to the interrogation, eyes bleary and a coffee cup gripped in one hand. He placed himself directly opposite Tom, with a tape recorder between.

"Where were you the night of Adelia Duarte's death?" Bailey began.

"I've told you. At Paul Harris's party at the Yacht Club. Surely you can verify that. Perhaps then you'll explain why the Nantucket police have decided to arrest the Baldwin family for every crime committed this summer."

"I've spoken to Mr. Harris, and I've spoken to a number of his other guests. Apparently there was a period of time during which you stepped out of the club to examine a boat, Mr. Baldwin?"

"I looked at a yacht that was for sale, yes," he said impatiently. "If you recall, I recently lost a vessel in that fiasco at the Town Pier."

Merry, sitting next to Bailey, touched him lightly on the arm. He looked at her and gave way.

"Was that boat insured, Mr. Baldwin?" she asked.

"Of course."

"And the insurer's name?"

"Water Rights. A Boston firm."

"I'm familiar with Water Rights. Interestingly enough, they also insured several commercial fishing boats that sank off the Massachusetts coast during the course of last year. Boats skippered by several of the men who crewed for Del Duarte's father, Joe. As you know, Joe, like Del, is recently deceased."

"What of it?"

"Does this pertain to the matter for which Mr. Baldwin was arrested?" Felix Harper said.

"It does."

"Because if it does *not*, I will advise my client not to answer your questions."

"Fine." Merry turned her chair slightly in Tom's direction. "Are you familiar with the corporations SeaCon and MariTrans, Mr. Baldwin?"

"Can't say that I am." His eyes flicked away from hers, and he rolled his shoulders, as though to ease the ache of his handcuffed wrists.

Merry deliberately gave him an instant to chew on her question. "You haven't heard of them," she said, lifting a publicity folder from a file, "even though, according to this quarterly earnings statement to which I'm referring dated May thirteenth, they were recently liquidated by their parent company—Oceanside Resorts? A company that lists Tom Baldwin as a member of its board of trustees?"

Baldwin studied her face an instant, and his own grew cold. If he could have, Merry thought, Tom would have punched her.

"The trusteeship is a recent appointment," he said. "I can't be expected to know everything Oceanside has done."

"That's a very curious statement, Mr. Baldwin." Merry ignored Matt Bailey's restive movement beside her. "A Jenny Dundee is listed as the chief executive officer of

Oceanside. Am I right in believing that Dundee is your wife's maiden name?"

A hesitation. "It is."

"How does this information bear upon the matter for which Mr. Baldwin was arrested?" Felix Harper broke in. "I must ask you to confine your questioning to the matter at hand."

"I'm with Felix," Matt Bailey said.

"And so the business of your wife's company is something you've ignored," Merry continued, her eyes never leaving the developer's face, "since its incorporation, which I see here was back in"—she paused, making a show of studying the earnings statement—"1997."

"Where did you get that thing?" he said suddenly, leaning painfully across the table, as though to snatch the quarterly report with his teeth.

"This information is a matter of public record, Mr. Baldwin."

"Merry," Matt Bailey said, almost seething, "could we hold the stuff about Baldwin's business and get on to the murder, please?"

"Certainly, Matt," she said graciously. "I was merely establishing background. And a motive for incriminating Jenny Baldwin."

"I did not incriminate my wife," Tom said.

Matt looked at her, then at Baldwin, and opened his mouth. Merry preempted him.

"Would you excuse us a moment, Tom?" she said, smiling sweetly. "Look after him, would you, Seitz?"

Matt followed her into her office. She closed the door.

"Here's the point," Merry said. "Baldwin's been hiding assets in a series of spurious corporations, most of them subsidiaries of a company incorporated under his wife's maiden name. SeaCon and MariTrans owned commercial trawlers that were deliberately sunk for their insurance value—three that I know of, but probably dozens insured by different companies around New England. The money was absorbed by Oceanside Resorts, Jenny's company, of which Tom's a trustee. Just yesterday at a selectmen's meeting, he was pumping a bid by Oceanside to rebuild the Town Pier with a commercial condo complex. It sounded like they bought it hook, line, and sinker. Tom denied any personal connection to the company in pushing for the contract, which we know is a lie."

"I still don't see what this has to do with Del Duarte," Matt said stubbornly. "You're derailing my line of questioning."

"Matt, try very hard to concentrate on what I'm about to say. From what I hear, the Baldwin marriage is on the rocks. A divorce proceeding would put Jenny on the defensive and make her cling to any money she could. It would also throw unwelcome light on Baldwin's corporate investments. But if Jenny goes to jail for murdering Del, Tom will get control of her assets."

"So he murdered Del and framed his wife?"

"Yes."

"He just screwed up on the fibers?"

"I guess so. A lot of people don't realize they leave a fabric trail everywhere they go."

Matt mulled this over. "Why Del?"

Merry flipped open her file and handed him the Registry of Vital Records fax. "He's Sara Duarte's father."

Matt Bailey whistled under his breath. "And did Del want him to divorce Jenny?"

"I don't know," Merry said. "I've no idea how she really felt about Tom Baldwin. I never even knew they were involved. She worked with him for five years, but when she left to have Sara, she stayed away for quite a while. If it was marriage she wanted, she took her time."

Merry paused, remembering Del's tight-lipped reaction when Tom tried to feed Sara at her father's funeral. "It looked to me like Del wanted to be left alone to raise her daughter as she chose. Tom may not have trusted her to do that. He may have been afraid she'd tell Jenny about Sara, and Jenny would file for divorce, and he'd lose his house of cards. So he tried to get rid of one problem—Jenny—by framing her for the murder of his other problem—Del."

"I think we should ask him," Bailey said.

"I've got one more area of questioning, Bailey."

He looked at her, and to her surprise, she saw a grudging respect in his eyes. "Go ahead," he said. "Just explain it to me later, will you?"

WHEN THEY RETURNED to the table, Tom Baldwin was staring intently at its surface, his expression impossible to read.

"Did you kill Mitch Davis, Tom, or was that your brother-in-law Jerry?" Merry said as she slid into her seat.

"What in the hell—"

"Detective Folger, I really must protest," said Felix Harper. "Mr. Baldwin has not been charged with the murder of Mitch Davis."

"Mitch Davis's death is related to the murder for which Tom Baldwin is charged."

"I would like my protest noted in the record."

"The Town Pier, Tom," Merry said. "The bomb. Oceanside received a shipment of the plastic explosive used to blow up a boat you owned. The marine superintendent was shot point-blank in the back of the head. Execution-style. Almost like a Mafia hit, I thought when I read the coroner's report." She waited for Tom Baldwin to react. He didn't.

"Poor Mitch. He was slated to lose, whatever he did. You had Jerry Dundee work on him for a year, telling him that if he didn't back the Oceanside Resorts plan for developing the pier—a plan that would bring you ridiculous amounts of profit, and that you'd finance from insurance fraud—you'd revive the scandal that ended his Coast Guard career. He had two young children. He couldn't afford to lose his job."

"This rambling is really inexcusable," Felix Harper said.

"Not to mention complete bullshit," Baldwin said between his teeth.

"I imagine Mitch hesitated for a long time," Merry continued. "Weighed the pros and cons. He'd worked so hard to give the pier a facelift; he'd outmaneuvered the selectmen, taken criticism from ignorant taxpayers, been the target of a lot of envy. He'd successfully rebuilt his life after a crippling mistake. And Jerry Dundee was asking him to throw his work under the bus." She leaned into Baldwin's face, forcing him to meet her eyes, to hang on every word.

"But better his work than his kids. You wore him down, didn't you? Mitch Davis set the bomb that torched the pier. He'd been with the Coast Guard. He understood explosives. And after Jerry got him the Plastech and saw that the job was done, he made sure Mitch would never talk about it. In all the smoke and confusion and chaos, nobody would hear a gunshot. And nobody would see who pulled the trigger."

"You've gone completely mad," Baldwin said. "You've made a single family the center of a fantastic conspiracy."

"That's not what Jerry Dundee says."

There was a moment's breathless silence. Tom Baldwin drew a shaky breath. "Jerry? You've—talked to Jerry?"

"I haven't. The NYPD has. We put out a national warrant for Dundee's arrest yesterday afternoon, and they picked him up last night. Told him you were in custody. He didn't hold out very long. Did you know he's an alleged hit man for the Castiglione crime family, Tom? Execution-style shootings are his specialty. New York was pretty glad to talk to him. They've been looking for a reason to put him away. I think you just gave them one."

Something in Tom Baldwin's face shattered. "Jerry talked? That son of a—"

Felix Harper placed a restraining hand on his client's arm. "I wouldn't say anything right now if I were you, Tom," he said. "None of this touches on the matter for which you were arrested." He looked at Matt Bailey, and Bailey looked at Merry.

An enormous weight lifted from her chest. Tom knew it was all over. Whether he confessed or not, the trail of evidence was there. Jerry Dundee's testimony would drown him deeper. However good a lawyer Felix might be, his client was trapped.

Bailey cleared his throat and looked down at his notes, trying to regain his focus. He'd last asked about a boat that Baldwin said he'd considered buying—while in all probability he was on Milk Street, killing Del and fram-ing Jenny.

"The evening of Del Duarte's death, approximately how long would you estimate you looked at the Yacht Club boat that was for sale?"

"I walked around it a few times. I glanced into the main cabin long enough to see it had an icebox instead of a refrigerator, and that was enough. I don't need an outmoded secondhand piece of junk."

"Guests at the party put your absence at roughly half an hour."

Tom shrugged. "Who's a judge of time at a party? They don't know how long I was gone. I couldn't tell you how long I was gone."

"Long enough to get to Milk Street, murder Del, wipe your fingerprints from the harpoon, and leave clean glasses by a bottle of your wife's favorite scotch," Merry said, her anger rising.

"You needn't respond to that, Tom," Felix said sooth-ingly. He looked increasingly less comfortable in his role, however.

"I had no reason on earth to murder Del Duarte."

"How would you characterize your relationship with Miss Duarte?" Bailey asked.

"Characterize? I don't know. She was an employee for years. A good kid. I was very fond of her. Felt bad as hell about the trouble she was in when she left. But she wouldn't take any help from me."

"Just a hundred thousand dollars when she got back?" Merry broke in.

"What?" Tom Baldwin looked perplexed.

"A hundred thousand dollars, Tom. In her bank

account. It corresponds to some certificates of deposit that were cashed in last week at the Pacific National Bank. Certificates in the name of Tom and Jenny Baldwin."

"I don't know what you're talking about."

"And you're saying Del was just an employee?"

For the first time that morning, Tom looked genuinely bewildered.

Merry pulled out the facsimile of Sara's birth certificate. "Mr. Harper," she said to the lawyer, "I'd like you to note that this is a copy of Sara Duarte's birth certificate. Please note the name of the father."

Felix settled his glasses on his nose and studied the fax. All expression dropped from his pale face, and his eyes slowly rose to meet Merry's. He understood.

"What is that?" Tom said.

"A copy of the form you stole from Del's filing cabinet. The one that shows you fathered her child."

"I fathered her child? *I* did? That's not possible," Tom Baldwin said. A look of panic came over his face. "I can't have children."

There was a moment's silence around the table.

"Are you certain?" Merry said.

"I don't have any, do I?"

"That could be your wife's difficulty, not yours."

"My doctor wouldn't agree."

"What exactly is the nature of your—problem, Mr. Baldwin?"

He looked intensely uncomfortable. "I had mumps. Low sperm count."

"That wouldn't preclude fathering a child. It simply makes it highly unlikely."

He considered this, picked up the certificate, stared at

his name typed on its face. "Little Sara," he whispered. "Mine. She never told me. Oh, my God." Tears pooled in his eyes. Unable to blot them with his hands cuffed, Tom was forced to let them trickle down his cheeks. It was a curiously humbling sight, coming as it did after so much bluster and anger. Merry glanced at Matt Bailey, and at Seitz, who shrugged in mute shock. They had watched Tom Baldwin bluff his way through an hour's worth of questions, with varying degrees of transparency, but his emotion now seemed absolutely genuine.

"Are you saying, Mr. Baldwin, that you had no idea Sara Duarte was your daughter?" Merry said.

Tom shook his head. Felix Harper reached over with a pristine white handkerchief and dabbed at his client's eyes.

"You didn't take the birth certificate from Del's filing cabinet the night of her death?"

"I told you," he said, his voice high-pitched and dry, "I didn't kill her. I'll confess to everything else—Felix, don't try to stop me, it doesn't matter anymore. I'll confess to the insurance fraud, the mess at the Town Pier, the plans for Oceanside. It's all true. I spent years laying the groundwork for it. But I never killed Del—I loved her. And I had no idea that beautiful little girl was mine. If I had, I'd have thrown up everything for her."

Despite the awkwardness of his cuffed wrists, Tom dropped his head to the conference table's cool surface, his face turned away from them, eyes staring at the wall. "Sara," he said. "Little Sara."

Chapter 28

MERRY LEFT THE station feeling more confused than when she had arrived. If Tom Baldwin was guilty of Del's death, his denial made no sense in the face of all that he had admitted. He was willing to claim responsibility for the Town Pier arson, not to mention insurance fraud and Mitch Davis. So why balk at confessing to Del's murder—unless he was truly innocent of it? And if Tom didn't kill Del, who framed Jenny Baldwin?

She stood blinking in the sunlight. A summer intern was busy in the station lot, washing a patrol car. It was then she saw Joshua Field.

He was standing with his bike on the public path that ran along Fairgrounds Road, looking like any other kid on a summer's Saturday morning. He wore no helmet and his hair was tousled as though he'd just rolled out of bed. His entire air was casual, but behind his narrow tortoiseshell glasses, Merry could feel him scrutinizing her. He'd been watching the station.

She walked over to him. "Hi, Josh."

He ducked his head in greeting, one hand on his bike's saddle and the other on the handlebars. He seemed at a loss for words.

"Waiting for your uncle?"

He shrugged and looked down the street, as though searching for a friend, or afraid of being seen by one.

"He's not being released, I'm afraid," Merry said. "He'll be escorted to Barnstable by plane later today, under the sheriff's protection. He'll be held there and arraigned on Monday."

"He didn't kill her," Josh said

"How do you know?"

"He wouldn't, that's all." Josh's fingers tapped the bike saddle nervously.

"Tell me about the night Del Duarte died," Merry said.

"I've been wanting to. I just didn't know if I should, or who was in worse trouble. Do you think Uncle Tom'll be convicted?"

"Could be."

"That's not right," Josh said. "She wasn't home."

"Del wasn't home? The night she died?"

"Not the woman. Aunt *Jen*. She wasn't home when she said she was."

"You mean, she has no alibi. No one could say she'd been home. That's slightly different."

He shook his head. "Nope. I mean *she wasn't there*. I went back, you see. Around nine o'clock. I left the house at seven, met some buddies, had burgers at the Atlantic Cafe, and ran out of money. They wanted to see the movie at the Dreamland and hit a couple of bars afterward. Nobody had any cash. So I went home."

"And your aunt wasn't in bed with a headache," Merry said, understanding now.

"The bed was unmade, like she'd been lying on it. I know, because I went up to her room. She kept fifty bucks in her upper left-hand bureau drawer, and I figured I'd put it back Monday when I could get to the bank. She took away my ATM card when I got arrested," he added, by way of explanation.

"She wasn't somewhere else in the house?"

"Her car was gone. I didn't think anything about it at the time. Just took the money and went back to the Dreamland—the show was starting in twenty minutes. She was in bed when I got home, though. And later, when she was arrested and said she'd been there all the time, I wondered about it. But I wasn't going to contradict her. It was too serious."

"It was, Josh," Merry said. "Serious enough to put your uncle in jail."

THE BALDWIN HOUSE seemed deserted when Merry drove up the drive with Matt Bailey and Howie Seitz. Mindful of the Dundee expertise with guns, they all had the instinct to move cautiously. Jenny met them at the door before they had time to ring.

"Where's Tom?" she said, looking past them. "Surely you've released him by this time?"

"Unfortunately not, Mrs. Baldwin," Matt Bailey said. "He's being flown to Barnstable on multiple charges of arson, fraud, and conspiracy to commit murder. Quite a list. But that's not why we're here." He cleared his throat and stood a little straighter. "Jenny Dundee Baldwin, I arrest you for the murder of Adelia Duarte. It is our duty to inform you of your rights. Patrolman Seitz?"

"You have the right to remain silent," Howie said. "You have the right to obtain counsel and—"

"Good heavens," Jenny said, with an amused smile. "We're not going through that nonsense again, are we? I heard it on Wednesday. You didn't have a case then. You don't have one now. Run along and find someone else to bother. I have to pack for the Cape."

She made as if to close the front door in their faces.

Despite herself, Merry was impressed. Dave Grizutto was right; Jenny Baldwin had everybody fooled. The private-school air and the conservative clothes, the unmade-up face and the plain brown hair. Unimpeachable marks of a respectable pedigree, cloaking the sister of a Mafia hit man. Money must be terribly important to her. And money had been her downfall.

Merry set her foot on the doorstep and leaned into the house. "One question, Jenny. Why did you report the missing fifty dollars? It was a small detail, but one you shouldn't have missed."

"I beg your pardon?"

"The fifty dollars. You said it was pilfered from your drawer. That was the word you used—*pilfered*. A word for a theft in the family, not a burglary. Did you know Josh had taken it?"

"Josh had nothing to do with it. The money was stolen when the bracelet disappeared."

"Actually, Josh says he took it the night Adelia Duarte was murdered. He was out with friends and returned to your house in search of cash before the Dreamland's second show, which was around nine-fifteen that night. Only you weren't in your bedroom when he pilfered your drawer. You were committing murder."

"That's absurd."

"I know. The whole thing is absurd. You must have discovered the money was gone a few days later, and wondered who'd taken it. Tom? Or Josh? If you were going to report the theft of the bracelet as you planned—to begin the process of incriminating your husband—you couldn't ignore the fifty dollars."

Merry stepped into the front hallway and, disconcerted, Jenny edged backward.

"You were afraid Tom or Josh might mention taking it, and say they'd seen the bracelet in your drawer when they did. You couldn't be sure. So you thought you had to admit you'd discovered the money's loss up front. But it was a detail that didn't fit with the story we were supposed to believe—that Tom murdered Del and framed you. We were supposed to think he'd taken the bracelet for that purpose, and left it near her body.

"But fifty dollars? Why would Tom pocket your fifty dollars? It was a detail that kept surfacing in the back of my brain."

"I don't know what you're talking about," Jenny said.

"Your plan. You came down with a convenient migraine the night you knew Tom had a party and Josh was supposed to be out all evening. You went to Del's house, wearing Tom's beige linen pants and silk knit sweater—he's only an inch or so taller than you, isn't he? Heels would take care of that. And Del let you in."

"I was in bed."

"Not at nine o'clock. Josh will swear to the fact that the house was empty and your car was gone from the garage."

Howie edged into the hall with a his phone in his hand. He liked to take notes on it. Matt Bailey was right behind him.

Jenny surveyed the three of them. Then she led them into her cool, airy living room with the view of the harbor beyond the windows. She sank down on the sofa. "I hadn't figured on Josh. I thought I'd worked everything out, but there was bound to be something I missed. I knew it—I just couldn't pinpoint what it was. The past twenty-four hours have been the worst."

"With Tom exactly where you wanted him."

"Yes. I was so close."

"You hate him that much?"

Emotion rippled over Jenny's face. "He brought it on himself," she said. "The way he's treated me."

"What was it?" Merry said. "The affair with Del, or the fear of losing the money?"

Jenny took her time answering. "Neither, really. He'd done the unforgivable—the *unforgivable*—thing. He'd given her the child he could never give me. Or never *would* give me. He didn't know what he'd done—I realize that. But *I* knew, from the moment I saw that child at Joe Duarte's funeral. She looked like Tom's baby pictures, every inch of her. She had the same bowlegged gait, and his mother's extraordinary red hair. *And he didn't see it.* I thought the entire room must know, must be looking and comparing and taking notes. I wanted that woman off the island, and her brat with her."

"And so you gave her a hundred thousand dollars to leave."

"You knew about that? I suppose you know about everything." Jenny's eyes dropped to her tanned fingers, obsessively smoothing a pleat in her cotton skirt. "She wouldn't keep it. She told me she'd decided to stay here. I'm afraid that made me—very angry. And so I had to do something."

"Did you know she kept a harpoon in her house?"

"No. I planned to spike her drink. But we never got around to having one. She didn't like scotch. I lost my temper—it's always been a tad uncontrollable—and she picked up the harpoon. I think she thought I'd be afraid of her. I wasn't."

"There were two types of blood on the floor," Merry said.

Jenny raised the long sleeve of her blouse and revealed a neat bandage on one arm. "I had a bit of trouble taking the harpoon away from her. I grabbed the shaft and wrestled her for it. I'm much stronger than I look, you know."

"You look strong enough."

She studied the bandage intently. "My, that dart was sharp," she said. "I had no trouble at all shoving it between her ribs."

"And then you left the scotch bottle with your fingerprints on it, and the pieces of copper chain."

"Well, that *was* the plan."

"Why, Jenny?" Merry said. "Why did you have to kill Del? Did the affair matter so much?"

"I didn't expect it to," she said, sounding surprised. "Tom told me about it after the girl left Nantucket—but of course, he never thought the baby was his. He thought she'd two-timed him, and it hurt his pride. That's why he made a clean breast of it to me. He felt like an ass. Wanted to make a new start. But I never could."

"Forgive him?"

"Oh, I suppose I forgave him—in the incessant way of married women. I forgave him. I just couldn't forget it. Couldn't trust him again. Every time he was out late, or missed an appointment, I'd wonder who it was this time. Until eventually I stopped caring. Or thought I did."

"And then you saw the baby."

"Yes. Tom would have thrown me out like a torn shirt if he realized Del had been faithful and the child was his. There'd be nothing to keep him, then. And suddenly I realized I didn't really *want* Tom anymore. What I *really* wanted was revenge. I wanted the money, the house, and Tom's life ruined. And I wanted to get away with it."

"You killed Del out of selfishness."

"She didn't matter very much."

"She mattered to me," Merry said softly.

"I'd like to say I'm sorry," Jenny said, folding and refolding her pleat with deft fingers, "but I haven't felt that way in weeks. I've felt—powerful. I've felt like I had a purpose. I could show the world that I was a hapless victim, and all the time it was Tom who would pay. I knew the shell game he'd been playing with my money, the boats that sank, the plans for the pier. He'd used my brother. No one would believe he'd balk at a simple killing. And framing me was entirely plausible."

"Just one thing," Merry said. "Why did you take Sara's birth certificate?"

"I wanted him to die not knowing," Jenny said. "I never wanted him to have the *satisfaction* of knowing." She lifted one wrist to rebutton the cuff of her blouse, hiding the bandage, and then stood up. "He knows now, I suppose."

"He does."

Jenny Baldwin reached for her lightship purse and placed it firmly over one arm. "Then I've failed all around. Well, gentlemen," she said, turning to Matt Bailey and Howie Seitz, " If we hurry, the sheriff can take us both on the same plane."

Chapter 29

Sᴜɴᴅᴀʏ ᴡᴀs Rᴇʙᴇᴄᴄᴀ's Quaker day of rest, and she was nowhere in sight when Merry pulled up before Peter Mason's door. Rafe, she knew, was at the Greengage; she'd seen the red Rover parked on Quince street, with its distinctive CRNBERY vanity plate. Peter was completely alone. She reminded herself to leave as quickly as possible.

He was in the kitchen at the back of the house, whistling cheerfully over the sound of running water, and her knock went unheeded. So she walked around to the deck and tapped on the screen, watching as his head jerked up in involuntary surprise, his eyes narrowing against the glare beyond the door.

"It's me," she said. "I came to tell you it's all over."

He shut off the water and stared at her, hands dripping. "Come in and talk to me," he said.

She pushed open the screen and walked into the kitchen. Set her bag down on the table. Pulled out a chair and slumped into it.

"What happened?"

"Do I have to go over it?"

"Eventually. I can't stand the suspense forever."

Whether he was discussing Del's murder or something

else, she didn't like to think. She brushed her blonde hair back from her eyes and looked at him.

"I want to thank you for sending me to see Lisa Davis. Talking to her unlocked the whole case."

"She called me after you'd stopped by. Apparently you made her feel a lot better."

"Only temporarily, I'm afraid. Mitch torched the Town Pier, Peter. And then was shot by Tom Baldwin."

"By *Tom?*"

"Well, his brother-in-law, actually. It's too complicated."

"You need a gin and tonic."

"What time is it?"

"Late enough," he said firmly. He fetched a lime and a knife, filling the room with the stark freshness of citrus. "Let's talk about murder some other time, okay? You need a break. I propose dinner *à deux*. Meaning, we both pitch in and scrounge something to eat."

"Is it dinnertime?"

"It could be. A summer evening with nothing ahead of us. Everything is open to negotiation."

"I'm so tired, Peter," Merry said, putting her head in her hands. "I haven't had time to realize how drained I am. All I can think of is Del. I thought at first she'd died because she'd stumbled on something important about Joe's death. But he probably *did* just fall overboard; sometimes the obvious is what happened. Instead she was killed because Jenny Baldwin was growing old and childless and unhappy in her marriage, and Del had youth and the love of Jenny's husband, and a child he never thought he'd create. Del died because she had so many reasons to live."

"This is going to take some telling," Peter said. "Here's your drink."

He listened without a word while Merry rambled through the history of SeaCon and Oceanside, Sara's birth certificate and Jenny Baldwin's brother. When she had done, she looked up and saw the shadows lengthening across the polished wood of his kitchen floor, and Peter's face very still.

"A long story," she concluded, "and none of it important, really."

"I wouldn't say that. You've solved several crimes at once."

"I'm not happy about it. I just feel completely alone. When I was little—probably about six—my father was called to a house on Milk Street where a woman had just died of cancer. She was lying in her bed, with a sheet over her face, and her little girl was crying in the room across the hall. They were all by themselves. Dad brought Del back to our house and put her to bed with me, and went off to find Joe drinking himself sick in the pilothouse of his boat.

"He could have locked Joe in a cell, but he didn't. Instead he slapped him into shape, got him back to our kitchen, and poured coffee down his throat until three o'clock in the morning. And when my mother committed suicide, Joe Duarte was right there in our kitchen, with Del, to pour coffee down my father's."

Peter reached for her hand, held it.

"Who'll pour coffee for me, Peter?" Merry said. "In the middle of the night, when disaster strikes again?"

"Is that why you're here?"

"I don't know."

"I wouldn't have you go to anyone else."

The intensity behind the words brought her eyes up

to his. She saw the unguarded feeling written on his face, and the decision he made not to take it back. He held her gaze an instant, and her stomach turned over. *Oh God,* she thought. *Oh God, no.*

Peter rose from his chair and knelt in front of her, her legs against his chest, his hands taking hers. He was alert and passive at once, the way an animal holds itself before springing, all the possibility of power and release poised in a muscular stillness. He said nothing, but the space between them filled with a static current, singing, alive, dangerously binding. Merry leaned away, fighting something akin to terror at his touch.

And then she took refuge in indifference. She could break this mood—reach for her purse, comment on the time, say something flip about murder making strange bedfellows. She opened her mouth to do it.

He saw the sardonic expression gathering, and laid his forefinger gently, inevitably, against her lips.

"You could break this mood in a minute," he said. "I know. And leave me jagged as a broken glass. You could do that. Merry, Merry—don't. It isn't necessary."

The touch of his finger on her mouth was like a cool seal to a pact struck long ago. She closed her eyes and reached for his palm with both hands, burying her face in it. She'd backed away from Peter once before, in the rose garden of a murderer, when he'd handed her a flower complete with thorns—a gesture implicit with the intensity and pain of offering himself. She had been afraid of him then, an instinctive fear born of ignorance. She knew him far better now, and knew why she was afraid. She wanted him more than anything or anyone she had ever known in her life. Peter Mason had the power to strip her of everything she was; the power to take her over, body and soul.

He lifted her face, a hand framing either cheekbone, his long fingers tangled in her hair. The gray eyes were burning now. "There's my girl," he said.

He took her in the shadowed half-light of his room under the eaves, the early June moonlight throwing his profile against the sloping wings of the ceiling, the sharp planes of his face picked out in black and white. He took her slowly, spinning out the midnight, making something holy from the ritual of shed clothing. He ran a finger like a burning match down the curve of silk covering her breast, then tore at the buttons of her blouse with his teeth until they fell in a rainy patter on the floor. He curled a hip under his palm, found the crease behind her knee with its faint dampness of sweat, dipped his mouth in the hollows of her collarbone.

Merry saw him outlined against the rafters, dark as a thunderhead hovering over her body, the power of his frame leashed by a terrible gentleness; it occurred to her that he was afraid that he might break her in half. She fought him over this—wanting to tear him loose, to force him into the tide that was sweeping the length of her body. She was a small boat, a wooden dinghy, the kind that fishermen used to launch in the surf years ago, meeting the sea just before its crest, knowing survival meant going through the wave, not foundering in it. She tried to tell him of the sea, of the wave curling in whiteness over her head, but her mouth was locked in his and he had taken her breath. She clung to him, to the pull and thrust of the current, feeling herself spiraling in a whirl-pool, drowning him with her. His fingers found her hair again, arching her neck back and her mouth up to his; she opened her eyes and saw his staring into her own, gray as the Atlantic under rain.

Much later, as Merry sat in her Explorer with the engine idling, forcing herself to go home, she watched the dog, Ney, round up the sheep in the early-morning sunlight.

"Stay," Peter said, leaning in through her window. "Stay here forever."

"I know why Alison left you." Her mouth felt dry.

"What does that mean?"

"You have power, Peter. I'm not talking about sex—or not *just* sex. I'm talking about the soul. About self-possession. Anyone who loved you would be completely controlled by you. That sort of feeling is what some women look for all their lives—a consuming passion to lose themselves in. I just find it frightening."

"Is that how this feels?"

"It does this morning."

"Consuming?"

"You bring me to my knees."

He turned to the climbing rose that trailed over the post-and-rail fence, tore off three perfect blooms, and brought them to her wordlessly. They spilled through the Explorer's open window in all the headiness of June scent. She looked at them and felt her throat constrict. Another offering of himself in the rose, an act painful in its honesty. He would never tell her he loved her, and weight her with a sense of obligation; he would make her choose him for herself. But the knowledge of love was there all the same.

Peter stood away from the car. A thorn had torn his

finger, and a bright bead of blood was gathering there. He seemed not to feel it. The sight of his hands brought back the sense of them on her skin, and she took a deep breath. She could not look at his face.

Merry turned the car toward home and fled down the drive, her lap filled with flowers.

Continue reading for a preview of
the next Merry Folger mystery

DEATH
IN A MOOD
INDIGO

Chapter One

"I COULD HELP," Nan Markham said. "I could."
Even to her own ears her voice was plaintive and young,
the voice of a neglected baby. "I could carry the water for
you. In my pail."

Nan lifted a dull-red plastic sand bucket and waggled it
tentatively toward her brother's unfeeling back. But Cecil
was absorbed in his digging, the castle's trench a widening perfection of scarp and contrascarp, the turrets rising
wetly against the blue-black of the surf. He had worked at
the fortifications for days—each afternoon when school
was over, and now for the bulk of Saturday. What the tide
and the weather destroyed in the hours of darkness, Cecil
patiently rebuilt, in a determined contest with time and
the sands. The two children were always out-of-doors,
despite the gloom of the deserted beach, the fitful showers of chill rain. Even immersion in this dispiriting spring
was preferable to being at home.

Nan brushed back a strand of bright-red hair and
hugged her sweatered arms closer to her body. The wind
scoured her cheek with stinging grains.

"Mummie said to let me help."

The last resort of the tagalong: the invocation of
Mummie.

Disgusted with herself and her eight-year-old weakness—disgusted with her brother and his silence and his solitary building—she kicked at the nearest rampart. "Stupid. Stupid old castle. I *hate* your castle, Cecil!"

Her wanton destruction left him unmoved. That was Cecil's way. He did not react like other boys—with a shove or a blow or the careful plotting of revenge. He did not offer curses. He merely looked at his little sister, incomprehension and tedium filling his face, and said, "Go away, Nan. There's going to be a battle."

And so Nan turned disconsolately from the rampart she had ruined and trudged off toward her secret place in the dunes to sit on a piece of driftwood and arrange a tea party. She used shells for teacups and her thoughts for friends. And Satchmo—her beloved Satchmo, his fur matted from repeated bouts with sand and salt water, his huge body shapeless from lying too long on the kitchen floor, his legs dangerously arthritic as he stepped each morning into the pounding surf—Satchmo settled down in the dune grass opposite her and waited eternally for his tea.

A gull cried from its perch a few feet away, and Nan turned to stare at it: malevolent dark eye, cruel mustard beak. It lifted one reptilian claw and flicked an orange peel her way.

What do the gulls do, she wondered, *when flying is not enough?*

The clouds were lowering on the rain-swept horizon, but before the iron grip of storm closed the sun's eyes forever, a faint glimmer of light shafted across the turbulent sea. Lord Cecil of Trevarre raised a hand to his brow and gazed intently at the enemy fleet and its forest of billowing black sails. In salute to the vanishing sun, a fourteen-pound gun roared from the flagship's bow, a challenge and a curse in its orange flare; and seconds later the ball whistled past Trevarre's noble head.

"Get down, my lord!" his lieutenant cried, and gripped his ankle in desperation.

"We shall not prevail by skulking within doors," Lord Cecil shot back, his expression both proud and bitter. "The castle can avail us nothing now. To the fore, lads, and show a brave face! Or die in the attempt!"

He sprang down from the breastworks, his feet finding soft purchase on the sand below, and raced to the water's edge, his standard raised high. The first of the enemy's landing boats were racing toward shore, filled to their gunwales with scores of men; in a matter of moments his own would be outnumbered. To die, then, and die nobly in defense of what he held most dear—this was his last, his only, destiny.

Gordon, his faithful retainer, appeared suddenly at his side holding the reins of his stallion, Satchmo; the mettlesome beast pawed the ground, his iron shoes ringing sparks—(no, not sparks, since the beach was sandy, not rocky like the beaches in England). The mettlesome beast pawed deep furrows in the shore's wet sand. Lord Cecil took hold of Satchmo's mane and swung himself into the saddle, his eyes fixed upon the enemy boats. As with one voice, the black-clad invaders cried aloud and jumped into the shallows, their brutal faces intent upon one man and his destruction—Trevarre.

A wave furled and crashed, mightier than its fellows, racing ahead to storm the beach's heights. But Lord Cecil and his small surviving band stood ready.

WATER POURED INTO the gap between Cecil's sneakered feet, foamed and swirled across his shoelaces, licked at the cuffs of his faded jeans. He gave a ferocious yell and thrust out his strong right saber arm, his invisible horse rearing high; then he tore down to the edge of the surf. The wave retreated in routed terror. Victory was in his very grasp.

Cowards. They had turned tail and taken to their boats, beating desperately against the tide to their black-sailed ships, rather than face his heroic band. Lord Cecil of Trevarre raised his saber arm in scorn and triumph and cried aloud. As if in answer, Satchmo neighed.

"Cecil! Cecil!"

He looked over to the dunes, exhilaration torn by annoyance. "What?"

Nan's bright head, crowned with a wreath of the first daffodils, emerged from the fringe of beach plum that fronted the derelict foundations of Codfish Park. January storms had swept several houses out to sea, and the remaining few looked likely to follow. Nan had probably scavenged the flowers from some abandoned front steps, like a camp follower rifling a battlefield's dead. As she scrambled up, the dog Satchmo groaned, a sound from deep in his blasted frame. He turned to stare at Cecil, something caught between his jaws, and then slowly, creakily, he trotted in Nan's wake. She ran pell-mell down the beach.

"Look!"

She was offering Cecil what looked like a twig— strange, since twigs came from trees, and there were none so near the beach. He took it from her fingers, his brow furrowed.

"I found it," she said, breathless. "In the sand, while I was digging. There are lots of others if you dig far enough."

And as he listened and turned the twig in his hand, Cecil felt the beginning of an inner excitement—something that seemed to spread from Trevarre's sea-drenched socks until it reached his noble heart.

For what Nan had found was a bone.

THE RAIN THAT had threatened all morning commenced in earnest an hour after lunch, as Peter Mason and Rafe da Silva grunted and strained over Meredith Folger's dining-room table. It was not that lunch had proved difficult to consume, or required a certain strenuous attention, but rather that the table itself was massive and dense, a veritable monolith in mahogany. And the table was sitting in the midst of Merry's front yard, imperiled by the sudden rain, and obdurately resisting its removal to the bed of Rafe's truck.

"Can I help?"

Merry was dancing around the two men as they strained over her board, feeling useless and very much like a *girl*. "I can get up on the tailgate and help you lift it from there—"

"Get outta the way," Rafe spat between clenched teeth. His perpetually tanned skin was streaming with something other than rain, and the distinctive odor of laboring male emanated from his T-shirt. "*Move.*"

Merry scuttled backward to the doorway of her family home on Tattle Court and felt her grandfather's arm encircle her shoulders. "Be glad you have help," Ralph Waldo Folger told her. "Even if it's as stubborn as the day is long. You aren't going anywhere with that table alone."

"It's not their need for gratitude that galls me, Ralph," she said, and crossed her arms against her damp green slicker. Her fingers were chill and reddening from the raw April day. "I could give them that. It's the female adulation. The groveling, you know? Just to get a lousy table moved."

"And a mattress, and a sofa, and a couple of easy chairs," her grandfather replied cheerfully. "Guess I'll check on that pea soup. You'll be wanting it, I expect, before long. You hardly ate anything at lunch."

Merry looked over her shoulder as he disappeared in the direction of the kitchen, feeling a sharp stab of doubt. Ralph was always worried about how much she ate—and though she would no longer be eating most of her meals in his kitchen, old habits died hard. She knew he would be knocking on the door of her apartment sometime this week, with a pan of lasagna, or a jar of soup, or some corn muffins he'd just whipped up. Another granddaughter might find his attention irritating—but, suddenly, all Merry could think about was that tonight Ralph would be eating without her.

She had dreamed of this day for months—all through the relentless snows of an unusually brutal winter and the rains of a late-blooming spring. Years of careful saving had finally reaped a reward: Merry had signed a year's lease on a small apartment—a guest suite over a neighbor's garage, really—that commenced this very weekend.

January had found her sitting rapt and silent in the glow of Peter Mason's fireplace, browsing linens catalogs; February was dishes and glassware. Did she want teacups, or mugs? Why not both? And what sort of wineglasses? She considered balloon- and tulip-shaped, hefted them in her mind, all but felt the misty beading of a well-chilled chardonnay.

In March, Merry abandoned economy and purchased the Islander's Special—a fifty-dollar round-trip ticket on the local commuter airline—for a weekend of mall hopping in Hyannis. There she bought cheap bookshelves and a small television, two lamps, an iron-and-glass floor vase Peter declared was an escapee from a medieval dungeon, a patchwork quilt handmade in China, and assorted throw rugs of sisal and hemp. She bought a garlic press and hand towels. Three excellently forged pots with steel handles. And a tin of English tea leaves—loose, unfettered, wildly redolent—and a sieve-like ball for steeping them. She ordered everything shipped to Nantucket by the next ferry and boarded her return flight feeling spent and slightly intoxicated. She was moving to her own home at last.

Gone would be the clutter of Tattle Court—the piles of junk mail on the dining-room table; the collection of nineteenth-century blubber-cutting tools from some forgotten Folger's whaling ship; the unfinished portrait of her brother Billy, awaiting her dead mother's hand. And gone, she thought, as she caught a snatch now of Ralph Waldo's singing over the whirr of the kitchen blender, would be all the comfort of wordless love.

Well, not quite gone. She was moving only three blocks away.

"Hey, Mer," Rafe da Silva said.

She emerged from her musings to find the dining-room table safely embedded in the truck, a plastic tarp shielding it from the rain. Peter was slumped on the bumper, his dark hair turning black in the downpour. Rafe leaned by his side.

"We need the keys."

"To the truck?"

"To your apartment," Rafe answered patiently. "There's no way that bed's going in the back with the table taking all that room. Besides, your neighbor's been bugging us to let her out of the driveway."

Tattle Court was grandly but optimistically named: in fact, it was little more than a sandy track divided among three houses. Rafe's truck had been blocking the exit to Fair Street for nearly two hours.

"Let's go," Merry said quickly, as she felt for the keys beneath her slicker and ducked out into the rain.

The flickering light of the ship's lantern, held high in Gordon's hand, threw Lord Cecil's broad-shouldered shadow monstrously across the sand. Trevarre stood silently next to his faithful retainer, his eyes intent on the bent backs of the two navvies grunting and heaving over the open pit. As a shovel lifted its burden of sandy soil, another bone glinted whitely in the fitful lantern flame—bones, the pirate's age-old signal of warning, left to guard a hidden treasure. A menace to the faint of heart; an invitation to the brave. Lord Cecil felt a stirring of familiar excitement. They must be very close now to the steel-bound leather casket, the gleam of jewels too long obscured from the light of day.

A clink of metal against metal—and he fell to his knees, thrusting his men aside, intent upon the smooth surface of the chest's domed lid. A moment of exertion for his prying hands; then the treasure came free—

CECIL SAT BACK on his heels in the sand, Nan wordless and awestruck at his side. Until this moment it had never occurred to him that the bones might be *human*.

And holding the thing like this in his hands—the cracked eye sockets encrusted with damp sand, speaking hollowly of death; the upper jaw devoid of its teeth—the fantasies of Lord Cecil, master of Trevarre, gave way to sudden terror. Cecil threw down the skull and took off across the dunes as though all the imps of hell were upon him, Nan shrieking behind.

Satchmo followed at a more measured pace, his aged limbs stiff with too much sitting in the wind and the damp, a stray bone clamped firmly, lovingly, in his jaws.

"MEREDITH — "

The voice was Ralph Waldo's, and it held that special evenness that signaled urgency—a holdover, perhaps, from the days when he knew crisis and had run Nantucket's police force himself. "Your father just called. He needs you out in Sconset as soon as possible. Which, by my way of thinking, is as soon as you've had something to eat."

"But I'm off duty!"

"I know."

Merry studied in turn the downpour pummeling the hood of Rafe's truck, Peter's patient face distorted by the streaming windshield, and the bed frame awaiting its place in Rafe's truck bed. Then she looked back at her grandfather. "What is it?"

"Something unique in my experience." Ralph pushed open the screen door and handed her a steaming mug of his remarkable pea soup. "A couple of kids just dug up a skeleton."

Chapter Two

SIASCONSET — OR SCONSET, AS it is pronounced
and most frequently spelled—sits at the southeastern
tip of Nantucket Island, facing squarely across the
Atlantic some fifty miles north of the dreaming wreck
of the *Andrea Doria*, the Italian luxury liner that was
rammed nearly amidships in the summer of 1956. It is
a charming backwater of a town roughly seven and a
half miles from Nantucket proper, known for its grassy
one-way lanes of rose-covered cottages; its summer
residents of ancient and hallowed pedigree; its small
gourmet grocery store where pâté and fresh strawber-
ries and fine cheese may be purchased during the summer
season, which ends abruptly in mid-September; and its
relative desolation during the winter months, when the
sole hotel and restaurant close their doors against the brisk
tides, and the summer people retreat, and only a hardy
few brave the relentlessly howling winds and the eroding
force of the sea. Sconseters firmly pronounce themselves
to be *Sconseters*, to distinguish themselves from Nantucket's hoi polloi, and the great cottages sitting high
in the shadow of Sankaty Light have a timeless quality,
breathlessly posh.

But now, in this wet and chilly April, the town huddled

forlornly between the gunmetal sky and the petulant sea, a lost dog curled at the island's feet.

The rain was torrential by the time Merry pulled up in the Gully Road cul-de-sac near the entrance to Sconset beach. Only two cars sat dully in the downpour, tires half-sunk in the grass at the road's verge. She recognized them both. Clarence Strangerfield's scene-of-crimes van, and Dr. John Fairborn's teal-colored BMW convertible, its canvas top darkened with rain. The rest of her team had made better time from town than she, being free of the obligation to down Ralph's split-pea soup.

Merry turned off her Explorer's ignition, jammed on the parking brake, and tugged the hood of her slicker up over her white-blonde hair. Then she thrust open the car door and dashed down to the edge of the sand. Her father had said the kids were waiting in a house in Codfish Park, the small settlement of cottages between the bluff and the eroding shore, but the kids would have to wait a little while longer. What interested Merry was the knot of uniformed and plainclothes men kneeling around a spot in the wind-tossed scrub just below Codfish Park. And so she began to slog through the wet sand, which was depressingly gray, like everything else about the day. It clung to her hiking boots with every step.

"Marradith!"

Clarence Strangerfield, the crime-scene chief. His peremptory greeting was flung over one shoulder, and his broad jeans-clad bottom blocked her view of the pit over which he knelt. Merry broke into a trot, fingers grasping the edge of her hood to shield her face. The effort *not* to get wet in the midst of a deluge is a peculiarly human one—as only humans wear clothes, and occasionally mascara—and abruptly, disgustedly, Merry abandoned it. While she closed the distance of five hundred yards between herself and the men, she took a mental census: Clarence; his assistant, Nat Coffin; John Fairborn—and Howie Seitz, his dark mop of curls glinting in the rain. Her father had sent her favorite first-year officer, the one she had trained and depended upon during the scut work of two murder investigations; Merry's spirits suddenly rose. It was too soon to declare the skeleton a result of *murder*, of course. It might be centuries old—the burial of an Indian, say, or one of the scores of men who first established Sconset as a seventeenth-century fishing colony. But the chief of Nantucket's police was clearly weighing other possibilities, like death by violence. And if he had sent his daughter and her favorite assistant, he might even let her investigate it.

"Hey, guys," she said casually as she came up to them. She laid a hand on Clarence's shoulder.

He grunted and heaved himself to his feet, hands on his bent knees for support. "Careful of the scene, now, Marradith."

She glanced around at the piles of disturbed sand, the torn beach plum, the scattering of small bones. The remains of a cement foundation, its house long vanished in January's waves, lay jagged and broken in what had once been a yard. A wilting daffodil, brilliantly yellow against the sodden sand, had been flung down beside a bruised-red sand bucket. "Like there's any evidence to preserve, Clare," Merry said tartly. "These are kids we're talking about, right?"

"Ayeh," the crime-scene chief said wearily. "And a dog. If you'll believe."

"The dog's taken a nip or two from a number of these

bones." Fairborn, the Nantucket police's volunteer medical examiner, offered Merry a gnawed gray example. "Look at the damage. Hard to tell what's dog and what's death trauma."

"Great. And you're sure they're human?"

"Well, the skull's a pretty good indication," Fairborn shot back, and took a drag on the cigarette he always kept lit between the fingers of his right hand. How a doctor could so imperil his health Merry never quite understood, but she accepted Fairborn's smoking as a sign that he was somewhat normal. The man usually behaved like a stand-in for God.

"Any idea how recently they were buried?"

"The utter lack of flesh or ligament articulation might be a clue."

"Ligament articulation?" Merry recognized the term from her forensics class—ten years back now, wasn't it? She just couldn't quite remember what it meant.

"Ligaments hold the skeleton together," Fairborn said, with what passed for patience. "These bones lost theirs years ago. They're completely disarticulated. Which means, in my view, that they weren't killed last week."

"Thanks, Fairborn. You're an immense help. Clarence?"

The crime-scene chief looked at Merry from brown eyes as large and soulful as a basset hound's and shook his head. "Ah've no idea, Marradith. Coulda been heah for yeahs, and the sand just worn away by the tides and whatnot this wintah. No tellin', rally. What we need is a good forensic anthropologist, and I'm not sure we'll find us one o' those at the state crime lab in Boston. But befarh we worry about that, Nat here has an awful lot o' siftin' ahead, don't yah, Nat?"

The youngest of the numerous Coffins raised his brown head and smiled cheerfully. Nat labored over a large mesh sifter Merry suspected was culled from Clarence's beloved garden tools; the crime-scene chief, as always, pursued his mission with precision and efficiency. No bone, no matter how disarticulated or long-buried in the Sconset sands, would slip from Clarence's grasp.

Merry surveyed the area silently, searching for the skull. She found it already bagged in plastic and set off to one side—incongruous and ghoulish and sobering.

"Alas, poor Yorick," Howie Seitz said as he followed the direction of her eyes.

"You never cease to amaze me, Howie. I had no idea you could be a fan of *both* Kurt Cobain and Shakespeare."

"Hey, a poet's a poet, Detective," he protested.

"Particularly when he's dead." Merry blew out a gusty breath—that failed in its object of lifting her sodden bangs—and turned away from them all.

The address her father had given her belonged to a house two down from the corner of Beach and Codfish Park roads—safe, for the moment, from the ravages of storm and tide—with neat ligustrum hedges by the door and the pale golden façade common to the island's newly shingled. Trellised roses ran the length of the catslide roof; a welcoming light shone in the window. No wonder the kids had come here for help.

Merry ran up the crushed quahog-shell path to the sheltered doorway, pushed back her hood, and stabbed the bell.

It was a man who answered her summons—nearly seventy, perhaps, with gnarled hands poking from the ends of a heather-blue sweater, and thinning salt-and-pepper

hair. The eyes behind his half glasses held a roguish twin-
kle that even the vicarious discovery of a skeleton had
failed to dim. He peered at Merry through his storm door,
nodded twice, then opened it wide.

"Detective Meredith Folger, Nantucket police," she
said, and held out her badge.

"Lenny Schwartz." He adjusted the glasses to peer at
the police shield, in much the same manner that a man
will gaze at the label of a wine bottle he has ordered, at
once knowing and ignorant; then he studied her, his eyebrows raised. "You're a detective," he said.

"Yes."

"I'm impressed. I didn't know Nantucket allowed
women to handle murder. How progressive."

"What makes you think this is murder, Mr. Schwartz?"

To Merry's surprise his face creased in a smile. "Well,
now—if you don't sound like the star of every police
show I've ever seen. Have I just talked myself into being
suspect number one?"

"That takes more than talk."

"Thank goodness," he said mildly, and led her into the
living room.

"My wife, Ruth." Lenny motioned to a broad-hipped
woman in a Shetland sweater sitting protectively close
to two young children huddled on an overstuffed sofa.
Both balanced Dixie cups of what appeared to be Coca-
Cola in their small hands and stared at her fearfully.
"And our neighbors, Cecil and Nan Markham. This is
Detective—Meredith?—Folger."

With the telltale hesitation of one who endures significant back pain, Ruth Schwartz stood up and extended
her hand. Merry shook it.

"We're so glad you could come," Ruth said, and glanced at the two children.

"I'm sorry that I have to intrude." Merry swung her leather purse from her shoulder and fished in its capacious depths for her laptop, then felt the square bulk of her reading glasses and pulled those out, too. "I could take the kids home and talk to them there, if that's more convenient—"

"I think perhaps you ought to do it here," Ruth Schwartz interposed, with what Merry read as a significant look. So home was not a congenial place for the young Markhams. "We've called their mother. I'm sure Imogen will be along fairly soon."

"In that case—"

"Please, take a chair. Can I get you anything? Soda? Coffee?"

"You know, a cup of tea would be great," Merry said gratefully. "It's really chilly out there."

"Yes. And the Daffodil Festival is only a week away—"

"Ruth," Lenny Schwartz said warningly. "The detective's tea."

"I'm going, I'm going." Ruth shot her husband a look, one that acknowledged her garrulousness as it reproved him for censuring it. Then she smiled at Merry and moved stiffly toward the kitchen. An imposing woman, gray hair drawn back in a loose bun, her high cheekbones still markedly beautiful.

"Weather's killing her back," Lenny explained, "and of course she refuses to lay off the gardening this close to Daffodil Weekend. She's got several entries in the show. But that's neither here nor there, right? You want to talk to the kids."

"Yes."

"You're really from the police?" a small voice said. Merry turned and found Cecil Markham's large gray eyes fixed upon her. "Why aren't you in uniform, then?"

Merry was struck by something in his tone—a refinement of accent she couldn't quite place—and she turned this over in her mind as she took a chair near Cecil and Nan. "It's Saturday," she replied, opening her laptop and settling her glasses on her nose. "And, besides, I'm a detective. A lot of us don't bother with uniforms."

"Oh." Cecil was obviously disappointed—and something else . . . Relieved? Perhaps a *real* policeman would have been too intimidating.

"Which one of you found the bones today on the beach?" Merry looked first at the small red-haired girl and then at her brother. The children exchanged a glance, then studied their cups of Coke.

"I did," the girl said finally. "Then Cecil came and helped. We thought it was buried treasure."

As Merry's brow furrowed, Cecil elaborated. "Pirates always leave bones on top of their jewels. To signal their mates and ward off the curious." There it was again—the unconscious formality, the stilted diction. As though he had learned to speak from reading books.

"Ah," Merry said. "I see. You kept digging, then, in the hope of hitting pay dirt."

"But then we found the—Cecil found the skull," Nan said in a thin voice. She shivered, her red curls shaking. "It was horrible."

Merry nodded thoughtfully and sat back against the chair's needlepoint pillow, studying the Markhams. They did not look like happy children—although any child who found a skull on the beach might be similarly sobered. "Nan," Merry said, "I'd like you to tell me something, if you can. Why did you decide to dig in that spot in the first place?"

"It was Satchmo," she said promptly.

"Satchmo?"

"Their dog." Ruth Schwartz appeared at Merry's side with a steaming mug of tea. "He's drying off in the kitchen. A dear old thing."

"Satchmo started the digging," Nan said. "He must have smelled the bones."

"Satchmo's a great digger," Cecil offered, "and he loves bones."

"But why were you sitting near the condemned houses at all?"

Nan's change of expression was swift and formidable. "Cecil wouldn't let me play."

"But there was going to be a battle, Nan!"

Merry turned to him. "And girls aren't allowed to fight?"

"Of course not."

"What about me?" she asked blandly. "I'm a police detective. We have to fight sometimes."

"Can you fire a gun?" Nan's voice was filled with awe.

"Yes. But I try to avoid it."

"Golly," Cecil breathed.

"So you were sent off to play by yourself while Cecil fought his battles," Merry said to Nan. "Why that spot anyway? It's an awful mess, with the houses gone and the foundations exposed."

"I didn't start out there, exactly." The girl's eyes narrowed with her effort to remember. "Satchmo and I were having a tea party. And then I saw some daffodils up near the concrete edge, and went to pick them. Satchmo started digging then, I guess."

"And what did you think when he found the bones?"

Nan shrugged—the catchall little-girl gesture of ignorance and indifference. "I thought maybe he'd buried them there himself. Satchmo's got bones everywhere. But then I saw a real little one—like a twig—and I wanted to show Cecil."

The doorbell sang out sharply in the quiet of the cozy living room, and Merry jumped.

"That'll be Imogen," Lenny said, and disappeared into the hallway.

"Miss Detective." Cecil's hand was tugging at Merry's sleeve, and his voice had grown oddly desperate. "Please tell Mummy it wasn't our fault. That we found those bones, I mean. Please tell her we didn't mean to do it."

And as Lenny Schwartz ushered Imogen Markham into the room, Merry saw why she intimidated her children.

She was a frail-looking woman, hollow-eyed and dark-haired, with two sharp lines running from her nose to the corners of her mouth. Her forehead was similarly creased, suggesting weariness and unwonted aging, although Merry decided the woman couldn't be more than forty. Imogen Markham wore a pair of faded duck trousers and a torn blue T-shirt under a jacket pulled hastily over her shoulders; the clothing hung upon her body. A tide of stale cigarette smoke permeated the room as soon as she entered it.

"Whatever did you have to run to the Schwartzes' for, then?" she asked, her voice deep with irritation as she looked at her children. Merry grasped at the sound of that husky voice, finding in it the explanation for Cecil's oddities—Imogen Markham was British.

"Hello, Imogen," Ruth Schwartz said.

Imogen ignored her and crossed rapidly to her son. She jerked the boy to his feet with one fluid movement of her arm. He hung his head. Nan sank miserably into the sofa.

Merry stood up and extended her hand. "Meredith Folger, Mrs. Markham. Nantucket police."

"You've done with the children, then?" Imogen Markham demanded, by way of greeting.

"For the moment."

"Right. Then we'll be leaving. Step smartly, Nan." Imogen wheeled for the door, mouth set and black hair rippling snakelike across her narrow back. Cecil dragged at her heels.

"Mrs. Markham," Merry called after her as Nan slid to her feet and took a reluctant step in her mother's wake, "I'd like to speak to you, if I may."

"What is it?"

Merry glanced at the children's averted faces. Nan had given up the battle not to cry. "Could we talk a moment in private?"

A faint, derisive smile flickered across Imogen Markham's face and was gone. "Whatever for? You think these kids hear anything?"

"Yes," Merry rejoined evenly. "I do."

Imogen rolled her eyes. She turned Cecil abruptly toward the Schwartzes' kitchen. "Go get the dog, mate, and take your sister with you," she commanded, with a slap to his behind.

The children scuttled off without a backward glance.

"Get on with it, then," Imogen told Merry.

"It's possible that what happened today on the beach might disturb your children for some time to come. You should expect nightmares at the very least. Possibly an aversion to the entire area. Maybe even an unwillingness to go out alone."

Imogen laughed derisively. "With all the violence on the telly? You think a few bones are going to unnerve my Cecil and Nan? You don't know kids, Miss Nantucket Policewoman. They're nasty little beggars. Haven't a sensitive bone in their bodies. It takes growing up to teach you pain."

"Then I'd say Nan and Cecil are growing up fast," Merry said softly, and bit back the words too late. Imogen Markham's face, if anything, became instantly more closed and unreachable. Nevertheless, Merry reached down to her purse and fished out her wallet. "I'm no psychiatrist. I'm only telling you what I've learned from experience. But I'd like to give you this."

Imogen took the small buff card from Merry's extended hand. "What's this?"

"A counseling service we recommend. In case you find your children are more sensitive than you think."

The woman looked at Merry for the briefest second. Then, deliberately, she tore the card in two.

WHEN THE MARKHAMS had gone—a silent and fulminating trio blackly outlined against the sodden sky—Merry took her leave of Lenny and Ruth Schwartz.

"You were very good to those children today," she told them. "I'd like to thank you, even if Mrs. Markham won't."

"Oh, we never expect thanks from Imogen," Lenny

said roguishly. "It's against her creed. She's a confirmed misanthrope. Any spark of gratitude would cause her face to crack."

"Sad, isn't it?" Ruth said a trifle wistfully. "They're such gifted children."

"Are they?"

Ruth glanced at Lenny. "Well, I think so," she said. "Not that I'm an authority. Nan is utterly delightful—a budding poet. The child asks the most curious questions—all about the *mentality* of things. Do dogs fear death? Are waves the sea's way of reaching for the shore when it wants to be human? She's absolutely enchanted with flowers, of course, and is always stealing into the garden when her mother's in one of her moods."

"Cecil lives entirely in his mind," her husband added, "when he's not living in his books. A daydreamer. Well, they both come by the imagination naturally."

"From—their mother?"

Lenny snorted. "Not Imogen. At least, not that anyone would be able to tell. No, from Ian. Ian Markham. He was a fairly famous sculptor, you know. Sank his boat and drowned in a squall about eight years back."

"*That* Ian Markham!" Merry exclaimed, jolted by memory. A flamboyant British expatriate—known for his charm, his daring work, his high-paying clients, and his sudden, tragic death. Markham had taken the island's art world by storm, if only briefly. "And his wife has stayed here all these years?"

"Kept the studio, the house, the whole artist schtick." Lenny nodded. "Stuck up a forest of NO TRESPASSING signs when the tourists started collecting on the front lawn. You'd think she loved it here in Sconset. Couldn't tear herself away. It's absolutely weird, I think."

"Now, Lenny." Ruth's voice held the mildest reproof. "We've no idea how Imogen feels about living here."

"The hell we don't," he rejoined. "You always know exactly how Imogen feels."

Or do you? Merry wondered as she walked swiftly down the Schwartzes' neat white path in the dissipating rain. Was it antagonism Imogen Markham wore upon her face—or a desperate shield against a too-painful world?

OTHER TITLES IN THE SOHO CRIME SERIES